PLAYGROUNDS

PLAYGROUNDS

Alan Gelb

G. P. PUTNAM'S SONS • NEW YORK

G. P. Putnam's Sons
Publishers Since 1838
200 Madison Avenue
New York, NY 10016

The author gratefully acknowledges the assistance of the
Virginia Center for the Creative Arts and the Mercantile
Library. Lyrics from the following songs are quoted
with permission:
    "I Love Paris," copyright © 1953 by Cole Porter.
Chappell & Co., Inc., owner of publication and allied
rights. International copyright secured. All rights
reserved.
    "Nature Boy," copyright © 1948 by Eden Ahbez.
    "Walkin the Dog," copyright © 1963, 1977 by Almo
Music Co. (ASCAP)

Library of Congress Cataloging-in-Publication Data

Gelb, Alan.
    Playgrounds.

    I. Title.
PS3557.E365P5   1987   813'.54   86-30441
ISBN 0-399-13277-5

Typeset by Fisher Composition, Inc.

Printed in the United States of America
1   2   3   4   5   6   7   8   9   10

For Karen, Noah, and Nathaniel

It is human to have a long childhood;
it is civilized to have an ever longer childhood.

—Erik Erikson

PLAYGROUNDS

PART ONE

1

Do your ears hang low?
Do they wobble to and fro?

"That's Charles, our head teacher," Charles heard Loretta tell the health inspector.

Can you tie them in a knot?
Can you tie them in a bow?

He looked up from the guitar long enough to see the woman jot down something in her book.

Can you throw them over your shoulder
Like a continental soldier?

He wondered what she was writing, this fiercely officious Latino woman who had come to judge them.

Do your ears hang low?

"Again!" the children cried, but Charles thought otherwise. He laid the guitar across his lap and looked out at the children. They were a splendid group—his kids; his *corps*—and the idea of their being judged by a stranger infuriated him. "Come on, Charles!" cried Hildy, the ringleader of the group. "Again!" Charles saw the inspector staring at him, looking for imperfections—lewd tattoos maybe, or sharpened incisors. He didn't like people staring at him; there was always the fear of recognition. He glanced at Loretta, who wore a huge, tense smile. It both amused and irritated him, this slavish obeisance to authority, and with a clear sense of purpose he picked up the guitar and once again began to strum it.

"Hello, lady. Hello, lady," he sang to the tune of "Frère Jacques," staring straight at the Inspector. *"How are you? How are you?"*

As if one head, the children turned to stare at the woman. Now it was her turn to be on display, thought Charles, enjoying her discomfiture immensely.

"Come on, kids. Sing it," he exhorted them, taking it from the top. *"Hello, lady. Hello, lady. How are you? How are you?"*

The kids started to sing in their ragtag way, smiling goofy smiles at her. She, in turn, attempted to alter her face into something friendly, but it was a losing battle. He had beaten her at her own game, he thought, rejoicing in his small victory.

We're happy for your visit,
We wouldn't want to miss it,
You're nice too.
You're nice too.

"Very funny, Charles," Loretta said to him later, in her office, after the inspector had left. "Absolutely hilarious."

"Oh, come on, Loretta," he replied. "Have a sense of humor."

She blew smoke through her nostrils. Whenever she did that, it made him think of a dragon. She was a big woman, physically big and emotionally outsize. It wasn't hard for her to look like a dragon, albeit a pretty dragon, full-breasted, slim-ankled, but with a dragon's temper that flared up too often these days and a dragonish need to control things that led Adina, the teacher who had just quit on one day's notice, to call her Big Mama behind her back.

"Listen," said Loretta. "When *you* start a day-care center and when *you* work your butt off to keep it going, then you can have a sense of humor about it, OK?"

Charles said nothing. What was there to say? It was precisely the kind of remark that had put an end to their relationship.

"Charles, I'm sorry," she said, catching herself. "That bitch gave me such a headache with that inspection. I thought she was going to go into my ears with a Q-tip."

He laughed. After everything was said and done, she was a smart, funny woman. He wished it had ended better than it had. He wished she hadn't so strong a need to lay blame.

"Look," he said. "If you've got such a bad headache, let me do lunch today and you take the kids to the park."

She bit her lip—one of her gestures. "I couldn't," she protested. "You've done lunch twice this week already."

"It's OK," he said. "I don't mind."

Of course he did mind, because it was a drag to make lunch, but the fact was it couldn't hurt to do a nice thing for Loretta. It pleased her to have people do nice things for her, and it was good to please her. He needed to please her. This had become his home, and he didn't want to lose it. He had lost too many things as it was.

"Are you sure?" she asked.

"I'm sure."

He helped her get the kids into the big wooden wagon that was used for group excursions. Aaron needed a hat to ward off ear infections and Molly needed her special bee-sting medicine and then, just as they were ready to pull out, Hildy remembered her gloves, which everyone told her she didn't need, it being so warm for the season, but Hildy had ideas of her own and kept everyone waiting until she located them.

"I guess we're ready," Loretta said finally, and so Charles helped her down the stairs with the wagon.

"Have a good time," he said, feeling a flush of warmth as he stood so close to her.

"Oh, we will," Loretta promised, looking at him and then looking away.

He watched them walk down the block. He felt very good, happy for the weather and for the order of things. "And hey," he called suddenly, "don't talk to strangers." She looked back at him and he grinned, underscoring the joke and disguising the slight wave of anxiety he sometimes felt, like a father, when the children went away from him.

A rocketship giggling in the park. Down they came, one after the other after the other. She loved this one little girl, a long stringy kid at the top of the slide, they called her Hildy. Funny name for a kid these days. She wore these gloves, this Hildy—it was only November and warm like June but she wore them anyway. Trina had seen their sort before—the trick was they were temperature-sensitive. If it was cold enough, little blue robots or UFOs would miraculously appear. Except it wasn't cold enough. But Hildy didn't seem to mind. Funny what makes kids happy.

Trina closed her eyes and pointed her face to the sun. It was too warm for November. She felt the sun's rays on her, tried to relax, tried not to hear anything she didn't want to hear, but she couldn't turn off the island lilt of the nannies, talking about hair spray. As she sat there, in the nannies, the field of nannies, she wondered what they made of her, coming here to the playground without a child. Like checking into a hotel without luggage. But she didn't care. It was what she liked to do. She just liked kids is all. There was that Hildy and this little black boy, they called him Olivier, with these robin's-egg-blue eyes that sent her a shiver. Another little boy—three or four—with pale skin and very black eyes. Petey she heard the woman call him. A big woman with beautiful hair, fox-red and gray, who was here in the playground with the kids three or four days a week. Just like Trina. Whenever she wasn't working—and she wasn't working—Trina came to the playground and just sat and watched.

She couldn't even say why she liked kids so much. She never expected to have them. It's just that she liked them is all and she liked to sit in the playground. It made her feel safe. And she was good with kids. There weren't so many things she was good at. She could embroider—butterflies, ladybugs, you name it. Around the hem of a denim skirt she once stitched a carousel of painted horses that could fly like the wind if you did the mambo. One winter, in Woodstock, she worked like a wetback embroidering denim jackets—piecework—and living on cornbread and Heinz beans. She knew how to embroider and how to stitch and how to live on Heinz beans.

She knew she'd never be rich. She doubted she'd ever be famous. The thing was she didn't really know where she was going. Once upon a time she thought she was going to be an actress. That was a while back already. It wasn't that she wasn't any good. There were times when it was clear how good she was. She could remember this one audition. She read Frankie from *Member of the Wedding*. The theater, once a bread-baking plant, still smelled of yeast, or so it seemed, and her voice flew about the space even though she thought she was whispering. When she finished reading, her spine was chills and she looked around and could see the gums of people with their mouths open.

But she didn't get the part. Who knows why? Maybe they were afraid. Afraid she'd fall into the role like some people fall through trapdoors or down elevator shafts or into dreams or out of windows, and maybe she would have. But she wasn't as afraid of her falling as everyone else was. She was ready to fall and she did.

But just then, as she sat there, feeling that falling, she heard it, the cries, and then felt those cries pass through her.

Maa! Maa!

The scream like a siren ripped through the playground, ripped through her. That Hildy. She ran across the playground, broke into the circle of nannies, who folded up around the child like a black sea anemone. In the middle was Hildy, shrieking, blood. The woman was there holding Hildy's twisty body while the two little boys watched. Trina heard a low sibilance in the air—the murmur of disapproval from the nannies.

"What can I do?" Trina asked the woman. "Should I get ice?"

"No. It's going to have to be stitched," said the woman, who was red in the face but firm in her manner of speaking. "We'll have to take her to the ER. Can you come with me?"

In the cab, the tall woman, who said her name was Loretta, cradled Hildy, just whimpering a little now, while Trina held the two boys on her lap.

"We'll call Julie from the hospital," said Loretta. "That's her mother. Look, it's already stopped bleeding. But it'll need stitching. God, will you look at me?" Loretta said. Trina looked; Loretta's pink jacket was spattered with blood. "This has never happened," she went on. "Not once in five years. But if it had to happen, just as well it's Hildy. She can handle it." She leaned over to kiss Hildy's ear; Hildy molded. "I didn't even see it. She told me she was trying to jump from one bridge to the other. Don't fall asleep, lovie," Loretta cautioned her. "You've got to keep them awake after something like this. Remember that," she said to Tina, as if she were staff.

The boys shifted restlessly but she held on to them. "You know, you're good with kids," Loretta said. "I've noticed you around the playground—wondered who you were. You've got a strange aura. You remind me of a war widow hanging around Arlington Memorial Cemetery." Loretta caught herself. "Oh shit. Listen to me. I'm always like this when I get nervous. You're not, are you?"

"What?"

"A war widow."

Trina shook her head.

"Oh, good," said Loretta, speeding. She rearranged the load of Hildy. "What are you?"

"Pisces," Trina said after a moment.

Loretta looked at her, grinned a little. "You're kidding, right?"

"Right," she said.

"So what are you? What do you do?"

Trina smelled the boys' sweetness as she thought of an answer. "I'm . . . mostly I waitress."

"Nothing wrong with that. Good enough money if you get the right spot. I used to do it too when I was acting."

"You were an actress?"

"Oh, sure. Isn't everyone in New York? Musicals. I was going to be the next Barbara Cook."

Loretta began to sing a little. "My White Knight." In this big operatic voice. She was weird.

"Stop," Petey said.

"They hate when I sing stuff like that. I'm only supposed to sing 'Polly Wolly Doodle.' Like I'm Burl Ives. Hey," she said, shifting into Hildy. "What's your name?"

"Katrina. Katrina Dunbar. People call me Trina."

"That's the greatest name I ever heard," Loretta said. "Hey!" she screamed at the cabdriver. "I could have walked faster than this. I've got a kid bleeding here, OK?"

"Lady! Don't let her bleed on my polstery!" shouted the cabdriver, who was an Armenian or something like that, with a lot of K's in his name.

At this, Hildy started to cry. "Jerk," Loretta muttered, pulling Hildy close. They got to the emergency entrance. "Pay him, will you?" Loretta said, walking on. Trina found enough money in her pockets and then followed her in.

"Jesus, what a zoo!" Loretta said. "Hildy, I'm going to call your mother. Stay here with Trina."

"No," Hildy said.

"Hildy, please . . ."

"No!" the child shrieked.

Trina bent low, put her face to Hildy's. "Don't scream. You'll hurt your ears."

Hildy looked at her like she was a little strange. Which she was. Loretta went off to find the phone. Trina held Hildy, had the boys at her feet. She hoped they wouldn't see something really awful: a man without a head.

"The first time I went to the hospital I was six," she said. "Guess what happened?"

There was a silence. No, not silence—there was the noise of the room. What there was was no response.

"Guess," she said again.

"We don't *know*," said Petey, with an emphatic shrug of his shoulders.

"OK. I'll tell you. I had a kid on my block—his name was Frankie Tuttle. We didn't get along. I guess you could call him my enemy. You know what an enemy is? No? Somebody you can't get along with. Anyway, those days they had peashooters. Little pipes—you blew peas at each other." She tried to make them understand; she put an imaginary pipe to her lips and blew. "Frankie Tuttle shot one in my ear and I had to go to the emergency room. Like you, Hildy."

"I want my mommy," Hildy said. "And I want her now."

"Sure you do, sweetie," Trina replied.

Loretta came rushing back. "Your mommy's on her way, honey," she called, and then, to Trina, "Her mother's getting a plastic surgeon. Good for her. First rule—first, first, first. Never have a child treated for anything if there's time for a parent to take over the situation."

Hildy's mother got there within ten minutes. Before Trina even knew who she was, she noticed the tall woman, moving quickly, straight thick dark hair down her back.

"Hildy!" the woman cried. "Mommy's here!"

Hildy bolted from Trina's lap and ran into her mother's arms, where she relieved herself, in sobs, of all that she had managed to hold in. They buried their faces in each other.

"Julie, she's going to be all right," Loretta said, touching her on the shoulder. "She's going to be good as—"

"Fine," Julie said, cutting her off. You could see she was hopping mad; Trina found herself a little afraid of her, had the impulse to hide behind the boys.

"I know you're upset," said Loretta, "but—"

"Why should I be upset?" Julie interrupted. "Why should I be upset? Just because I spend thirty-eight dollars a day to have my kid taken care of and here she is with her head—"

"All right," Loretta cried. "*All right.*" Her face, which in repose was a large smooth white oval, a perfect canvas for an actress's expressions, was now beet-red, with twisted features.

"How did it happen?" demanded Julie, who was very pale and who was clutching Hildy, crying even harder now. "Can you tell me just how the hell it happened?"

"She hit her head jumping from one bridge to another. It *happens*. Even at thirty-eight dollars a day," Loretta said with some bitterness.

"It *happens*?" said Julie, lifting Hildy to carry her to the nurses' station. "We'll talk later."

Loretta put out a restraining arm and held Julie fixed for a moment. She leaned over and put her hot face against Hildy's. "I love you, cupcake," she whispered. Then she straightened up and, heading for the exit, instructed Trina to bring the boys along.

When they got back to the Center, Loretta gave the boys over to an obese black woman named Darcy, and led Trina into her office.

"Sit down," she said to Trina, who sat down, looking at the walls which were plastered with candid photos of the children and a blowup of Loretta herself looking fleshy in a swimsuit at the beach.

"You want tea?" asked Loretta. "Or bouillon maybe?"

Trina shook her head.

"I'm going to have the bouillon. It's all salt and I've got heart disease racing through my family history like brushfire but it's protein, baby, and let's face it— those amino acids are what's going to get me through a day like this." She opened up a can of College Inn broth and inserted an immersion coil. Then she lit up a cigarette, a Saratoga. "You smoke?"

Trina shook her head.

"Damn. I'm the only one in the Center who does. I feel like a criminal. Ma Barker. But I never smoke so the kids can see me." She puffed and put a finger into the bouillon, which hadn't yet warmed. "I told you you were good with kids. Did you ever think of doing it as a job?"

"No," said Trina.

"Waitressing is all right but the legs go. And a lot of time you want to kill the people. I used to get these Diamond Jim Bradys—out with their girlfriends, double-thick chops, cigarette in the rice pudding, and a five-percent tip. That happen to you?"

"Sometimes," Trina said with a little smile.

"Working with kids—well, it's damned hard work but it's also kind of uplifting. Even when the money stinks."

"How bad does it stink?" Trina asked.

"As bad as it can. People make more money cleaning other people's stoves than they make taking care of other people's kids. It's the way it is." She felt the bouillon again and frowned. "Listen, I'm not used to hiring off the street but I'm caught shorthanded." She looked up and stared directly at Trina. "I think it's worth our while to talk about this, don't you?"

"But don't you have to . . . know something?" Trina asked.

Loretta shrugged. "You've got to be able to learn. But the kids'll teach you. Listen, they like you—I could see it. I knew it right off. I'm a very instinctive person. You've got to be able to trust your instincts when you work with kids. You've got to play by your gut. You start intellectualizing around kids, you can just pack it in. They've got built-in bullshit detectors."

"I never worked with kids before," Trina said. "I took care of my little cousins a lot, but I never really worked with kids." She forced herself to look directly at Loretta, who scared her a little. "What happens if they don't like you?"

Loretta took a puff off her Saratoga. "They let you know it," she said. "But why wouldn't they like you? You're nice. Think of all the old hags taking care of kids over on Park Avenue. The ones with the white uniforms and the chests like rolltop desks who keep their kids strapped up with harnesses until they're around four or so. Next to them, you're Snow White."

Trina smiled.

"Hey. A real smile. The first one." Loretta put a finger into the bouillon again. "Fucking coil. The other thing is that none of the kids like *everyone,* but all of the kids like *someone.* You'll see—somebody'll fall in love with you. You'll fall in love with somebody. This place is like a net. We all form connections, and these connections—whether they be teacher/child; child/child; parent/parent; parent/ teacher—they support us, hold us up. Even today, with Hildy and Julie—listen, I like Julie and all but she's alone in the world with the kid and even though she makes a bundle—she sells space for Condé Nast—she's got this Woman Alone attitude, like the world's out to screw her if she doesn't watch out. But still, she's part of the net and so's Hildy and so am I and you could be too if you want to be."

Trina stopped smiling. She looked down at her hands, which were too short and white as grapefruit pith, except for a half-moon of dried blood which was there for reasons she couldn't remember.

"You want to say something," Loretta observed.

Trina looked up at her with the pond-green eyes that her mother always said were her best feature but that she took for her worst. "How do you kow I'm OK?" she asked. "How do you know I don't have TB or that I'm not an ax murderer?"

Loretta inhaled from her Saratoga and held the smoke in her sinuses, so long that Trina watched in fascination, waiting for the release. "Well," she finally exhaled, "as far as the TB, you'll have to take a physical—state law—and in terms of ax-murdering, your former life is of no great significance here. I don't care whom you've slept with or whether you eat fish on Fridays or if that's your real teeth with the poppyseeds stuck in them."

Trina reflexively put a hand to her mouth. She'd eaten a bagel hours before— poppyseed—and now she felt caught at it, silly, and wondered if she liked this Loretta.

"Listen," said Loretta, snuffing out the Saratoga and pouring the tepid bouillon into her mug, "the first thing is my kids. Anything happens to my kids, I rip the liver out of whomever, and I'm not kidding. I know I told you how I'm instinctive and all that, but don't get me wrong. This place has rules. This place has structure. You'll be watched. But I can tell something about people by now. I can tell you've got what to give and haven't gotten to give it. Am I right?"

Trina felt something ignite behind her eyes. She blinked a few times.

"So?" said Loretta. "You want to sleep on it?"

Trina listened to the shriek of a child from beyond the door of Loretta's office. "When would I start?" she said, smoothing her hair on top.

"Kiddo, you already did."

2

LOUISE STRONG DOWELL wasn't alone. Like many other scientists in New York City, she was researching a cure for the dread illness—indeed, scourge—of AIDS. Her husband, Bill, was frightened by her work, and certainly she could see why, because it was a disease whose essential nature was its mystery, and whose secondary aspect was its astonishing death rate. Of course she herself was not in contact with the victims. She held a fellowship in biochemistry at Rockefeller University and had never personally laid eyes on any one of those poor young men who were dying off at the untimely ages of twenty-eight, thirty, thirty-one, thirty-three. Still, Bill was frightened because of the children and nagged at her constantly. She consoled herself with the knowledge that her work was of vital importance and, second, with the conviction that, in time, Bill would cease to be her husband.

They had been married now for fifteen years. A long time by modern standards. Longer, indeed, than the marriage of her own parents, which had groaned along to its pewter anniversary. No, no—she was being facetious. She couldn't have begun to tell you which the pewter anniversary was. In fact, the union of her parents had lasted twelve years and now her father was eight years into his second marriage. Her mother, on the other hand, had become a sort of prioress of Lower Education, acting as principal for an esteemed progressive school on the Upper East Side of Manhattan, and forswearing, as prioresses would, the idea of remarriage.

Louise and Bill had met in Cambridge. Bill was a student at the Harvard Divinity School; Louise was at Wellesley. They dated for six months before they went to bed together. Bill had, in that period, reoriented his life. He enrolled in the Business School, where he did fairly, and, away from the yoke of his calling (his was a family of ministers, going generations back—the clergy of Rhode Island), he seemed to be ready for her. They were both virgins. This they found out on a cold evening in January. They had gone to dinner at Café Budapest—she hated the heavy food; she lived on greens and whole-wheat bread—and then to hear Van Cliburn with the Boston Symphony. She told Bill that he looked like Van Cliburn. He laughed, but it was true—he did. He had kinky red hair; he was tall, thin, faunlike. In acerbic moments, she thought he had the look of a divinity student who comes out at the YMCA. Yet she found him attractive. The fact was that they looked rather alike. Since her marriage, she had made a point of studying couples and found that, in a great many instances, the spouses possessed strikingly resemblant physical characteristics. Like Bill, she was tall, thin, pale, had heavily lidded eyes, thin lips, and long spatulate fingers. No one had ever told her she was beautiful, not even Bill, but she would age well and, if she lived to be really older, she would suddenly become one of the best-looking of the bunch, with ankles and wrists that would advertise the fineness of her bones while all the "cute" women would already have assumed the shape of overmixed muffins.

She and Bill had left the concert, ate Häagen-Dazs, which was just then a new thrill; and then returned to her room at Wellesley, where Louise made Earl Grey tea and offered Bill damson-plum jelly and Uneeda biscuits. The night outside was vile; a cold resinous rain pelted down, coating the trees and the sidewalks with ice.

"Will you stay the night?" she asked, prepared, at twenty-one, to finally break the rules.

Bill suggested they go back to his place, but she didn't want to. She liked the goose-down comforter that her cousin had sent her from Eddie Bauer.

Louise lit votive candles, which she had bought in preparation of just such an occasion, and they undressed. She thought, again, that their bodies looked alike, not just the longness of them, the thinness, the lack of fat, the finely sheathed muscle, but a pearly luminescence about the skin, fair skin, to be kept shielded from the sun.

To report that they didn't know what to do would make the scene seem pathetic and/or comic. Looking back, she supposed it had some of these properties. But it also had the quality of beauty. She hadn't seen male genitalia except for her cousin's, when she was twelve, at Lake Champlain, and renditions of assorted statuary and artwork by Renaissance artists. She thought Bill's genitalia were quite beautiful. Long, thin, conch-colored, the soft blossomy testicles—she wanted to kiss them at first but she didn't and then subsequently she felt embarrassed to do so. For his part, he attacked her breasts like a starved foundling and made them sore. His erection was tentative; it failed them twice during coitus.

Thinking about it now, she wasn't sure then that she knew a penis was supposed to work any differently.

When it was done, they lay, as everyone lay, looking at the ceiling.

"I'm sorry," he murmured.

She didn't know what for. His sexual amateurism? His violation of her hymen? "It's all right," she whispered back.

They tried again and then many times again; it got better enough for them to marry and then it got worse. They went to a psychotherapist for counseling and had to go through the entire catalog of their sexual incompatibility: impotence; frigidity; pain; abstinence. The therapist asked her if she'd ever had any hysterical pregnancies. They stopped going to the therapist. They turned to vodka and found that they were able to relax a little and enjoy each other more. She was even able to achieve orgasm occasionally. When it came, with a shuddering heat, he drew back from her, almost in a state of alarm. What did he think it was? she wondered. St. Vitus' dance? It was only her body enjoying something. She thought, given everything, she had the right to enjoy something.

As she sat at her desk going over some notes for a lecture she would give later that evening, and thinking about all the things she'd been thinking about, the phone rang. She knew it would be Bill, calling to set up their lunch date.

"Hello?" she said, picking up. She had a phone voice just like her mother's—high, fluting, overly genteel.

"Hi," said Bill. "How are you?"

"I'm fine." She paused. "How are you?"

"Fine. Are we on for lunch?"

"Of course." She looked at her watch. "Twelve-fifteen?"

"Yes. That sounds fine."

"I'll see you then," she said, hanging up.

He didn't know she had a lover; if it were up to her, he'd never know. She didn't want to hurt him and the fact was that the lover wasn't nearly as important, as an individual, as was the fact that she now knew that she could make love well. The thought of it held her fixed for a moment—she felt a sudden welling-up of pity and tenderness for her Bill. Over the years, he'd become very dear to her, like a brother or a very, very close friend, and she didn't want to lose that ever. Add to that the fact that they had two children and you could see why the predicament was severe. She hoped, very deeply, to make the first steps toward a solution this afternoon, at lunch, just the two of them.

Although it was unusually warm for the season, Bill felt winter coming on. There it was, in the sense of fatigue one felt invading one's movements, and in the boys' resistance to waking up and starting the day. He felt sad with winter coming. One of his pleasures was picking the boys up by five and then heading into the park with them for ball. He loved baseball, football, soccer. He'd never been very good at any of it, but he was a sport, and in college, when he didn't make the teams, he at least distinguished himself as a cheerleader, devising a number of cheers that were still in use today. He hadn't told anyone this, but he suspected that Dennis, his older boy, was a natural athlete who, one day, would be cheered rather than cheering.

He walked along Fifth Avenue, looking for flowers. Because of the presage of winter that he'd been feeling all day in his bones, he had the impulse to bring Louise some spring—a nosegay, his mother might say. Maybe the flowers would cheer them all up. God knows, he could use some cheering, for in fact he was in a sad and terrible mood and was looking for a way out of it. Louise, for the fourth day in a row, had been out of the house by seven. It was up to him to wake the children.

He had to lift them, carrying them bodily into the kitchen, barking at them to eat their Cheerios. It was no mean piece of work. Then he had to pack Denny's lunch. It was he who stood there pulling the strings from the celery stalks lest, God forbid, his brave son should encounter such monstrousness. Then, when they sulked over getting themselves dressed and became involved, though it was strictly forbidden, with their action vehicles instead of their clothes, he became sinisterly quiet with them until Dennis started to whine. Poor Dennis. Little Petey, three years his brother's junior, could stonewall Genghis Khan, but with Dennis the slightest disapproval broke him to pieces. Sometimes—oftentimes—it worried him. He wished he could yell or scream instead of lowering his voice. He thought perhaps that lowering his voice was not the very best thing for the children, but he couldn't seem to remember not to do it.

He went into a tiny florist's shop called Aunt Betty's Garden. It was precisely the sort of name that trapped him every time, like a fly in amber. Louise once accused him of living inside a Norman Rockwell painting. That stung, but perhaps it had some truth to it. He wished things were easier. At the age of thirty-eight, he had begun to experience the deeply unsettling and sad feeling that he had made mistakes he could no longer rectify. At thirty-eight, he was a grants administrator for the Pendleton Foundation, which funded a wide range of research projects and humanistic endeavors. At thirty-eight, he was haunted—was that too strong a word? he wondered, and then he decided that it wasn't—by the feeling that he should have entered the ministry, as he was expected to do. It was a source of pain to him that the Spirit had so little, so frighteningly little, to do with his life.

"May I help you, sir?" said the woman in the flower shop. Aunt Betty perhaps—she certainly looked like an Aunt Betty.

He looked around. "Something simple," he said, with the appropriate shyness of a man buying flowers. "Violets maybe?"

She gave him an amused and tolerant smile. "Always lovely, sir, but I'm afraid unavailable this time of year. Some freesia perhaps?"

Yes, the freesia would do fine. The woman wrapped it in green tissue and he left with a smile on his face, as men are supposed to leave flower shops, although the smile was supposed to be considerably less shaky than his was.

It had been a very long time since he had brought his wife flowers. That's why the violets, the freesia—he was aiming at understatement. Louise was not the kind of woman to whom you gave birds of paradise, dahlias, passionflowers.

It had been three months since they slept together. It wasn't as though he hadn't asked, he thought to himself with a thin smile. She was, God knows, awfully clever at finding excuses. She even went so far as to have her body manufacture a host of not-terribly-serious bacteria to ensure her of a continuous span of vaginal infections. There were times when he wanted to come right out and ask her if her cunt was rotting away. Through nonusage, corroding like a bucket with a puddle in it left behind a shack.

Oh Lord.

Like the fin of an arctic shark, the wind, out of nowhere, cut across his cheek and made him pull his coat tightly around him. Winter. He couldn't believe it was winter so soon. He wondered if they would ski this year. He'd like to, but he couldn't get it together without help. For a ski trip there was altogether too much to choreograph; he'd need help. But when he thought of the boys out there, in the snow, hale, ruddy-faced, and then Denny's grace on the slopes—he could already ski—he couldn't imagine not going. He owed the children something. Yes, in fact, he owed them quite a lot. Thus far, it must be said, he and Louise had fallen down on the "home-atmosphere" front. The least they could do was make up for it in the winter-sports division.

He walked faster, wanting to walk away from his thoughts. The bitterness was so unlike him. He was a person who dreamed of clouds. He had an emphatic, profound regard for the celestial. He had never lacked for something to believe in.

When they married, in that time-smoothed white church, small, clapboard, forget-me-nots lining the paths, forget-me-nots in her white arms, the smell of sea, the salt glaze on the rose windows, the sound of the surf off Watch Hill crashing against their vows, he had expected it to last forever. His species, he was sure, was meant, like swans, to mate for life. But, ah—*ah*—where was it written that they were meant to be mated happily?

He was unhappy. She had done that to him. True, he had other problems—his job, his *work,* was not enough. He hadn't managed to do anything really fine in his life. And the children—no, he loved the children with what at times seemed to be an ecstasy. He could look at them—in the bath, asleep, all the cornball times and places—and feel strange, high, exalted, confused. Ether on a white cloth—he could feel drugged by his love for them. Then, other times, they seemed strangers. He hated them for their anger, their will. There were times when they seemed psychotic to him, autistic or schizophrenic. Then he worried that he had done that to them. And then, moments later, when they were coloring or building with blocks, he worried that he could ever have had such thoughts in the first place.

Was something wrong with his family? Was something deeply wrong with *him?* He had never wanted anything less than to be the best husband and father he could possibly be, he thought as he walked through the gates and into the cool green yard of Rockefeller University.

Before he opened the door to her office, he watched her through the glass window. She seemed calm and busy; her very high white forehead seemed capable of springing forth progeny. He could tell that she wouldn't want to be pulled away, but what choice did he have?

"Sorry," he said as he entered. "You look busy."

She smiled. "I am."

"Ah. Well . . ."

"But the world will just have to wait. Let me just wash my hands, will you?" she said, brushing past him and heading for the john.

While she was gone, he walked around the laboratory. He always felt oddly excited and unadmitted here—like a child taken up to see the cockpit. The equipment fascinated him. But he couldn't touch. She might catch him at it and, then again, there was the germ thing. He wished she didn't have to do the kind of research she was doing. He looked at the vials on the counter. If what she was working on had anything like the toxicity of botulism, let's say, then each vial might well be adequate to destroy the world. It made him feel uneasy to know that Louise was so empowered.

When she returned, he could smell her cologne in the air. Damask rose. He wondered why she had put it on. As a gesture toward him? As an effort to cover up the formaldehyde or the sweat or whatever it was that had finally managed to assault her senses in the bathroom?

"You look lovely," he said. "Here," he added, thrusting the flowers he had been holding behind his back at her.

"Oh, my," she said, taking them, smelling them. "Aren't they lovely?"

"You should put them in water," he cautioned. He watched as she took a beaker and filled it with distilled water. This sensitivity, to use the distilled water, sure to make them last much longer, made him feel good and bad at the same time. She was careful—only he knew how careful—but, beyond that, it looked like she was doing her best to make things last.

"Ready for lunch?" she asked brightly.

"Yes. Let's go," he said, offering her his arm.

They remarked on the chill in the air as they walked across campus. Once beyond the gates, they felt pitched into the rhythm of the city and, by design or by accident, kept bumping against each other as they walked down the street. The restaurant was two blocks away; they always went there for lunch, whenever, that is, they had lunch.

She ordered a zucchini quiche; he ordered vegetarian chili. As they waited for the food, they spoke about the children.

"Denny wants to go to Ezra's house Friday night for a sleepover," Bill said. "I told him he could."

"Oh. Fine."

"Perhaps we can get Darcy or someone for Petey that night. I'd like to go see the new Bergman. It's supposed to be very good."

She frowned. "I'm expecting I'll have to work late Friday." She looked down at the table and then up at him. "You can go if you want. What's it called?"

He paused before replying. "I don't recall."

"I don't know. I haven't much liked his recent movies."

"But he has to be seen, don't you think?" Bill said, unable to keep a note of peevishness out of his voice. "I can't imagine missing one of his films."

"I suppose," she said, sounding uninterested.

He couldn't help smiling. "Do you remember when we saw six Bergman films in a row that summer?"

She smiled. "God, yes. One of those things you can only do when you're young."

"The Seventh Seal. Wild Strawberries. Winter Light. Through a Glass Darkly." He couldn't remember the others. They faded into the blur of memory, into that happy time that seemed so much happier now.

"I just hope they don't give him a lot of sugar," she said as she sipped at her mineral water.

"Who?"

"The Normans."

"Oh, I don't think they will . . ."

"They *ply* Ezra with sugar. That's why he's fat. Why they're fat. I bet they eat Fruit Loops for dinner."

"Come on. They're very sweet . . ."

She smirked.

"Poor choice of words," he said with a small laugh. "I'll just tell them that Denny can't handle sugar."

"He can't," she said firmly.

"I know he can't."

He felt a certain heat of shame. She must have known that he broke the rules; she must have known that there were sundaes and David's cookies and, yes, even the occasional Devil Dog. She must have known that there were times when her dietary principles made him sick.

"Petey can handle sweets much better," she continued.

"Yes, I know." And so Petey got the occasional frozen yogurt when Denny wasn't around. "I've been meaning to ask you," he said, "but you've been so scarce this week . . ."

"I know," she said firmly. "It's been a difficult week. I don't want to have to apologize for it."

He considered several responses, but decided, in the end, that he was best off not to address what she said. "There's a feast at the Center next Friday night . . ."

"A feast?" she said, amused. "A sacrificial feast? Will they serve roast child?" She didn't like the Center. She thought the people were dippy and that the entire place could have been considerably more hygienic. At one of the rare parents' meetings she had attended, she gave a long discourse on sterile conditions. Loretta, however, was not one to be cowed, even by Louise at her most scientific/ officious, and told her firmly that if she wanted a sterile environment she had come to the wrong place.

"It's a Thanksgiving feast. Everybody brings something. A covered-dish supper. I thought we could bring brownies or something."

"And get our brownie points," she muttered.

"What's that supposed to mean?"

"I don't know," she said, and she didn't.

The waiter came over with their food. The process of placing the dishes on the table, pouring water, and asking if they needed anything else took a minute, long enough to cool them.

"Will you mark it on your calendar for next Friday? The children will want us both to be there."

"I don't think I can go," she said, poking at her quiche.

He stopped eating. "Why?"

She gave a small sulky shrug. "Something may come up. A seminar . . ."

He felt a lump forming in his throat. "Don't you want to do anything as a family anymore?"

She stared at him. "No," she said. There it was—no.

He looked at her; he felt afraid. "What does that mean?"

She laid down her fork. Was she finished? She ate like a bird (a vulture, he thought, remembering an old joke). Her eyes, which were unusual but not pretty, large, opaque, and dimly blue, betrayed nothing. "Don't you think it's time?" she asked.

"Time for what?" Time for talking? Time for help? He didn't know what she meant.

"Bill, I haven't been fair to you . . ."

It was true, he thought with a wash of relief, she hadn't. "That's all right," he said. "We can get back to—"

"No, no," she said quickly. "I'd like you to listen to me."

Again he felt the fear; he listened.

"It's been a long time coming. You know that. It's been a long time coming . . ."

"Fifteen years?" he said. "Is that a long time in your book?"

"Look, if you're not going to help . . ."

"I *always* help," he shot back.

She took a deep breath. He could see her start to tremble.

"You know it hasn't been right between us," she said, poking at her quiche. "Not for a long time. We're growing but we're not growing together."

"Where did you get that from?" he wanted to know. "*Cosmopolitan* magazine?"

He watched the tiniest flicker of a smile play across her lips. The idea that she would read *Cosmopolitan* magazine was so improbable that the remark made little sense and couldn't hurt her. "You married me when I was twenty," she said. "Twenty years old . . ."

"All right, now don't make it sound like I stole your youth, please. I was twenty-two. It seemed, at the time, we were in love."

"We were. We *are*." She trembled. "I love you, Bill. Please don't ever think I don't. You're very dear to me."

The lump became immediately enormous, wild and cancerous. "You're playing with my life. Our lives. Our children's lives."

"I don't think I am. I think we'll all survive. I think we'll prosper."

You're very optimistic, he thought. You're very confident. You're very wrong, he wanted to scream at her. "Can't we try to get help?" he said. "People *have* been helped, you know."

"We've tried that."

"We can try again."

"This is not something I need help with," she said. "There's no deep, dark thing here that can be analyzed away or that *needs* analyzing away. I know what needs to be done. I need space. I need time . . ."

"Come on, Louise," he said, trying to make his voice sound paternal. "We haven't made such demands on your time. I think we've done a pretty fair job of giving you—"

"Bill, understand!" she cried. "This is what I want."

And so you shall have it. He felt something leach out of him—something ineffable and irretrievable. "What do you want to do?" he asked. "How do you want to do it?" He put his fist up against the pulse in his neck. "I don't know how to do it."

She pushed the quiche away and leaned back in her chair, letting him know that she was ready to talk turkey. "I think we should try a trial separation. Six months. Nothing legal, of course. And then we'll reassess."

"Reassess?" he said. "But you haven't answered my question. How do we do it?"

She thought a moment. "Well, I suppose you move out." She checked his stricken face, softened her tone. "That's generally the way it's done, isn't it?"

"We can't afford that," he cried. "Two residences in New York City on our incomes? Are you crazy?"

She frowned; she didn't like the noise he was making in the restaurant. "Do we need to go somewhere else?" she asked. When she saw him settle down, she continued. "You'll manage," she said. "You know you're very resourceful when it comes to things like this. You'll find a sublease . . . something."

"What about the kids?" he said. "What about them?"

"We'll share responsibilities, of course."

You? he felt like screaming. *You*? Do you even know which toothbrush belongs to which kid? "You're never out by five," he said. "How will you pick them up? You'll—"

"I'll make arrangements," she said firmly. "Please stop. We're not the first ones in the world this has ever happened to."

He felt the room darken, spin. "Is there someone else?"

"No."

"But there will be?"

"Oh, Bill."

He seized her hand. He held it tight. He could be very strong. She didn't even know how strong he could be. "Don't," he said.

"You're hurting me . . ."

Those words. Prelude to murder. Oh yes. He wanted to kill her. He wanted her really to know what it was to hurt. "I love you, Louise," he said, feeling the lump explode, and the tears, those acid tears. "Don't do this. We shouldn't do this."

"Bill, stop it," she said, her eyes growing larger but no brighter. "Why are you doing this?"

"Fifteen years. You can't just throw away fifteen years."

"Stop it!" she hissed. "Just stop it now!"

He let go of her hand. She rubbed it. Her face was redder than he had ever seen it, which made him feel good and scared both. "You're acting much worse than I ever thought you would. You're entirely vindicating my decision," she told him as he sat there not wanting to look at her. "It's no use, Bill," she said, softening her voice again, feeling a pity for him. "I've made up my mind."

You've made up your mind.

"I need space."

You need space.

"And time to think."

And time to think.

"Do you understand?"

He looked at her in such a way that she knew he didn't. Who'll help you sleep at night, Louise? he wondered. Who'll massage your neck? Who'll mix you your drink? Who'll listen to you crying three times a year that you've got cancer and you're going to die? Who'll love you the way I do?

"Yes," he said finally, letting it go. "I understand."

3

THAT FIRST DAY, Trina followed Hildy around. Sure, it would have been nice if it were the other way around but it wasn't and Trina wasn't proud. She needed to think that someone knew who she was. At first, Hildy wasn't letting on that she did and Trina felt like the kid who's always left out, the one who misses the bus to summer camp and gets there after everyone else has chosen a bunkmate. Not that she knew the first thing about summer camp. You didn't get to go to summer camp when you grew up in Fleischmans, New York.

Everyone always asked her about the name of her hometown. Most figured it for the birthplace of yeast. Is there a Yeast Hall of Fame? some of the funny ones wanted to know. The fact was that it had nothing to do with yeast—or margarine, for that matter. It was just this little town in the Catskills, with two kosher butchers and a lot of summer Jews.

She grew up there. Her father worked with his hands and was a Communist. Her parents had moved up to Fleischmans with a bunch of their friends who held the same political convictions. A collective, they called it for a while. Her father, Joseph Rudy Dunbar, started as a trucker and went on to carpentry, plumbing, landscaping, and, finally, poultry farming. He raised some of the finest geese in New York State. Funny about that—she was always afraid of geese. Even now, when she saw a child feeding geese in the park, going too close, she wanted to run and scoop her up, that's how fearful she was of a goose's temper, its hiss, its bony clicking tongue. When her father died—emphysema, at fifty—the geese died with him. It wasn't that they pined for him or anything; there was just nobody who wanted to take care of them. Trina was afraid of them; her mother could have cared less. Her mother, Carmel Dunbar née Horowitz, had never taken to the rural life as her father had. Even though both of them came from Brooklyn, only her father was the one able to make the change. Maybe it was because her mother was Jewish, from a long line of tailors and seamstresses, those who lived by the cloth instead of off the land. When her father died, her mother moved straight over to Kingston, which may not have been a city by New York City standards or even by Jersey City standards, but which was certainly a city by Ulster County standards. There she opened a hobby shop, where she sold knitting supplies, pottery supplies, lapidary supplies. She wrote a column for the local newspaper on "Hobbies and Collecting." She sold antiques from her home— juice glasses with oranges and strawberries painted on them; toast racks; cranberry glass; that sort of thing. She survived. She lived to tell the tale.

Trina looked around the room, made sure she knew where Hildy was. By the time all the parents had dropped off the kids—so many faces, baby tears, people staring at her, little bodies that needed to be held—Hildy was beginning to feel

the eye on her and came over with a book. *Curious George*. Trina read it twice as
Hildy stared at her, instead of the pictures, memorizing her, cataloging her.

"You got red hair," Hildy said.

"Yes. You've got brown."

"And freckles."

"Uh-huh."

"Do they hurt?"

"What?"

"The freckles."

Trina shook her head. "Freckles don't hurt."

Hildy laughed, and Trina wondered if she had been joking. The idea that a
three-and-a-half-year-old child could make such a joke scared her a little, but she
loved it.

She loved the meeting too. Ten kids in a circle. One of the teachers, Charles,
led things along. She sat there, quiet as the quietest child, and watched him. He
was good to watch. He had the most beautiful hands. She always noticed hands;
his were long, white, strong hands. Christ hands, she thought, but as soon as she
thought it, she wished she could have thought it away. It was the sort of thing
that got her into trouble.

"Does anybody have anything they want to say today?" asked Charles.

"I do! I do!" cried Hildy.

She waited a moment, until she was sure that all eyes were on her. "Red is my
favorite color," she said.

"Why?" asked Charles.

Trina watched as Hildy thought this over. "It's the color of ketchup," she said
finally.

Charles couldn't help smiling. "Anyone else?" he asked.

A little boy named Aaron stood up.

"You can sit down and tell us, Aaron," said Charles, who was very peaceful, but
had an edge to him that Trina wondered if anyone else could see.

"My grandma wanted to give me rice pudding," Aaron said. "With raisins."

It was weird, Trina thought. The disconnectedness of it all made Trina think of
group therapy, which she had never been in, but which she had an image of, from
the movies maybe.

"Rice pudding!" cried Olivier, the little black boy with the dazzling blue eyes.
He started making a noise that sounded like "Eeow."

"Hush up," said Darcy. "Rice pudding is good as it comes!" she said indig-
nantly.

"My grandma wanted to give me rice pudding," Aaron continued, "but I didn't
want it . . ."

"Eeow," Olivier hissed, his eyes bright with mischief.

Aaron, a sensitive child, burst into tears and crossed the circle to sit with Darcy,
his pillow, who cradled him in her arms, massive Easter hams.

"Do you want to finish, Aaron?" asked Charles, who sounded magically patient
and kind.

Aaron shook his head.

"You mustn't jump on other people's words," Charles told the group. "And you,
Aaron—you must use your words."

"I don't want to finish," Aaron murmured against Darcy's endless breast. "I want to go home. I want my daddy."

Charles glanced at Trina—to see how she was taking it all? Trina wondered. "Your daddy will be here later, Aaron." He looked around, collecting the circle with his eyes. "We have a new teacher, everyone," he announced. "Her name is Trina. I think some of you already know her."

"I do," Hildy said.

Trina looked at her; just then it felt like no one would ever say a better thing about her.

"I know her," said Petey, and then Olivier said it too.

"You'll all know her before the day is through," said Charles, and then he smiled at her, the smile so warm, like a blast of heat off a passing train or some warm wind raking the beach in June.

The day was long for her, very long. She was used to working hard—Lord knows, the dinner shift at Harding's was no picnic—but the fatigue brought on by meeting needs, urgent child needs, was a new thing for her. Not only was she working nonstop—changing diapers, cleaning spills, spreading peanut butter on rice crackers—but she was already, so soon, just like that, one of the sources the children turned to for comfort.

By midday, she knew all the children. Olivier, big, brown, those blue eyes, faster, stronger, liking to push, liking to see others fall down. Aaron, who fell down a lot, who cried, who hid, and who could make the others laugh when he wanted to. David, big, blunt, red-headed, uncomplicated, Huck Finn at three and a half. Molly, dimpled, rosy-cheeked, beautiful, shy one minute, stage center the next. Petey, who was like a midget, so serious, so together, so competent; you figured him to become a great man. Martha, loud and fat and incredibly alive. Hildy, of course, who was her friend already. And then there was Caitlin. Caitlin was Down's-syndrome. The only one all day who didn't complain.

"She never complains," Loretta said, later on, when she pulled Trina into her office for tea. "You can see how hard everything is for her. Every little thing. But she's brave. God, she's so brave. And really, on balance, so on top of it all. I wish her parents were that on top of it all."

"What's wrong with her parents?" Trina asked.

Loretta shrugged. "They're decent people. God knows, if anything they're decent. And the thing about parenting a child like this—one of the things I've learned since we started mainstreaming handicapped children—is that you can't sit in judgment on the parents, regardless of how they act. That's particularly true in the case of Caitlin's parents. You see, they can't have another. This is what they've got."

"Is that so bad?" Trina wondered.

"No," said Loretta, lighting a Saratoga. "She's the sweetest, best, brightest little girl. She could grow up to become one hell of a woman. I think her mother knows that." Loretta smiled a little. "Her mother's a lioness. She's this teeny little woman, about four-feet-eleven, with little doughy features. She looks like a Hummel figure. But you talk to her for three minutes and you get the sense that she will swim across the Atlantic with Caitlin strapped to her back, if need be."

"What about the father?"

"Patrick? He's a big Irish lug. Salesman type. In fact, I should say, a salesman. Works for AT&T. Makes *mucho dinero*," Loretta said, rubbing her fingers together in street body language. "Worked his way up the hard way. He comes from some little town in upstate New York, so does she. They're bona fide high-school sweethearts. Came to the Big Apple, played cards right, and then whammo. Along comes Big Problem."

"Caitlin?"

"Good guess." Loretta put out her half-smoked cigarette in the dregs of her teacup. "Listen, I don't want you to get the wrong impression. The man is a good man. You need a favor, you need to have a chest of drawers moved maybe? He'll come over on a Saturday morning, you can count on it. And, as far as Caitlin goes, he's got all the right moves, but somehow his heart isn't in it."

"Why?" Trina asked.

Loretta laughed. "You're a gossip. Terrific. I knew it."

Trina flushed a little, played with her spoon.

"Come on. I wouldn't have hired you if you weren't. Half of the game is getting to know the principals, gathering and conveying the information. Hell, we're taking care of their *kids*. Eight hours a day. We damn well better know who we're dealing with."

"Then why isn't his heart in it?" Trina asked more confidently.

Loretta thought a moment. "He had a dream," she said. "And then it turned into a certain kind of nightmare."

"What kind?" Trina murmured.

"The kind you can't wake up from."

At three o'clock, Sam Sloan sat on a bench in Central Park near the Eighty-ninth Street entrance. He had sat on that bench since 12:45. Recently he had begun a novel set in Central Park. It had, as its hero, a rabbit named Junius. Since becoming a father, nearly four years ago, Sam had made a place in his life for anthropomorphism. Not that he was interested in giving the world his version of the Berenstain Bears, but he would certainly be pleased to leave behind a legacy that could be entered in the literature alongside *Charlotte's Web* or *Bambi* or that greatest of anthropomorphic classics, *The Wind in the Willows*. His novel, which was so far untitled, featured a rabbit—Junius P. Adams—who had the odd life experience of being a less-than-urban creature in the most extreme of urban circumstances. In the course of telling Junius' story, which would be a great adventure story, full of risk, deviltry, bravado, and escape, he would provide a history of the park, a veritable monograph on Olmsted's landscape design, and a near-catalog of the botanical varieties to be found in New York's great oasis. He thought the book had a distinctly commercial ring.

It was time for a book with a distinctly commercial ring. Or should he say it was time for a book that was a success. In the last thirteen years, he had written four novels, two of which were under a pseudonym and had to do with virginal young women losing their hymens in remote climes of the world like Turkestan or Lapland (the latter was a little difficult to pull off, but the money was good); one of which had gone unpublished; and the fourth of which was a highly literate dog story that would not have made him much money at all except that it was optioned for the movies by a faded forties film star who was an animal lover and who happened to be married to the ketchup and condiment king of America. Now, at each meal, which was often hamburger (he was in charge of dinner), he and Liv would toast "the ketchup king" as if they were saying grace. Lately, this had seemed an old joke, he reminded himself to tell Liv.

Liv had suggested he not return to literate animal stories, but he told her that he loved animals. Anyway, he didn't like her interfering in his work. He didn't interfere in hers. Nothing did. She was a third-year associate with the prestigious law firm of Comley, Wizan, Frank & Wishnograd, in their Trusts and Estates division. She made $69,000 a year and had been pretty much assured that she would make partner, whereupon her salary would take off into the stratosphere. Sam, who in addition to his writing did editorial work for his former employer, a small publishing house called Ernest Wesson Books, made, in a good year, let's say a cool twenty grand.

Liv didn't seem to mind. She loved what she did. She loved counseling rich Park Avenue matrons on sheltering their trusts—or whatever the hell it was that she did. As she put it, "she didn't like to bring home the office with her." And so they seldom talked about their work, which was a far cry from the days when they had first met, as junior editors at Ernest Wesson. That was a while ago, however, and the fact was that Liv hadn't waited long to get herself into a more lucrative profession. She knew that money was important to her and, on the few occasions when they fought about it, she let it be known that she wouldn't be without it. And she wasn't.

Now she was six months pregnant. When the time came, she would take a short leave from work, give suck, and return to her office. He couldn't help smiling a little as he thought of it. She was a hell of an achiever. And she didn't achieve at the expense of her family. Her family, himself included, loved her very much.

Sam closed up his notebook—he had written three pages today, a fair effort—and headed toward the Center. He had promised Aaron that he would take him to the carousel today. There wouldn't be that many more carousel days; they closed it up for winter. As he walked, he framed, in his mind, a scene in his book in which Junius' friends, a family of mice, take up winter residence inside the cavity of a gilt-and-turquoise carousel horse.

Just as Sam reached the Center, which was located on the ground floor of a brownstone on Eighty-ninth Street, he saw his friend Nancy Poole. The sight of her, coming down the street in the opposite direction, filled him with a certain pleasure that he hesitated to examine.

"You're early," he called.

"No, I'm late!" she cried. She was a big girl—probably an inch taller than he— and had regular, almost plain features that he had come to think were rather beautiful. She looked fresh and robust, like a russet apple or something, and in his hornier fantasies he could imagine her in some tacky nineteenth-century painting with loosely laced bodice and ewer upon head. "I told David I would be here by two, but the deliveryman from Bloomingdale's was late, of course."

"Why two?" he asked, as they headed down the brownstone stairs.

"He told me this morning that his nose felt funny."

"Poor oogums," he teased.

"Stop it," she laughed. "Seriously, he never complains."

"Did you call?" he asked.

"Yes, they said he was all right, but . . ." She trailed off.

"But you wanted to see for yourself," he finished for her.

"Right."

As soon as they entered the big, bright room, the group of children moved toward them like a wave. "Hi, Mommy!" David called. He was such an open child, Sam thought. Big, healthy, vigorous. Sam watched as Nancy picked him up and hugged him.

"Hello, Aaron," Sam called to his son, who had stayed behind, out of the wave, to do something with Lego.

Aaron looked up but said nothing.

"Same to you, buddy," Sam said.

Charles came over. Sam liked Charles very much. He thought Charles was extremely intelligent and conscientious. And Aaron loved Charles utterly.

"Hi, Charles. Did you have a good day?" Sam asked.

"Fine. No problems." He paused. "He got a little sensitive when he wasn't allowed to complete a thought at meeting."

Sam nodded, a little concerned that he didn't care as much about it as Charles seemed to. Then he noticed a woman looking at him. He nodded hello.

"Trina," Charles said, "this is Sam Sloan."

"Hi," said Sam. "Are you working here?"

Trina nodded. "I've just started."

"Good luck. You'll need it."

"Don't mind him," said Nancy, turning around. "I'm Nancy Poole. Welcome. The children are wonderful."

"Yes, they are," said Trina.

Nancy and Sam got the children together and headed out.

"She seems nice," Nancy said, out on the street.

"Probably a little spacey," said Sam. "Loretta likes to get them spacey. Then they imprint on her, like baby geese, and follow her anywhere."

"Oh, stop it," Nancy laughed. "You're wicked."

He grinned. "Would you folks like to join us? We're going to the carousel."

"The carousel?" she said, a touch of wistfulness in her voice. "We haven't been there in ages."

"So come."

"I don't know. I haven't even started dinner yet."

"You haven't even started dinner yet?" he said, throwing the words back at her. "You live in New York City. Welcome. There are such things as Chinese restaurants."

"Justin doesn't like highly spiced foods," she said.

"Then let Justin eat the rice."

"Ho, ho. Wouldn't that be funny?" she said with a sly grin.

"Come on," he said with a sudden urgency. "Come to the carousel."

They took a cab, drawing off the financial resources of their respective spouses. Nancy's husband—Justin—was in leverage buyouts or venture capital or some such and evidently took it in hand over fist. At least Nancy never seemed to have to worry about how or where she spent her money and, consequently, David, who was such a sweet kid that it was doubtful he would ever be spoiled, seemed to have everything: more toys, more clothes, more pairs of shoes, more everything.

"I want a Checker cab," Aaron complained.

"I know you do," said Sam, "but cabs are hard to find on Central Park West."

"We could go to Broadway," Aaron said.

"Jesus," Sam cried. "Walter Winchell here. Mr. New York."

"I want a Checker cab," Aaron continued, with that terrible whine he worked constantly to perfect.

"Listen," Sam said, "shall I have the cab turn around and take us home?"

There was a silence.

"Huh?"

"No," Aaron managed.

Nancy shot him a look—an I've-been-there-many-times-before look. But still he wondered if she really had. Aaron and David were such different kids. Sometimes it was hard to figure how they were the best of friends. For one thing, David must have been a good fifty percent bigger. Aaron was very small; he didn't make the charts. Of course, it wasn't difficult to trace the source of his diminutiveness. Liv was tiny, barely over five feet, with the slimmest of wrists and ankles, but she overcompensated. Maybe Aaron overcompensated too. He seemed more aggressive than David, who could, however, when pushed too far, swat his small friend with an absolutely bearlike gesture. Justin, David's father, was tall, but, according to Nancy, David really got his meaty hands and canal-boat feet from Nancy's father and grandfather, who operated a dairy farm together in New Jersey.

They got off near Tavern on the Green and began walking through the park. The sky, as they walked the short distance to the carousel, was turning slate.

"Do you think this is a good idea?" Nancy asked.

He took it as a rhetorical question. When they got to the carousel, it was deserted but, thank God, not officially closed.

"Me first!" Aaron screamed, pushing his way in front of David. Sam sighed and shook his head. He and Nancy secured the children onto the horses and then stepped outside to the other side of the fence. A hurdy-gurdy version of "Tie a Yellow Ribbon 'Round the Old Oak Tree" started up and then the carousel went into its act—up and down, up and down, around and around and around. Nancy and Sam stood there, looking for the boys to wave to each time they came around the bend.

"This is one of the greatest spots in New York," Sam said.

Nancy looked at him.

"Really. It is." He pointed. "Look at them. They're so happy."

It almost choked him up to see Aaron so happy. There were times when it occurred to him—deep within him—that his son was maybe not such a happy kid. Why not? He loved him. He loved him absolutely. This son of his—this smart, crabby, high-strung, funny son of his—was the most important thing in his life. Well, there. Maybe that was just the problem. Maybe his son shouldn't be the most important thing in his life. Sam's mother always used to tell him that he and his father and his brother were all equally important to her. Psychoanalysis later disproved this to Sam, but, at the time, he felt there was something reassuring about those words. But even if he lied to Aaron the way his mother had lied to him, he doubted he could pull it off. Because he was convinced that his mother really believed that everyone was equal in their family, whereas, in his family, he didn't believe it for a moment. For all the problems they had—and they had many—he loved Liv, but not the way he loved Aaron. Oh, in the beginning, maybe. Yes, in the beginning. Those first years, when he wasn't with her he dreamed of her. They had enormous fun in those days. They were both very active—they loved to play tennis; to go cross-country skiing; even, when they had the dough, to go downhill. Through a fluke, they were able to rent a cottage near Stockbridge for next to nothing and they went there year-round, escaping on the weekends. They were both into cooking then, and they would have cook-offs. She used to do elaborate breakfasts—*bauernküchen* and apple crepes and stuff like that. And he would do these highly complex ethnic dinners, shopping during the week for weird ingredients like masa farina and nasai goreng. And there was so much time to read then and they were so very serious about it. They'd always read the same thing at the same time and then they'd discuss it. One summer they read all of Richard Yates; one winter all of Walker Percy. God, they were ambitious then. They'd get into the car and drive an hour down dark, twisty country roads to Rhinebeck, to the Upstate Films, where they could catch old foreign movies like *The Earrings of Madame de . . .* and *Ossessione*. And then there was the sex. No joke, but he could bring her to tears those days. It was beautiful. Sweet, pure, beautiful.

"Sam," Nancy said, nudging him, "they're finished."

No, they weren't. The boys began to negotiate. They got another ride, but finally it was time to go. Aaron gave him lip about going, but he told himself that he was the parent and Aaron was the child and so he got him off the horse.

As soon as they started to head out of the park, the clouds gathered into what looked like a vortex, something from Oz.

"Run!" Sam cried, and they all started to run, but Aaron was never from the great runners and, after a minute, he started to cry, stamping his feet, biting his knuckles, and Sam had to dash back and scoop him up.

"Don't cry, don't cry," Sam whispered. It must have been so frightening, Sam thought, to see the sky blacken, and to see yourself left behind. "Don't cry," he said again, kissing his son's soft round cheek.

They had to wait under an awning maybe ten minutes before they could get a cab.

"This was a mistake," said Nancy, in the cab.

"Come on. A little rain. Big deal. Live a little." A great big farmgirl like you, he thought to himself.

She nodded. "You're right, I guess." The cab stopped in front of her building—one of the really good buildings on Riverside Drive. Immediately, Aaron, with David's measured assistance, began to raise a stink about wanting to go upstairs to David's.

Nancy shrugged. "You want to?"

Sam looked at her. "But you haven't even started dinner."

She grinned. "That's OK. You can help me chop onions."

"I cry," he warned.

"It's OK. I'm used to crying."

He never failed to be bowled over by her apartment. It was huge, rambling. He and Liv enjoyed a perfectly respectable two-bedroom that would soon become too small when the new baby came and that they would live in, regardless of cramped space, for however long it took for the building to go co-op. But this place—this was the big time.

David and Aaron ran off to David's room and left Sam and Nancy alone together in the kitchen.

"Tea?" she asked.

He thought about it a minute. "You have any bourbon?"

She looked at him and then she grinned again. She really had a nice grin, Sam thought. She went to the liquor cabinet and pulled out a bottle of Jack Daniel's. Only the best, of course.

"You're not a secret tippler, are you?" she asked, pouring him a shot in a very expensive crystal highball glass.

"What's the secret?"

"You know. Drinking in the afternoon and all."

"Beats the morning," he said. "Anyway, if I were in publishing or advertising or whatever, I'd have a couple of belts at lunch every day, so what's the big deal? Househusbands deserve at least that, right?"

"Right," she said, with some hesitation.

He knew that she was bothered by the appellation "househusband." She was very conventional and probably believed that men should leave the house every morning in a uniform. But he didn't care. He liked what he did. He liked having his work occupy a small, manageable part of his life. He liked being the one whom Aaron called for in the night. And he liked bothering people. "Wanna join me?" he asked, with a grin of his own.

"Are you kidding?" she laughed. "You've have to scrape me off the floor."

Suddenly there was the sound of screeching from the bedroom. Aaron's screeching. Nancy got ready to go, but Sam put up a restraining arm. "Let them work it out," he said. They stood there for a moment—more screeching and the unreasonable fear that David, twice his size, was sitting astride Aaron, crushing his rib cage. Nancy pulled away and Sam followed her down the endless hallway to David's room. There they found Aaron, red-faced and screeching, with David, looking abashed, holding an action figure.

"David," Nancy said in the hushed voice she reserved for reprimands, "you must learn to share."

"Aaron," said Sam, the voice of reason, "stop screaming and use your words."

They mediated a few more minutes, into a truce, and then left them alone, as they headed back into the kitchen. Sam picked up the bourbon where he had left off.

"Those damned action figures," Nancy fretted as she rummaged in the vegetable bin for onions. "They bring out the most aggressive forms of behavior."

"Aggression goes with being a boy—it's part of the territory. The figures give them an outlet. That's not the problem," Sam said. "The problem is that Aaron can't handle it."

She gave him a look. "Come on, Sam. 'Can't handle it'? He's not even four."

Sam felt himself about to get into an uncomfortable position, but he already had one leg in. "The littlest things ruffle him. I look at David. He's so calm, so affable . . ."

"Aaron's a different kind of kid. He's intense. He's brilliant . . ."

"I don't want him to be so brilliant. A little less brilliant, a little more relaxed . . ."

"Well, as Loretta says, 'you get what you get.' You're brilliant, Liv's brilliant, and Aaron's brilliant."

There was a silence. For shame, for shame—but all he could think of was that she had called him brilliant. He wasn't used to getting compliments. He felt touched and even rather excited.

She began to chop the onions. "Let me have a board," he said. She hesitated for a second—this was new to her, a man chopping in her kitchen—but she supplied him and soon they were working alongside, Sam sipping from the Jack Daniel's as he chopped.

"And don't think David doesn't have his moments," she said, picking up the thread. "Let me tell you, he knows how to wake up screaming in the middle of the night."

Sam was shocked and a little pleased to hear this. Night terrors were not Aaron's affliction. "What's that about?" he asked understatedly.

She shrugged.

"Have you talked to Loretta about it?"

She nodded. "She feels he's pressured."

"David? Pressured?" Sam said. It was like imagining the statue of Atlas in Rockefeller Center feeling pressured.

"Yes," she said decisively, going at an onion. "David. Pressured."

She didn't seem to want to talk about it any further. The kitchen was quiet except for the sound of blades passing through onions.

"They're quiet," Sam pointed out. "Is that good?"

She smiled a little. "They wouldn't really hurt each other. They really love each other. They're so different and they complement each other so beautifully." She looked up at him; her eyes were full of tears. She tore off a piece of paper towel and dabbed at her eyes. "Damned onions."

"Don't you have a Cuisinart?"

"Yeah, but I don't like it for onions. It purees them."

"You have to get the technique down. On, off. On, off. On, off."

"Doesn't work for me," she said.

"I think you just like to suffer."

She stared at him, then she turned back to the onions. "You shouldn't worry about Aaron," she said. "He's a wonderful child. He's fascinating. He's got a wonderful father who's always there for him."

Compliment Number Two. He wasn't quite sure what to do with it. "Sometimes I think that's his problem," he suggested.

"What?"

"That he's got a father who's always there for him. Maybe he'd be better off having a father who went to work in the morning, came home at night. A role model of a man out in the world." He laughed—a little hollowly. "Jesus, you should see him when I have to actually put on a tie and jacket and go somewhere. It's like Coronation Week."

She laughed and dabbed once more at her eyes. "Come on, Sam," she said. "You're crazy if you don't think he's incredibly lucky to have you. Justin puts on a tie every morning of the week—what a thrill. Do you know how much David gets to see him? I have to call his secretary to remind him when he's due to spend an hour with his son!" she said in a rare outburst.

"No, you don't."

"The hell I don't."

"That's awful," he said, putting down the knife, the onion work getting to him, searing his nostrils. "Jesus," he said, "who *cares* if the onions come out a puree?"

"I care."

There was a tense silence. She chopped grimly. "He wakes up screaming 'the bad man is going to get me,'" she said, almost to herself. "'The bad man.' Well, you don't have to be Sigmund Freud to figure that one out, do you? And you know what Justin does? He screams at him. *He screams at him.* I want to kill him . . ."

She stopped herself. She was an extremely private person. He didn't talk to her more than a hello or a how-are-you for the first year he knew her. The first year he knew her he didn't think very much of her at all. Funny, wasn't it, how you came to know more and more things about a person. First little things and then more and then more and then the person whom you once thought plain and excessively shy for an adult took on a certain worthiness, a certain interest, possibly even a kind of fascination.

"I don't know what I'm talking about," she said, covering her tracks.

"Yes, you do."

Two tears fell down her cheeks and she didn't bother to pretend it was the onions. He touched her hair. Honey-colored hair. She let his hand rest there a full beat and then she reached up to touch his hand that was touching her hair. Friends, he told himself, but then why, when he let his hand fall away, did they decide to check on the children who had, after all, been playing so nicely.

4

"HERE. LOOK. The Care Bears," said Anna, going after her daughter with a favored T-shirt she now wanted no part of.

"No," Molly returned, running away.

"Yes," Anna said, cornering her and pulling the T-shirt over Molly's head. "Now we've got to hurry up," said Anna, "because Trina's waiting for you."

Trina had immediately established herself as the chief lure for Molly. Frankly, Anna couldn't figure out what it was that Molly saw in Trina; as far as Anna was concerned, Trina seemed pretty low-amp. "I'd go so far as to say she's rabbity," she told Michael one night.

"Hmmnh?" said Michael, who had been reading *The Wall Street Journal*, something new for him.

"I said she's rabbity."

"Rabbity?" Michael repeated, not looking up. "As in cuddly-bunny or potentially rabid rodent?"

"Whatever," said Anna, feeling a flicker of irritation. She and Michael had been
married five years, after a courtship that was complicated but supremely romantic. These days, however, she worried that he wasn't listening to her the way he
used to and she worried that she was boring and she worried about the fact that
she couldn't lose the seven pounds that would return her to her fighting weight
and she worried about the fact that all of her worries were making her sound like
those women who were always writing in to Ann Landers for advice. Most of all,
however, she worried about the thing—the lump—in her breast, which she
hadn't even told Michael about yet and which she was going to see her doctor
about today. She was sure it was just a cystic thing, but still it was harder than
others she had had and it should be checked.

"OK now," she said as she dressed Molly for the cold. "Tights next." She pulled
a pair of red tights onto her daughter—it amazed her how rigid Molly could make
herself when she was feeling uncooperative. It was like this biological defense
mechanism, the way an armadillo rolls up into a ball or a cat bristles.

"A little help here would be appreciated," Anna grunted as she picked up Molly
and pulled the tights tight.

"I want an English muffin," Molly said.

"That's a total *non sequitur*," Anna said, slipping on and Velcro-ing a sneaker.
"We were talking about cooperation, not muffins."

"I don't want to go," Molly whined.

"Oh, now," said Anna. "Trina would miss you and so would Hildy and Martha
and Caitlin." She always included Caitlin because it made her feel good to know
that Molly was growing up in a world where the handicapped were not hidden
behind closed doors.

Molly whimpered a little and made Anna feel rotten. Lately there had been so
much in the news about child abuse in day-care centers and how one indicator of
a problem was if your child complained a lot about going. Well, the fact was that
Molly, God bless her, complained a fair amount about everything (too much
attention, Anna's mother said), and, in fact, she only complained before she got
there and once she got there she was fine. Which led Anna—and Michael—to
believe that it was getting dressed and having to rush out into the cold that she
objected to rather than any abominations at the Center.

Still, for all of the benefits that Molly seemed to derive from day-care—the
community, the social skills, the fact that she was being cared for by accomplished educators rather than refugees from the islands—Anna was still subject
to attacks of guilt. Molly was a baby and yet, four days a week, she had to be
hustled into her Oshkosh and hustled out the door because Anna was a working
mother. Three days a week she worked at *Gotham*, a giveaway consumer magazine where she was an editor for a batch of columns that had very little to do with
each other: book reviews, film reviews, discount shopping, terrace gardening,
personal software. (Anna was learning quickly. It had only been this last year that
she had learned "personal software" did not mean Kotex.) One day a week she
wrote P.R. for a friend's bakery concern. Anna's business card read "writer—

public relations—promotion." Everything but electrolysis, she sometimes joked, though it wasn't so funny. It was a small thing, her career, but her own. And the fact was that they needed her money. Michael's architectural practice was doing well enough, but still there were dry spells—*cash-flow problems* was the correct terminology—and at least her money, such as it was, was regular. She paid for day-care, at the staggering tune of thirty-eight dollars a day. Civilians thought Michael and Anna crazy for spending that much, but what was the choice? She didn't want to send her kid to a place where she would get trench mouth every time she drank a cup of apple juice. There was enough in the world for her to worry about.

"OK, lovie," she said to Molly, "now the sweater."

"Itches."

"Doesn't," Anna said. "It's acrylic."

"Itches," Molly said, running away.

Suddenly there was this woman of thirty-six running after a three-year-old with an acrylic sweater advertising Snoopy.

"Let her be," Michael said, entering the kitchen.

Anna looked up at him. He was beautifully dressed. Funny, when she first met him, he dressed like something left over from the Harvard-Yale game of 1958. Baggy pants, boxy jackets, frayed Brooks Brothers shirts, Weejuns. She had given him a lot of things; one of the things she had given him was pizzazz. Now he wore Italian suits and Italian shoes. He had the physique for it: slim all the way. Now he spent more money on his clothes than he should—"he had an image to protect," they joked, but it was true, for his practice had moved in the direction of interior design for the very rich.

"It's thirty-two degrees out," said Anna. "That's freezing on the Fahrenheit scale."

"If she's cold enough when she gets outside she'll want to wear it. If she's not cold, she doesn't need it."

"So you assume a three-year-old knows when she's cold enough? Have you ever heard of hypothermia?"

"Christ, Anna," he said, sitting down and reaching for the paper. "She'll be wearing *layers,* won't she? She's got on an undershirt and a shirt and a coat, right?" He looked for the Home section of the *Times,* for it was Thursday, and he had to see who had gotten in that he knew.

"*You* didn't dress her," Anna accused. "How do you know what she has on?"

Michael frowned. "Fine," he said. "I'll get her to put on the sweater."

"Forget the sweater," Anna snapped, as Molly watched with interest. "Why don't you just take her this morning and deal with it, OK? I've had enough."

Michael looked at her. "Are you OK?"

She nodded. "I'm fine. I've just had enough this morning, OK?"

Michael stared at her for another moment. "All right," he said.

Anna watched him eat his All-Bran. Every time one of these silly spats erupted, she wondered, in spite of herself, where they were headed. Not that she doubted that they had anything but a committed relationship, but they didn't seem to enjoy each other the way they used to. Part of this—most of this, she'd have to say—had to do with having a child. The combination of two people working and raising a kid added up to one thing: more work. More work than anyone could handle. They tried to be terribly organized. They tried to cook Sundays, to use their Seal-a-Meal, to freeze away dinners for the rest of the week. But, ah, the best-laid plans—Sundays rolled around, came and went; the Sunday papers; the birthday parties and the bar mitzvahs; and nothing got done. So there was the week: she'd pick up Molly at the Center by five; go shopping; home by six; cook dinner; Michael would be home by six-thirty; dinner would be finished by seven-thirty; bathtime for Molly over by eight; storytime and sleep-inducing concluded somewhere between eight and nine. And then there would be fatigue and TV; sometimes knitting; telephone-talking; and maybe a little s-e-x, as they said "in front of the child."

"Will you be home the usual time tonight?" Anna asked.

"Yes. I think so." He tried smiling a little; he didn't like these fights either.

"What shall we do for dinner?"

"I don't know. Something easy. Omelets."

"OK."

They had omelets at least twice a week. What a different kind of life they led from the generation that came before. Her mother, even though she'd worked as a school librarian, always had a hot dinner on the table. The idea that Anna sometimes gave Molly dry Cheerios for dinner probably would finish off her mother altogether.

"OK, Molly," said Michael as he rose from the table. "Let's hit the road."

Anna gave Molly her down coat and her chewable vitamin, which was a sort of reward-cum-transitional object for her trip to the Center. Then she leaned over and gave Molly a kiss. Actually, a "supersmooch," she called it.

"Have a fun day," Anna said. "I'll see you later."

Then she looked at Michael and he looked at her. "Sorry," he said in a whisper. She kissed him hard on the lips.

"I'll call you later," Michael promised, and Anna watched him go, knowing he always kept his promises.

It was one of those miserable mornings, Michael told himself halfway to the Center. Just one of those terrible, crummy mornings. He had just strong-armed Molly into her sweater, and was in a sweat having done so. The thing was she had started to tremble en route to the Center. For two blocks, he had tried to reason with her.

—You'd be a lot warmer if you put on your sweater.

—Why don't you put on your sweater? I'll help you. We'll get it done very fast.

—If you don't put on your sweater, you're liable to catch cold and that wouldn't be any fun, would it?

She responded with a studied lack of response. It was this that always drove him crazy. *I'm talking to you!* he would find himself screaming, and the fact was that he wasn't ordinarily a screamer. But this morning he had run the gamut, the full repertoire: warnings, cajoling, threats, repetitions, pleas. Finally, he took her in hand—his hand that could suddenly seem very large, a monster's hand—and holding her, he stuffed her, howling, into the sweater. That was a block ago, and still she howled. Everyone who passed gave him a look, and he returned, involuntarily, a stupidly apologetic smile. By the time he got to the Center, his smile hurt.

"Listen," he said to Molly as he bent down and began to think of a way to make sense of something that made no sense at all. "When you're intent on making a fuss about something that should have been no fuss at all . . ."

The wailing accelerated, leading Michael in new directions.

"Now, you just stop it. *Right now*," he bellowed in a whisper.

Molly looked at him in amazement, then fright, as she edged into tears once more.

"Oh God," Michael said mournfully, with disgust for himself and, he had to admit, for his daughter. "What are you crying for? You should hear yourself."

He should hear himself, he thought; he was saying all the wrong things. "I'm sorry," he said, kneeling down. "I'm sorry this had to happen," he clarified, putting it on the inevitability of the happening rather than on any fault of his own. And, even as he said it, he had the sense that it was wrong, too, knowing as he did, in his heart of hearts, that the sweater, an acrylic sweater for all that, would hardly make a difference in the cosmic scheme of things. "Don't cry," he said, even as he heard an inner voice warn him never to tell a child not to cry.

"What's the matter with her?" he heard.

He turned around. It was Martha. A three-year-old Jewish mother if ever there was one. She was quite large for her age and somehow, in her pinafore, she had a sort of pigeon-breasted look. "Why are you crying, Molly?" she asked, with her language that had always seemed perfect, as if it had been given to her full-blown, the better to ask questions and offer advice with.

"Martha, stop," said her mother, Heller Norman. "My little *yenta*."

"You shouldn't cry, Molly," Martha continued in her advisory tone that was unique among the children at the Center. "It isn't worth it."

Michael and Heller exchanged glances and Heller shrugged. "She got that one from her grandmother."

"Ah," said Michael. He found Martha a very strange child and often wondered why Molly included her in her circle of friends. One reason, Michael supposed, was a basic function of the Center. Everyone was a part of this community, this extended family; special attachments were made but the whole prevailed. Sometimes Michael complained that it was like living in a small town. Or, more to the point, like living in a Levittown.

"I don't get what you mean," Anna would say.

"Sure you do," Michael would insist. "Did you ever see *No Down Payment*?"

"What's that? A movie? I guess so."

"You would know if you did. It's about these young marrieds who move into postwar tract housing and what happens to them."

"Oooh. Are we young marrieds?"

"We should live so long." Almost everyone with children they knew in New York City, including themselves, was anywhere between thirty-three and forty-three years of age. New York parents, it had to be concluded, were late starters. "Anyway, these young marrieds all have to deal with these very real problems. Not enough money, not enough housing . . ."

"Just like us."

"You got it. Except that even they had more. There was still the idea of the single-family house. And now everyone we know is clamoring after an apartment with a convertible dining room."

"For $380,000."

"Exactly."

Exactly. All of them in need, even the rich ones, trying to make something livable of a city that had, in Michael's opinion, deserted the family. It made him sick when he realized that his parents and his grandparents would have considered him one of life's unfortunates, living in their tiny brownstone apartment with the front room, almost a closet, done over for Molly and her toys, her Lego, all over the apartment, the pieces strewn like waste on the floor of a plastics factory.

He was stopped at the door to the big, open room, brilliant with primary colors, by Loretta, who was wearing a kerchief around her head and who smelled bracingly of Ajax.

"I got in early this morning," she said, picking up in the middle of things, a habit Michael found disconcerting. "We had a prospective parent in yesterday who wrinkled her nose and said the place wasn't clean enough. Do you think it's clean enough?"

She was obviously conducting some kind of poll. Michael, who didn't do well with being put on the spot, could only reply with blunt honesty, "It could be cleaner."

Loretta snorted. "Oh. Another one of those anal types, eh?"

It was just the sort of remark that made Loretta impossible for him. Anna got along gangbusters with her—they both had a manic energy and they could work out a kind of riff between them, like a comedy team with no straight man. But as far as he was concerned, she made him uptight and quieter than he even was normally.

"Well," he said, "if you don't buy it, why were you in early this morning cleaning?"

"Because I've got to put up with anal types. I've no other choice," she joked, in a not very friendly manner.

Charles, who had been overhearing this exchange, came over. He always wore deerskin moccasins and Michael noticed that he moved soundlessly. "She's just in a rotten mood," he said, throwing a long sinewy arm around Loretta's shoulder. "She always gets that way when she takes a sponge in hand."

She shook his arm off, playfully one would assume but there was a surge of anger there too. "Mr. Piggy," she said. "What can you say about a man who had to have his *van* exterminated?"

She walked off. It was a snotty remark, as snotty as they come. He felt embarrassed for Charles, who, however, didn't seem embarrassed in the least. Charles smiled—an apologetic, carefree, sexy smile. Everyone suspected that Charles and Loretta had once gotten it on; Michael felt like he had just seen proof of it. Of course, you couldn't tell who Charles was fucking; he had a kind of spiritual physicality—or a physical spirituality—that touched everyone. He was a physical man. He liked to touch people. He touched women, he touched men, he touched kids. It always seemed he had his hands on people. "He's handsy," Anna said about him, but it wasn't the right word. It implied a dirtiness, and there was nothing dirty about Charles, even if he had to have his van exterminated. He was tall and thin and he dressed every day in starched white shirts which he ironed himself and clean jeans. He had a thick, closely cropped head of silver hair, premature, and brilliant blue eyes and cheekbones like an Apache. Anna thought he was terrific-looking. All the women did. And all the men liked him. Everyone loved him—his soft tender voice; the way he always had a child hanging from him; his mystery. His mystery was talked about at every social gathering. Some said he was a reneging husband who was working with children because he had left his own behind. Some claimed he was an ex-heroin addict because you never got to see his arms. Michael wasn't sure why there were so many stories about him, except that he really was a man of mystery.

"Michael," said Charles, sensing that he was being scrutinized, wanting that stopped before it went too far, "have I told you that you're a really great dresser?"

Michael, taken aback, shook his head. "Uh, no. Actually, you haven't . . . lately," he added, as sort of a little joke.

"You're a really great dresser," Charles said. "And you know why? Not because you put colors together well, though you do. Not because your suits are impeccably tailored, though they are. But because you look comfortable in what you wear."

Michael looked at Charles. This was a guy with a good line. Maybe he was a state witness given a new identity. Maybe he was a CIA man. "Thanks, Charles," he said. He glanced at the official-looking clock on the wall with its generously proportioned Roman numerals. V to IX. Time to go. He looked around the room; he found Molly in a cluster of children, being read to by Trina. The eastern light of morning shone through the great high windows, shooting rays onto Trina's hair, which in the afternoon, when sometimes he came to pick up his daughter, seemed the color of a mouse; but now, in the morning, in that morning light, her hair had streaks of copper. Her face, which when seen in passing on Broadway or on line at the bank seemed blank and plain, now seemed radiant as she read aloud of twelve little girls in two straight lines who smiled at the good and frowned at the bad.

He was almost loath to interrupt her. If he could have sneaked away, without telling Molly, he would have. But they had a rule against it: the sternest rule. They were never to break her trust. And so, from his vantage point where he could watch her tiny heart-shaped rapt face, frowning at the bad, smiling at the good, he moved toward her. She looked up. In an instant, her face changed. There was a flicker of fear that darkened her face like a shadow.

"Don't go, Daddy."

He knelt down. Her lower lip had started to tremble.

"Have a good day, booby," he said. "Mommy will pick you up."

"Don't go, Daddy."

She threw her arms around his neck. For a little girl she had a powerful grip.

"Don't go."

I've been cruel to you this morning, he thought as he hugged her back, a feverish closeness. Then he looked up; there were Trina's eyes. She put the book down. Her eyes were strange, he thought as he watched her put her arms around Molly, who had begun a keening noise.

"We'll watch Daddy from the window," Trina said, gentling her with her voice. Trina nodded to Michael, suggesting he go. And so he went, reaching out just once to touch Molly's Chinese-black hair.

All the way down the stairs he heard Molly's pitiful cries. He felt a weighing-down of confusion and loss, guilt and fear. When he got outside, on to the sidewalk, he looked up, and, through the old glass, he saw her shining rippled face, trying hard to be brave. He waved, turned to walk, didn't look back. All the way to the bus, and then beyond, he tried not to think that something was wrong.

What if I die? She sat there, forbidden thoughts, but she couldn't help thinking them, she couldn't keep them away. What if I die? How could she not think it? All morning long, getting Molly off, then the shower, where she had first felt it, three days ago or was it a week? She knew—everyone knew—that you didn't put off going for a week. Not when it was hard. This one was hard. Like a pea. But everyone put it off. Didn't they? Oh, maybe there were a few people who didn't. There were some people who didn't squeeze pimples either. Good people. Perfect people. She was a good person, but she wasn't a perfect person. That's why she waited. What if she died? What if she found out that the days—two, three, four— she had waited had made all the difference? Into the lymph. Swimming into the lymph.

She looked around the swank office and tried to calm herself. There were Leonard Baskin prints on the wall. The furniture was covered with heavy camel cotton. Very nice offices. Very nice. Her gynecologist, Rose Mead, was just about her age. And doing very well, thank you.

Anna picked up a copy of *Savvy*. Now she knew she was in New York. In any other gynecologist's office in any other part of the country, you'd find a nice *Redbook*. You could clip a nice reassuring recipe for Swiss steak or pineapple boats. Not here. Here you had to read about the problems of women who made "in six figures." She'd never make "in six figures," unless you counted the decimal points. She sat holding the magazine unopened on her lap.

What if I die? What would Molly do? What would Molly *do*? Oh, Molly, I won't leave you. What would Michael do? How would he explain it to her? Mommy's gone to heaven. Would he use the term? She hoped so. She wanted to believe in heaven. Clouds. Clouds. She wanted him to use "heaven."

Never die before your child is six.

She read that somewhere once. *Redbook* maybe. Good practical information. Yet she wasn't quite sure what it meant. She guessed it meant that your kid couldn't handle it if she was any younger than six. Would Molly's life be ruined? The thought made her fill up with tears. What if I die? Would he take Molly to the grave? Is that how Molly should remember her? No. She'd make a tape instead: ". . . Molly, it's Mommy. I love you, Molly. Always remember, Molly. Mommy loves you . . ."

Oh God. Would he marry another woman? Would that other woman be called Mommy? Would it be the best thing for Molly? With no one looking, she reached up to touch the lump beneath the brown jersey. The lump. Oh my God. This one was different. She could feel the difference. She would die. No, she wouldn't leave Molly. If she did, she'd come back, in Molly's dreams. She'd watch over

Molly, she wouldn't let Molly get hurt. She would never let Molly get hurt. . . .

"Now, just look at you."

She looked up. Rose Mead. She looked at herself. She was crying.

"Come," said Rose, who was Chinese-American, beautiful, married to one of the most beautiful WASP men Anna had ever seen. Rose threw an arm around Anna's shoulders. "Something's up."

"You guessed, huh?" Anna said bravely, smiling through her tears.

She had the examination and then, in Rose's office, they talked. It was not a nice lump, said Rose, who didn't look happy.

"I've got cystic breasts," Anna said lamely.

"I'm going to send you for a mammogram," Rose said, picking up the phone.

She sat there listening to Rose Mead make arrangements. She felt a deep sickness in her gut. Will I die? she wanted to ask.

"Will I . . . will I be out by five?"

"Yes, I'm sure."

"I've got to pick up Molly." With that, the tears came again. The tears exploded. So sudden. It was like she vomited tears. Rose came to her, touched her hair. "Anna."

"What if I die?"

"You're not going to die, Anna."

"I'm scared."

"Of course you are."

"What if I die? I have a child. I have a little girl!"

"Anna, you will not die. OK? You will not die." Rose put her face very close to Anna's. "OK?"

I have to call Michael, she thought. "I have to call Michael."

She took the phone in her hand. It rang three times. The new girl, Lesley, picked up. "Hi. It's Anna. Is Michael there?"

She waited a minute.

"Hi," he said. "What's up?"

"I . . ." She looked at Rose Mead, who was watching her. "I need you, Michael," she said.

5

IT WAS THE FRIDAY after Thanksgiving. The Center was closed and almost everyone was on holiday. Except Louise. And except Dr. Howarth.

Bill Dowell sat in Dr. Howarth's office and wondered what to say. It was funny, Bill thought. He had started out this relationship tongue-tied; he continued in it tongue-tied. At the tune of seventy-five dollars a session, it was an extravagance to remain tongue-tied.

The first time he had come to see Dr. Howarth had set the tone. Bill had been referred by a woman he worked with and had arrived very nervous, not knowing what to expect. Coming into the dim, small chamber, done in burnt earth tones, he saw Dr. Howarth for that first time and stood there like a fool.

"Excuse me for not getting up," Dr. Howarth had said, extending his hand. Bill had remained standing, staring down at Dr. Howarth and his hand. Then, collecting himself as best he could, he shook it.

"Why don't you sit over there?" Dr. Howarth had suggested, indicating a tweedy club chair.

Bill did as Dr. Howarth suggested and, sitting there, tried not to stare but of course this was impossible. Dr. Howarth was a dwarf. Dr. Howarth was a dwarf in a wheelchair.

His friend had not told him anything—later she would claim that she hadn't wanted to intrude in his "process"—and so, for quite a few moments, Bill, that first time, didn't say anything. What was there to say? He wanted to leave but how could he do such a thing? Still, he doubted that a dwarf would be able to relate to his problems.

"You didn't know?" asked Dr. Howarth.

Bill shook his head.

"I might have told you on the phone," said Dr. Howarth, putting out the cigarette he had smoked down to the filter, "but, frankly, I've gone beyond the need to announce it, if you know what I mean."

"Yes," said Bill. "I know what you mean."

Over the years, he had gone in and out of therapy with Dr. Howarth. He hadn't necessarily gotten "more in touch with his feelings," as the lingo would have it, but he had come to think of Dr. Howarth as a great human being. One of his fantasies had to do with getting a clean bill of health and then having regular lunches with Dr. Howarth, whom he would then call "Fred" and they would be friends, very good friends. Indeed, Dr. Howarth would make a worthy friend for anyone because Dr. Howarth was a man who, despite the fact that he didn't clear four feet, knew what it was to be a man, to love and want to be loved, to have children, to hate your children and to love your children, to want to live and to want to die.

"How was your Thanksgiving?" asked Dr. Howarth.

"Fine."

But over the course of the session, he told Dr. Howarth more about his Thanksgiving and how it hadn't been fine. He and Louise had decided, for the sake of the boys, to celebrate together, and to defuse the intimacy they had invited a few friends and neighbors to join them. It would have been a fine day, except that, for a change, Louise hadn't held up her end. Something had come up at the lab and she flew down there, on her ten-speed bike, her cape blowing in the wind, like science's answer to Mary Poppins, breaking her promise to make it a family day, and breaking her promise too to provide the sweet-potato pie and the salad. So Bill had to take the kids—always an operation—to buy the pie ready-made and, instead of a green salad, some coleslaw, which didn't really go at all.

"So what did you say to her?" Dr. Howarth asked.

"Nothing much. We didn't really have a chance. The guests stayed late and then we had to clean up. When I began to say something, she told me that she was sorry but it was an emergency. What could I say?"

"I don't know. What could you say?"

He couldn't seem to figure it out in the next twenty-five minutes. He kept telling Dr. Howarth that he was "annoyed."

"She wants to annoy me and she knows just how to do it."

"How does she annoy you?"

"She makes it seem that her work can't be interfered with, that it's inviolable. She makes it seem that her work is holy and my work is totally expendable. She doesn't seem to realize that I am one of the most important people in grants administration in this city! And hence in this country!"

And hence in the world, he told himself, feeling like a complete idiot.

"She could lose a few hours here and there," Bill added. "So a couple of more people might die of AIDS. That's life," he said bitterly. "The thing is she probably won't even make any breakthroughs. She's a workaholic, but how much does she actually get done?"

"What do you think she does with her time?" asked Dr. Howarth.

"Who knows? Stares into space. Or worries about cancer. She does a lot of that."

There was a silence and Bill rushed to fill it. "Her mother had a breast removed when Louise was nine or ten. It made an impact on her. Of course her mother's as strong as an ox and her grandmother and all her great-aunts are still alive so things look good, genetically speaking." Bill stared at the Matisse on the wall. "Sometimes I feel sorry for her. I don't think she understands yet what she's done. She's a good person, really. It's just that she doesn't give very much. Like with the kids. They'll paint a picture or something and I'll feel . . . warm."

"And she doesn't."

"No." He said it again. "No."

"So Louise has never experienced *nachas,*" said Dr. Howarth.

"What's that?" asked Bill. Dr. Howarth frequently threw in Yiddish. It was, he claimed, his second language; sometimes Bill wanted to remind him that it wasn't the second language of everyone who lived in New York.

"*Nachas?* Oh, it's a sort of pride. A joy. The literal translation, if you go back to the Hebrew, means 'pleasure of the spirit.'"

Bill stared at him for a moment. "No," he whispered. "She has never experienced *nachas.*"

When he left, a few minutes later, he realized, once again, that he hadn't spoken of his rage. *His rage.* Like all the times she called Dr. Howarth his "troll." Sometimes, when he would suggest that something she had said was perhaps less than sensitive to him, she would roll her eyes and ask him if his "troll" told him to say that. Then he wanted to smack her, to smack her till she cried. She didn't cry easily. In fact, she almost never cried. She cried when her father remarried. Imagine—that's the time she chose.

But how could he tell Dr. Howarth all of this?

—She calls you my troll.

It was not just that it would be rude, that it might hurt Dr. Howarth's feelings. After all, a dwarf is one thing, a troll quite another. No, it wasn't just that, because the fact was that Dr. Howarth could take it. No, the thing was this: the thing was that if he told Dr. Howarth what she said, then Dr. Howarth would know what

Bill had kept secret from him and maybe even secret from himself. The thing that Dr. Howarth would know was that despite everything Bill said in her favor, there were times when he suspected that his wife was not a very kind person after all.

Trina was taking care of the boys. As Bill returned from Dr. Howarth's, he wondered what kind of reception he would get from them. They would jump him, sure enough. Those times when they felt they weren't getting enough and they held on to him, making it seem like they were extravagantly happy to see him— he hated those times. Once Dennis had ripped the back pocket of his suit pants that way.

He opened the door to the apartment. He still had the key; it wasn't, and probably never would become, a lock-changing situation.

"Hi."

He waited a moment. There was nothing.

He looked out the window. They had a park view. He didn't. In his new place— a sublease on 111th—he had a view of an old lady who sat day and night decaying in her window. Down below, so tiny, he could see Trina and the boys. They were playing with a great big red balloon. She must have brought it with her. She seemed to have a lot of surprises. She dressed strangely, in denim with miles of embroidery. Crocheted bags, filled with not only tissues and gum but also odd things: shells, stones, pieces of bark. Petey told him that she brought things into the Center, things she found. Caterpillars, desiccated worms, jeweled green beetles, sycamore pods, mica. Maybe she was a witch, he thought, without alarm.

He put his coat back on and headed downstairs. When he got to the park, he stood at the stone wall and looked down to the fields below. It was a gray day, middling cold. But she had them out, running, running. The balloon, as big as a giant's head, was floating just above them and then it floated down and they took turns beating it back up again. They seemed to be alone in the park, except for a man running a weimaraner, and their laughter, unimpeded, flew up to him. How small the boys looked, legs like matchsticks. Just the way he had been when he was a child. Did they eat enough? They lived on peanut butter and oatmeal bread—that's what they lived on.

He headed into the park, down the long winding ribbon of path, past the bare trees. With a sweet taste in his mouth, he anticipated their surprise and their pleasure. Very slowly and deliberately, he walked, coming close to them before they saw him. Dennis, always so aware, so tuned in to him, was the first to notice and to let out a howl.

"Dad!"

He was six and a half; he had gone from "Daddy" to "Dad." He came bounding over, threw himself into Bill, a hug, a tackle. Bill grunted and then picked him up, made a wild circle spinning him around, made as if to let go, to send him sailing into the river, and Dennis shrieked and there came Petey, shrieking too, looking for action, and he got it, a spin around, as he shrieked louder, and Bill felt his heart pounding.

"How have they been?" he asked Trina, setting Petey down, ignoring the pleas for more, more, more.

"Good," said Trina. "They're always good."

He laughed. "Stick around," he said.

She nodded. "OK."

He looked at her. She had a quality that didn't seem exactly of this world.

"Come on, Daddy. Play. Play!" Petey demanded.

He wished he could have told them he was tired and gotten away with it. The fact was that he *was* tired—at times like this, this lonely holiday, profoundly tired—but it wasn't fair to the boys and so he joined the game.

It must have been twenty minutes before they let him sit down again. Then he went to the bench where Trina was sitting, her legs curled up beneath her. She was knitting.

"What are you knitting?" he asked, breathless, all sweaty in the cold.

"A shawl. For Loretta. For Christmas."

"Oh, really? That's nice." He paused, and looked out at the field. Maybe in a month they could go cross-country skiing here. "I'm told that it costs almost as much to knit something these days as to buy it. Because of the price of wool. Is that true?"

"No." She knitted one, purled two. "It's not true. Anyway, my mother owns a hobby shop. She used to give me a lot of free wool."

"Aha. But there's still your time."

"I have lots of time," she said. She knitted one, purled two. "In the evenings," she added, looking up at him. He saw that she was staring at him. Her eyes, so large and green, riveted him. "I have to do things with my hands in the evenings. Otherwise, I get nervous. I knit, I sew, I embroider." She smiled a little. "I'd like to make something for the boys. Vests maybe. Do you know what colors they like?"

"Oh, no. Really, it's too much . . ."

"No. Really," she said. There was a flush to her cheeks and her neck. "I'm sort of a one-woman industry. I love doing it anyway." She paused. "And I love the boys."

He stared at her and then he looked out at the field, the boys. "They *are* good boys," he said.

"What colors do they like?"

"Oh Lord. Let me see. *Manly* colors. Black, as in Darth Vader. Silver, gold. That sort of thing."

She laughed. "I don't think I could knit in those colors."

"Well, then, how about blue? Blue's always nice."

"Yes," she agreed. "Do they like trains?"

"Trains? Yeah, I guess they like trains. They don't feature largely in their experience, but I guess they like them. Why?"

"I thought I'd put trains on their vests. Do you think they'd like that?"

He smiled. She was very sweet. "Yes. I think they'd like that."

Petey came running over. "Dennis won't let me have the balloon . . ."

"Work it out," said Bill.

"But he won't let me . . ."

"*Work it out.*"

Petey looked at his father. His mouth became small. He was trying to decide whether or not to appeal the decision. Then, in a flash, he turned and was gone.

"That's good," Trina said. "The way you did that."

"What else can I do? If I didn't do that sort of thing, I'd be busier than your average criminal-court judge."

She bent forward a little bit; she pushed some of her red hair off her face. "You're such a good father."

He stared at her. "Oh . . . I'm okay," he said with a grin.

"Petey starts missing you every day around two o'clock. 'When's my daddy going to come? When's my Daddy going to come?' He adores you. Sometimes it's almost as if nobody else exists."

"Yes. Sometimes it is," Bill said. It could feel like a burden. But he would never let it go.

"Doesn't your wife mind?"

"What?"

She took a glance around; the boys were there, out of trouble. "That they only talk about you."

How should he field this one? He could be staunch. He could be wry. "She manages," he said, opting for the wry.

A cold wind blew and she pulled her bulky sweater more closely around her. "You're very understanding," she said, implying that she understood little and that she wanted things explained.

"It was my choice," he said. He looked down at his hands and then looked up and out over the field, making sure that the children were all right. "Louise never really wanted children," he said, not sure why he was speaking so personally. "She said she had enough in life, with her work. I believe her," he said, turning to look at Trina, wanting to convince her of it. "It's different with creative people."

"She's a creative person?" Trina asked, and Bill thought he heard something like regret in her voice.

"Oh yes. She's a scientist. Scientists are creative people." He turned to her and smiled. "I'm not a creative person. I once thought I wanted to be. I once thought I wanted to be a pianist and then, after that, a bassoonist. I played both instruments very seriously."

"And?"

"And nothing." The sun was setting; he looked up and squinted. "Something happened—I don't remember what. There was a long siege of bronchitis and then there was Vietnam and I taught in Roxbury." He grinned a little. "I feel particularly stupid saying that bronchitis cut me down in my prime, but in a way it did. I lost my momentum and I never got it back."

She stared at him; he wasn't sure she believed him. "I'd like to hear you play," she said. He thought about that. He looked for the hollowness in the line and it didn't seem to be there.

"You would?" he asked—the boyish grin.

"Yes." She smiled. "I would."

"Then you shall."

There was a look—they held it.

"And then," he said quickly, "Louise has so many fears. She was so afraid of the process. The pain, the blood." He looked out at the field: the red balloon seemed slightly smaller, softer, puckered and overripe. He wondered when they would notice. "But I insisted," he said, taking a certain pleasure in the words, rejoicing in the tangible proof, out in the field there, that his uxoriousness was not complete. "And after we had Dennis, I insisted again. That was a little harder"—he grinned—"but I wanted Dennis to have a sibling. I never had a sibling. Do you?"

She thought a moment. "I had a sister," she said. "She died."

"Oh. I'm sorry." He looked at his hands. "I'm really very sorry."

"Yes. It was sad."

"Anyway," he said, forcing himself to go on, "I made up my mind, early on, that fatherhood was going to be the really important thing in my life. I didn't have that growing up and I wanted to make sure that my sons had it."

"I didn't have it either," she told him.

Just the, the shade of thick blue clouds rolled down over the fading sun and suddenly it was night. "It's late," he observed.

They rose together, acting quickly.

"Boys!" he shouted. "Boys!" He waved them in, but they weren't coming. "Boys!" he shouted once again. The boys started to run across the field. There was enough light to see their white skin.

"They'd stay here all night if they could," Trina said.

"Isn't it the truth."

She looked at his back, broader than she had first noticed, beneath the tweed coat. She felt her hand ache to touch the coat, the back.

"That was a nice talk," she said, and he turned to her. He looked at her. "Yes," he said. "We must do it again."

"Yes," she said. "We must."

She walked down Broadway, in the night, the fourteen dollars heavy in the pocket of her jeans, the jeans that were flared at the bottom, only slightly flared but even so too much. His money. One old ten, four old singles. When he took them from his wallet—his wallet the color of a good old saddle—it was like something tasting bad in her mouth.

Though she needed the money—she needed whatever money she could get—she didn't want it in her pocket, on her person, in her account. She was angry at it and wanted it spent. It wouldn't be hard to spend, she realized. She walked into Zabar's. The air was heavy with the smell of cold sausage and butter and smoked fish. She went for the salt—pickles, gherkins, salami, Liptauer cheese. The fourteen dollars went as fast as it came. When she was out in the street, she was holding a shopping bag full of good food and she didn't want to eat it alone.

She was only two blocks away from Loretta's. She had been to Loretta's a bunch of times, for meetings and pickups and stuff. She had never been to Loretta's just like this. She couldn't be alone now; that much she knew. If she were alone now, she might do something terrible.

She was supposed to wait to be buzzed in when she got to Loretta's building but a man with a giant poodle was coming out and she slipped her way in. In the elevator, she saw her face disfigured in the round shiny disk set up to show you dangerous corners.

She got out on the fifth floor. She stood in front of Loretta's green door for a minute or two, listening for something, anything. There was nothing but silence.

What would she do if she wasn't there? What would she do if she *was* there? She rang the buzzer, first lightly, then with more force. She heard the peephole creak; she stood there, not knowing how she should show herself. The door opened. There was Loretta, in a yellow chenille robe, washed too many times, all pilled up, a Turkish towel wrapped around her hair.

"Well, hi there," Loretta cried, seeming happy to see her. "What brings you here?"

Trina shrugged. "I was passing by. With all this food . . ."

"Zabar's. Just what I need. From your lips to my hips."

"Did you eat?"

"Does it matter? Come in, come in."

Trina handed her the shopping bag and came in.

"I'm so glad you just stopped by like this," Loretta said while she put out two crazed, blue-glazed faience plates. "It's so neighborly."

"But it looks like you were in the middle . . ."

"Oh, I'm just giving my hair a treatment. Split ends, you know? Oh Lord, look. Farmer cheese. My favorite."

"We used to make it," Trina said, faraway. "It's not hard."

"That's right. I forget you were a farmgirl. Somehow I never think of you as a farmgirl."

"Braids might help," Trina murmured.

Loretta gave a look and then broke out laughing. "You always surprise me. That's your magic. That's what the kids pick up on."

When they finished eating, Loretta cleared the table and then came back carrying a joint and a bottle of Beaujolais.

"I don't do that," Trina said. "Not anymore."

Loretta shrugged. "Suit yourself. Nobody's going to make you. But listen," she added, giving her a good look, "you're among friends."

Trina watched Loretta light the joint and pull smoke into her lungs, holding it there. "So where were you today?" Loretta asked, on the exhale.

"Taking care of Petey and Denny. Louise had an emergency at the lab," she explained, hesitating on the 'Louise.' She was a brilliant, accomplished woman, Bill's wife—she was a scientist.

"Oh, did she? So what else is new?" Loretta smirked as she took another toke. "It's amazing just how hard some people work," she added, with a big wink.

Trina poured some wine. It felt sharp and good on her tongue. "What do you mean?"

Loretta held up her hands. "I tell no tales," she said, then smiled—the grass was working. "Poor Bill," she sighed. "He's a lovely man—kind of a sad man. He's one of those people you describe as 'the last to know.'"

The last to know what? Was he dying? "I don't understand," Trina murmured.

Loretta made a face. "She's been seen. Louise. Someone saw her, with a man, at a hotel in the Catskills. She was supposed to be on a conference. I'd say she was *in* conference." Loretta giggled and then sobered. "Poor Bill. He doesn't seem to know."

Trina felt strange, a little dizzy, from the wine. "Why doesn't he know?"

"Because that's the kind of guy he is," said Loretta. With a sudden goofiness, brought on by the wine and the dope, she made the sign of the horns. "'Riba, 'riba," she crowed, making no sense at all, and then she burst into sheer narcotized laughter.

It was the warmed wine, the shame for Bill, the pity for Bill, her feelings for Bill, strong and not yet sufficiently understood, and the sense of duplicity everywhere, that made her turn so deeply, violently red. Loretta, who noticed almost everything, was quick to notice this too.

"Aw, sweetie," she said, "look at you. What did I say?"

Trina shook her head. She felt numb and heavy, but she managed to pull herself to her feet.

"Where are you going?" Loretta asked.

"Home."

"No. You just got here."

Trina felt a weakness, a sudden tremor. She didn't know what she was about anymore. She hadn't known what she was about for so long a time. "I've got to go," she whispered in the littlest of her voices.

Loretta stood and took hold of her by the elbows. "Don't go. You're upset. Please. Don't go. Tell me what it is."

"I don't know what it is," she said, in that same voice. Then her face stretched tight—it seemed to change—and her voice assumed a harshness it almost never had. "I don't know what it is."

Loretta put an arm around her. Trina could smell the hair treatment, harsh with an overlay of orange and cloves. With her other hand, Loretta reached out to push back the hair that had fallen into Trina's eyes.

"I really don't know what it is. I guess I was sad for him, sad for the boys. Anyway, you're good at making people feel better," Trina whispered, liking to be in her arms this way.

"It's what I do," Loretta said. "Mother to all," she added, mocking herself. She stroked Trina's hair tenderly. "Did you know I have a son?" she said, almost in a whisper.

Trina looked up at her; she hadn't known.

"Gregory," she said. "He's seventeen now. He hasn't lived with me for four years."

"Where does he live?"

"Florida. Captiva."

"Captiva?"

"It's an island. Captiva Island. He's with his father. My ex-husband, Jordan. Jordan owns a motel. The Scirocco. It's no joke," Loretta said, as she continued to lightly stroke Trina's hair. "That was the name of Errol Flynn's yacht. And there you have it. Jordan was a stockbroker. Then he found the sixties—or the sixties found him. He decided to sow his wild oats."

"But what about. . . ?" Trina began, but didn't say the boy's name.

"I lost him," said Loretta. "Just that simple. Jordan had too many nice shiny things for him and I lost him. He's been away four years and he doesn't even want to come here for vacations," she said, her voice sounding suddenly throaty, "but I make him. Then he comes and sits in front of the TV—*Silver Spoons, The Facts of Life*—all that unending shit, and when I can't stand it anymore and I shut off the goddamn thing, he gives me that stupid smirk of his and I want to kill him. But I don't because he's my son and I guess I have the fantasy that someday he'll love me again."

There was a silence for several long minutes, as Loretta ran her fingers through Trina's hair. "So," said Loretta at last, "I've poured out my soul and liver. Now it's your turn to spill some secrets."

"I haven't got any," Trina said quickly.

"Oh, ho ho ho," Loretta snorted.

Trina turned to go, but Loretta put out a hand to stop her. "Don't go," she said. "You seem so alone. Really. I worry about you."

The red room was like a heart, Trina thought as she stood there, not moving, The air seemed thick and sweet and she felt something pulsing.

"Stay," said Loretta.

She let Loretta lead her over to the sofa and she lay down there, suddenly very tired.

"You can stay the night," Loretta said. "I don't want you to be alone. You shouldn't be alone."

Trina squeezed shut her eyes; they hurt. Somewhere, from upstairs or next door or outside, there was the sound of muted salsa and it beat in her head and hurt so that it felt good when Loretta touched her lightly at the hairline and the temples.

"Sometimes I want to get too close," Loretta whispered, "and then you can tell me. But give it a chance, Trina."

She closed her eyes and Loretta watched her sleep.

6

IT WAS GRANDMA LOU GARVEY'S recipe. One-two-three-four cake. Rich, moist, but light. And it only got better with time. Corinne had baked it three days ago, wrapped it in foil. This morning she took it out to frost it. Caitlin's favorite colors—pink and yellow, of course. She was pure girl, all the way through.

Thanks again to Grandma Lou, Corinne also knew the fine art of making butter-cream rosebuds. All that stuff—how to make butter-cream rosebuds; how to make radish rosebuds; how to spin sugar—it had all skipped a generation. Corinne's mother couldn't have cared less about how to spin sugar, unless there was money in it. She was a businesswoman; she owned two beauty salons in northern Syracuse. She'd always pushed Corinne and her sister to make something of themselves. And Corinne had toed the line, coming in second in a high-school class of over four hundred. When it came to figures, Patrick always said she had a steel-trap mind. Her mother wanted her to be a CPA. Even now, as roses belched out of her pastry tube, Corinne had to smile. In the period when she was growing up, other mothers wanted their daughters to become Natalie Wood or Sandra Dee or, failing that, a Lennon Sister maybe. But her mother wanted her to become a CPA.

And she would have been a CPA, if it weren't for Patrick. He lived down the block from them and she had known him since she was five. In fact, she had been crazy for him since she was five. He was two years older than she, but it had seemed like more. She was then, as she was now, tiny and brittle. Her bones broke too easily. She always had something in a cast. He, on the other hand, was big and bluff, high-colored, rollicking, with the funniest, most peculiar laugh, a high-pitched hyenic cackle that came in jags and that had him thrown out of many a class in which he was otherwise beloved. Everyone loved him. He was kind and cheerful and heroic on the playing fields and smart enough but not too smart and tender. She married him when she was nineteen.

Her mother, of course, died over this. Her mother had herself been a child bride and her experience with marriage had not been a good one. Corinne's father had deserted when Corinne was seven. She had almost no memories of him. All she could recall was a glum, saturnine presence that had sat nightly in the rose velveteen chair. She even had a memory—a very dim feeling—of being glad when the presence was removed.

Her mother then started her business and quickly made something of it. She preached a gospel of independence; promulgated their image as survivors, as women who didn't need men. But Corinne didn't buy it for a moment.

She kept her eye on Patrick. When Patrick was sent to Vietnam, she wrote to him, sent him magazines, sent him a pair of red rag socks. It didn't occur to her, until much later, that red socks might make a good target for the enemy, and he never pointed it out to her either. They grew very fond of each other, a long-distance fondness. Up until then, she had only known him tangentially, as one of the boys in the neighborhood, and even though he'd always been very friendly to her, the truth was that he had always been very friendly to everyone. But that was the thing about wartime—you could push closer to a boy you always wanted to be close to and everyone would think you were performing your patriotic duty.

When Patrick came back—migraines, exhaustion, medals—she became the one he talked to. She learned how to bake and she brought along cakes. Her mother took every opportunity to make fun of her. "If it isn't Betty Crocker." "If it isn't the Pillsbury Doughgirl." Corinne didn't care. She knew what she wanted and she positioned herself.

The more she visited him, the more she became sure of her ability to heal him. He called her "Little One." She called him "Big Guy." She stood there now, in her bright kitchen, the pastry tube in hand, and felt a curious mingle of shame at their corniness and pleasure in their innocence. They were in love and they did the right thing, the natural thing: they got married. Her mother gave them a Danish wedding. No, not Danish as in Denmark—no raft of herring, aquavit, and fresh flowers for them. Rather, "Danish" as in prune, cheese, or cinnamon raisin. Danish and coffee after vows in the living room. Oh well—her mother was her mother. And as long as she had Patrick, she didn't care.

The wedding night. It was good. She was a virgin, but she wasn't scared. She was proud. She felt like she had been entrusted with something very valuable, very precious and powerful, and she had taken good care of it, the best possible care of it, and so it was her gift to give and so she gave it. She was a virgin, but she didn't play any games. She let him know that this was what she wanted and that she would want it again and again and again, and forever.

She licked the pink cream from the pastry tube and then tossed it into the sink. Done. Now, next—the cheese board. The party wasn't just for Caitlin and her friends; the party was for grown-ups, the other parents, the teachers from the Center, anyone who cared about Caitlin and wanted to rejoice in the fact that she had more than merely made her way to a fourth birthday.

The party must have been costing more than three hundred dollars. It was lavish. Maybe it was too lavish—she didn't care. And she didn't care about the money. (Well, maybe she cared a little about the money. Unlike Patrick, who was now used to making big bucks, Corinne could remember when they first came to the city and didn't have enough money—literally did not have enough money—to buy tuna, so wound up eating Wonder Bread for two days straight.) She was just so proud of her little girl.

She thought she had the greatest little girl in the world. She didn't care if no one else in the world seconded the motion. She knew that her little girl was just something else. When she was born, people told her to forget it. Well, she forgot those people who told her to forget. One woman, also in lying-in, asked her if she was going to keep her. Keep her? Oh Lord, she could remember that so well. That was when it was all so raw and the world was very dark and her husband didn't even want to see what they had made. Keep her? she screamed at this woman in the corridors of New York Hospital. Keep her?

It really was time for a cup of tea. She had worked very hard. She'd been up since six, and until eleven had had to deal with Caitlin wanting into everything. She had finally gotten Patrick to take her with him to the supermarket. He didn't like to do this because sometimes she could be wild and once she had pulled down a display of Progresso soup and he told Corinne that "he felt every eye in the store on him" as he picked up the cans. So what? she had wanted to shout. So just what were they looking at? A man with his daughter. A man with his daughter who was a Down's-syndrome child. Big deal. This morning she had put her foot down; this morning she had told him that he had to take her with him.

—But look how wound-up she is already.

—I don't care. You have to take her. It's your problem.

He liked to refer to Corinne as "The Boss." To make himself sound like Harry Truman or something. Sometimes he called Caitlin "Little Boss." Well, that was his way of dealing. She couldn't take that away from him; it wasn't hers to take away. Anyway, he was a good man. Look what he had provided for them. All this. She could look out her kitchen window and see the reservoir. She could see the sunlight dancing on the water. The kitchen was so bright she could grow her own herbs. She liked to cook—she didn't know why. Maybe as a response to her mother; maybe because of the order of cooking, the fact that if you mixed milk and flour and butter you got a roux and with that roux you could go far.

He was a good provider. They had come to New York and he had gone to work for AT&T. He had worked himself into a sales position where he was now making a base salary of $125,000 a year with commissions well beyond that and a program of benefits that was as good as anybody could hope for. He was a wonderful salesman. He had a sort of fakebook of every kind of joke, and he laughed, with his crazy laugh, louder than anyone and everyone laughed with him. Not at him, with him. He believed in what he had to sell and he found something worth liking and something worth connecting to in just about everyone he did business with. He could make you feel that what he had to sell was the best of the best and often it was. He could make you feel, about almost everything he touched, that it was not only worth having, but that it was vital to have.

But behind every great man is a woman, she thought, sipping her tea, looking out at the reservoir. A little woman. Or, a variation on that: no man is a hero to his valet or to his wife. If anyone ever asked her—like, let's say, Barbara Walters— what the essence of a marriage was, she would know what to say. She would sit back, straighten her shoulders, and say, "Barbara, the essence of a marriage is *shared secrets.*" Barbara would blink a few times and ask her to clarify. "What I mean, Barbara, is that nobody knows you the way your spouse does. Nobody knows that secret self that you keep hidden from the world. And, in a good marriage at least, nobody can help your spouse with that secret self the way you can."

She let that float around a little, took the last sip of tea, and then she washed out her cup. Her back hurt. There was always something that hurt. When she was young, there was always something in a cast. Now there was always something that hurt. She wondered if there was a connection but didn't have the time to waste on the question. Guests would be here in an hour. She looked out through the serving window into the living room and saw that everything was not perfect. She had much to do.

By the time Patrick McIver had gotten out of the Food Emporium, he was in a sweat. Caitlin had kept trying to climb out of the shopping cart, and when he turned his back for a minute, to look for festive napkins, one of those bitch old ladies with an inch of white powder all over her face swooped down, to the piped-in tune of "Chariots of Fire," and told him that "you must never leave a child unattended in a shopping cart." Particularly *that* kind of child was the implication, but at least the old bat had the good, sane grace not to articulate it. At the checkout counter, Caitlin kept trying to stop the conveyor belt. He worried she would somehow get her fingers caught, and so, to distract her, he kept her plied with whatever sweet stuff was handy—a family-size box of Good 'n Plenty—and then worried that she would choke on it. Choke to death. And then what would he do? And so, almost as soon as he gave it to her, he had to take it away, and wasn't that fun, wasn't that just swell, as she screamed, full volume, the loudest scream in the history of the world, made Fay Wray look like Tweetie Pie, this little daughter of his, turning blue on her birthday as he tried to sell her a bill of goods about cooperation and coexistence.

It all seemed so hopeless, out there, on Broadway, her screams ricocheting. It all seemed so goddamned hopeless. Look at her. Just look at her. Everyone said they were docile. Well, hell—they hadn't met Caitlin. She knew how to get to him. She knew how to make his chest hurt. Yes, with that scream she could make his heart hurt and he took his hand, his big red hand, and placed it against his chest, feeling his heart hurting, feeling pain in every pocket of his soul. And then he was touched on the shoulder, as he knelt there, and he looked up and saw that it was Olivia Sloan, with a tentative smile, a look of concern on her face, letting go of the hand of her son Aaron, who went straight to Caitlin and made her smile.

"Hi," said Olivia, whom he knew well but didn't. "One of those days, huh?"
"One of those days," he said, flashing a grin.

"*But,*" she said, holding up a slim, delicate finger, "I sense a problem. This is her birthday and we are going to her party in one hour and here you are, *comme ça.*"

He stood up, and let Caitlin run around with her friend. "Yes," he said. "Here I am. *Comme ça.*"

She gave him a broad smile that mitigated the archness of her tone. He could never tell about her if she were as pretentious as all get-out or if, in fact, she was just that way, a Seven Sisters girl, Radcliffe he guessed, and beneath that porcelain exterior beat a little bit of the old chicken soup. She was a Jew, even with that name. Stanislasivitz, no doubt—something like that. Not that she looked like a Jew. Her hair was wheat-colored; her features small and delicate. But she was a Jew. A smart Jewish lawyer. Her husband, Sam, was some kind of a writer or something. Nice guy—kind of touchy, maybe, not the kind you'd slap on the back—but sort of nowhere. Stayed home—what did they call it? Househusband? Jesus, what a thing to call yourself.

"Birthdays are very exciting," she said, in that precise, prim, almost mincing way in which she expressed herself. "Sometimes much too exciting."

"Yeah. Well, we're letting her get it out of her system. Right here on Broadway. You are there."

She laughed. "Can I do anything to help?"

Something in him reflexively bristled. "Help" was a word they liked to keep scarce in their vocabulary. "No, we can manage."

He sensed, by the look of doubt that flickered across her face, that he had put her off too strongly. "Corinne's got everything under control," he said. "You know Corinne," he added with a grin.

"Oh yes," she replied. "I know Corinne." She looked down with a smile at the children. Caitlin, he saw, had her mouth open and he had the impulse to tell her to close it, but he didn't. It was something they worked on very hard and, to a large degree, they were successful. She avoided the vacant stare, the dropped jaw of the hopelessly retarded.

"Well, I just figured," said Olivia, "if you needed someone last minute to pick up juice or anything. Actually, I have to confess," she confessed, "we're just on our way to pick up a present for her."

He didn't know why she had to confess that, but he nodded anyway.

"Oh Lord," she sighed, "last-minute living. Need I say more? Sam was supposed to attend to it yesterday, but he had a dental emergency and so here I am, late as always, and wondering what to get her. How do you feel about Barbie?"

"Barbie?" He had no idea what she was talking about.

"As in Barbie Doll." She gave an apologetic variation on her smile. "I can't bear it. I think it's smarmy and sexist and awful, but every little girl I know would kill for it and a birthday is a birthday and I figured if you didn't object, maybe I'd get some outfits, like ice-skating or tennis or whatever . . ."

She stopped suddenly. He stared at her. Then he looked down at his little daughter, in her green down coat with her blond-red hair just like his and her big feet, so big that whatever she wore, even the patent-leather Mary Janes that she loved more than life itself, looked like space shoes. He felt touched and he didn't know why. Even as Olivia Sloan waited for his answer, he tried to think of what it was that had touched him. And then he knew. The idea that somebody—any-body—would worry about issues of sexism around his little daughter, when all her life, all her four years, they had more than they could do to worry about things like teaching her to think, teaching her to keep herself clean, teaching her to keep her mouth closed. Oh, it was nice, it was *nice,* to think of a time, maybe this time, when they could worry, along with everyone else, about something in the air, something that might not be good, about influences instead of realities.

"Of course, if you just don't care for it," Olivia said, "it's no problem. There's plenty of other . . ."

"No," Patrick said. "It's terrific. Really it is. She'll be tickled pink. Won't you, honey?"

Caitlin looked up at him. For a moment they stared at each other and then, just like that, they smiled together, at the very same time. He reached down for his little daughter and, like Tarzan, in one fine swoop, he hoisted her and placed her atop his broad high shoulders, looking back just once to wave and then heading home, to await their guests.

From the bedroom, with the shades drawn, too dim for the day, a brilliant fall day, too warm this late in the season, Anna could hear their voices, their breakfast voices. Michael liked to make pancakes on Saturday. He would get so *involved,* and Molly would get involved too, and usually it would sound something like this:

Michael: OK, now. We need a tablespoon of baking soda. Not baking
           powder. We did the baking powder already . . .
Molly: I wanna do it. I wanna.
Michael: OK, OK. I said you'd do it. Careful now. Don't spill it. OK. Very
           good. Now, where are those oats we pulverized?
Molly: Here, Daddy.
Michael: Oh, good. Very good. Now, *add pulverized oats*—good—and now
           we'll add the buttermilk and the beaten eggs . . .

Generally, after about a half-hour or so of this, she was called upon to make a Great Lady entrance, in her not-very-great robe, and they would make a fuss over her, and it would be fine.

But now, feeling a chill in the room, she pulled the covers up. She would not rise for pancakes this morning. The treatment was such that she could barely keep down anything livelier than melba toast.

Rose Mead has said she would get her life back and that it would take time. She believed Rose. Rose had taken good care of her. Other doctors would have wanted the whole breast removed, gone, just like that, but Rose felt, in light of the early detection and other properties of the lump, that they should go with a lumpec-tomy. This precipitated mass hysteria—her mother, flying in from Brooklyn, crying that if it were a choice between her breast and her life, why did she even have to think about it? Why did she have to spend even two minutes, two lousy minutes, thinking about it? Why didn't she just get rid of it? And then Aunt Bea, who was a nurse, chimed in and then her cousin Marjorie called from

Bakersfield, California, to say she'd been through it all and that was six years ago and she felt good as new and yes, she and Charlie had as good a love life as ever.

It was awful.

Finally, she sat her mother down—her poor mother—and explained to her that her chances, at this point, with a lumpectomy were no better or worse than her chances with a mastectomy or even a radical mastectomy. It was all a matter of hanging in. If she lived beyond the five-year mark, she could begin to think of herself as a survivor. Until then, no one knew.

Five years. Molly would be eight. When Anna went in for the "procedure," Molly had stayed with her parents. Molly didn't ask any questions. Molly wouldn't know what questions to ask. Mommy was going on a business trip. Thank God for working mothers and their business trips. For each night that she was away, Anna left a tiny gift in a tiny box. A little figure of a ballet dancer in red shoes on a bed of cotton inside a tiny red cardboard box. A delicate piece of chocolate molded in the shape of a horse inside a tiny gold cardboard box. Each day, when she got the gift, it would be like a little visit with Mommy. It was really a very terrible thing, a great saddening thing, to think that if she died now, Molly would not remember her.

She told that to Michael, the day after the operation. At first, he had said nothing. He sat there, the way he could, not saying anything. She couldn't stand that.

—You're not saying anything, she said.

—It's not true.

—Yes, it is. Studies show that children who lose parents before the age of five, or maybe even six, retain no memories of the deceased.

The word hung there, ugly, like a great gray bolt of cobweb hanging down from the ceiling in an uncleaned room. Deceased. It made him angry.

—You don't know what you're talking about. You really don't. You read some dumb pop-psychology article in *Redbook* or whatever and that becomes your *gospel.*

With that, she broke down crying. Sobbing. It was so unlike her. She and Michael had this kind of exchange twelve times a day and it didn't mean anything. No, it meant *something*—it was their marriage. They wrestled with each other, all the time. It's what they liked to do, and there was still plenty of time left over for other things. But what was this? She was crying. And as she did so she felt, more than she had before, like a different person.

—Hey.

She saw him through a film. She thought he was beautiful, her husband, as he thought she was beautiful. They were making a life together. Bastards! Bastards! Her tears were hot on her face.

—Hey. Anna. Come on.

He reached out to take her hand. He had as beautiful a hand as she had ever seen. Smooth white marble strong clear nails. His hand was cold. Oh God. This was so hard on him. His mother had died of cancer when he was still a boy. Once before, years before, she had found a lump and she had asked him to feel it. Go ahead just feel it. But he wouldn't. He went with her to the doctor but he wouldn't touch the lump and when they found it was no more than a cyst, they didn't bother to talk about it or the fact that he had refused to touch it.

—Come here (she had whispered).

She took him by the hand and pulled him up to the bed. At first he kept his feet on the floor but she wouldn't stand for it so he kicked off his shoes—his Italian shoes—and joined her, on the bed. Like a boat, on the sea, just the two of them, holding each other, and wondering what the message in the bottle would be.

"Pancake, Mommy!" Molly cried, rushing into the bedroom.

Anna leaned down—their bed was high and brass—and pulled Molly up.

"No," she squirmed.

"Squirm germ," Anna whispered into her tiny silken shell of an ear.

"Squirm germ," Molly giggled back to her. Look at the face. Look at the *punim*. *Shana punim*, Molly's grandfather, Anna's father, called it. *Lichte punim*. Face of beauty. Face of light. "Come on," Molly said. "Pancakes."

Anna made like a great lady. "I couldn't possibly, my dear."

"Breakfast!" Michael called.

"Come, Mommy," Molly insisted, pulling at her.

Anna reached out to touch her rosy cheek. "I don't know, kiddo," she said, but there, in the twin blue wells of Molly's eyes, she thought she saw something. *Something*. A premonition of loss. An augury of sorrow. Anna rose from the high brass bed, descended, and took Molly's hand, letting her lead the way to the breakfast table.

When he saw her, standing there, in the white robe he had bought her two years ago, something tightened in his throat. But he smiled anyway. And then, when she came closer, he kissed her and hugged her to him.

"You smell like batter," she said.

He smiled. "Batter up," he punned, making it sound suggestive even though he hadn't any idea whether or not the pun made any sense.

She smiled a little—too little—and went to sit down. She looked wan. Yet somehow the reality of her illness still seemed unreal to him.

"I don't think I'm going to have any pancakes," she said, her skin so pale, with a grayness at the hollows of her neck and at her temples. "But they smell wonderful."

"They're johnnycakes," Michael said. "They're very easy to make. Molly practically made them by herself."

"Good girl," Anna said. "But eat them quickly and get dressed. You don't want to be late to Caitlin's party."

Of course, she almost wound up being very late. They had to practically push her out of the house on the weekends. Ever since she was eight months old, it had been her job to get out of the house at least three mornings a week, in the cold rain snow hail sleet, and now, on the weekends, she wanted nothing more than to hang around in her jammies and mukluks and play with her set of Cabbage Patch colorforms that her grandma—Michael's stepmother, the widow of his father—had gotten for her the last time she visited.

"Do you want your pink or your green?" Anna asked, holding up two garments.

"Pink," Molly said. "No. Green. Green!"

"Good choice."

Moments later, with her coat on, her navy-blue dress coat, Molly stood for them and preened. Michael watched Anna watching her.

"Are you sure you don't want to go?" he asked.

"Come, Mommy! Come!" Molly cried.

"Thanks," she said, out of the side of her mouth, to Michael.

"Maybe it would do you good."

"No." She shook her head. "I can't believe you're being so insensitive."

"I'm *not* being insensitive. I'm thinking of you being inside on a beautiful day when you could be—"

"I don't give a shit about beautiful days!"

"Mommy!"

They looked at Molly. Normally she was robust, rough, and ready, but in this outfit, she took on the role of the little princess. It would have been funny if they were in the mood to laugh.

"Molly," said Michael, "just go into your room for a few minutes, will you please?"

"No," she said, her jaw jutting.

"Leave her alone."

"I want to talk to you," Michael said. "Molly, go," he ordered, but Molly wouldn't. She stood there, with her arms crossed.

Anna looked at him. He looked so upset. Why was she doing this to him? Her eyes filled with tears. "I can't go. Everyone's going to look at me and think she has ancer-cay."

"No, they're not . . ."

"Yes, they are. They're going to look at me and think she has ancer-cay and she'd going to ie-day."

"Anna . . ."

The tears started to come, rolling down, despite every effort to keep them back. She didn't want Molly to see them, not today, not when she looked like a little princess. "Oh, God," Anna said. "Don't you love this conversation? Pig Latin. Why couldn't I have arried-may a man who knew Yiddish?"

He smiled a little. Then she smiled a little—she couldn't help it. He didn't know any Yiddish. When they first met, he asked her, even though he was technically a Jew, what the word *mensch* meant. She couldn't believe it. He had never eaten stuffed derma. She put her arms out for him; he came into them. They held each other close. "Not yet," she said. "I'm not ready yet." He couldn't say anything. He couldn't make any words. She kissed him on his eyes, shut tight, and then she bent down to run a hand lightly over Molly's shiny black hair. "You have a good party. And when you get home, we'll do something nice together. Something special. OK?"

"What?" asked Molly, a little sullenly.

"Oh . . . play a game."

"What game?"

"What game, what game. I don't know. What game do you want?"

Molly thought a moment. "Candyland."

"OK," Anna said, looking up at Michael. "I promise, when you get back, we'll do Candyland."

For a moment, they all stood there. "OK," Michael said finally and he took Molly by the hand and Anna watched them go.

*   *   *

It was a quarter to eleven. Charles was early. He took a ride in the brass elevator, his favorite elevator, the one with the seat in it, from the better days when there'd be some little Irish elevator operator sitting there spinning yarns and how-de-dos, not like now, with the menus from the Chinese restaurant littering the floor and the word "LAO" carved into the cherrywood paneling in three different places.

Julie and Hildy lived on Riverside Drive, upper Riverside Drive, once grand, then lousy, and now sort of grandish again. Julie had a beautiful apartment. She collected art deco and the living room, mirrored and mauve and sleek as a set from *Top Hat,* looked out on the Hudson River. He liked to wander around the apartment when he babysat for Hildy. Julie hung her dresses—her beautiful dresses—on a coat rack, like they were sculptures out there for everyone to see, and her beads and her strands of fake pearls were hung all over the four-poster bed, like offerings to some kind of goddess of goods.

He liked to lie in Julie's bed. Sometimes, most times, when he babysat for Hildy, after he gave her a glass of Ovaltine with a raw egg mixed into it (at Julie's instruction; her area of great madness); after he gave her the bath; after he wrapped her up in one of the big pink bathsheets; after he got her into her jammies, and read to her from *Bread and Jam for Frances* or *The Story of Babar,* and told her to turn over onto her tummy, and rubbed her back, and sang her "Day-O" like he was Harry Belafonte or something, and looked at her, as she slept there, not a pretty child, but a distinctive one, and a survivor, a gutsy lady like her mama, an Amazon of human proportions, he'd close Hildy's door and then off he'd sneak to Julie's room. Julie's room was all Laura Ashley grays and pinks and smelled mightily of lavender. She was one of those modern women who made in six figures but who still liked to put sachets—Crabtree & Evelyn sachets—in all the bureau drawers. Then he'd lie down on Julie's bed and close his eyes and breathe in, smelling it all. Once he had masturbated on her bed. Rubbed his cock against her white chenille bedspread. He was very neat about it when he came and wiped himself clean with one of her Kleenexes—the Kleenex she kept in a crewelwork tissue box—and he didn't feel at all guilty about it. He was quite desirous of Julie Nolan. He wanted Julie Nolan to be his.

He fully expected this to happen. He was very good at getting people to fall in love with him. Part of it had to do with the fact that he really liked women. He always thought he had a lot of woman in him. There was a period when he slept with men and women both—that was in the days when *everyone* slept with men and women both—but then he stopped. He felt foolish. He was really a man and he really liked to watch a tall woman take down her hair. He was a very tall man, six-feet-four, and Julie Nolan was a very tall woman. She was six feet easy. Just right.

Yet she wouldn't go out with him. He never knew her to go out with anyone. She was terrific-looking, with dark, lustrous hair like an Iroquois maiden's, big long bony feet and long bony hands and kneecaps like rock formations, and a big wide mouth with big teeth. Lesser mortals might have called her horsey-looking and maybe she was. But a fabulous horse. A lot of the little girls at the Center were wild about this toy sensation called My Little Pony. Well, in his private erotic moments, Charles Tucker thought of Julie as My Big Pony. He'd love to see her run naked on the beach. He'd love to see her naked anywhere. She was, however, a hard case.

He got out of the elevator on the seventh floor. His lucky number. The vestibule was gracious, a relic from a gracious time when there were always little tables to put your hat down on, and mirrors for checking to see if your nose was shiny. His nose wasn't shiny—in fact, he had a long, hawkish nose that reminded some impressionable women of Sam Shepard—but he checked himself out in the mirror anyway. What he saw was okay with him. He was thirty-nine years old. He'd been through war and tumult. He had scars, but not the kind you saw looking at your face in the mirror. Still his eyes were clear; his skin was healthy; his hair was thick and gray, which turned on so many women you'd be surprised; and all that age had done to him was to make his face leaner and a little more dangerous. It didn't stop anyone from looking.

Before he rang the doorbell, he stopped to listen. This was an old habit, one which he picked up in those days when it was quite necessary for him to know what went on behind closed doors. It was something he'd gotten so good at that his ears could hear through oak what other people couldn't hear through plywood.

"I told you, the green dress isn't for this time of year," he could hear Julie saying.

"I want it," returned Hildy.

"Do you want to look ridiculous? You do not wear that fabric this time of year."

It was some conversation, Charles thought.

"It's getting late!" he could hear Julie cry. "Are you going to change or not?"

Mistake: offering choices. Why couldn't his parents ever learn? They were "modern" parents. They talked too much. They couldn't keep their traps shut.

Don't you think it would be better Perhaps we should think about doing it this way If you'd listen to what I'm saying you would see that the only thing we should really be talking about now is how best to . . .

Bullshit. Why did so many of his parents sound like fucking analysts? Kiddies couldn't handle those choices.

He pounded on the door. He liked to pound doors. Doorbells were effete inventions. He pounded again. Three fists. Fist Fist Fist.

"Who is it?" (annoyance).

"Charles," he grinned.

She opened the door. She was flushed. Her pile of crow-black-blue hair framed red cheeks and a thundering brow with two sharp creases like apostrophes over her large deep darting green eyes that reminded him of tiny trout in white water. "Oh," she said. "You're early."

He was always early to her. One, he couldn't wait. Two, he liked to catch her unawares, like today, to find a piece or two of the mystery.

"Can I help you with something?" he asked, utter courtliness.

She made a face. "Yes. Hildy."

"Hey hey Hiladerry," he called.

"Charles," Hildy cried, running. "Do you like my dress?"

So he would be forced to choose between Daughter, in a light cotton kelly-green dress with plaid trim that made her look like something out of Sherwood

Forest, and Mother, who stood there tensely, those eyes darting. "Great dress, sweetie," he said.

Julie stared at him for a moment. He knew she found him wildly attractive. He wondered if she thought of him at night. How could she not? He thought of her every night and made believe his pillow was her belly.

"Can I get you some coffee?" she said coolly.

"Sure."

They went into her kitchen, which was very big by urban standards. She had made it into a country kitchen. She had big copper cookware, which was, amazingly, never tarnished. She had mason jars filled with everlastings. Behind the glass doors of the cabinets she had redware and spatterware. The only thing that was off was a box of Crispix on the gateleg table.

"I don't know what to do with her," Julie confessed, with a grin that didn't fool him a bit. "She's so obstinate."

"Takes after her mama."

"Oh, stop it," she said, and he thought he saw her cheeks go redder.

"You're a beautiful woman when you blush," he said, with a mouthful of Danish.

"Oh, Charles. Come *on*. Give me a break, will you?"

He shrugged. She condescended to him. She made a pile selling space for Condé Nast and she did smashing well in life without a man, getting all the clothes furs jewels daughters she needed without a resident cock, thank you very much, and she figured him for a laid-back puss-cat because that's what he wanted them to think and he guessed that she guessed he was one of those guys who liked to give back rubs better than anything else. He'd like to get down with her, show her a thing or two. "That's what I'm trying to do. Give you the break of your life."

She rolled her eyes, but he wasn't put off; the fact was she liked having him around. He babysat for her at least once a week. She was always running off somewhere. Not that she was a delinquent mother—hardly; in fact, a little delinquency would have been a spring breeze in that system—but she had a raft of responsibilities. She had to see and be seen. Four nights a week she had some kind of cocktail party or business dinner or whatever. She knew, when she had decided to become a single mother, that the exigencies of her life and the demands of her job were extreme, but she was full of energy, fiercely organized, belligerently conscious of her responsibilities, proficient about hiring on friends, neighbors, colleagues as part of her support system, and so she made a go of it. But the effort involved—the awful effort—had to take its toll on Hildy. Where? In the nervous smile, the way she pushed other kids, the way she talked, so blazingly loud, talking through everyone else's talk like the Great Buzzsaw of the Old West. Hiladerry. Sometimes he just wanted to do something so quiet with her. Take a bath. Sponge her sweet peach back. Of course, in these days when the city was fingerprinting its day-care workers, it would not be wise for a man his age to take a bath with a girl her age, even though his desire was only to give her his warmth. He'd best keep a low profile. If ever they got around to fingerprinting employees of private day-care centers, he'd have to find a new career. Test-flying fighter jets. Stuffing the fortunes into fortune cookies.

"Is it cold out?" Julie asked.

He grinned at her. He really wanted to take his hand and place it alongside her cheek. "Not for me."

"She catches cold so easily."

"You still subscribe to the cold-draft theory of colds? You must be the last woman alive to do that."

Hildy was watching them with undisguised interest, which Julie noticed. She took Charles by the elbow and led him out of the kitchen into the foyer.

"You shouldn't try to make fun of me in front of her," she whispered. "It's absolutely inappropriate."

"Oh, come on. Don't take it so seriously. You know I think the world of—"

"You just shouldn't," she said, with sudden fierceness. "I don't tell you how to do your job and . . ."

She stopped, realizing she had painted herself into a corner.

"That is my job. Children. Next point." At once, he felt pleased by her lapse, so uncharacteristic, so unlike her to make a mistake, and outraged at the thought of her trying to put him down. "You're much too hooked into the idea of 'jobs,' if I do say so."

She stared at him. She took a deep breath. "Don't let her eat a lot of crap at the party, will you?"

"OK."

"Corinne McIver always has the whole spread. Candy, chocolate, cake, ice cream, soda even."

"She's got a lot to celebrate."

She started to say something, then thought about it. He watched her, waited. "I'm not always like this," she said with a sharp frown.

"Like what?"

"You know. Shooting my mouth off and all that."

"You always shoot your mouth off." He reached over and with his big hand he touched her thick dark hair. "It's one of your best qualities."

He watched her watching him. She got that blush again—faint but no mistaking it—and her lips parted slightly, as if to say something.

"What are you doing?"

They turned; it was Hildy. Watching them, eyes big as lanterns.

"Oh boy," said Julie, under her breath. "Mommy got a boo-boo," she said, "and Charles was making it better."

"Mommy got a boo-boo?" Charles said dryly.

"Yes," she said firmly. "And Charles will get a boo-boo if he's not careful."

"I'm never careful," he said. "One thing about me is I'm never careful."

"Go to the party, will you?" Julie said, her eyes shiny.

"I'm going. I'm going."

Trina put the dishes in the sink. She rarely had company to her apartment but then Barry wasn't company. Barry was her friend; she had known him almost the whole time that she had been in New York. They met in acting class. He played the Dauphin to her Joan in a scene from Shaw. Neither of them was good at understanding that kind of sacrifice.

From the beginning, he took her under his wing. She guessed she looked like someone who needed taking care of. She repaid him by laughing at his jokes and thinking he was wonderful. He needed the ego support. Because of his lisp, his very small size, his spiky blond hair, his tiny hands that flapped around like flippers when he got excited, his repertoire was limited. What can I play? What can I play? was his constant lament. The Fool. Ariel. Puck. Some Molière. Beckett. *Charley's Aunt.*

—Let's face it. I will never play Willy Loman.

—No. You will never play Willy Loman.

—Not that I'd want to. And I will never play Hickey in *The Iceman Cometh.*

—No. You will never play Hickey in *The Iceman Cometh.*

—Nor Othello.

—That is safe to say. You will never play Othello.

They would laugh. He was one of the only people in the world who could make her laugh. Sometimes she felt like the sphinx, half-buried in sand, paws dug in, ugly with the nose worn away leprous from the gritty wind, waiting there, waiting. But he knew what buttons to push; he knew how to make her laugh, even if the laugh was dry and rough, like a cold pipe getting started.

When they weren't laughing, they exchanged survival strategies. Restaurants to work in. Cleaning services to work for. Freebies. She got him working as a sub at the Center, even though he claimed to hate children and referred to them as "beasties." Still, the place was right for him. He could be a clown there but, maybe even more important, it was small enough, a built-in community, like a small town, and served him well as a source for endless gossip. She, on the other hand, generally kept her mouth shut for no one knew better than she that people had secrets and that secrets were best kept shut up.

As she washed, he stood beside her, drying and going on with his general dishing of everyone connected with the Center.

"The one I can't figure out is Nancy Poole," he said. "She's so sweet, so nice. What is she doing with that husband of hers?"

"I don't know," Trina said, trying to get egg off the Melamac. "Maybe she loves him."

"Your views of life are primitive," Barry said. "'Maybe she loves him.' 'Maybe she doesn't love him.' You've got to start thinking with more sophistication. Maybe she loves his money. Maybe he's a father figure to her. Or maybe he's the only guy she's ever laid."

"Barry. Stop," she said.

"I *beg* your pardon."

"Can't some married people just be happily married?"

"When I see it I'll believe it."

She didn't say anything. She just kept on washing. She was bothered by what he said. Even though she never expected to marry, part of her wanted to preserve the dream. White lace. Seed pearls. *Peau de soie.* Her sister had dreamed of nothing else. A great big fat wedding. The getaway car with shoes tied to it. Trina wasn't immune to all this. The sight of newlyweds on church steps in the sunlight could still unravel her. "There's nothing wrong with marriage," she said. "There's nothing wrong with people making a life together."

Barry said nothing. He dried the dishes. He frowned. He looked like a reprimanded lapdog.

"Darcy should be here any minute," Trina said, glancing at the clock.

"Why you had to arrange to have her go with us I'll never understand."

"I told you, Barry. She wanted us to sign this big card she made for Caitlin."

"She's beyond the pale, that one. And that sister of hers. Sybila. What a name. The pair of them together give me the willies."

"You have to understand them," she said. "It's a cultural thing . . ."

She trailed off, not really completing her thought. She really didn't know what she was saying, hadn't any idea. Even though she almost finished college—Syracuse, then NYU—she was very unsure of herself. She felt like she never really understood the meanings of words like "empirical" or "epistemological" or even a word like "cultural." Those kinds of words got stuck in her head like clots.

"Sybila scares the hell out of me. I've seen her on the street, talking up a storm to herself."

"Her and half of New York," Trina said, putting the last dish on the dish drain, scouring the sink, turning off the water, drying her hands. "People like Darcy and her sister," she said. "They've got a hard life."

"Tell me about it," Barry said, folding the dish towel and putting it on the counter. "Why does Loretta look for life's losers?"

Trina stared at him. "What do you mean?"

"You know what I mean. The wanderers. The flotsam and the jetsam. The lost and found. People like Darcy. Charles. People like you and me."

Trina didn't know if she should answer, but then she did. "I guess," she said, "people like us have the time for children."

They walked along Central Park West, the four of them. There was a cold wind. Barry was wearing a sheepskin coat much too big for him. He'd gotten it from the Good Will and now he was lost in it, like a mouse in a barn. Darcy was carrying the huge card—gigantic, like those oversize pencils or paper clips you see in children's museums, like Darcy herself. Her sister, Sybila, walked behind Darcy. She was rail-thin where Darcy was fat. She had on a cheap challis kerchief—cream-colored with stamped orange roses and fern—and she carried a cane and limped, due to an injury to her ankle that she had sustained in a fall on last winter's ice and that had never healed properly. Trina walked behind her, looking at the rough skin, the color of ash, on Sybila's heels as they exposed themselves with each step, lifting out of the cheap pink sandals.

"She goin' to see this here card," Darcy laughed, "and she goin' think it circus time!"

"Nice card," Barry agreed.

"She love big things, that girl. I bought her this here Hershey kiss last Christmas? I had her mama's permission. Lord, it was this big. She see it, her eyes pop out like cuckoo clocks," Darcy cried, laughing so loud that people on a passing bus looked at her. "Guess that's why she like me." She paused. "'Cause I am not small!"

More laughter. Trina smiled. Darcy was wearing an imitation Persian-lamb coat, cocoa-brown, that made her look like a giant stuffed animal. What could be warmer than to mold into her, yards of flesh, the soft of her haunches?

"She one pretty little girl," Darcy said.

When they got to the corner of Ninety-second Street, Trina saw Bill Dowell and Petey waiting at the light to cross the street.

"Trina!"

It was Petey calling. She felt the wind in her face. She waved and he waved back to her. Bill waved. As she crossed the street Petey hopped on first one foot then the other like he had to pee. He was so happy to see her. He ran to hug her around the knees and she picked him up and held him in her arms.

"It got cold, didn't it?" Bill said, his skin pink. "Just since we went out."

"Mr. Dowell," Darcy cried, making her way across the street, all three hundred pounds of her. "Hey there, Mr. Dowell."

Barry rolled his eyes at Trina. Darcy was the only teacher at the Center who called parents "Mr." or "Mrs." No matter what anyone said or how many times they said it.

"Petey, lamb," Darcy said, bending down to give him a kiss that he writhed away from. "Ain't he the sweetest?" she said to Sybila, who occasionally cooked at the Center and whom all the children knew by sight at least.

"Oh yeah. He sweet."

Trina saw Sybila smile at Bill. Her teeth were wasted. He looked at Trina and she smiled at him. Out of the corner of her eye, she could see Barry looking at them. Barry was too much. She felt like he knew every secret of her life. But he didn't.

They went through the beautiful brass-and-glass lobby, swans etched on the glass. Bill stepped aside to let the others go first into the small elevator; she waited with him for the next car.

"Where's Dennis?" she asked.

"He had a sleepover last night," Bill said, and then laughed at little. "He's such a little macho number sometimes but don't you know he forgot his six inches of Original Crib Blanket and I had to rush over with it, express, at ten o'clock, all the way down to Seventy-seventh Street."

Trina smiled and shrugged. "He's only a kid."

"Yeah, well, he wasn't even embarrassed in front of his friend. Big shot."

"Why should he be embarrassed?" she asked.

Bill considered this for a moment. "I don't know," he said finally.

The elevator came back to the ground floor; the door opened. Petey ran in to hold the button and Trina felt Bill's hand on her back as he led her in. The touch made her hold her breath and she waited for him to say something, anything, and he did.

"So Caitlin is four," he said. "Incredible."

"Can you imagine how happy they must be?" said Trina.

"No," said Bill, undoing his plaid scarf and folding it into a neat square. "I can't."

"You know, I don't think they love her any the less for it," Trina murmured. "Sometimes I think they love her more. I guess that would be hard for some people to understand."

"Yes," he said. "I guess it would."

"But not for me," she said. "I could love her to pieces." She paused; she licked her lips. "Would it be hard for you?" she asked. "To love someone who wasn't altogether right? Who wasn't a hundred percent?"

He stared at her. "I don't think so," he said. "No. It wouldn't be hard for me."

For a moment, she searched his face and then she decided to believe him.

*   *   *

Corinne worked in the kitchen, watching the party through the serving window. It was hot in the kitchen—the southern exposure; the water on for coffee; the oven heating up the tiny cheese strudels—but she didn't mind. The party was a good one; she'd made a good party. She had cleaned and cooked; had the windows washed; bought flowers; made loot bags for the children. She was a good organizer—a great organizer. The only thing she'd fallen down on in the organization department was their offspring. One like Caitlin—bless her, bless her—was one thing, but then not to have another . . .

She didn't wish to adopt. She only cared to have something totally good and well-made come out of her union with Patrick. They were such a good team. Look at them now. She in the kitchen; he circulating among the guests. Ready smile, glad hand. Host. No one of them had ever seen him cry. No one but her. She had seen him cry like a baby. Disappointment didn't come easy to him. She looked at her baby, Caitlin, sitting on Darcy's table of a lap, looking at Darcy's oversize card. Her little girl had a lot of people who loved her.

What a lot of good people there were out there. Growing up, she had never felt very warmly about people. Coming to New York, she had felt less so. She always felt that people here looked on her as though she weren't good enough. Not tall enough, not pretty enough, not well-dressed enough. When she worked at Time Inc., in financial planning, she always felt that others got ahead of her because they looked better than she did. Then, when she had Caitlin, she felt that her stock had gone lower still. Until she went to the Center. There she felt surrounded, embraced. Not that any of them were like her, but it didn't matter. They were her world; she was theirs. Their children were hers; her child was theirs.

She dried the dishes and watched the kids through the serving window. She was so absorbed by what she saw that she didn't even see someone come up behind her and grab her ass. "Patrick!" she hissed. He was already high as a kite!

"Are ye goin' to be watching the festivities through that little window the whole time, Mrs. McI?" he asked in the Irish brogue he affected whenever he'd had too much to drink.

"Don't be a fool, will you?" she snapped, brushing away his hands.

"Come on out, luv."

"I'll be out in a minute," she said, all blushed, embarrassed to have been caught in the act. "Some of us are working today. You go attend to our guests, will you please?"

He bent down—from so high—and kissed her. "I love you, lovie."

"I know you do," she said, and she did.

She wiped the last cup, put it all on a tray to carry out. From the window, she could see Patrick pour himself another one. Drunk. Always at something like this. You know what they say about kids? Transitions aren't easy. Well, transitions aren't easy for anyone. She might as well stop counting. Later there would be a fight. And tears—his. He'd start blubbering something about "his little girl." And then about "his little girls." She'd have to hold him, stroke that giant head of his, that melonhead, and later, in bed, she'd make it all right. Poor oaf, she thought— what life has dealt you. She could have cried right then. But she didn't. Oh, what a job to be a wife. What a job to be a mother. She picked up the tray and headed into the living room, feeling very happy and sad.

Happy Birthday to you,
Happy Birthday to you,
Happy Birthday dear Caitlin,
Happy Birthday to you.

Patrick was loudest of course. But Corinne wasn't singing at all. Trina knew, because Corinne was next to her. Caitlin looked more like a Down's-syndrome child than she ever did, because she was so happy and because her mouth was wide open, and so everyone sang louder, Darcy's voice the thing of beauty in the room, and Trina, in that circle, pressed against Bill Dowell and felt him press against her. If she didn't have someone for herself, she would go mad. She needed someone—she needed it. Loretta looked across the circle at her and winked—just a happy wink, nothing conspiratorial. Barry had his arms around Aaron and Molly, and Sybila stood there, framed by a window, her kerchief with the orange roses still on her head. Charles kissed Corinne like the mother of the bride when it was all over and Patrick shot everyone with his video camera.

Then Barry played the clown. He had a funny hat—a black pirate's hat—and sang "I Know an Old Lady Who Swallowed a Fly" and "My High Silk Hat." He played games with them and had them howling.

As the kids howled, Bill tapped Trina on the shoulder. She was kneeling and she had to look up at him and he looked tall. He was smiling. He had beautiful lips. She rose and they went to a quiet spot by the window in the long foyer, hung with cheap baskets.

"I wanted to talk to you about Wednesday nights," he said, not quite looking her in the eye. "Wednesday nights I could really use some help. I've got a standing meeting on Wednesday nights and can't get home until seven. I'm really in a jam."

"Couldn't you switch with her?" Trina asked. He was so jittery and pale and sweet; she wanted to hold his face in her hands.

He shook his head. "She has a concert series on Wednesday nights. She makes time for that," he added, with a more overt bitterness than usual, perhaps for her benefit alone, but she didn't care. She'd take it. She'd take whatever she could get.

"I'd like to help," she said. "But I'm so awfully tired after the Center . . ."

"I know, I know. It's terrible of me to even ask. But the kids love you so. And I'd make it worth your while . . ."

Worth her while. Money. Money. She hated that. She felt something freeze up inside of her. "All right," she said. "We'll work something out."

Business done, there was nothing left to say. She started to move away, but he put out a hand to stop her. He stared at her. They could hear the howling. Their faces were very close. "We're so lucky to have found you," he said. "You just appeared. Just like that. At just the right time."

She looked at him and then looked away. "Hey. I'm not a miracle, you know. I'm a regular real live person."

He stared at her, ready for this. "No, you're not. You are a miracle. Straight from heaven."

They looked at each other. It had begun. They stood, close, silent, until Petey came to find them, and led them by the hand back to where the party was.

PART TWO

7

LOUISE'S MOTHER had called at four o'clock to announce a migraine and to tell Louise that she could not take the children for dinner. Louise asked her mother if she had had any caffeine. Her mother told her that she did not wish to be grilled. Louise said she would be at the school by five.

When she hung up, she felt her own head begin to ache. Her mother's simple suggestion of a headache could immediately start one up in Louise. It had always been so. In so many ways they were alike. They looked alike. They had the same shoe size. On a voice test, their voices would probably match. And, like Abigail, Louise would probably be a better grandmother than she was a mother. Indeed, it was their alikeness that made Louise fear for her breasts. Her mother's left breast had been removed at forty. Louise was thirty-six. She was scrupulous about her breasts, but you could only fight genes so much.

Of course, there were ways in which they differed. Abigail, for one, had married an exciting man. Louise's father, John Strong, was well-known. He was an attorney and a theatrical producer. He had produced shows with Tallulah Bankhead, Walter Slezak, Barbara Bel Geddes. Louise remembered all of these people visiting their home—or at least she remembered stories about them. Once, when she was at Wellesley, Louise's father had come to stay at the College Inn for a weekend. She felt wonderful to show him around; he felt wonderful being shown around and flirted with the girls and made them laugh. Their big dinner was at Locke-Ober's, where he was well-known. He had three Gibsons. All through dinner, she stared at him, thinking him marvelously handsome, even with the liquorish flush. His hair was, and had been for most of his adulthood, silver snow. He wore it a little long but impeccably barbered. Everything about him was impeccable. He had once been named a best-dressed man. His shirts and ties were Turnbull & Asser. His suits were Dunhill, always dark. In his pocket, he always kept an immaculate white linen handkerchief—Belgian or Swiss, with the monogram hidden in the folds, but there nonetheless. They sat in the plush heavy comfort of Locke-Ober—she ate Dover sole and consommé, she remembered—and he told her a dirty story about Tallulah Bankhead. The first time he met Tallulah, he told her, he had gone up to her suite for a business meeting and she had received him *au naturel.* "May I take your clothes?" she had asked him (he imitated her husky voice perfectly). He had politely declined and they had gone on to become great friends. Louise remembered feeling so adult, there in Locke-Ober's, being told that dirty story by her father, who always treated her like a princess.

She could never figure out why he married her mother. Oh, she'd heard the official version many times. He was at Harvard; she was at Wellesley (yes, another sameness). Abigail was interested in theater then, and so of course was he. They had worked together on a production of *Right You Are.* She had been luminous then, he said—or she said (Louise got the sources mixed up). But as soon as they married, things began to chill. The needs of their union were at odds with Abigail's needs. She wanted to be able to express herself. She didn't want to be just an attorney's wife. He tried to bring her into his theatrical endeavors, but she wouldn't be his assistant. She wanted to have an identity of her own. She enrolled at the Bank Street College of Education; she got her master's degree. She went to teach at the Soames School. She was never happier. Everyone loved her.

There followed a more extensive upheaval—therapy, women's groups, what-have-you. She left her husband. It wasn't what she wanted. Louise, as a girl, had hated her for it. There simply wasn't a good enough *reason.*

Louise packed up her briefcase and turned off the lights in her lab. She was uneasy about leaving this early. For one thing, she almost never left this early and felt really peculiar about it. For another, she had taken time today, during lunch, to visit with her lover in his office. She was quite sure no one knew about the affair, even though their trysts went on right here at the university. But they were careful for, like herself, he was married—very married. He lived in Riverdale, with a Danish woman who sculpted and their three teenage children. His name wasn't important. In fact, she never used his name. Loose lips sink ships. He was, for his part, just as concerned with discretion, if not more so. He had no intention of dissolving his marriage. When she told him that she and Bill were separating, his large hazel eyes grew even larger.

—Don't worry. It's not on your account (she had said).

And it wasn't. She was by no means in love with this man. This was no *Brief Encounter,* no bittersweet romance. This was an excellent arrangement—nothing more, nothing less. He was a good man. He had a brilliant mind. They respected each other professionally. He was also physically attractive. American, but of Danish descent, he had dark blond hair, all over him. He was also an eager, ardent, talented lover. But the thing that was so excellent about it all was that it worked. *She* worked. All along, with Bill, she'd been so afraid that there was something really wrong with her. Now she knew that she worked—that she could achieve orgasm if she set her mind to it. There wasn't anything wrong with her. Probably, in the right hands, there wasn't anything wrong with Bill. What was wrong was *them.* They didn't work together. She didn't know why she had waited so long to find this out for herself.

She took a bus to the corner of Ninety-fourth Street and walked the block east
to the Soames School, where her mother was director—one hesitated to use the
word "headmistress" these days—of the primary school. She and Bill had enrolled Denny there when he was five, against her better judgment. She had really
wanted her sons to go to Horace Mann or Trinity—one of the very curriculum-
oriented schools where they would be worked as hard as they could be worked so
that by the time they were eighteen, they would have as complete an education as
most people would ever have and they'd only be just beginning. But there was a
problem. Denny had a learning disability. It was probably a mild dyslexia, although he was just getting to the point where that could be legitimately diagnosed. Bill—and Abigail—were insistent about his going to a school where "he
wouldn't be judged a failure at six." At first, she resisted them, claiming that to
send him to anything less than the best would be to judge him a failure. But her
mother said there were "different kinds of bests" and Bill spoke passionately
about his own experience of frustration and inadequacy at Boston Latin. Bill,
although his academic credentials certainly wouldn't indicate such a thing,
sometimes seemed to her to be not quite in the front rank of intelligence. Once
she had taken a class with him over at Harvard—social anthropology—and she
had done much better than he had. Still, she could only resist so much and so she
let Denny go to the Soames School in the end. There he learned reading by color
group and math by color rods. Louise's father sometimes joked that his grandson
would grow up to become a set designer.

At Ninety-fifth Street Louise entered the brownstone that had housed the
Soames School since its inception thirty years ago. It always seemed to Louise to
be underscaled, like a leprechaun's cottage. This appealed to Bill, she thought.
He liked things small—small schools, small cars, small analysts. She walked up
the two flights to her mother's office and knocked before entering.

"Come in," said the high, fluting voice—just like her own.

The room was dimmed—a migraine dimness.

"Poor Mother," Louise said. "You didn't eat chocolate, did you?"

"No, I didn't eat chocolate," said her mother, lifting the cold compress from her
forehead. "I wish you wouldn't treat me like a criminal when I get one of these. I
don't treat you like a criminal when the situation is reversed."

"I'm sorry," Louise said, her own ache starting to escalate. "Do you think it will
be a really bad one?"

"No. I don't think so." She pressed the compress against her left eye, staring at
her like a cyclops. "You're late."

"The traffic was impossible."

"I knew you'd be late."

Louise suddenly wanted a cigarette very badly. She smoked three a day, even
though she worried about it. Still, it settled her nerves. "Only ten minutes," she
pointed out, trying to ignore her urge. "How's Denny?"

"He's all right. He's in the gym now." She paused a moment, wrinkling her
nose as if to sneeze. "He cried today."

Louise looked at her. "Oh?"

"Miss Dergin told me. In art class. It seems he spilled paint. He got terribly
upset. She told him not to worry about it, but of course he did. He started saying
that he wasn't any good. That it was all his fault. She brought him to see me."

"Is that appropriate?" Louise asked.

"What?"

"That she bring him to see you."

There was a silence in the room as Abigail stared at her. "That's what you're worried about?" Abigail said. "Well, don't worry. At Soames, we let our principals be grandmothers and our grandmothers be principals. We're funny that way," she added.

"Is that what brought on the migraine?" Louise asked, looking past her mother's shoulder to a huge collage in greens, blues, and yellows that the K-2 had done.

"It's common in situations such as the one Denny's living through for the child to assume responsibility, to blame himself," Abigail went on, ignoring Louise's question. "It's something I advise my parents to be very sensitive to."

But I'm not one of your "parents," Louise wanted to cry. She suddenly felt so angry, but, what's worse, she knew her mother was right. That was the thing about her mother—she was always so damned right. More right than even Louise was, and Louise was just about as right as anyone she knew.

"We've never suggested to him," Louise said evenly, "that he or Petey was in any way responsible for the situation. I don't understand why he would even begin to think that . . ."

"You don't understand," her mother said, leaning forward, making the effort even though her face was white with the migraine pain. "You really don't, do you? You never could understand things that didn't read $X + Y = P$. But this isn't a formula, Louise. This is the *psyche*. I'm worried about Denny's *psyche*."

"All right, Mother," Louise said, standing. "I understand. Thank you for telling me." She headed for the door, but then, when she got there, she turned around. "I know you think it's all my fault. Not Bill's. Not your precious Bill . . ." She stopped herself; her head was throbbing. It was too much, too much. She stared at Abigail. She looked old and weak and Louise wanted to hurt her, but not too much, not irremediably. "You know, Mother," she said, pulling herself together. "Sometimes I think Bill should have been the man you married. You two would have worked very well together."

"Perhaps we would have," her mother said.

A moment followed and then Louise turned and headed out the door.

Through the observation window, she watched Denny in the gym. He was playing basketball. She didn't think she had ever seen him play this before; she thought he seemed very good compared to the other boys. He had such a lovely body. If you took her body and Bill's body and you put grace on top of it, strength and fluidity, you'd get Dennis's body. Petey didn't have that kind of body at all. Petey's body was very frail and narrow. But Petey had the brains and Denny had the beauty. Yet, as much as she would have expected herself to value the one above the other, she surprised herself by not doing so. She valued immensely Denny's beauty. He would have all sorts of people falling in love with him in this life of his. And that was important. She looked at her father. He hadn't been the best—he was known, he was well-known, but he wasn't the best—and yet he had what Denny had: the ability to make people love him. That didn't come to her naturally, nor did it come naturally to her mother. They were like two sibyls: hard to hold. Bill, on the other hand, was the other extreme: he oozed all over you. Petey was more like her: he knew, knew, knew. Sometimes she looked at him, as he slept, and through his thin papery eyelids she could see the meat of his brain, or at least she thought she did.

She went down the steps and into the gym, struck in the face by its warm, moist sweat smell. Little boys' sweat was sweet if not too much of it was in one place at the same time. "Denny!" she called. He turned; his face lit up. She stared at him approvingly: his blond hair; clear skin; features even and well-defined. He could be selling grape drink or cereal on TV if he'd had a different kind of mother, she thought. He ran to her and hugged her around the waist. She hugged him back. "Come on, now. Go get dressed. We've got to go get Petey."

They got into a cab and headed through the park to the West Side. She had the cab wait as they went in to get Petey—an extravagance but she was a mother alone now and she deserved certain extravagances. As she walked into the Center, she saw Loretta standing with the fat black woman, whose name escaped her for the moment, and the small, pale girl they called Trina.

"Hi there, Mrs. Dowell," the fat black woman called.

She murmured a hello to everyone. Then she looked around for Petey, but she didn't see him. "Where's Petey?" she asked.

"He's asleep," Loretta said.

"What?" Louise cried. "He'll be up all hours."

Loretta shrugged. "What can I tell you, Louise? He looked like he was coming down with something. His eyes weren't right."

"He said his throat hurt too," Trina said, almost in a whisper.

Louise felt her head begin to rip, filled as it was with razor blades, with knives. Loretta didn't like her; she made no bones about it; she let Petey take a late nap. "All right. Where is he?"

"In the back," Loretta said.

She found him on a cot. He was warm. Oh God, he was getting sick. She picked him up and he molded into her, his wet gummy lip against her neck. Her head hurt and she felt furious with him and furious with herself for feeling furious with him. "I think he has fever," she announced as she headed through the main room. "You should have called, you know."

"It just came on," Loretta said. "Maybe an hour ago."

"That's no excuse," Louise said, her face white, like her mother's had been.

"I don't need an excuse," Loretta said.

Louise looked at her. There was definitely something unpleasant about Loretta's face, something vulpine. She shouldn't be trusted with children.

"Give him a Tylenol," Loretta said, handing her one.

Louise snatched it from her and headed out the door. The cab was waiting. She was glad, at least, she had thought of that. When they got home, she put Petey to bed and went to call Bill first thing. But there was no answer. She couldn't believe it: there was no answer. What would she do tomorrow? She couldn't miss work, she simply couldn't. She had a big day planned. She would try him until she got him, she resolved. Bill would take care of it. He had to.

*   *   *

This time, as the first time, as the second and third times, Trina bought fresh flowers. The daffodils were coming in already, because it was late into February, and she bought a stalk of tuberose as well. One stalk of tuberose could fill her small place with scent. She bought Spanish sparkling wine and oranges and vanilla coffee beans. Also she bought some old lingerie at a second-hand store called Screaming Mimi's. The color lilac. She felt shy to wear it at first but then, in the right light, she was a redhead and the color was good for her. It exceeded her budget to have a lover, but she could think of better places to cut back.

It had been so long since she'd had a man in her life. For a while, she had so many men in her life—that's all she could seem to do. Collect men. Like her mother collected Staffordshire pug dogs. Big men, small men, pale pink brown dark yellow and white men.

She looked at herself in the mirror now. She'd found something else at Screaming Mimi's. Old perfume bottles with atomizers. She sprayed on perfume. On her white shoulders. She had filled one of the bottles with a perfume she had mixed herself. A spicy scent. It went back to her Woodstock days. Those days when everybody mixed their own. Sometimes she felt about a hundred years old.

She was thirty-five. She looked younger. Once a week she put plain petroleum jelly all over her face. Nothing like it. She hadn't a line. Her body was good too. She didn't exercise a lot, but she exercised regularly. She walked. She did moves in the morning, before she got dressed. And there were certain things that she got from her mother. Her mother was like a monkey. At seventy, her mother still picked up things with her feet. Her mother could pick up a pencil with her feet. Like her mother, she could pick up a pencil with her feet or a quarter or maybe, on a real good day, a dime. Monkey-legs.

She felt better, having a lover, than she'd felt in ages. She felt complete. And wasn't he a gentle lover. She'd had rough lovers, plenty of them. They weren't much. Anything could be rough, any animal. You get something angry enough it can be rough. But a gentle lover . . .

She'd had lovers with better bodies. Oh, she'd had lovers with bodies like statues. She'd had lovers with better faces. She'd had lovers with emerald eyes. Tiger's-eyes. She'd had lovers with nipples like rosebuds. But it didn't matter. None of that mattered. It didn't matter that her lover's skin was as white as chalk or that his legs were so skinny his kneecaps stuck out like headlights or that his hands were cold or that, in the shadows, his thing looked like the sad old hooked nose of a little old Jewish man. She smiled a little. She touched her breasts, wrapped in silk lilac. None of that mattered. He was a gentle lover.

She went to see about dinner. She was making a noodle kugel and a green salad. She hadn't eaten meat in seven years. She didn't want to think about baby lambs carved up for chops—no. She didn't want to think about veal.

She put some foil over the kugel. Lately she'd gone back to some of the things her mother made, her grandmother made. Kugels. *Tsimmes.* She never thought she'd go back to those things. She didn't think of herself as a Jew. She was a Citizen of the Earth. It was the only thing made any sense to her. When her sister died, she wouldn't sit *shiva* with her mother. Her mother sat on a two-gallon pickle barrel. You've got to sit on wood. She didn't know why, even now. She didn't know why those Jewish lawmakers wanted to give you a sore ass when you lost someone you loved.

The doorbell rang. She looked through the peephole. Bill. She opened the door. He kissed her and handed her a box. Poppycock. Something she never knew about before he came into her life. Fancy Cracker Jacks. The best Cracker Jacks money could buy. She liked having someone to buy her the best. She liked too that he knew her tastes were pretty low—Cracker Jacks, jellybeans—things you could buy at a circus or a rodeo.

"Look at that negligee," he said, looking. "Jean Harlow."

She turned for him. "You like it?"

"What do you think?"

They embraced. He smelled good. He always smelled good. He smelled of nothing but clean skin. She didn't want to think about all the times she'd been with men who smelled bad.

"What's that?" she asked, noticing what he was holding in his left hand, a kind of suitcase.

He didn't say anything. Just opened it. "My bassoon," he explained, as he saw her staring at the pieces.

"Oh, Bill," she cried, thrilled. "Play it."

"After dinner."

She never had a man play a bassoon for her before. Nor a violin nor even the harmonica. She'd always had to bring her own music. She loved music but she didn't play anything real. She was one of those Original Finger Cymbal Girls. There were times when she worried if she was good enough for him.

"You like the dinner?" she asked.

"Mmmnh," he said, lifting a forkful to his lips. The cheese pulled, like taffy, and she saw him look a little uncomfortable as he dealt with it. "What's it called?"

"Noodle kugel. *Lukshen kugel.*"

"Kugel? Is that a Jewish dish?" he asked, holding a little in his mouth.

"Yes," she said. "From the tribe of the Hebrews," she added, teasing him.

He looked at her. He put the lump of kugel in his cheek and grinned. He didn't know she could make a joke like that, she thought, as she watched him swallow. There was a lot he didn't know about her.

"Are you Jewish?" he asked.

She shrugged. "My mother's Jewish. My father's people were Dutch. Didn't you ever see my wooden shoes?"

He looked down below. There were her feet, with painted toenails red.

"Not there, silly." She rose and went to the bookshelves, came back with two wooden shoes. "They were his mother's," she said, and as she said it, the smile faded a little. He noticed this and put his hand on her hand.

"Sometimes," she said, looking past him, "I get sad when I think about him."

"What was his name?" Bill asked.

"Joe," she said. "Joseph Rudy Dunbar."

"What did he do?"

"Oh, he did a lot," she said, touching the pulse at her neck. "He did a lot of things."

"Has he been dead long?"

Not long enough. She pulled herself up and went to stand next to him. Her lilac silk was against his cheek and he pressed his face into her belly. "Let's not talk about him," she said as she leaned down to kiss him.

*   *   *

The bassoon music filled her apartment. She felt she was in a cave: one candle; the smell of musk from her home-brewed perfume; the shadows on the cold walls; the low moan of the reed. His face, as he played, was full of love. Already she had forgotten what he told her the music was. Something by Schumann. Prelude and numbers, she thought. He looked like he was making love to Schumann. She watched his lips work, his cheeks blow in and out. She imagined him giving head to Schumann. As she watched him, she felt the tingling all the way through her. The lilac silk scratched at her nipples and she felt a pulse. She looked at his feet. He'd taken off his shoes and socks. His feet were long narrow white. Cavefish. All of him was hers, she thought. She wanted him all for herself. She wanted him to get her out of whatever she was in. When the music ended, she didn't say anything for a while. She didn't even look at him.

You don't know anything about me, Jack.

"That bad, huh?" he said finally.

She turned to look at him. "If I could do something like that," she said, "I don't know how I could do anything else."

There was a whisker of silence. "What do you mean?"

"It's all I'd want to do. Every minute."

"I'm not that good," he said, putting down the bassoon. "You only think I'm that good because you don't know anything about it."

"I think you're that good," she said. "I know you're that good."

"You only hear the good parts," he said. "But every minute I play I hear my failures."

She stared at him. "That's wrong to do," she said. "I don't do stuff like that. If I only thought of my failures, I couldn't go on."

"Well, therein lies the difference between you and me."

She rose and went to where he was sitting. She took his hands and put them on her breasts. "You and me aren't so different," she said. "We want the same things."

"Do we?" he said. "Show me."

She put a hand into his lap. Combustion. She wanted; she wanted. She wanted to take him away from himself. She undid the buttons on his shirt. She was fast. One year she'd worked in a ward for mental cases. She got good at buttons, great at knots. Then she had to run because the future was there and had an eye like a yolk and looked straight at her. She touched the ridges of his chest his nipples the color of fallen plums then sweet on her lips shivering the slope of his belly the tough girdle of muscle at his waist the swell the mast of his cock rising in the wool suit pants he'd worn all day that smelled close and sour of him and the dry cleaners and the heavy burden of not making music. She wanted him to make music. Always, always.

She felt his cold hands on her upper legs. The backs of her upper legs. She wished his hands weren't so cold. She moved so that his hands were on her ass, the flesh there thick, not so sensitive, and he kneaded her ass and she moved her lips back to his lips where they exchanged their tongues back and forth back and forth like mating snakes.

She pulled off the lilac threw it somewhere. Her breasts were small but felt big to her. He took them in his mouth, first one then the other. When she couldn't stand it anymore she wrenched them free and then knelt beside him, undoing his buckles, pulling the pants down, the chaste white underwear, pulling them off, kissing his cavefish then his calves those knees then his specialness, his stalk, she fed on it, felt it slip down her throat, ate it, swallowed it, then coughed it up and started all over again.

Then she reached down to touch herself. Her cunt was wet with fire. He hadn't done something for her yet, maybe had never done it, so she hadn't asked him for it, but now she did, lying back on the rug, shoulders against the sofa skirt, pulling him down on her, hooking her legs over his shoulders, forcing his head down, moving her hips, and he touched his lips to her, seemed to freeze there, but she said Do it Do it and he did it, not like some had done it but he did it, and then, when he wanted in, she let him in, and she heard his cry as he fell down her deep, her bottomlessness, but she held him like a baby—*Baby*—and they rocked together and when he cried again she kissed him hard and held him tight and wouldn't let him go until she was ready to go too and then they floated out on the raft of her smile and were there.

They must have slept an hour. She woke first. Tenderly she touched him.

"Oh," he said. "God."

"You want something?" she asked.

"No." He shook his head. "I'm OK."

She touched his cheek. "I didn't tell you before, but I think Petey started to come down with something."

Immediately his face alerted, as she knew it would. "What?"

She shrugged. "A little fever. Your wife came to get him. Had a little to-do with Loretta. She's . . ." She stopped herself. What? Scary? A bat out of hell? A nutcracker? "She seemed kind of nervous about it."

"Louise isn't great when it comes to sickness," he said, sitting up too fast.

"Some people aren't," she agreed, although she wondered what his wife *was* great at.

"She gets into these severe hypochondriacal phases. If she's bruised, she's sure it will turn into cancer. She's so worried about her breasts. Her mother lost a breast to cancer."

"What does she need them for?" Trina heard herself say, but it was a mistake, because Bill looked shocked and a little offended. She got out of bed and went to pee. He never spent a night in her bed. He wouldn't now. She wanted to tie him down and keep him there. He was always with the kids, sometimes with his wife and the kids. They still did holidays together. She hated his wife; she thought she was a sick bitch and now, as she sat there, she hated Bill for not hating his wife too.

When she went back in, he was already getting dressed.

"Where are you going?" she said.

"I'm going to go check on Petey," he replied, without apology or anything.

"I think he'll live," she said.

He turned to look at her. "I want to see him."

She didn't say anything. She watched him pull his socks up over his bony ankles, his cavefish.

"I guess he won't be at the Center tomorrow," Bill said.

"No. I guess he won't."

"I'll take a sick day," Bill said, planning aloud. "It's really Louise's responsibility tomorrow, but I guess I'll have to be with him. She wouldn't know what to do with him."

She could see he was loving the idea—being at home with his little sick boy, making him toast and jam. Oh Lord, she thought, she wanted someone to take care of her that way. No one had ever taken care of her that way.

"I'll call you tomorrow," he said, kissing her lightly on the lips.

She watched him go. From the window, she watched him get into his car. It wasn't until he was gone that she saw he'd left his bassoon. With great care, she withdrew it from its case. Carefully, she put it to her lips. She blew, but nothing came out. Then, for a long while, in the light of the dying candle, she sat with it on her lap and fingered the keys noiselessly.

8

A WEEKEND TO THEMSELVES. Anna could hardly believe it. They almost never left Molly, weren't sure they even wanted to, but this time Anna's parents had insisted. It had been so long. Go somewhere, somewhere nice, her father had said, I'll pay for it. They didn't need him to pay for it. Michael had a trust and there was plenty of money somewhere, even though the illness and the demands of having his own business had caused them to pretty much go through their yearly allowance and Michael was reluctant to disturb the bedrock of his portfolio. But her father wanted to do for her. Suddenly everyone wanted to do for her.

For a while they flirted with the idea of the Hamptons—off-season walks on the beach; a driftwood fire—but in the end Michael wasn't comfortable with the idea of spending the money. Through the years, Anna had thought she'd cured Michael of his lifetime habit of parsimony and self-denial, but illness, she had come to realize, leaves nothing the same. For Michael it had brought back all the old fears, pulled off the scab on his depression, which was his own illness that he had to live with and conquer. Now that she'd gotten over what had once seemed the worst of it—the shock of it, the terror—she could put aside the selfishness of the sickness in order to discover another "worst" of it: what it had done to Michael. As far as she was concerned, she was feeling good now. She was sure that she was going to lick this stupid thing, be done with it. She was the eternal optimist—she liked herself that way—but Michael was not. Michael suffered.

Still, they'd have a good weekend. She'd see to it. They had decided to stay in the city, do all the city things they couldn't do with a child around. Like brunch. Brunch was one of those things that disappeared when you had a kid. She and Michael talked a lot about brunch and now, this weekend, weekend of weekends, they would sleep late, go to brunch at a good restaurant, and have spicy Bloody Marys with eggs Benedict. Her weight be damned. She had found a way to lose weight.

"What do you want to take with you to Nanny and Pop-Pop's?" Anna asked Molly that Friday night as they packed Molly's bag.

"Glowworm," Molly said.

"Oh. Glowworm. Of course." A cuddly, smiling green worm with a battery inside so that it lit up if you squeezed it and could ward off the terrors of the night. "What else?"

Molly thought. "Mrs. Tiggy Winkle."

So in went the Mrs. Tiggy Winkle doll.

Michael came in with some laundry and Anna packed socks and some of Molly's little panties. She folded them very neatly, these appurtenances of her daughter's femaleness.

"Mommy," Molly said. "Why do I have to go?"

Michael and Anna looked at each other. "You don't *have* to go, Molly . . ." Anna said, half-prepared to cancel all plans, not sure why she was so ready and even so eager to do so.

"But I want to go," Molly declared.

"Good girl," Michael said.

"Don't say 'good girl,'" Molly scolded. She hated to be codescended to, Anna thought, even if she was only three.

"Oh. OK. Bad girl," Michael said.

That made Molly laugh and so they laughed and then the doorbell rang.

"Nanny and Pop-Pop," Molly cried, running to the door.

Ah, the cries. Oh, the joy. *Shana punim. Lichte punim.* Kisses. Squeezes. Groans of unbearable delight. *Is my big girl going to Nanny's house? And is Nanny going to give you cherry blintzes? Yeth. Nanny gonna give me chewwy bwintzes.*

Amazing, Anna thought, how immediately a child could regress in the presence of grandparents. If only somehow it could be bottled, it would be a great weapon against the Russians. In a flash, you could have them regressing all over the battlefield, so that they'd wander about, totally oblivious, not listening to a single command.

"Did you pack her hairbrush?" Anna's mother asked Anna.

Anna worried about her mother obsessing over Molly's hair as she had once obsessed over hers. It almost seemed a reason to cancel the weekend. But not reason enough. "Yes, Mother. It's packed."

"Now say bye-bye to Mommy and Daddy," Anna's mother said, smoothing Molly's hair, smoothing the collar of Molly's coat.

"Bye-bye," said Molly, with this huge shit-eating grin on her face. She was going off to Candyland, and they weren't.

"Bye-bye," they said, with kisses, hating to see her go.

So then they were alone. Really the first time they'd been alone together since she'd gotten sick. It felt weird, Anna thought.

"She certainly didn't seem too upset about going," Michael said.

"No. I don't think you could say she was."

"I wish they wouldn't talk baby talk to her. I've told them time and again."

"Grandparents' prerogative. Anyway," Anna said vampishly, giving it the go, "let's not talk about *her.*"

He laughed and then they kissed—weird again, Anna thought, with a self-consciousness that rose in the air like steam.

They had plans to meet Liv and Sam Sloan for dinner. Liv had just had the baby last week, and the nurse was still with them. She'd had a girl—Freya—and Anna had put together some of Molly's baby things to bring them. She'd washed and ironed all the baby things and now, seeing them in a pile on top of the bedroom bureau, she felt, for a moment, weak with nostalgia. "Look, Michael," she said, holding up a teensy yellow stretchie with embroidered ducks on it.

He looked.

"Can you believe she was ever so small?"

"I can believe it," he said.

She put the baby things in a shopping bag and they headed out. The night was cold. At least for her. She seemed to be more vulnerable to the cold than she used to be. She sat close to him in the cab, and she took his arm and put it around her. "I'm cold," she said.

"Yeah," he said. "It feels like snow."

They were first to the restaurant. It was their favorite Chinese restaurant. Sometimes Anna thought they could actually be Chinese for the amount of Chinese food they ate. They sat down and Anna asked for noodles. She had periods when she couldn't face anything, and then she had periods when she was ravenous, like now, finishing off the noodles by herself. "There they are," Michael said, and she turned and saw them and waved.

It was an entrance—a real entrance—for they had just brought a new production into town. Liv had this big grin on her face. A new mother's grin. They all hugged and kissed.

"You look incredible," Anna told Liv, as Liv took off her great big down parka. "How do you feel?"

"I feel fine," said Liv. "A little tired."

"Bullshit," Sam said. "She's just saying that. This one drops them in the field. Got a pelvis like a laundry chute."

Liv laughed and then Michael and Anna followed suit. The remark was a little strange, Anna thought, but then Sam, though likable, was a little strange too. Though it never quite came out, you always had the feeling that somewhere down there was an angry vein you didn't want to open up. Probably a result of being around the house too much, she thought.

As they ate, they talked about the baby. "What's this name?" said Michael. "Freya?"

"You don't like it," Liv said, putting down her chopsticks. Anna shot Michael a look. As successful and motivated and competent as Liv was, she was still a very sensitive person. Once Anna had seen her burst into tears when she had come to pick up Aaron at the Center and Aaron had thrown a fit because he wanted Sam instead. She had told Liv then that Molly did that all the time—and it was true—but Liv wouldn't believe her.

"No, I like it," Michael assured her. "I just never heard it before."

"It's Norse," Sam said.

"Oh," said Michael. "Norse."

"Yes," Anna teased, unable to resist. "Norse is very in these days."

Even Liv laughed a little over that. "Sam's grandmother's name was Fanny," she explained. "We had to name her after Sam's grandmother, for reasons I won't go into. Of course we couldn't name her Fanny."

"Why not?" said Anna. "It's very French."

"Not with 'Sloan' it isn't," said Sam. "The fact is that F is a really terrible initial to work with. Florence, Fern . . . you know what I mean? Finally we came across 'Freya' and since it's always been Liv's dream to have a battle-maiden for a daughter . . ."

"Thank you, Sam," Liv said.

A bit of tension, Anna and Michael noted with an exchange of glances. Perfectly normal for a postpartum situation, Anna supposed, but that's the way it had been going for Sam and Liv for a long time now.

Halfway through dinner, Liv wanted Sam to call home. "You call if you're so worried," he said.

"Thanks," she said. "Nothing like indulging the new mother," she added, pulling herself up and going out to call.

When she got back, she didn't say anything. She just sat down.

"Well?" said Sam.

"I thought you weren't worried."

Sam smiled and turned to Anna and Michael. "This is what I have to put up with."

"Poor Sam," Liv said, finishing off the platter of twice-cooked pork.

When the fortune cookies came, everyone, of course, had to read theirs aloud.

"'Waste not, want not,'" Liv read.

"They knew you were coming," said Sam. "The original Ball-of-Foil girl." He turned to his own fortune. "Ah so. 'The apple falls far from the tree,'" he read, and then balled it up and threw it over his shoulder. "Shit. Not only are these fortunes not fortunes—they are *proverbs*—but they've got them wrong. I want my money back, lawyer lady."

It was Michael's turn. "'A man's home is his castle,'" he read.

"Hear that, woman?" Sam said to Liv.

Anna looked at hers. "Oh, these really are dumb," she said, tossing hers into the center where Michael had thrown his.

"Come on. Let's see," Michael said, retrieving it.

Anna turned to watch the fish in the tank—kissing gouramis—but then she turned back to look at Michael, who seemed white-faced, or was it the strange light you sometimes get in a Chinese restaurant?

"'Gather ye rosebuds while ye may,'" Michael read, for not to read it would be even worse.

There was a silence.

"We'd better get back," Liv said. "My tits are getting sore."

Anna watched as Liv nursed the baby. For a moment, all she could think of was breast, breast, breast. "How's Aaron doing with all this?" she said finally.

"Aaron?" said Liv. "You know Aaron. He's never very laid-back about things. I guess he's a little jealous."

"A little jealous?" said Sam, from the kitchen, where he'd gone to get a beer. "We're talking Medea here, folks."

"Oh, Sam. You're always exaggerating," Liv said irritably.

"Hey, don't get on my case," Sam said, with an unfriendly grin. "I make only so many allowances for hormonal rushes."

"Lil," Liv called, removing the sleeping Freya from her breast. The baby nurse, a very old black woman in a pink quilted housecoat, pink hair rollers, and pink slippers, padded out and carted the child to the nursery to be changed and bedded down. "She's wonderful," Liv whispered. "You hardly know she's around."

"Until she goes to sleep," Sam said. "Then she sounds like a pulp mill."

"Jesus, Sam," said Liv. "Talk about hormonal rushes . . ."

Anna caught Michael's eye. It was getting time to excuse themselves.

"You vill plis not embarrass ze company, plis," Sam said with a Sid Caesar-like German accent.

"Oh, you goof," Liv said, with some fondness. "They're not embarrassed. You're not embarrassed, are you?" she asked them, with her characteristic forthrightness. "They're not embarrassed," she told Sam. "They know us."

There was another silence, which Michael broke. "So how long are you going to be out from work, Liv?"

Now it was time for Sam and Liv to exchange glances. "Well, I've got this leave but something's coming up . . . I may not be able to finesse my way out of it . . ."

"Oh, Liv," Anna said reflexively.

"They've really been very good about it," Liv rationalized, "but tax season is upon us."

"Yeah," said Sam. "They've been great about it. They actually make allowances for the reproduction process at Comley, Wizan. But don't worry about little Freya. Mommy explained all about the tax season to her."

"Very funny," Liv said sharply.

There was an even more strained silence. Sam twirled the bottle of beer in his hands. "Hey, I'm sure these good people do not wish to sit around on their free weekend and watch us go at each other," he said equably. "Now do you?" he asked Michael and Anna.

It was their chance—their instruction—to leave.

"Actually," Michael said, "we *were* going to a late movie."

"Oh," said Liv as brightly as she could. "What are you seeing?"

"*Micki and Maude*," said Anna, and then, to be polite, "Wanna come?"

Of course there was no chance of it, but Liv and Sam went through the motions—*It's supposed to be very funny but it's kind of late and Dudley Moore's last three films were such bombs I guess we'll pass this time*—and then they all kissed each other good-bye. "Thanks so much for the things, guys," said Liv.

"Oh, I'm sure you'll take good care of them," Anna said. "Just remember we may want them back someday."

Michael took Anna by the arm and led her out the door.

"Jesus," Michael said in the elevator.

Anna said nothing. She had begun to feel something. She wasn't sure what. A sadness maybe.

"I give them six months at the outside," Michael said.

"Oh, please," said Anna. "Lots of people go through that sort of thing when there's a new baby. It's perfectly normal."

But she knew it wasn't perfectly normal. Later, as she stood on line at the

Thalia, all she could think about was Liv and Sam and what they were doing to each other. She felt cold standing on line—other people did too; she could see that—and she moved closer to Michael, into him, into his dark gray wool topcoat. Why were they doing that to themselves? she thought. One of the hardest things—but maybe also one of the best things—about what had happened to her, Anna thought, was that she had been imparted this new knowledge, this special wisdom. *Don't waste your life,* she wanted to counsel people. *Don't be cruel to each other,* she wanted to hector them. You don't know what you're throwing away.

Michael got seats for them and she went to get junk. Popcorn and Pompoms and Coke. Michael used to get on her for that in the old days. *The old days.* Nowadays he didn't say anything. The fact that he didn't say anything depressed her for a moment, but she put it aside as quickly as she could.

It was a stupid funny movie. Dudley Moore had two wives. A lot of slamming doors. But, for all the laughs, the movie had a curious effect on her, unshared, she was sure, by anyone else in the audience. It was the babies. The movie had two babies in it and these two babies, on top of Liv's baby, were more than she could handle. She thought of her body and what was happening inside of it. Wasn't she, in a manner of speaking, giving birth to something just as she sat here? Cells. That's all a birth was, that's all conception was. A congregation of cells. But here she was—waiting for that time bomb to go off inside her—that congregation of cells that didn't lead to new life but to something bad, something *malignant*. For a moment, as she sat there, in the laughter, the light from the screen flickering just enough so that she could see Michael laughing too, and it was good to see him laughing, it was good, but, for a moment, just a moment, she felt a pain of hunger in her body that she thought would make her faint. She wanted a baby. She wanted to do it for Molly, to give her something else. She wanted to give Michael something else. She wanted to give the world something else. She wanted her cells to fall together right. She wanted a baby.

"What's the matter?" Michael said later, over coffee.

She shook her head. "Nothing."

"You didn't like the movie?"

"No. It was fine." She paused. "It was fine."

"What's the matter?" he asked. "Something's the matter. Is it Liv and Sam?"

She thought a moment and then she nodded. "Yeah. It's Liv and Sam."

He stared at her. "No, it's not."

She picked up a spoon and played with it.

"Look at me," he said. "Stop playing with that spoon." He stared at her intently. "Did you find something?" he forced himself to ask.

What a question. She looked at him. "I want a baby," she whispered. "I want us to have a baby." She watched his face twist; it was terrible to watch; it hurt her. "Why not?" she wanted to know.

"I don't believe this," he said.

"Come on," she said, deciding to jolly it up. "Didn't you want one when you saw them in the movie? And when you saw little Freya? You love babies. Didn't you want one?"

"I do not fucking believe this."

She felt her jaw begin to tremble, and she put a hand over it.

He looked at his hands, as if they weren't real to him, and then he spoke, very slowly and quietly, so that she had to strain to hear him. "We're hanging on," he said. "We're hanging on by our fingertips. And you're talking about another baby . . ."

"OK, Michael," she said. She didn't want to hear this. She'd die if she heard this. "It was just an idea. Just a lousy idea. Forget it."

"Not even to mention the medical ramifications . . ."

"I said forget it!"

They stared at each other. She jumped up, pulled on her coat. "Sit down," he said, but she was out the door.

She stood on the street and tried to get her breath, but she couldn't get her breath. It had gone to her lungs. Oh God, she thought. What have I done? What have I done to Michael? She turned; through the window she could see him paying. She pulled the collar of her coat up around her cheeks.

When he came out, she started to walk ahead of him, very fast. They were only two blocks from their house. He walked behind her. In the elevator, they said nothing. There was nothing to say. She wasn't angry at him. She was angry at the world.

When they got into the apartment, they still weren't talking. She hung up her coat. He was kneeling down to gather the things that had been pushed under their door while they were away. A menu from Szechuan Plum. A flier from a twenty-four-hour locksmith. The apartment was curiously quiet, almost barren, without Molly there. She wondered why he didn't stand up, why he just squatted there, his coat on, the junk in his hands.

"What is it?" she said at last.

He didn't say anything.

She felt scared and she felt her heart ache. She leaned over, touching his shoulder. "What?"

"I can't stand this," he said, not looking at her.

She didn't say anything. What could she say? She left her fingertips on his shoulder. They stayed that way for a moment—a jelly of time, nothing moving, all still.

"I can't stand this," he said. "I can't stand it."

"What do you want?" she asked, her voice rippling through the tears she was holding back. "Do you want to go away?" she said. "Do you want to leave me?"

He whirled around and threw his arms around her waist. He buried his face against her. Against her breasts. He hadn't been this close to her breasts in so long . . .

For a long time it was just that they were crying. That's all. They hadn't done that before. Not much of it. A little maybe, here and there. She guessed they were waiting for Molly to be gone. And now she was.

"Michael," she whispered, cradling his head.

"Why do you have to talk about the things we can't have?" he said. "We can't have those things. I can't give you those things . . ."

"Oh, Michael."

"I knew you'd get sick," he said in a voice throaty with things, lots of things, rage, grief, hate. "I knew you would."

"I'm not," she said. "I'm not."

"You can't leave us," he said, digging his fingers into her.

"I won't." She took his head in her hands and lifted it so they were looking into each other's eyes. "I won't," she whispered.

She took him by the hand. She pulled him up. To his feet. They went into the bedroom. Together they lay on the bed, he in her arms, his face against her breasts. That's just how they lay for a long time, no sounds except now and then a siren or some loud sick car. After a while, with the deliberateness of someone with a job to do, someone whose job it was to take care of others, she pulled off her sweater, rolled down her pants.

Come on, she said.

He undressed, quietly, with a curious sense of shyness, or was it shame.

They met again on the bed. Halfway. They were like new lovers, except that they seemed to know each other from some other place, from some other life. Like new lovers who have come to a place for reasons that go beyond simple reasons, they were patient, slow, sure of themselves despite their frailties.

When it was over—and it had not been easy—they lay entwined, staring at the ceiling or at the dark or at the big nothing that for now, just now, didn't seem so scary. They didn't have to say anything, but they did, because they were in that habit and because they liked that habit, and then they were off, to sleep, together.

9

IT BECAME WARM. Even though it was not even spring yet, something warm had come up from the Gulf. The forsythia would be fooled, Trina thought that morning when she woke up and threw open the window. The warmth touched her cheek like a hand. It made her want the farm. She thought of their cow—how good she smelled on those first warm days of spring. She never touched milk anymore. Once you'd tasted milk the way she had tasted it, there wasn't any point in drinking the store-bought kind. So she drank tea—black-currant tea—and she sat there on her fire escape in her bathrobe with the faded pink roses on it.

Later that morning she told Loretta she wanted to take the kids to the park.

"Damn," said Loretta. "Is it that time again?"

She'd never heard anyone curse the impending spring before and said as much. Loretta laughed a little, ran a hand through her thick graying hair. "Time goes so fast," Loretta said. "I look at the children—babies—and now they all look grown up to me already."

Trina and Darcy made sandwiches. Usually Darcy cooked a hot meal for the kids, sometimes with he sister Sybila. But today it didn't seem to make any sense at all to stay in for a hot meal. They made cream-cheese sandwiches on whole-wheat bread. Then they had all the kids put on their coats. Some complained—the ones who never liked to go outdoors and some people are like that—but Charles held up a hand. "Everyone's going," he announced.

So everyone went. The children held on to a rope and they crossed Central Park

West and headed into the park. She was in the front. Charles was in the back. Darcy was singing a song to march to:

>   *. . . Mary Mack, dressed in black,*
>   *Silver buttons all down her back . . .*

Before long they were at the playground. David, the most physical of the group, led the charge to the fort, which they could climb and stand atop, feeling mighty.

"I love to watch them here," Charles said to her. "Don't you?"

She looked at them, thinking of how long she'd been coming here. "Yes," she said. "I do."

"It's like a laboratory. You can see them—their personalities—come out. Look at David. He doesn't stop for a minute. He'll run himself ragged and then he'll fall down and then he'll cry."

"He reminds me of this yellow dog we had," Trina said. "This big yellow dog, most of it a Golden. He'd jump all over you. Finally you'd have to chase him away with a stick."

"And Olivier, keeping pace."

And Olivier was like a cat. No—stronger than a cat. A puma maybe. Big and sleek, with a dangerous side.

"Then there's Aaron," Charles said.

She looked at Aaron. He wasn't very good at physical things, so already he'd made up an act. He'd start to climb and then he'd fall down and have all the other kids laughing. He did it again and again. She wondered though how much he liked it. Or would he like better just being able to climb up high.

"I love the girls," said Charles. *"Les girls."*

He meant fat little Martha and Molly and Caitlin. The bridge party. They were sitting on a bench. Martha was gabbing and Caitlin was listening and Molly was looking beautiful, a job she was very good at.

"You see Hildy?" Trina said, pointing.

Hildy was at the top of the highest slide. Sheena the Jungle Queen. She was more boy than girl, except when she didn't want to be.

"And then there's Petey," Charles said.

She saw Petey, draped over a tire swing, just rocking back and forth, back and forth, looking at the ground.

"Our thinker," said Charles.

After a while, she went over to him and knelt down to his level. Always get down to their level, Loretta had taught her, if you want them to even consider listening to you.

"What are you doing?" she asked.

He kept rocking back and forth.

"Secret?"

"I'm not doing nothing," he said. He had the sweetest little voice, like a baby, and a mind with force and strength like a man.

"Are you having a good time not doing nothing?" she asked.

He nodded.

"Me too. I like doing that. Sometimes I like best to just sit in a chair. Can't be any chair. It's got to be a big soft chair. And then I close my eyes and I don't go to sleep but I dream."

"I don't like to dream," Petey said.

"No? Why?"

"I see scary pictures."

She thought of him afraid and she wanted to reach out and touch him. What she really wanted to do was hold him. She loved him the most; him and Hildy. They were like her children. But even with your own there are times when you can't go too close. Like now. Times when you just had to have the talent for stillness and wait for it to come.

He came off the swing and sat on her lap. He smelled good, like warm on a cold day. She tried not to hold him too close.

"Knock knock," she said.

"Who's there?" he answered, knowing all the jokes.

"Ima."

"Ima who?"

"Ima in lova with youa."

He laughed. She touched his black hair. She thought he'd grow up to be a handsome man. He was made well, with fine bones, good color. But you couldn't always tell the way a living thing would grow. It had its own secret pattern, and would do what it wanted to do.

"You hungry?" she asked.

He shook his head.

"You're never hungry."

He reached for the necklace she was wearing—a blue-glass string of beads—and held them. "I like this," he said.

She took them off and put them around his neck.

He smiled. "Now I'm you."

She unclipped one of his mittens and put it on her own sleeve. "And I'm you."

They looked at each other and laughed.

Charles gave out the sandwiches and poured juice. He made himself, too, into the bee chaser. Of course, they're not really bees, he reminded everyone constantly. Bees are good. The world needs bees or else the world would be like a piece of coal. Those are yellow jackets—*wasps*—and they live in the ground, too mean and grubby to build themselves a hive or, failing that, a paper nest like any proper wasp would. He had no compunction about killing yellow jackets and, in fact, tried to do just that every chance he got.

"Charles," called out Hildy, "I don't want cream cheese."

"Eat it," he said. "None of us here are so privileged that we can afford to turn up our noses at good wholesome food."

Hildy grinned and went back to her sandwich. She was teasing him; he knew that much. The children knew his philosophies, and they knew what would anger him, and they liked to see his anger. It was all right: he liked to show it. If ever there came a time when he couldn't find his anger, he'd pack it in. Mosey on up to the Great Perpetual Care Home in the Sky.

He didn't know, when he had started doing this, that he loved children, but he did. He also loved the way of life. The sense of community, the sharing. He felt it was the way children should be raised. Sometimes, when he'd go to the East Side (although lately he'd begun to see it on the West as well), he'd look at the babies strapped into their carriages, wheeled along by the nannies, so many of whom had children themselves that they never got to see, children back home on the islands, Jamaica, Grenada, Barbados, Haiti, most of all Haiti, the poorest nation in the world right on our doorstep, and he'd feel like going over to those carriages and pulling off those rotten harnesses, setting those children free, liberating them, watching them turn from little blobs with their silly little buntings into explorers, baby astronauts, entering new worlds. That's what his children were like. Over the last two and a half years that he'd been at the Center, he'd watched them all grow and now they were exquisite—brave and strong and vital, even little Caitlin—and he'd been a part of that growth.

It was Loretta's doing. She was an indomitable woman, a remarkable woman. Times between them were not what they were, but still he had the greatest love and respect for her. When they were lovers, which they were for a period of six months, it hadn't been good. Oh, not the sex—the sex had been too good; it made the ending of it hard. She was a juicy, loving woman, who didn't find a part of the human body alien to the touch, and in fact there were nights when he still longed for her. But like many big strong women, she had a secret fantasy. She wanted, somewhere in the world, to be little and weak and taken care of. She wanted that place to be in his arms. No—in his heart. She wanted him to take care of her, but it was his conviction that the only person he could take care of, in that final sense that she was talking about, was himself.

When they broke up, she made herself, in his regard, doubly strong and started acting like a queen who has to get rid of a bold and bad consort. She contradicted everything he said. She tried to drum up feeling against him. But he wouldn't let her. He finally told her he wasn't going anywhere, that he wasn't ready to go. So they made a kind of truce and kept at it. Sometimes he wondered what she would have done to him if she'd known his secret. He wouldn't put it past her, in that vengefulness that had gripped her, to turn him in to the authorities.

For two and a half years, he had been Charles Tucker. Before that, for just short of a year in Lawrence, Kansas, he had been Eugene Knight. In the years of 1979 and 1980, he had been Richard Driver in Madison, Wisconsin. For two years before that, he called himself Jacob Barnes and lived outside of Tacoma, Washington. In the beginning—those first two years—he had been many more places, had many more names. Eugene Gant. Thomas Buchanan. James Tyrone. Way back when, in what seemed another life, he had been a graduate student in American literature.

Through those years, he had worked every kind of job where you're not watched too closely and you don't have to join a union and few people know you or care about you. For a long while, he was a carpenter's assistant and then he worked for a cleaning service and at points too he worked the fields, picking onions, picking dates. Along the way, he discovered children. Gradually, it seemed to make the most sense to him. Not only was the profile low, but it was a way for him to stay with the work he had first set out to do. He found himself in a position where he could inculcate values. Of course, there was much to learn and he still spent his evenings cooking up cheap dinners and then reading, reading, reading. Sometimes he toyed with the idea of getting a Bank Street degree—he'd audited a few courses—but then he'd tell himself he was deluding himself, that he couldn't stay anywhere this long, not even here. But he couldn't help deluding himself, he thought. It was human nature. He thought a lot about getting Julie Nolan to fall in love with him, and about becoming a father to Hildy, who didn't have one and who needed one, who needed him, and of making a life.

But the thing about his life, the thing that had saved his spirit when he was so close to losing his spirit, was the knowledge that he was making a difference. He told the children that they had to listen to each other. He told them that there were people suffering all over the world and that they had to be kind to people and to share what they had with those less fortunate than they. And it wasn't only the kids—it was the teachers too. He helped Darcy and her sister—helped them use the system, to find what was available to them, to teach them whom to complain to when they had so much to complain about. And Trina—he was going to work on Trina. She was too far away. He was watching her closely and he was making sure she didn't get any farther. Soon, when she trusted him, he would try to pull her back in. But you had to be careful. It was like a fish. If you made the line too taut, it would snap. You had to have a net below. But then that's what Loretta always said, that they were a net, all of them together, and if they were careful, no one would slip through.

After lunch, he asked Darcy if she would sing. She had the most beautiful voice. If she had been born into any other world, they would have built a palace for her and all she would have had to do was sing. But she was born into this world. And she was fat. And her glasses were taped. And she was too loud and too needy and she wasn't pretty enough to make enough people listen to her. But he listened to her, and of course the children did too:

> . . . Samba-le-le was a show off,
> Threw a stone at a mango . . .

He watched the children's faces. They didn't see anything in Darcy except beauty. He was so glad that he was one of those people in the world who saw her beauty too. It made all he'd gone through seem worth it.

> The mango fell down,
> Broke on his head,
> Point to something that's red.

He remembered the red bandanna in his back pocket. Twisting around, he pointed to it and the children laughed and so did Trina. Funny, that red bandanna, being so small, was one of the few things he'd been able to carry with him all these years. A souvenir, he thought, almost falling back down through his memory, but then it was time to point to something blue.

Soon it was time to head back. The children needed their naps. If they didn't get their naps, they'd start growling by three o'clock, pawing the ground. Trina buttoned coats, and tied hats. As soon as she put Olivier's hat on his head, he threw it up into the air, and broke the line. She told him to stop it, to put it on his head, but he didn't listen to her, only listened when Charles told him what to do.

Everyone listened to Charles. He was a man. Tall, strong—his long arms coiled with veins. Sometimes, watching him, she wondered what it would be like to go to bed with him. Barry told her that he had heard—on the grapevine—that Charles and Loretta were once lovers. She imagined them, beautiful together, but then she wished she could stop thinking about things like that. She wished that when she looked at Charles she didn't have to think what his lips tasted like or whether he'd be fast or slow, whether he'd love up her breasts or bury himself below.

She had sex on the brain. It shamed her. The family curse. She could remember her mother talking about the first time she'd seen her father with his shirt off—his hard stomach, his strong back. She remembered the first time her mother told her to stop walking around in her panties. Wasn't she too young then to be told not to walk around in her panties? Her sister's breasts, big when she was twelve. The kids used to call her Marilyn Monroe. Trina, four years younger, couldn't imagine she'd ever have anything like that. And she never did . . .

Molly tugged at her sleeve, said she had to pee. Trina took her over to a bush. "Let go, Molly."

Molly let go. The stream sizzled on the ground. Trina remembered a time when she was five and wet her pants in school and the teacher called her a baby. My, they had teachers in those days. The ones that did it until they dropped, with iron-gray curls and big old tits never touched by any other hand but their own, the kind who didn't like half-Yid little girls from Bolshevik farms.

They walked down the road toward Central Park West. Darcy began to sing again.

> . . . *Mary Mack, dressed in black,*
> *Silver buttons all down her back* . . .

She wasn't sure whether she liked that song or not. It gave her a funny feeling. All over she was starting to get a funny feeling. The day started out warm—first spring—but by now she was feeling cold. She wouldn't be seeing Bill until the day after tomorrow. When his wife took the kids. Sometimes she wished he wasn't as good a father as he was. Sometimes she wished he wasn't a father altogether. Sometimes she wished there wasn't even such a thing as a father.

At the bottom, and across the street, she saw Darcy's sister standing there. As soon as Sybila saw them, she started to scream.

"You give me back my money! She took my money!"

Darcy hunched her shoulders, made her fat massive and thick. "What you want? You get goin', girl!" she cried. "Get goin' now!"

Sybila's hair, weeks dirty, stood away from her head like a cone. Her dress, time-stretched yellow cotton printed all over with faded strawberries, was held together in front by a safety pin. As she came closer, Trina could see her skin, like dusk, leading down to thin, parched breasts.

"You stealin' from me again! Whore! Dirty rotten whore!"

Darcy looked around. Her face was starting to blow up; her eyes were becoming silvery with rage and fear. "Now you shut your mouth. You shut it now or I shut it for you. I put you away where they never let you out."

Trina saw the children watching it all—a play. Some of them—Hildy, Olivier—had smiles on their faces. She felt a touch on her shoulder: Charles. Take them back, he said, and as she walked down the street, she turned to see Charles with his arm around Darcy, who had a fist in the air, shaking it near her sister's hatchet face.

Most of the children were asleep. She had to spend some extra time with Aaron, who was full of questions.

"Why were they yelling?" he asked for the third time.

"They were having a fight." She stroked his hair. "You and David fight. You and David yell at each other."

"No."

"All the time," she said, making it a lullaby. "All the time."

Then they were all asleep. She looked around the room—the cots, the sleeping faces. She felt powerful, like a good witch who had spread good pollen.

With them asleep, she felt her own bones begin to ache. She needed tea and then to close her eyes. She went in the back, and then she heard Darcy's voice. She was sitting with Charles and Loretta and going through a box of Kleenex.

". . . she crazy," Darcy said, crying. Her tears were huge beads that seemed to fly from her eyes like the tears of people in comic strips. "I can't take it no more. I can't."

Charles was patting her back, which heaved, and Loretta held her hand.

"She gonna kill me one day," Darcy wailed. "Put sumpin' in my food. She know about poison. She know all there is to know about poison."

There was a silence. Trina guessed Charles and Loretta were thinking about Sybila cooking meals at the Center. "Is she under a doctor's care?" Loretta asked finally.

"Oh Lord, Loretta," Darcy moaned, "she been to more doctors than you could shake a stick at. She been to every doctor . . ."

The rest was lost in new tears. Charles and Loretta looked at each other.

"If you feel she needs to be institutionalized . . ." Charles said.

"For her own safety," Loretta added.

Darcy looked at them. Her crying stopped and her eyes were huge now. "Oh, never," she said in an appalled whisper. "I could never do that. Don't you know what them places is like? She been in one of them places when she was younger. I could never put her back."

What a good sister, Trina thought, wanting to tell her so, but not wanting to go any closer. What a sister of sisters.

Darcy sighed heavily, then wiped her nose. "I gotta take her back to Dr. Weissman," she said with renewed conviction. "They gotta adjust her medicine. That's what they gotta do. She was takin' sumpin', doin' fine." She shook her head. "She have such a bad life. A *bad* life. You know it's what she ate? Yeah. The paint. Dat's right. When she was a little girl. My mama had to leave her alone days. Left her in the apartment. She ate paint that got lead in it. A whole year my mama had to work like that, before she made nurse and got somebody to stay wif her. A year of eatin' lead."

Trina saw Charles's face tighten. Loretta offered up the cup of tea.

"I never got left alone," Darcy said. "My auntie always took care of me and I never ate no lead. So don't you see how I gotta take care of her? She my sister. Who gonna take care of her if it ain't me?"

The question hung there in the air. Trina stood still a moment, and then she went back into the room where the children slept. She listened to their breathing, watched their dreaming faces, and then fixed the blinds so that the shafts of light were gone. Then she lay on the beaten-down olive-green sofa and, like the children, she let herself drift off to sleep.

10

"HELLO. IS THIS Ellie Hedwig? Hi. This is Nancy Poole. I'm calling for NY NARAL? Can you attend a meeting on March 3 at the Ninety-second Street Y? Well then, how would you feel about calling some of the names on the list you received? You would? Great. Thanks so much."

Nancy hung up the phone and drove a fat red line through the tenth of ten names that had been issued to her by the New York State chapter of the National Abortion Rights Action League. It was an honest day's work and the experience of it was invigorating. At Cornell, she had been political-minded—of course that was going back fifteen years—but everything, in the way of life, had intruded and so she had put aside all of her political interests until just a few weeks ago when Liv Sloan had cornered her at the Center and asked her to make calls for NARAL. Liv, who was as persuasive as Nancy felt herself to be ineffectual, kept insisting how good Nancy would be at the job. Nancy wondered who might not be good at this job, which consisted of using a phone—Helen Keller, perhaps?—but of course she said yes. Liv was hard to refuse, even though Nancy didn't much care for her and wondered why Sam was married to her and wondered if, indeed, Liv realized just how unsatisfied Sam was with their marriage. Anyway, and perhaps more significantly, there was no good reason for saying no, Nancy having nothing much better to do.

She was probably the only mother at the Center who didn't work. She didn't know why she said "probably"—she was definitely the only mother at the Center who didn't work. Even Heller Norman, who had just about as many money worries as Nancy, had some kind of part-time paid job with the American Jewish Council.

It wasn't that she didn't want to work. She used to work. She had worked her way through Cornell. She had managed a tennis club; she had sold time for a local radio station. When she and Justin came down to New York, Nancy went to work as an administrative assistant to Irving Herman, who ran a huge barter operation and who always carried with him an insignia of dried white Gelusil at the corners of his mouth. Irving loved Nancy—she thought he must have seen her as a piece of prime *goyim,* a way to give his operation some "class"—and he wanted to take her into the business in a big way. And it so happened that she really was good with people. She could have been a crackerjack salesperson. For a while she took credits toward an MBA at NYU and felt like she was really onto something. But that's when all the business with the babies started. It took forever to get pregnant. She'd never been regular with her periods, and then, when she did manage to conceive, she had two miscarriages. Then they found that her endometrium was insufficiently rich, so they endowed her with something called Clomid. That got her pregnant again and this time she held on long enough to have an amniocentesis and then they found out that the baby—the fetus—had spinabifida.

She had a salting-out. She gave birth to it—well, not quite "birth," but she groaned and panted and screamed for seven hours and then it effaced and then . . .

And then she joined a support group. Twelve women who had given birth to dead things. Most of them would never have a normal child. It was not what you'd call a fun group. So many tears. The Doeskin Twelve, one of them joked.

Most of these women had done the whole New York trip of psychotherapy and consciousness-raising groups and were freely expressive of their feelings; Nancy was not. But finally, one night, she had to talk.

"When I tell people about it," she said, "they look at me, all surprised. You? they say. And I say, Yes, *me*. And you know what they're thinking? How can a big healthy gal like you have problems in the childbearing department?"

With a pelvis like mine, big as a dinosaur bone, what could be the problem?

Even now, she could still start shaking if she thought about it. She was big and strapping and presumably made for childbearing and she hated it. She wished sometimes she looked like Liv or even Louise Dowell. She wished she had ankles and wrists that a man could encircle. She wished she didn't have shoulders like Terry Bradshaw and that her hair, which everyone marveled at, wasn't as thick as a horse's tail and wasn't the color of "new-mown hay" as Justin had described it in their courtship. She wished she had an aspect of delicacy about her.

Justin, who was from Jersey City and who had grown up knowing only smog and dark-haired, dark-eyed Jewish and Italian girls, used to tell her she reminded him of sunrise and country mornings and that awful new-mown hay. When she had taken him home, to meet her father and her grandfather, he went around the farm for two days with this idiotic grin on his face, like some Jewish Fresh Air Fund kid feeling an udder for the first time.

She knew that Justin married her in part to get away from everything he had grown up with. His mother, Vivien, was everything that Nancy was not. Nancy's first meal at the Pooles'—né Polonsky a few generations back—was like a fraternity hazing. Everything short of Vivien turning to Justin and saying, "Does she like mashed potatoes?" They were less than thrilled to see her, you might say. Perhaps it would have been better if she had been a less obvious *shiksa,* but Nancy was not a less obvious *shiksa.* She realized she was one of life's prototypical *shiksas,* like Suzy Chaffee or Kate Smith. But when the adjustment was made—and it really didn't take *that* long—Nancy believed that Vivien and Mort were finally pleased that Justin was getting married at all, since to them his entire focus seemed to be away from anything domestic and toward everything that had to do with himself. Vivien, in a rare burst of generosity, took her shopping at Loehman's.

She always knew Justin would be incredibly successful. He had a lean, hungry quality; unlike Vivien, Nancy never even thought of fattening him up. The first time she saw him, in an introductory economics class at Cornell, where they were both freshmen, she took a good look and said, *For me.* She wasn't usually that decisive a person, but oh, the tensile quality of that boy, his unruly dark hair, that thin face which, if it had been any thinner, would have been hatchetlike but she thought instead of eagles and hawks, with his large thin nose and his almost frighteningly aware eyes that looked like they could sight a rodent from an altitude of a thousand feet. The truth was that he made her ache. As it turned out, the two of them were the best students in the class and, although she was willing to admit that by now this might be apocryphal, she remembered being even better than he was. Soon enough, they began to study together. She could have studied better by herself. She couldn't take her eyes off his thighs, which were like thighs that a starved whippet might have, and which worked constantly, up and down, up and down. And his hands. His mother wanted him to be a concert pianist. Her golden boy. With hands like that, maybe he could have been. He was very vain about his hands. As soon as he started making money, he treated himself to manicures.

When they slept together—she was eager to and let him know it—she found out that he was a virgin. Not that he bled on the sheets or anything, but one of Justin's salient characteristics was his compulsive honesty in intimate situations. His late blooming did not affect his performance. He was an ardent lover, as she knew he would be, and he wanted her so many times that first night that she developed cystitis. He was an achiever, her Justin. Even though he was late at the starting gate, he was determined to be the best ever. And for a long time, for her anyway, he was.

Then, when she began to feel like this might be forever, they came apart. After a year together, he announced they had to part.

—Why?

—Because I need to have other experiences. I grew up Jewish uptight. I lost out on so much.

—It isn't all it's cracked up to be, you know. Variety, that is. When you're onto something good, you ought to stay with it. You're smart. You should know that.

But he had made up his mind and so he went on to other blonds—the complex was unmistakable. She decided to try football heroes again. For a while, she enjoyed the substantiality of them, but then she longed for Justin's grace, his fine bones, the sharp planes of his face. When they got back together again, as she always knew they would, he told her that she was right, when you're onto something good, stick with it. But, she sometimes thought, it was never again quite as good as it had been, and she didn't think he'd ever really forgiven her for having more experiences than he did and, moreover, for having experiences while he was out having experiences.

Because, you see, Justin was essentially a child. A brilliant, charming child, but a child. He wanted to have what he wanted to have when he wanted to have it. And she'd made a life out of giving him what he wanted. The one thing that he didn't much care about, but that she insisted on, was David. As far as he was concerned, after the amniocentesis—and the spinabifida—they should stop trying. He didn't like to lose; he knew, he told her, when to "cut his losses."

—But it's not a "deal," Justin. It's my life. I'm not ready to "cut losses."

So she made him keep trying. And now, for a second child, she wanted him to keep trying again. This was silly, he told her, and maybe it was, because he hardly ever spent any time with David anyway. She was, in fact, surprised that he was as poor a father as he was. She had expected him to be one of those dads who are always *doing* something with their sons: collecting coins or stamps or bringing home a telescope or a microscope and showing their sons what human hair looked like magnified ten thousand times. But he wasn't that kind of father. He was no kind of father at all. His range of response to David went from benign to irritated, with never a stop along the way at loving or tender or concerned. Poor David. He'd never think back on his father with love; he'd never know what that was like.

As she went about the house, straightening up, she thought about the fact that she had been taking care of nothing but men for twenty-five years. Daddy, brother Edwin, Granddad, Justin, David. She could write a book. Both times, when she was pregnant, she secretly rejoiced at the news that she was carrying a boy. What would she do with a girl? She didn't think she had the patience for a girl. But David—her patience was endless for David. She couldn't believe how much she loved David. He looked more like her than like Justin, and she was glad for it. This surprised her, and she wasn't sure why. Maybe because she always thought Justin was beautiful and she wasn't, although she realized that many people would think it was the other way around. But one of the things David did was to make her feel beautiful, because he was beautiful and he looked like her and showed her the ways that a pug nose and square shoulders and hair the color of new-mown hay could be beautiful. Maybe one of the reasons, she thought, that Justin didn't love him enough was that he didn't look enough like him. Can't you get his hair cut? he kept saying to her. When the fact was that David had hair just like hers, fast-growing, on the thin edge between luxuriant and unmanageable.

It was no secret that the appeal she held for Justin had diminished. Dwindled. Evaporated? Close. The memories of the sex they had once had were now just that: memories. When they got into bed—which most nights now they did at different hours, like shifts—there was a sense of exaggerated politeness, like two strangers forced to share a camp bed in the wake of a flood or a forest fire or some other natural disaster. But then that's what they were—a natural disaster. Weren't they? For what was more natural than two people—two married people—falling out of love?

She lay down on the bed now. Why was it so late in the morning and the bed had not been made? She didn't know where the days went; she was falling down on the job. She fell down—on the job—to the bed. It had been so long since she had felt voluptuous. She wasn't even sure anymore what it meant to be voluptuous. The word connoted all the things one stayed away from these days: heavy cream in regular coffee; cigarettes; dark dense beer.

They used to go away for weekends. They had an inn in the Hamptons that was really like a private home, except better than any private home they'd ever been in. It was run by an eccentric Englishwoman who looked like Alec Guinness in *Kind Hearts and Coronets* and she served bangers for breakfast, which was always good for a laugh or two, and in the winter, and they went a lot in the winter, she pulled out the hot-water bottles and they brought with them a bottle of whiskey which they drank neat and Justin always took along a brace of joints that he rolled fat and they'd make love for hours and then go down to the kitchen for Mrs. Velentin's thick white bread with butter . . .

She pulled the pillow close to her. She pressed it against her vagina. It was no use thinking about what went wrong: things went wrong, that's all. All she knew was that she wanted to have a weight on her. She felt utterly, utterly empty. She thought of Sam. She just liked him. She liked his dark, curly hair going gray, and his eyes, when he smiled, and his smile, his sort of curvy smile. He was a curly, twinkly, curvy guy, she thought, touching her breasts. Sometimes she noticed him looking at her. He would stare at her and then she would look at him and he would give this comical little jump of the eyebrows. She couldn't tell if it was unconscious—his alarm at being caught in the act—or just another of those funny little things that he did which was why all the kids liked him so much and why she liked him so much.

She wished two people could go to bed together without anyone getting hurt. She wished they could just leave the boys one afternoon, playing their violent little games, and go into the bedroom and close the door and play their own violent little games. But think of all the people it would hurt: Justin (what did he care?—he must have been getting his rocks off somewhere for he certainly wasn't getting them off with her); Liv (maybe she deserved it anyway, spending all her time at work when she should have been at home, instead of having her husband take care of the new baby); David and Aaron (what they didn't know wouldn't hurt them); Freya (this was getting ridiculous).

Maybe, she thought, closing her eyes for just a moment, it was something to think about.

The babysitter had left early for an audition but Freya obliged with a nap and Sam sat down to steal some working time on his novel. You remember: Junius P. Adams. The rabbit in Central Park. Junius was up against Francis Callaway, a Norway rat with three wives, one of whom, Iris, was a white rat who had once been the pet of a little boy. Junius has glimpsed her once or twice—this desperate, vulnerable creature longing to escape—and he has fallen in love. Junius seeks the advice of an old street-smart New York-type squirrel named Moe, whom Sam liked to think of in terms of Walter Matthau. This afternoon, he was working on a scene between Junius and Moe.

He sipped his coffee and retyped a page that had only one mistake on it. He thought he should probably invest in a word processor. A Mac or a KayPro? He wondered if his novel was an embarrassment. It was the kind of novel that could easily be an embarrassment. On the other hand, if it were good, it could reach an enormous number of people, as *Watership Down* did. Some days he thought it was good; some days he thought it was an embarrassment. He hadn't shown it to anyone yet. Not even Liv. Certainly not Liv. Liv didn't even like the sound of it. She was so damned literal-minded sometimes.

—Who's going to want to read a novel about a rabbit in Central Park?
—Lots of people.
—*Lots?*

That wasn't why you sat down and wrote something anyway. Many times a bestseller was a happy accident perpetrated by someone with a unique vision: *Watership Down;* the Kit Williams books; even *Jonathan Livingston Seagull.*

But what if it just wasn't any damned good? That was the thing. He was thirty-six years old. He had commenced Act Two. He hadn't anything much to show for Act One. He wasn't Moss Hart. He wasn't Steven Spielberg or John Updike, who had started to publish in *The New Yorker* when he was in his early twenties, or Julian Schnabel. Nobody had heard of him. He was a late starter with no backup. He had no good jobs waiting for him if the writing didn't work out. Of course he *had* published—it wasn't like he was totally absurd to have stuck with it. Only moderately absurd. And every day, as he sat down to write, he felt the big fear upon him, the clammy chilly feeling of failure that put its mark on every moment of his professional life.

He sipped more coffee and then the baby cried. It was funny, he thought, as he listened, how differently his son and his daughter cried. Aaron had this awful, awful cry. It was like the cry of the vivisected in the old *Island of Dr. Moreau;* it was the cry of the tortured in Argentina and Uganda. No one could sit still for it. Six adults could be sitting around having a lovely dinner, eating stuffed mushrooms and sipping at Pinot Chardonnay and talking about Caravaggio or the Eurythmics, and then the cry would come and it was panic, sheer visceral reaction, as people overturned their chairs and ran into each other and beat their heads against the walls. But Freya was so different. Her cry was the cry of a little pussycat caught up an apple tree. Not a towering oak, but a sweet little apple tree. Freya's little mewing sounds began and then became a little more injured, working into a whine.

He rose from his desk and went to her crib in the next room.

"Aw, aw," he said. "What's the matter?"

He picked her up and she looked around, trying to find a nipple somewhere on his flannel shirt. She had on her little birdy face—the face that made Aaron sometimes call her Tweety Pie—and her head tended to bob a bit also, like one of those cheap little plastic birds you buy in Chinatown.

"You're hungry, little girl?" he asked.

He went to get her bottle and then they sat down together. "You're going to get fat, little girl," he warned, as she sucked and swallowed and blissed out. He really didn't know why he said that, he thought as he wiped away some crust at her left eye (he hoped she wasn't getting a clogged tear duct). She could never be fat. They were such a skinny family. Liv hadn't put on a pound in their ten years together. In fact, she was one of those people who burned up their body fat and then went to work on the protein and you could see the map of blue veins at her temples. She would be this skinny old lady. And he would be this skinny old man. With a fat little belly right below his belt. Just like his father. His father, who was a retired civil servant, was remarkably into noodles. Not pasta—he had never heard the word "pasta." He was into noodles with butter and salt and he was into the study of Talmud. When he became a widower, he was newly retired and he went off to live in a retirement village in Margate on the Florida coast. He wore his white hair long now, like a prophet, and he tried, long distance, at AT&T rates, to engage Sam in talmudic discussions. Sam had periodic nightmares—sweaty, wake-up-in-the-dark, reach-for-the-wife nightmares—in which he turned out just like his father. One of the most positive things in his life was the fact that he couldn't imagine Aaron turning out like his grandfather. Or, for that matter, like his father.

His son was a strong, practical child whose danger was rigidity and unchecked ambition. He could push himself into a state trying to realize the goals he set for himself. In that respect, Sam supposed he was very much like Liv. He hoped Aaron wouldn't grow up to be something like Vice-President, Financial Planning, for Pfizer or General Foods. He thought it might be good for his son to become a scientist. He had that kind of mind. Already, he was better than his father at doing puzzles, and could more quickly put together a puzzle of Woody Wood-pecker that had eighteen pieces to it than Sam could.

The baby started to cry again. Correction: Freya cried. He had to stop calling her "the baby." He hated to admit it, but what he really wanted to call her was "that baby." Somehow, she still felt like a stranger to him. He could no longer recall the point at which Aaron had stopped being a stranger and had become a piece of him—his arm, his leg, his Aaron—but he feared that Freya wouldn't ever get to that point.

He put her over his shoulder and jiggled her around. What he used to do for Aaron was play Alberta Hunter and James Cotton records.

—*You've got the blues again, Aaron. You've got those lowdown colic blues.*

It hadn't worked for Freya. It seemed to alarm her. For a while she liked the soundtrack of *Gigi* but that, too, began to pall.

He gave her back the bottle but now she wouldn't touch it. She made an awful face, as if she had been asked to suck W. C. Fields's nipple. He placed her on her back, across his knees, and began to sing "This Land Is Your Land." She took the occasion to manufacture cheese, which he quickly wiped away, wishing the word given to this particular excrescence wasn't quite so vivid.

He glanced at the clock. Time to go. It was this operation that he dreaded more than anything. He'd rather change five dirty diapers in a row than have to get a baby dressed to go outside. Not that it was even cold. But it was March and there were chills in the air and the baby had to wear an undershirt and a shirt and tights and booties and a sweater and it was a major production number.

"The itsy bitsy spider went up the waterspout," he sang, and she shrieked and he tried to sing louder than her shrieking but that was dumb, wasn't it? It only made her shriek louder. He tried, in a whisper, to sing "Mairzy Doats." But after a few bars, he felt assaulted by the incredible stupidity of it and so cut himself off. What exactly was he doing with his life? he asked himself.

He managed to get the baby dressed and into her stroller. She was a handful. She seemed denser than Aaron ever had, but at least she was on the docile side. Aaron, almost from the moment he was born, strained against the changing table as if it were the rack.

They got out onto the street and headed toward the Center. For a moment, even in this preview of spring, he felt crushed by the daily drudgery that had somehow become his lot. How had it become his lot? Somewhere along the line, really much too early, he had surrendered to it. Oh yes, he and Liv had long made believe that what they had was an experiment in living. But he knew better. He knew that it was really an experiment in avoidance.

At the corner of Eighty-ninth and Broadway, the baby started to cry and he stopped to have a look. He wished she was ready for bagels. He leaned down and touched her bald head, with its jaunty red cap. If she were anything like Aaron, she would be bald until she was two. Is there anything sillier-looking, he thought, than a little bald baby girl? She took a look at him and made herself all mouth. The Gaping Maw. He picked her up. She seemed to be able to attach herself to him in some way, some primordial/marsupial way. He felt her close dampness. He cradled her on his arm that seemed enormous and thickly matted with hair, and he smiled back at an old lady who was smiling aggressively at him, wanting him to see how she approved of this new way of doing things. The old lady stood there watching him, like a show, which maybe he was, and he carried his daughter and pushed the stroller toward the Center.

"Now, now," he said meaninglessly, "now, now."

But she couldn't seem to stop crying. The immature digestive system, he told himself. But maybe it was more. Maybe she sensed that he didn't love her yet. *Yet*. With Aaron, he'd loved him as soon as he popped out. There he was, covered head to toe with mucus, like some giant booger from some giant's nose, and he thought his son was the most beautiful thing he had ever seen. With Aaron, he never worried about time or money or freedom. He wanted this son. In fact, he had to convince Liv of it, for she was disinclined.

—We're just making a go of it now. Why not wait a little? I'm only thirty-two.

—*Only* thirty-two? Women have been grandmothers at thirty-two.

—How nice for them.

—Come on. You won't have to do a thing. I'll do everything. I'll deliver it even.

He remembered her laughing. That was the way he won her over, then and always. She laughed and he entered further and she laughed. Who was the stronger of the two? That was a toughie. She was never quite sure he really loved her and he realized that she was never quite sure and that was what made her vulnerable when everything else about her was very strong and so he rarely told her he loved her and when he did it was in an oblique way.

He stood before the Center. The baby gurgled and clawed at him. He rang the intercom buzzer and someone asked who it was.

"Sam Sloan," said he.

They rang him in. He parked the stroller in the vestibule and carried up the baby in his arms. When he got inside, he saw that there was a birthday party going on. Everyone was wearing pointy hats and there was half of a very large watermelon stuck with pink candles.

"Daddy!"

He waved at Aaron. "Whose birthday?"

"Mine," said Loretta, her mouth full of cake and on her head a crown that someone had picked up at the Burger King. "Have some cake."

He couldn't say no, even though the cake was too pink for his taste. Trina cut him a piece and all the kids watched as he ate. "Mmmnh," he said appreciatively.

Aaron came over to check things out. He peered at his sister. "She looks hungry," he said disapprovingly.

"Thank you, Dr. Spock. Will you please sit down?"

Aaron sat down and Sam put the baby in his lap. Was there a sweeter sight in the world? There, at the age of three and a half years, was the beginning of caring—the beginning of caring about someone other than oneself. The fact that he was perfectly capable, a moment from now, of dropping the baby against the pointed edge of a table did not diminish the act of caring. Sam placed his hand on Aaron's damp neck. A current passed through: Sam—Aaron—baby. He heard the click/whoosh of a Polaroid. He looked up and saw Charles smiling. They were keeping some kind of "immortal-moments" record at the Center. It was a bit too intrusive for him, but he smiled anyway. And then Nancy Poole came in.

When had he started to think of her as beautiful? Always before he had thought of her in ways that were non-Liv, anti-Liv: tall, soft, big, buttery. Now those words seemed beautiful to him, a standard of beauty.

"Hi," she said. "Whose birthday?"

"Loretta's," he told her.

"Happy Birthday, Loretta," she called with a wave. But whatever cheer she had manufactured soon dissipated. She seemed to have a lot on her mind; her face couldn't hold a smile. Even when David came bounding over, her smile, which for him was usually endless, kept going in and out, the sun through the clouds.

"You want to do a little park action?" he asked her.

Her smile started again. He knew how to get her to smile—with language constructions the likes of which her Yuppie husband would never indulge in. "Sure," she said.

They gathered the children and headed into the park. The weather was turning; everything was in bud. You still needed a coat, but not for long. The children, anyway, had begun to fight the good fight against coats and sweaters, mufflers and thermal underwear. All the baggage that made a winter with children indefensible anywhere but in the Sun Belt.

"Look at the magnolia," Nancy said.

"First one out," Sam said.

"David! Aaron!" she called. "Look at the magnolia."

But they were running ahead. "Forget it," he said. "If it doesn't fire live ammunition, they're not interested."

They sat in the sandlot playground. This was one of those big modern jobs—lots of redwood and hemp, soft sand all over the ground. Sam had been coming here with Aaron ever since Aaron could hold his head up. It was really meant for older children—teenagers swung from the swinging ropes like street-smart Tarzans—but then Sam had always thought of Aaron as an older child. He fretted like an older child; Sam wished he could relax more.

"Aaron's having a hard time with that rope," Sam said. "Look at his face. God, he's tense."

"Did you ever notice," he asked Nancy, "that when you go on vacation, it's like you've got a different kid? The tensions drain out and they're suddenly *kids*—mellowed out, cuddly, happy."

"We never go on vacation," said Nancy.

"Sure you do. What about that place in Quogue last summer?"

"That was a vacation? Justin saw more of the phone than he did of us."

"Hmmnh," Sam said, stroking an imaginary beard, "I detect some anger, no?"

"Stop," she whispered, her voice seriously strained.

"Hey."

But she wouldn't look up.

"Hey. You're not yourself."

She played with a length of black vine she had plucked from a tree on the way in. She wrapped it around her fingers, wrapped it tight.

"Have you tried getting some help?" Sam asked.

She looked up from the black vine she had twisted around her pinky and ring finger. "No," she said.

"Why?"

"There isn't any help for this problem."

"There's always help," Sam said. "Even the most intimate problems . . ."

She laughed. He stared at her. "I'm sorry," she said. "You just suddenly sounded so unlike yourself."

There was the briefest moment of silence. "Who did I sound like?"

"Dr. Ruth," she said.

"Screw you," he returned in thick *mittel*-European accent.

They laughed; then, again, some silence.

"We just don't love each other anymore. That's all. We did once—although it seems so remote now; it's hard to remember—but then we stopped. The subscription ran out. We got canceled. We folded out of town . . . whatever."

"So why don't you end it?"

She sighed. "Do you have a cigarette?"

"You don't smoke."

"Yes, I do. When I have a conversation like this, I do."

He gave her a cigarette; he lit it for her. He watched as she smoked it, obviously knowing what a cigarette was about.

She blew smoke all around her. "Come on, Sam," she said through the smoke, "didn't you ever hear of staying together for the children?"

"You've only got one, Nancy."

"And I'm not going to let anything happen to fuck him up."

"Now, that is definitely one of the least insightful remarks I've heard this month."

"Give me a break, will you?"

There was a silence. Sam stared at the boys and then laughed a little.

"What's funny?" she asked.

He shrugged. "I was just having this fantasy of the two of them, on those tires, having the same conversation as we were having. 'They just don't love each other.' 'So why don't they end it? . . .'"

Nancy giggled. The sound was rude and she immediately suppressed it, her expression grim, as before. "You have such a vivid imagination," she said.

"Yeah. That's me. Imagination is my middle name."

"Liv is lucky. I should have been with a man who had imagination. I have none. I'm too earthbound. Feet of clay . . ."

The baby started to whimper. Sam picked her up, burped her a little. She went back to sleep. She was really a rather easy baby.

"She's so sweet," Nancy said.

A squirrel came bounding over to them. Twittering noises, everything twitching. "Look," said Sam. "He likes us. We must radiate provender or something."

Nancy stamped her feet. "Go!"

"What's the matter?" Sam laughed. "I figured you for an animal lover. Cows, pigs, geese . . ."

"Oh, spend a little time on the farm, see how you like it. Anyway, we're talking about squirrels. Maggoty, lousy, potentially rabid . . ."

"Wait a minute. Are you talking about *squirrels*? They're cute," he said, betweeen cheeps and sucking noises he was making for the squirrel's benefit. "In my novel, the squirrel—Moe—is sort of the civil engineer, very interested in sanitation . . ."

"I'm not kidding!"

He stopped the cheeping. "You're not, are you?"

She shook her head.

"I'm sorry," he said. "I guess I got carried away. All that anthropomorphism I'm involved with. I'm sorry."

"It's OK," she said. "I guess it's silly. I'm just kind of tense, I guess. I don't know . . ."

Neither of them saw it coming. His first thought was a bat—it was dark and seemed to fly—but then he saw it was the squirrel, onto her lap, and her scream, and then off her lap, and her scream, and the squirrel up a tree, and her scream, and the four dark marks of its tiny muddy paws on her denim skirt. She stood up and screamed again and burst into tears and shook and seemed to . . . deliquesce before his eyes and he stood up too and put his arms around her, holding her together.

"Sam." She shook. "Sam."

"It's OK," he said, "it's OK." He put his hand to the back of her head, feeling her thick straw-colored hair. She buried her face against his neck and trembled in his arms. "It's OK, sweetie, it's OK." The baby started to cry and with his other hand he rocked the stroller back and forth. "Oooh, oooh," she kept saying, shivering head to toe.

He patted her back, noting the solidity of it, the muscularity. She looked up at him—her eyes seemed huge and swimming in the tears.

"Oh, Sam."

They looked at each other. Others started to gather. "She OK?" asked one of the nannies, craning forward to see. He nodded. He patted her back. The children got off the ropes, ran to see what was happening.

"Mommy! Mommy! What happened, Mommy!"

"David!" She pulled him close; he had his arms around her leg. "It's OK, baby," she said, pulling away from Sam, bending down to pick up her son. "Mommy just got scared by a silly squirrel. It's OK."

But it was too late. Seeing Nancy afraid that way, David twisted his face up, and then came the tears. He bawled, his sturdy little back heaving.

The baby started to cry in earnest and Sam picked her up and jollied her around.

"What's the matter?" asked Aaron, the voice of reason. "Why is everyone crying?"

"Nancy got frightened by a squirrel," Sam said, cooing to the baby.

"By a squirrel?" asked Aaron, incredulous.

"Why don't we go?" Sam suggested, and Nancy agreed and they headed out of the playground.

They went back to her place; she put up tea. "Herbal?" she asked.

"No. The real thing. It's no time for fenugreek."

They laughed. The children were in the other room and quiet.

"Should we go see?"

She shook her head. "As far as I know there are no sharp objects around."

He looked at her. "Maybe," he said, "after what we've been through, some of your good Jack Daniel's would be good."

"Bourbon and branch water?"

"Yeah."

She turned off the kettle. "Why not?"

She had hers with plenty of soda. "What exactly *is* branch water anyway?"

"I don't know," he said. "It doesn't sound like something that should concern us right now."

Then they sat there for a while, without talking, sipping from the bourbon. They were very close. When he went to take her hand, she didn't protest.

"You've just had a baby," she said.

"I know." He looked around, at the stroller parked near the front door. "She seems to be sleeping."

She looked at the field of fine brown hairs on the back of his hand.

"What are you thinking?"

She brought his hand up to her lips. Then they looked at each other. "That we're opening up something we might never be able to close. Do we want to do it? Is it wise?"

He touched the back of her neck. Her hair was so thick and soft. "I know," he said. "I'm not one of life's great planners. I've never been able to take the straight path from A to B."

"What if we're doing this for all the wrong reasons?"

"What are the *right* reasons for doing this?" he wanted to know.

She touched his cheek. "Where would we. . . ?"

He leaned over and kissed her softly on the ear. "We'll work it out. I have every confidence."

"We couldn't do it here. I'd feel . . ."

"Of course. I understand. We'll work it out."

"No more, Sam," she said, as he kissed her neck, but he wouldn't stop. "The children . . . David . . ."

And then the baby started to cry and this time it was Nancy who ran to her and picked her up and held her.

11

Katrina Dunbar.

She signed her name in all the places she was supposed to. She made out her check—payable to Motor Vehicles Bureau—and then she went into the big room to take the written test.

It was hard but she had studied for it and her memory was working more clearly now than it had been for a long time. But the fact was that she had never been much of a student. It was hard for her to study; it was hard for her to learn things she didn't care about. Spanish, chemistry, math—she had especially been a math disaster, the formulae floating aimlessly, purposelessly around in her head.

She grew up being told she didn't do things well. Let me pour that, let me carry that, you're just going to spill it anyway, you don't look where you're going and that's my best Wedgwood pitcher . . . It was the music she had grown up to.

Her mother was a competent person. There was almost nothing Carmel couldn't do. Her gift for numbers was legend; her account books were models of their kind. The amazing thing was that she wasn't rich. But she wasn't hurting any either. The sale of the land—two hundred acres in Fleischmans—was the cornerstone of the fund, but Carmel knew how to invest and even the hobby shop turned a profit.

Money, money—her mother was always going at her about money.

—Look at you. Hand-to-mouth. Penny in your shoe and not a care in the world, ay?

It got even worse after Phyllis died. Phyllis had been the level-headed one—held down a factory job, saved up from it—but when the sickness came, all her savings went down the drain. She had insurance—which was more than Trina had before she went to work at the Center—but insurance didn't cover everything. Carmel wound up spending a lot of her own money before it was all over and it was clear that the money wasn't going into a good investment. The whole thing made Carmel more Carmel-like than ever. After the funeral, there was a fight in the kitchen over money.

—Hand-to-mouth, ay? And Carmel will take care of everything, ay?

So, Trina thought, the message of Phyllis's death was that she should be putting money away for her own death. Then just go fuck yourself, Trina had shouted. The memory thundered now, and she shook her head, shook it right there, in the big room at the Motor Vehicles Bureau, with all the pencils scratching, with all the people concentrating on U-turns.

It turned out she knew the answers. She knew her left-hand signals from her right-hand signals. She knew all there was to know about three-point curves. She knew that she wanted to drive. She didn't have anything to drive, but she knew that she wanted to learn. Carmel had learned late in life. But she was awfully good at it, took it real seriously. Now she was one of those women in late middle age—cigarette, kerchief, dark glasses, car coat, car seat, Monza. Zipping along. WNEW and the Make Believe Ballroom at top volume. Smoking/driving/coughing to Frankie and the Morning Report from the Chairman of the Board.

Later, when they told her she had passed, she felt good all the way through. Now she had it: her learner's permit. Her permit to learn. Things were getting better; her memory was working better; her skin, in the morning mirror, was looking less dry; her hair looked better. As she headed back to the Center, she caught glimpses of herself in store windows and didn't think she looked half-bad.

Back at the Center, when she told them about the learner's permit, they kidded her a little.

"Look at her," said Barry, subbing that day for Darcy, who had gone to the clinic with Sybila. "Look how radiant she is. You'd think she just won a chair at the National Academy of Arts and Letters or something."

"Hey, better than that," said Charles, putting his long stringy arm around her, "she's going to learn how to drive."

She ignored them both and put on her apron. It was her turn to cook this morning. Cooking was another thing she never much liked doing and wasn't good at. Everybody else at the Center cooked incredibly. Charles made all sorts of thick, spicy vegetarian stews, with brown rice and green peppers and coriander and tamari. He made them up as he went along and never had any disasters. And Loretta was the greatest baker—her grandmother had owned a bakery—and only used honey and whole-wheat flour. But Darcy was the real miracle cook: sweet-potato pies, fried chicken, something called pecan delights. She should have been set up in her own business, everyone always said. But Trina couldn't cook to save her life. Maybe it was all the time she'd worked in restaurants. She didn't think anybody who'd ever worked in a restaurant could really enjoy cooking. The smell of old used grease stayed with her, like a film she couldn't rub off.

"What are you making today?" asked chubby little Martha Norman, as Trina gathered the ingredients.

Martha's favorite thing was to kibitz in the kitchen all morning. It reminded Trina of her grandmother, back in Brooklyn: cups of tea all day long, dry zweiback, gossip.

"French toast," Trina told her. As she beat the eggs, Molly and Hildy came over to watch. "The secret," she told the girls, "is the vanilla." They watched as Trina measured out two teaspoons of vanilla and poured it into the egg batter.

"Now we've got to soak the bread," she explained.

She sliced up two challahs and then got the girls to help with the dipping. Aaron came over too—sometimes he liked to help out in the kitchen, even though he rarely ate—and then she had the whole operation going. She stood back, drank a glass of milk, watched them. When she'd first started here, she used Carmel's voice all the time in the way she spoke to the children. *Watch out, you're going to drop it, let me do it.* She didn't ever realize it until Loretta told her.

"You tell a child he's going to drop something and I can assure you—one hundred percent—he's going to drop it," Loretta told her. "And you know what? I don't give two shakes of a rat's tail if a kid does drop something. We've got mops, we've got brooms, we've got a brand-new Hoover. Who cares? I'm not going to inhibit my children's sense of competency for the cost of a mixing bowl."

It was one of the finest things Trina had ever heard. She thought of Carmel—the rages over broken nickel-and-dime saucers and teacups. She thought of all that fine sheer Communism ending in accusations of clumsiness and the grim gluing of chipped porcelain.

"OK, let's fry it up," she said.

She had each of them place dripping slices of challah into the pan. The egg spread and sizzled; she watched them watch, their faces rapt.

As she removed the slices from the pan, she placed them on a platter and dusted them lightly with confectioner's sugar and cinnamon. She would have liked to slice an orange thin as an onion and garnish the plates with it, as they had done in one of the restaurants in which she had worked, but she knew the children would object.

She watched them eat. Some of the children asked for more. They all had different styles. Some, like Hildy and Olivier, were stuffers. Some, like Molly and Petey, were pickers. And then you had Aaron, who had never actually been seen eating anything. "Is it good?" she asked, bending down to Petey.

He looked up and gave her his smile. "My daddy cooks this."

"I know," she said, touching his fine dark hair.

She'd had his daddy's cooking and it was good. Things in the blender: hummus; babba ganoush; red and white gazpacho. She loved having someone cook for her. She'd never had that before—before Bill.

"The only man who ever cooked for me was my father," she told him one night over dinner.

"Was he any good?"

"Heavy. Very heavy. At the time it tasted good, but, looking back, it was very heavy stuff."

(That night, if she remembered correctly, they'd been eating a soup made from buttermilk and something green.)

"It's strange," Bill said—he had a faint white buttermilk mustache—"how when you're a kid, your frame of reference for food is almost exclusively what your mother serves you."

"What did your mother make for you?"

"Oh God. Horrible stuff. Frozen fish fillets with cream of mushroom or cream of celery dumped over it. Cherry Jell-O mixed up with beaten egg white. Vegetable purees that looked like they came up from the drain. Mother had a passion for the offbeat vegetable. There were always new things to be tasted and appreciated. Kale and kohlrabi and Swiss chard and salsify. God knows where she got them—special torture-your-children mail-order catalogs maybe."

"Do you still see much of her?"

"Oh sure."

(She remembered him buttering a pita bread for her, handing it to her, watching her eat it.)

"You know what a wise man once said?" he asked.

"No. What?"

"That you know you're a grown-up when you get to eat whatever you want."

"Who was the wise man?"

"Me," he said.

That afternoon, she stood by the door, waiting for him to come in, the children all wired, running around her. Transition, Loretta always said, was the hardest part of the day. In the mornings, when they were left, the kids cried and clung to her, and she had to make room for them in her lap and read them Babar stories or *The Little Engine That Could*. And in the afternoon—the late afternoon—there was a new set of tears as the mommies and daddies came in, and they wanted the daddy instead of the mommy or the mommy instead of the daddy, or they didn't *want* to put their coats on or they didn't *want* to talk about how their day was, and sometimes they'd have to be carried out, shrieking, not even wanting the bagel or the whole-wheat pretzel that had been offered.

"Did she have a good day?" asked Anna Diamond as she came in to get Molly, who avoided her, hiding in a huge corrugated cardboard crate that had been painted and turned into a playhouse.

"She had a good day," said Trina. "She wanted to do water play all day long."

"That's the toilet learning," said Anna.

Molly was joined in the cardboard playhouse by Hildy and Aaron, David and Olivier and Petey. Suddenly Anna was crouching down, licking her chops, shaking the playhouse. "I'm gonna huff and I'm gonna puff and I'm gonna blow your house down!"

The children squealed.

"Not by the hair of my chinny-chin-chin," Anna cued them.

"Not by the hair of my chinny-chin-chin," they squealed.

"And I'm gonna huff and I'm gonna puff and I'm gonna . . ."

Trina watched her. The poor thing. Her smile was so happy. How could she be so happy? She had something wrong with her. They hadn't taken the breast yet, but well they might. Look at all the things that can go wrong with you. Phyllis just kept on getting those bruises. She'd look down at her legs and there would be these . . . *blossoms*. Purple and black and yellow, all over her legs. And she'd say, I must've bumped into a chair. Some chair. And then her gums began to bleed. The blood seeping out of her gums. Aplastic anemia. Like leukemia—a first cousin—but she couldn't remember what the difference was. She knew how they were the same: you died of them.

They asked Trina for her marrow. The marrow from her bones. Take it, she told them. The needle was as long as an arrow. But that was okay: she was never really afraid of needles. She didn't want to see Phyllis die. She didn't want to see her sister die. Phyllis was her sister: she didn't want to see her die. Oh, they had their problems. They were different—very different. Phyllis always acted like she knew where she was going. This is my life plan, she'd say. I'll marry late; I'll have one child; I'll continue my work; we'll have separate bank accounts. It made Phyllis angry that Trina had no life plans.

—How do you make a life plan anyway?

—You sit down with a pencil and a pad. That's all. Fifteen minutes out of your day to get your life in order.

But, oh—the *dis*order. It wasn't until she fell down deep into the sickness—so deep, and Trina would look at her, her eyes pale, hands outstretched, a face trapped beneath the ice—it wasn't until then that the *dis*order came out. The secrets; the layers of lies and then the window open, opened wide in winter, and the frigid wind cutting into them like a knife . . .

"Penny for your thoughts."

She looked up. Charles. She felt all her nerve endings rise up. She wanted to crawl into his arms. She wanted to wrap herself around him, have him in her, in her, all the way. God, she thought, what was wrong with her, God.

He smiled at her; she could see his long, thin eyeteeth. "What are you thinking about?"

"Driving," she said, forcing herself to calm.

"You stick with it," he said. "You're going to be one good driver."

And then, a moment later, Bill came in. Oh, look at him—look. He wore a yellow shirt and a red tie. She loved that combination.

"Bill," she called.

He looked around and smiled. "Hi," he said. Petey was in his arms. Petey loved being in his arms. *She* loved being in his arms. "How was his day?"

"Oh, fine," she said. "He fell in the park. Bruised his knee. Didn't you, Petey?"

Bill rolled up the pants leg of the Oshkosh. A blossom, purple now, yellow in a day or two.

"Did you put on ice?"

"Oh, sure."

He kissed it and then smiled at her again. "And how are you? Any falls in the park today?"

She shook her head; her smile came slowly, like something tiptoeing out of a cave. "I got my learner's permit."

"Hey! That's great! Petey," he said, "Trina got her permit."

She stared at him. "Will you help me, Bill?" she said suddenly. "Please. I don't know who else to ask."

He looked at her and, she thought, took too long to answer.

He wound up taking her to Yonkers.

"Yonkers is a good place to learn how to drive," he told her. "In fact, one of the few things Yonkers is good for is learning how to drive."

She was nervous. Bill was patient, but still she was nervous. They parked on a side street—it was called St. James Place, like in the Monopoly game—and there was a curtain of elms overhead, and neat white houses, some with flags.

"Here you have your brake and here you have your accelerator," he began.

"I know that, Bill—"

"Please," he said, holding up a hand. "Hear me out."

So she heard him out. First he told her all about how a car works. The pistons, the carburetor. She felt her head begin to fill up, but she willed herself to keep it clear. This was her chance, she thought. After he quizzed her—and she'd gotten the answers right—he let her put the car in gear and pull away from the curb.

Oh, it felt good. To move like that, her hands on the controls—it felt good. They went very, very slowly and there wasn't any noise at all—it reminded her of those boardwalk vehicles in Atlantic City.

"You keep your car so nice," she said. "It purrs . . ."

"Don't talk. Just concentrate."

She concentrated. When she saw a stop sign, half a block ahead, she jammed on the brakes. He was thrown forward; she heard the slap of his hands, defensive, as they hit the dashboard, pushing it away.

"Whoa. Gently . . . gently."

She went more gently. She went very, very gently down green streets. She hadn't been behind the wheel of a car in years and years and years. Her father was a great driver; her mother didn't learn until a few years ago, but now she was a great driver too. So look, Trina thought, there's nothing to worry about: you come from a long line of great drivers.

He had her turn at the intersection of St. James and Princess. She made the turn neatly, but came almost to a halt.

"Keep up your rhythm," he told her.

Her father was a fast driver—so fast. Driving to him was like breathing or eating or sleeping—something he did so naturally; something he had no problems with. He had been a truck driver. To Florida and back; to Cleveland, St.

Louis, Fort Wayne. He said he couldn't stand to drive with her, that she was too slow.

"Turn here."

She turned onto Wisteria Lane. She tried to keep up her rhythm. Twice her father had taken her out. *This is where you put your hands: one on one side of the wheel, one on the other. I don't ever want to see you with less than two hands on the wheel. Driving's got rules. You break the rules, you risk your life and others'.*

"Watch out for that car," Bill said.

Can't you go any faster? she remembered him shouting at her. He had her stop on a dirt road near the landfill. *That's the worst driving I ever saw. You're worse than Phyllis and I always thought Phyllis drove like she was blind. Where's your rhythm, Trina? For Christ's sake.*

Then she had burst into tears. An explosion of them—hand grenades going off in the fawn-colored Plymouth with the rust starting on the fender.

"OK, now," said Bill, "pick up some speed."

And the crying only made him bark more. Except that he wasn't barking—he was shouting. And still she cried. And then the car was silent except for those honking noises she made. And then he had his arms around her.

No no no. I'm sorry, baby. I'm sorry.

The incredible softness of his old, often-washed flannel shirt, her face pressed against it, the pleasingly stale mash of tobacco and Lifebuoy, hair and sweat and witch hazel.

Don't cry. Don't.

He hugged her close. He put his lips to hers. Years, it seemed, had gone by without affection and now this kiss, the gentlest kiss as he cupped her face with his rough hands, and she stared at him . . .

I don't ever want you to cry, Trina. Never.

And then another kiss, holding it, both of them, and then she made a noise, pushed him away. She fumbled at the ignition, her hands not working well, and in her haste she turned the key the wrong way and it made that ugly screech, that shriek, that metal scream, and he was on her again. Didn't I tell you! he shouted. You could wreck a car that way, damn you!

"Watch it! Trina! Watch it!"

She awoke. A boy on a bike. Her brakes screamed. The car skidded to a stop. She and the boy stared at each other for a moment . . . then he laughed and pedaled off. Her heart was going double-time. She didn't want to look at Bill. She felt her head would split open in two.

"Where were you?" Bill demanded.

"Don't shout at me," she pleaded, making her voice so small, so small it almost faded away.

"Dammit, Trina," he said, without patience, "you weren't concentrating."

"Don't," she said. "Don't."

He looked like he was going to say something but he didn't. They got out and changed places. He got behind the wheel, and she leaned back and closed her eyes, and he drove them south, to the city, without music and without words.

They stood at the door to her building.

"Aren't you going to come in?"

He shrugged. "It's getting late."

She looked down at the sidewalk. Two Chunky wrappers: someone had gone on a binge. It made her want something sweet, made her want it desperately.

"Come up," she said.

He decided he would. She held his hand as she turned on the light in her apartment and found it as she had left it, the cat where it had been, looking like it hadn't blinked once.

"Are you thirsty?" she asked.

He thought a moment. "Hungry."

She remembered that they hadn't had dinner and all of a sudden she felt ashamed. She hadn't taken good care of him. "I'll make you something," she promised.

He nodded. "OK."

She opened up the refrigerator. At least she had fresh eggs. And a couple of scallions that she couldn't remember buying. And sour cream. The makings of an omelet. She broke the eggs and beat them.

"Need help?" he called.

"No." She didn't want him in here, in her privacy. "Put something on."

He turned on the radio. She kept it tuned to a country station but he fiddled with it till he got classical. She beat the eggs to Brahms. She melted butter and she threw in the eggs; she covered the pan and counted to sixty. Phyllis had taught her how to make an omelet. Phyllis was the only female in the house who liked to cook. It was she who, on their father's birthday, made the lemon cake he loved. Phyllis told her there were certain things she had to learn. She had to learn how to make an omelet. She had to learn how to boil eggs, make a stock, roast a chicken. These things she knew, she thought now, with a certain sense of satisfaction, as she lifted the cover and spooned on the sour cream and the scallion, which her mother always called a spring onion.

It was a large omelet of many eggs and she cut it in half and slid each half onto a plate and put bread on the plates and sprinkled on pepper and salt. There was no wine; there was no beer. Anyway, she hadn't lost her taste for something sweet. There was the full bottle of seltzer she had picked up last night. There was a jar of strawberry preserves. She remembered her grandmother, Ada, mixing the jam into the seltzer. It was apricot then and the old-fashioned siphon in true-blue bottles, but she'd just make do with what she had.

When she came into the living room, all of it on a big bamboo tray she had from Phyllis, he got up, as if to applaud, but only just took the things from her and set them down on the pine table that she also had from Phyllis.

"Look," he said, and she saw the delight. "It smells great."

They sat down. He picked up the seltzer, which had red strands of jam floating in it. He looked doubtful. She explained what it was, and still he looked doubtful, but they touched glasses anyway. "*Santé*," he said. She smiled. She tasted the drink. It was as she remembered: sweet, strange. It evoked all the things she liked to remember: her grandmother's kitchen; the endless drive from Fleischmans to Brooklyn; halvah and raspberry slices; potatoes and prunes; unborn eggs.

"Like it?" she asked, even though she could tell he didn't and was too polite to tell the truth.

"It's interesting," he said.

"That's what people say about drinks made from ginseng," she replied, without a smile.

"No, really, it's . . ."

She stood up too quickly and reached for his glass. Too quickly she turned to the kitchen. He lied to her. Trina, he called, but she didn't stop and she didn't know what she was doing. Out of the corner of her eye, she saw him jump up and come after her. She didn't know why she was running from him—she didn't know what she was about, what she was doing—all she knew was that she was moving quickly away from him, too quickly, looking behind her to see that he was far enough away, looking behind, not looking ahead, and then, when she turned, she saw that she was right at the hard porcelain lip of the sink and there wasn't time to change course, and she hit the sink straight on, there was the splinter of glass, a shattering at her feet, and one keen sliver sank into her palm like a thorn.

He was next to her; he was looking at her. She had bare feet. He looked at her like he didn't know what to do, until she put out her arms and then it was clear. He reached for her; she leaned into him. He lifted her out of the mess she had made. He carried her into the living room. She held out her palm, afraid of having the glass go any deeper.

"That's a nasty thing," he said, examining her hurt.

"Help me get it out," she said.

"Do you have a tweezers?"

"In the bathroom."

While he looked for it, there was the time to think, but she couldn't, she couldn't think. There had been too much this day, and now this, and she had no explanations, none at all.

It wasn't more than a minute or two before he came back with the tweezers. He made her hold out her palm very flat and straight.

"Stop shaking," he told her in a strong voice she didn't recognize. She was trembling and she couldn't keep her eyes off the glass shard that stuck upright in her palm like the North Pole. She'd always had a fear of having things pulled out of her—that moment, endless, when you and the thing that impales you have to become separate.

"Don't," she said.

"Don't be silly," he said, holding the tweezers glinting sterling in the incandescence of the low light. "You can't just walk around with it."

"It'll work itself out by itself," said Trina, pulling her hand away.

"You really are being silly," said Bill. "All you need is one second of courage."

She didn't know if she had a second of courage in her.

"Trust me," he said.

It's what she said to her kids. Every day she said it: *trust me, trust me, you can trust me.*

She gave him back her hand. He took it and held it very gently, very tenderly. She wished her hands were beautiful, but they weren't. "It'll hurt," she murmured.

He shook his head. "No, no," he soothed. "I wouldn't hurt you."

He held the tweezers and peered at the hurt through glasses he seldom wore. "Steady now," he said. He concentrated like a diamond-cutter. Like a diamond-cutter he moved with confidence and skill. "There!" he said. He held up the shard to the light. "Big enough little bugger, isn't it?"

It was—it surely was.

"You want it?" he asked. "As a keepsake?"

She shook her head, without smiling.

"Any others?"

She looked at her arms, her hands; she bent down to look at her legs. "No," she whispered.

"You were a lucky girl."

He folded the shard in a tissue and went to throw it away. When he came back, he was carrying a bottle of hydrogen peroxide.

"I don't need that," she said.

"Of course you do," he said. "Haven't you ever heard of infections?"

When it was all done, they sat there for a minute looking at each other. Then she reached for him. "I love you, Bill," she said. He came to her. His shirt sleeves were rolled up above the elbow and there was a thick blue vein that ran down his forearm into a darkness of hair. "I love you," she said, all filled up with tears, and he kissed her solemnly on the cheeks and on the lips and on her eyes. "I love you," she said again, as she drew him down to the rug, wishing this was the first day of their lives, that they were born together, just now, here, Adam and Eve, and that they would discover everything together for the first time and that nothing had ever happened before, nothing.

12

A MOTHER AND HER DAUGHTER.

A daughter and her mother.

Mi madre, su madre.

Anna sat on the bench, eating the Oats 'n Honey granola bar she'd brought along for Molly, and watching Corinne push Caitlin on the swing.

Falling sick had turned her drastically sentimental.

Of course, she'd always had that bent. As a girl, she would be out for days over *A Tree Grows in Brooklyn* or *Hi Lili*. And she was not the only one. She remembered legends of her mother, as a young woman, being helped from the Paris Theater, circa 1945, during a screening of *La Symphonie Pastorale,* which had something to do with a French country curate educating and falling in love with a blind girl who had been raised like an animal, and her mother, on the sidewalk, having to be revived with cool compresses.

But the fact was, heredity aside, it was beautiful and touching to see Corinne and Caitlin together. Corinne was really an excellent mother. Sturdy yet yielding; loving yet firm. Anna was filled with admiration for her, and lately had begun to seek out her company.

Part of it had to do with the fact that she'd come to value Corinne as the antithesis to the New York mentality. Corinne had lots of money, but she didn't seem to care about money, save for the security it created in Caitlin's behalf. Corinne didn't care about clothes; she didn't care about theater, restaurants with mesquite grills, or any of it. What she cared about was her husband and her child.

Anna supposed that wasn't a very fashionable attitude, but, in fact, it was what had come to seem of greatest importance to Anna. Her husband, her child. There is something about being sick. (*It's called mortality, hon.*) There was something about being sick and about knowing that in all the world there are very few people who are bound to being at your side—whose very *job* was to be at your side—and it was these people who would bathe you when you were foul, who would hold your head when you vomited, who would change your sheets when you had soiled them . . .

Sometimes Anna felt like she was living a great adventure. She was a sort of explorer, going into a country that was strange, with its own language, its own rules, its own peculiar customs. No one could understand it if they hadn't been there. She imagined it was like describing the South Pole to someone. It's very white; the spaces are wide open . . . How inadequate. The thing was you lacked a certain frame of reference if you hadn't been there yourself.

Maybe that's why she felt she could talk to Corinne. Corinne had been there . . . or at least somewhere near there. This place where things were unknown; where there was an empty feeling that felt like something bottomless; a black hole that defied nature at the very time it was the essence of nature itself.

"Mommy, did you eat my granola bar?"

Anna looked up. Molly stood in front of her, very angry, her hands on her hips. Where and when did she learn how to put her hands on her hips that way? This Basic Female Posture. Who taught her? She certainly hadn't.

"Honey, I didn't think you wanted . . ."

"Mommy!" she cried, her face screwing up with tears. "You're bad!"

Then there was a very loud wailing. Fuck her, Anna thought. She cut off any further explanation; there would be no explanation. Let her cry. But the crying was so injured, and Anna's vulnerability to it so vast, that Anna tried again. "I'll give you another when we get home . . ."

"It was mine!" Molly said furiously, stamping her feet.

This was what the books called a tantrum, Anna thought. You walk away from them and give them room and let them have it. Anna went over to the swings, where Corinne was discreetly watching them.

"Excuse me," called Anna in ridiculously refined tones, "have you, by any chance, a blunt instrument?"

Corinne gave her a sympathetic smile. "I've got some rice crackers in my bag."

"I don't think they're heavy enough for the job."

Corinne pushed the swing; Caitlin's mouth hung open and the swing squeaked. The sound of the swing squeaking made Anna feel sad. She looked at Corinne, looking at Caitlin as she pushed the swing and hummed "Singin' in the Rain."

"Do you ever feel like you can't manage?"

Corinne, surprised but not too surprised, looked up. "Only every day."

"When every day?" Anna pushed.

Corinne said nothing, pushed the swing. Corinne was Gentile and closemouthed; Anna suddenly felt crude and pushy and very Jewish. "I'm sorry. It's personal and . . ."

"No," Corinne said quietly. "It's OK. I'm thinking." The swing squeaked, like a mouse caught on glue. "It's really hard for me," she said, "when I can't make her understand. Once I lost her in a department store for a minute and she was so scared that when I found her she couldn't even see me. It was like she was blind and I couldn't make her see me, I couldn't reason with her, I couldn't just say, 'Mommy's here.'"

"Is that any different than any kid?"

Corinne shrugged. "I don't know. I don't have any other kid."

Anna nodded. Caitlin looked up at the sky, throwing her head back like a girl on a circus pony.

"But I think I'm going to," Corinne whispered.

Anna looked at her. "Come again?"

Corinne covered her mouth, as if she wanted to keep the words in, not knowing why she had let them out. "I think I'm pregnant," she finally whispered.

"Oh, Corinne," Anna breathed.

"I *think*." She covered her mouth again, then forced her hands down to her sides. "I don't know why I'm even telling you. It's ridiculous. Please—don't tell a soul."

"Of course I won't," Anna promised.

Corinne let the swing come to a stop. Caitlin scrambled off and over to Molly, who sat, still disgruntled, on the bench.

"Patrick doesn't even know yet." She looked at Anna; her eyes, which were the color of stone, seemed brighter than Anna had ever seen them before. "But I know," she added, again in a near-whisper.

Anna hugged Corinne, who stood stiffly in the embrace. "I know this is going to turn out well," Anna said as she pulled away. A kind of bubble floated through her and then burst: resentment, jealousy. She didn't want anyone else in the world to have pleasure or good things. But then she chased it away: she was happy for Corinne, so happy. "There's that new test," Anna said. "Chorion something. At nine weeks they go in through the vagina and take a sampling. It tells you everything an amnio tells you and you get the results in your ninth week."

Corinne smiled. "A chorionic villous sampling. I know about it. I'll have it done in Philadelphia. That's where it originated and that's where they have the lowest rate of spontaneous abortion."

Anna reached out to put a hand on Corinne's shoulder. "Listen," she said. "I know it's going to be okay."

"You do?" Corinne replied.

"Yeah. I do." And she did. With the intimations of mortality had come the full blossoming of her intuition. She fancied herself a kind of divining rod, a medium, a healer of others if not herself. "It's your time."

The chord of faith that Anna struck spoke deeply to Corinne, whose Catholicism had lapsed but had by no means vanished. She took Anna's hand and gripped it fiercely and her expression was fierce as well. "There's nothing we can't do if we believe that we can do it," she said to Anna, who stared at the small pert features, evenly placed beneath the ash-blond pageboy, strained now by the intensity of her words.

"I know," said Anna after a moment, returning the pressure of Corinne's grip. "We're very brave, aren't we?"

Corinne said nothing—smiled.

"It's good to be brave," said Anna.

"Yes," said Corinne. "It is."

"I've found that the only real price to being brave is constipation," Anna cracked.

Corinne said nothing—smiled.

I never expected to be having this kind of conversation, thought Anna, *but then that's life, isn't it, the endless and miraculous mystery.*

"I'll take care of Caitlin when you go down to Philly," said Anna.

"Oh, that would be nice," said Corinne, still holding her hand, seeming not to want to let go of it.

"Mommy!"

"That's Molly," Anna said, like she had eyes in the back of her head, and she went to her, prepared to make peace.

There was traffic on the way to Philadelphia.

"Shit," said Patrick. "The fucking eastern seaboard. The highways on the eastern seaboard are totally inadequate."

"Will you lay off the eastern seaboard?" said Corinne, who was knitting a cotton sweater for Caitlin. She was nervous and needed to do something with her hands and she had made the sweater more complicated than it needed to be so that she not only had to use her hands but had to think about what she was doing as well. "You're getting to sound like an old crank, one of those old geezers who go on about fluoridated water or whatever."

"Ay, whaddya say?" crowed Patrick, cupping his ear.

She laughed; he was silly. She knit two, purled one.

"I sure hope these doctors know what they're doing," he said.

"I sure hope so too," she replied sarcastically.

"I don't know. This procedure is totally new. The amnio has only a tiny percentage of risk . . ."

"I'm not going through an abortion in my seventh month," she said, wanting to put an end to this.

"An abortion at any point is—"

"Let's not start that again." Patrick's brand of Catholicism was considerably more orthodox than her own. "I don't plan to raise two Down's-syndrome children. The Good Lord will understand, I'm sure. Damn!" she cried.

"What is it?" he shouted.

"I dropped a stitch."

"Oh, great. A fucking stitch. You scared the shit out of me."

She smiled a little. "Sorry."

She went on knitting; he boiled in the traffic.

"We're going to be late," he said.

"No, we're not."

"You know something? You're getting that tone."

"Which tone is that?" she replied.

"That earth-mother tone. See all, know all."

She looked up from her knitting; his redhead's pink complexion was pinker than normal. "Paddy, my boy. I know you're as nervous as I am, but please don't be mean."

The traffic abated; he opened the car up on the road and they sailed into Philadelphia. *It better be good, it better be good.* He took some pleasure, or at least found some relief, in the way the BMW handled, and the way the tape of the Beatles' *White Album* sounded at sixty-five mph. On the steering wheel his hand tapped along to "Rocky Raccoon."

He had always wanted to own a very expensive black car and now he did. Some of the favorite memories of his boyhood had to do with his going to automobile showrooms with his dad. Dad was an automobile nut who had kept his Chevy Impala running for twenty years, and the two of them, throughout Patrick's childhood, had had their eye on a Thunderbird. Patrick used to like to look through the glossy books of custom colors in the showrooms. Fawn, burgundy, lemon, silver blue, silver gray. But he always came back to black. Just a weird kid, he guessed. The thing was that a black car—always shining, always waxed— looked to him like power. And he wanted power. He never knew how much he wanted it until it was almost too late. When he was an Army grunt, when he had to go first, to see if it was safe for someone else, then he knew he wouldn't be content with the way things were. Then he knew he wanted more, he wanted his piece of the pie. He worked hard for it—he wasn't one of those who didn't know how to work for what it was he wanted. He'd make good. Long nights, extra work, work on weekends. *Hey, Earl, let me take a pass at that this weekend.* Always keeping the boss in sight. Getting into the same elevator as the boss if it meant trampling some poor secretary's arches. Keeping your eyes open. Keeping your goddamn eyes open. Learning that big onyx cufflinks weren't the passport to success. Learning that priest and rabbi jokes went over like a lead balloon in the wrong circles. Forgetting vacations. Getting it into your head that vacations were for other people, the boss or the also-rans. Not for you. A weekend with the wife at Gurney's Inn every year is all. Working your nuts off. Watching your nuts turn to talc. And then the goodies start to come. The salary incentives, the benefits package, the stock options. Office with carpet. Office with schefflera. Cufflinks, sterling silver, shaped like Tylenol capsules. The nuts begin to grow back. You join one of those health clubs. Not the kind that smell of sweat, no. The kind that smell of sandalwood. The kind that sell eight-dollar chef's salads in the dining room hung with asparagus fern and you eat it, or maybe your six-dollar Reuben, with a glass of Perrier with a twist of orange in it and you look out at the girls practicing diving, their tits bobbing like buoys, and you've got it made, right?

Wrong.

Because then God plays his joke. You're doing too good, Patrick McIver. Let's face it, you're just a little bug and you're doing too good. So he figures to play a trick with the chromosomes. You spend nine months waiting for the blessed event and she puts alphabet strips running around the ceiling of the spare room like a frieze. A is for Alligator, B is for Bear, C is for Crow, D is for Deer . . . and she knits for nine months straight, all the time asking you if she should put trains on the sweaters or penguins or clowns or Christmas trees. And the nine months go by—name books; Lamaze classes; you even learn what a layette is—and then she feels it. It's her time and she feels it. You carry her bag, already packed, set to go, and the Lamaze bag too, with the lollipops to suck on when her mouth gets dry and the pink Spalding to squeeze with all her might when the going gets tough and then it starts, the panting and the nurses telling her not to push and you look at her face, plum-colored with the effort but strong too, strong and unafraid, and him telling her to *breathe out, breathe out, breathe out, breathe out* and someone yells, The Head! and she's pushing, pushing all the blood and the mucus—how can anything good be born of all that blood and all that mucus— and there she is, in the doctor's palm, sticky and marbled and alive and kicking, and there are tears on your cheeks, your cheeks are wet with tears, you are crying . . .

"What are you doing?" Corinne cried. "You missed the turnoff, you dope."

"Oh, shit. Why didn't you tell me?" He slammed the palm of his hand against the steering wheel. "Why didn't you say something?"

"I thought you knew!"

"Don't *think!*" he told her.

She thought of saying something else to him, but she didn't. She held her tongue. This was a hard day—one of the hard ones—a day that anyone could make mistakes. So why should she make it worse? She firmly believed that one of the things that was best in their marriage was the fact that neither of them was looking to administer the killing blow. Both of them knew how to back off, how to let the other save face. "So we'll be a few minutes late . . ."

"Half an hour!"

"So we'll be a half-hour late. Big deal. Who cares? Just drive."

They were actually twenty-two minutes late. The nurse, who was obese and who wore a pin that spelled out, in rhinestones, LOVE, seemed peeved with them and was short as they asked questions pertaining to all the forms they had to fill out, which were really duplicates of forms they had already sent in the mail. But Patrick told her a joke about a nurse and a gorilla that jollied her up a little and by the time they went into the room for the procedure they were old friends. Such was Patrick's magic, Corinne thought.

"This is Mr. and Mrs. McIver, Dr. Roohifar," the nurse introduced them.

The doctor shook their hands. He was Iranian and had a large hairy mole on his chin. Corinne wondered why he didn't have it removed. Perhaps it was too deep; perhaps they'd have to scrape bone. Dr. Roohifar explained the procedure to them again, although they had already seen an explanation of it in the mail. It involved a transcervical passage of a specially designed catheter followed by the aspiration of a small amount of the developing trophoblast.

The obese nurse, whose name was Mindy, prepped her and then she was on the white sheeting, her legs up, and Dr. Roohifar approached her with the catheter.

"Just relax now," he said. "It will be no problem."

She hated having things put into her, hated it. She looked straight up. There was Patrick's face—large, pink, a moon. She breathed in deeply, breathed out, breathed in, breathed out. *If it's a boy,* she breathed, *I will name him Conrad after my granddad and we will call him Con.* She felt it enter her. *Conrad McIver. A good strong name. And if it's a girl* . . . oh, pain, a little jab of pain. She reached for Patrick's hand and held it; he wouldn't let her go. *And if it's a girl,* she breathed, *her name will be Laurette because it's a beautiful name, Laurette McIver, and because I love it.*

A white room. Lamps. White sheets. Something wet: sweat. Loud music somewhere. On the bed. Men around her. Men in white. Pushing. Pushing. Patrick. Where's Patrick? Pushing. Pushing. Ah—now. Ah—there. It's done—it's done. Why don't they show me? Why don't they hold it up? They have no faces. Only masks. Hold it up. Hold it up. Ah—there it is. Where? There. But—wait. A white cat. Upside down. Eyes like stars. Sparkling.

"Unnnh," she heard herself say.

"Wake up. Come on."

He was nudging her. She opened her eyes. There was a pool of drool on her collar. He was waking her up. She felt disgusting. She must have had a bad dream. They were passing through New Jersey. She saw a sign that said "Elizabeth-Goethals Bridge." Close to New York.

"I was dreaming," she said.

"Sounded like a good one." He began to make little yelping, scratching noises, like a dog having a bad dream.

"Oh, stop it," she said. She sat up, pulled her collars straight, searched in her bag for a Life Saver to eradicate the gummy feeling from her mouth. "What was I saying?"

"Push."

"What?"

"Push. Push."

She nodded. "I don't even want to tell you what I was dreaming."

"Good. I don't want to hear."

They were soon at Michael and Anna's apartment. It was very late for Caitlin. Surely she would be sleeping. Corinne sat in the car while Patrick went up to get her.

"How was it?" Anna asked, at the door.

"No problems," said Patrick. "Corinne got through it OK." He looked around.

"She's in Molly's room," said Anna. "They're asleep."

"How was she?"

"Oh, fine. Fine. She asked for you guys a couple of times, but nothing very heavy-duty. She had a good dinner, they took a bath together, story time—that sort of thing."

He smiled. She took him into the bedroom. It was a moderately frilly bedroom, mostly yellow with white trim and white shutters on the window and framed prints of pastel people with smiling moon heads. On the bed were two little girls, one in a pink nightgown, the other—his—in red pajamas with feet. She lay on her back, snoring, her mouth open wide, and in her repose was the fullest reflection of her damage, but he realized, as he bent down to pick her up, that he had missed his time with her today. She made little whimpering sounds of protest as he arranged her in his arms. "Aw, pudding," he whispered into her ear. She put her arms around him, and dug her face into his neck.

"Thanks," he whispered to Anna. "We owe you one."

"Forget it," said Anna. "Tell Corinne I'll call her in the morning."

"Will do."

She closed the door. *We owe you one.* She hated that. She didn't know why people had to say things like that. She didn't know if she liked Patrick McIver at all.

But maybe she was being unfair. The thing was she didn't like beefy men. She liked men with fine bones. That was the first thing about Michael she had fallen in love with. She loved his bones. She loved his hands and feet. She didn't want to think about Patrick's feet. They must have looked elephantine. Michael's wrists were as slim as her own. A lot of people said they looked alike. They didn't really—or if they did it was just because the truism that all married people begin to look alike had, as with all truisms, an element of truth in it—but she liked the idea nonetheless.

She loved Michael's slim wrists and bony ankles, his Adam's apple, the veins on his forearms and calves, his cheekbones. She loved seeing his workings. She loved the whole anatomy of him. When they first became involved, she could spend all night looking at him. That summer he was reading all of Robert Stone and she was pretending to reread all of Jane Austen. But she didn't reread all of Jane Austen (in fact, she had never read *all* of Jane Austen in the first place). Instead, she held on to *Northanger Abbey* night after night and peeked from behind it to study him. He was perfect, and she never tired of looking at him. Then they'd finish reading—and peeking—and then they'd make some tea and put on music—they were very into Joni Mitchell then—and they'd neck and then they'd go to bed and make love and it was wonderful. It was wonderful because it felt so good and it was wonderful because together they had done something, *accomplished* something. In the beginning, Michael had been unable to sustain an erection. He had a history of chronic depression and he had become impotent. He told her he never expected to love a woman. But she didn't listen to him and she fell in love with him and she made love to him and she cured him.

Now it was his turn to cure her.

She sat there for a moment and then she rose and there were aches and pains. The thing she hated the most was the aches and pains. No—the thing she hated the most was the exquisite awareness of the aches and pains and the questions, the constant questions, it raised. But not to worry: everything was under control.

She went to put on Joni Mitchell. *Blue.* She poured herself a glass of red wine and listened to Joni sing about the wind coming in from Africa.

She wondered if she'd ever get to Africa. Or Venice. Or Stockholm or Prague or Rio. She looked at the clock. 10:08. She wished Michael were home. He was always working late these days. Molly was hardly getting to see him. Forget Molly—*she* was hardly getting to see him. He had just been in Milan for a week. He left a chart for Molly of riddles and clues to a week's worth of gifts to appease her in his absence.

Tonight your gift will be seen
In something that is hanging and green.

He hid some rainbow stickers in the spider plant. And the next night in the washing machine and the next in the piano bench. Molly loved it. She couldn't wait for him to go away again. For her part, Anna got pearls—beautiful baroque pearls they could ill-afford.

She wished he were home. Sometimes she wondered if he'd still love her if she had a breast removed. Or two. Would he? Oh yes, he'd stick by her—he wasn't the sort who'd actually do anything so horrible as walk out on a woman in her condition—but would he leave her anyway? Emotional withdrawal—is that what she could come to expect? His mother died of cancer when he was twelve; he'd conditioned himself to a life of withdrawal until he met her. But now she could feel him slipping back into it—the absences, the forced smiles, the delayed reactions.

She couldn't altogether blame him. A person needed his defenses. When the doctor told them—*there's every reason for hope; amazing success these days; caught it early*—she saw the hope wash out of him. There—he had let it ooze, out of him, away, into the leaching fields, and it was gone. Now they had everything less—less talk, less sex, less kissing, less holding. Sometimes they massaged each other. Sometimes they did this relaxing exercise they had learned in Lamaze. *Relax your toes, relax your arches, relax your heels, relax your calves, relax your thighs* . . . slowly, slowly all the way up to the scalp. When they made love—and it was always more gently now, as if she might break—he neglected her breast. To be fair, he was never much of a breast man, but he was surely less of one now.

She sipped again from the red wine. Why didn't he love her breast? It didn't seem fair. They had taken out the sickness; all that was there to show for it was a red scar, promised to grow paler. She had loved him when he was sick. She had loved his sick part. She had taken his sick part into her mouth when he had let her, and she loved it and she believed utterly that because she had loved it it had gotten better. But he wouldn't do the same for her. He wouldn't take her sick part in his mouth. He wouldn't help her find the cure.

At 10:52—she blessed digital clocks for their accuracy—she heard the front door. She made note that before he came in to see her, he hung up his coat. Why not? she thought. It was a very good coat. A Hugo Boss.

"I'm home."

She didn't say anything for a moment. She wanted him to find her. He followed the music and found her.

"Hi," he said.

"Hi."

He crossed over to kiss her hello.

"What's happening?" he asked, sitting down to pull off his shoes and then his socks.

She had the opportunity to look at his bony ankles and did so objectively. They held up, she thought, sipping again at the wine.

"Did you have dinner?" she asked him.

He shook his head. "A sandwich at five. I'm starved."

"I'll get you something," she said, starting to get up.

"No, it's OK. I'll do it."

He went to the refrigerator. He came back a moment later with the cottage cheese. As he scooped into it, with an apparent relish, the thought occurred to her that he was one of the few people in the world who turned to cottage cheese when starved.

"How's Molly?" he asked.

The daily question. "Fine." She drained the red wine; she wouldn't have any more tonight. "Caitlin was here till about an hour ago."

"Caitlin?"

"I told you. Today was the day that the McIvers had to go to Philadelphia for the chorionic villous."

"What's that? It sounds like a religious ceremony."

She didn't laugh. "It's an early amnio," she explained.

He ate some cottage cheese. "So how'd it go?"

She shrugged. "I'll let you know when the results are back."

He shook his head. "Odds are sort of against them, aren't they?"

She watched him eat the cottage cheese and felt a strange cold fury. "What do you mean?"

He ran the spoon carefully around the bottom of the container, getting every curd. "Don't the statistical odds of genetic error increase year to year?"

She hated his language. Scientific language—what was it doing in his mouth? "Maybe they're not that concerned with statistics," she said, spitting out the last word.

He looked up at her; he had not been prepared for her anger. "Maybe they should be," he said.

"She wants to have another baby," she replied, too sharply.

He put down the cottage-cheese container. "Something troubling you?"

"No."

There was a silence. He didn't know where to go from here. Usually she was open and direct; it was those very qualities that had led him to fall in love with her. But she was changing and he didn't know how to deal with the fact that she was changing. "Are you angry about something?" he asked, openly, directly.

She got up and brought her wineglass to the kitchen. She wasn't answering him and suddenly he felt furious with her. She wasn't being fair. It seemed the worst crime: she wasn't being fair.

He watched her wash out the glass. She noted him watching her; it made her weaken a little, sag a little. "I'm just tired," she said.

So what was there for him to say? OK. Let's drop it. He didn't want to drop it. "I'm tired too," he said.

"OK," she replied dully. "You're tired too."

She turned off the water and wiped her hands on the dishcloth. "I'm going to bed," she said, brushing past him.

He stood there for a moment. His mouth was dry and he had no real awareness of what it was he had done. All he had done, as far as he could see, was come home. Work late, much later than he would have wished, and come home. Help himself to a little nourishment. Make a little conversation. And now this . . .

He went into the bedroom. The lights were already out; she was in bed with the blanket up to her neck. He felt at a distinct disadvantage, arguing with someone in the dark. "You're not being fair to me," he accused.

"You're right," she muttered.

"It's not fair for me to come home, after a day's work, and to be greeted with this . . ."

"I know. You're right. I should have greeted you with a dry martini. I'm sorry."

"Do *you* think it's fair?"

There was a silence and then her anger. "Fair. Fair," she cried. "What the fuck is fair?"

He stared at her. He could hear her breathing. Why was she breathing so heavily like this? Anxiety took over. He stood by the edge of the bed, his hands at his sides. "Are you all right?"

She didn't say anything for a long moment. "Yeah. I'm all right."

"Did anything. . . ?"

But he left the question unasked; unasked questions hung all over the place, like tinsel.

She rolled onto her back and covered her face with her arm. "Jesus, Michael," she said, "we can't even have a goddamned fight anymore."

It stung. It also ended the hostilities. He stood there another moment or two, then he put his hand on her leg beneath the blanket, but it reassured neither of them. "Good night," he whispered.

He went into the living room and sat on the sofa for a long while. From where he sat he could see the Empire State Building. Having it as part of his view had increased his fondness for it. It was a skyscraper; its needle scraped the sky. Tonight it was blue. He didn't know why. He didn't think there was any blue holiday happening just now. Did the color have something to do with the weather? He thought he'd once heard something about that. Blue for hail? Blue for sleet? Blue for fire-and-brimstone? Or was the thing his personal moodstone? An architect's conceit if ever there was one.

From the terrace he could get a better view.

They were lucky. They had forty square feet of air rights. In the summer they grew petunias and cherry tomatoes and geraniums. Molly played with a watering can out there when the weather got too hot.

He couldn't imagine life without a terrace.

Sometimes—lately not seldom—he'd be in bed or lying on the couch and the room would seem to list, the whole apartment would seem to list, and he'd feel himself being pulled to the terrace. He'd imagine a rope to hold on to, to keep himself from being sucked off, sucked right through the bars, but nothing he could hold on to would be strong enough to forestall the irresistible force.

He felt it now, the apartment listing, everything listing.

He went out onto the terrace. It was cold and the sky preternaturally clear. Sometimes he had fantasies of setting up a ladder to put in a hook to hang up a plant. For a long time now, in the summers, he had wanted to hang some fuchsia. And then, atop the ladder, as he reached to drive in the lead sinker, he might reach too far. The ladder might tilt. And before he knew it he might be falling.

But how could he leave his Molly all alone in the world?

He looked down at the city of New York. Bright lights, action.

It was a cliché—nothing less—to suggest that someone might feel alone here.

He waited until midnight, when they turned off the decorative lights on the Empire State Building, and then he went inside.

*   *   *

Breakfast was messy—Caitlin was still in the habit of broadcasting her scrambled egg—but Corinne didn't care. She felt strange today—good-strange. More alive. Hopeful. Yet feeling hopeful made her feel afraid too—it was strange.

When Patrick came to the table, she searched his face for the same feelings she was having. But he kept his eyes averted from hers; he kept them in *The Wall Street Journal.*

Caitlin was so excited after breakfast when she realized that Patrick was going with them to the Center. He usually got to his office by eight-thirty and so beat them out of the house, but today he was actually going with them. Caitlin ran all the way there.

"I should do this more often," he said.

"You do what you can," Corinne assured him.

When they got to the Center, Caitlin announced to everyone that her daddy was here.

"Oh, my God," cried Loretta. "It must be a holiday." She turned to Darcy. "Did I forget a holiday? Guy Fawkes Day? Ascenscion?"

Darcy looked at her like she was a crazy lady.

"OK, Loretta, lay off," said Patrick, giving her a big rough squeeze.

She gave him an elbow to the ribs and they laughed. Corinne's eyes sparkled as she watched them. They didn't really like each other but that didn't stop Patrick, which was why, Corinne realized, he had risen to the top of the heap.

They kissed Caitlin good-bye. She never complained anymore about being left, and they waved to her as she stood by the window, enfolded in Darcy's arms. Then they got into a cab. They had to be down at NYU Medical Center by nine. They were getting the results of the chorionic-villous sampling this morning.

"We are going to hit traffic like you wouldn't believe," he warned.

"Don't worry. We'll get there."

"Why you had to schedule an appointment at the peak of rush hour I do not understand . . ."

"I told you, it's the time they gave me. Why are you giving me such a hard time?"

"Who is?"

"You. I made it early because I thought you wanted to get back to work . . ."

"I'm not going to work today," he said.

She looked at him. Not going to work for Patrick was like missing the Super Bowl for most Americans. For Patrick, every day at work *was* the Super Bowl. The only other time she ever knew him to miss work was four years ago when he was out for three days with a nearly terminal case of the Hong Kong flu.

"Why?" she asked, even though she could figure out the reason.

He shrugged.

The reason was clear. If the news was bad, he had made up his mind to be with her. If the news was good, they would celebrate. What would they do? An afternoon movie, James Bond if there was one, and a jumbo bucket of hot buttered popcorn. She put her hand in his.

They got to the hospital on time. Her doctor, Dr. Waterman, who had an office in the hospital, kept them waiting, naturally. She leafed through *Parents* magazine and thought about writing down a recipe for a souffléd sweet-potato dessert pie.

At 9:23 they were admitted to Dr. Waterman's office. He was very young. Younger than they were. To compensate, he seemed to make himself eccentric or befuddled. He wore awful green suede shoes and he looked like he combed his hair with a rake. But he was a sensitive person, with a dry and disarming sense of humor, and his office was lined with degrees and accolades from America's finest academic institutions.

"Patrick, Corinne, please—sit down," he said.

They sat. There was a call. Dr. Waterman—she didn't know why she couldn't bring herself to call him Michael, but she couldn't—told the nurse to hold all calls. A drastic plunging feeling happened in her stomach and she reached for Patrick's hand. But Dr. Waterman didn't seem to notice. He looked through her file for a moment and Corinne thought she would die. Then he looked up. "Phila-delphia likes you," he said, flashing a slightly snaggletoothed grin.

She felt the plunging feeling again, and then an incredible spreading flush of warmth. Patrick's hand was squeezing hers so tight, but not too tight, not too tight.

Dr. Waterman pushed his glasses back onto the bridge of his nose and in his gravelly and strangely inflected voice he continued the report. "Clean as a whis-tle. No Down's. No neural tubes. No nothing."

There was a silence.

"I'm not sure I understand," said Corinne slowly. "Are you saying that there are no problems with this fetus?"

"None," said Dr. Waterman with a grin again. When he grinned, Corinne thought, he reminded her of Ollie on the old *Kukla, Fran, and Ollie* show.

Patrick and Corinne looked at each other. "What about the amnio?" he asked Dr. Waterman. "Could the amnio show something else?"

Dr. Waterman shook his head. "Wait a minute," he said. "Don't confuse me. There's not going to *be* any amnio. Everything we need to know—chro-mosomally, that is—we got from the chorionic-villous sampling."

"In other words," Corinne began.

"In other words, barring any other pitfalls, you're going to have a healthy baby."

The plunging feeling again. The tightening grip on her hand.

"Any questions?"

She shook her head. Patrick remained immobile.

"Do you want to know the sex?"

"Not yet," Corinne cried. It was too early. "Not yet," she murmured.

"OK, listen. Why don't you two sit here for a few minutes," Dr. Waterman suggested. "I have to check in on a patient. I'll come back and if you have any questions then, I'll try to answer them."

They were alone. She tried to memorize this moment. The time: 9:32. The color of the walls: rosy-beige. The art: Galerie Maeght reproductions. The trans-parent plastic womb. Patrick in a charcoal-gray Chaps suit with a brown stripe. A yellow shirt. A tie with ancient madder pattern. From the nurses' station came canned music. "All of Me."

Years. Years. It had been years. She had never given up hope. It was not her place to give up hope. It was her place to try. And she had tried and tried and tried and she had succeeded. She had a baby in her. Caitlin would have a brother or a sister. She hoped, for many reasons, it would be a boy and then she stopped herself. It wasn't right to hope for anything but the best.

She looked at Patrick. He was breathing heavily. She got up from her chair and went to stand beside him. At first he said nothing. She touched his shoulder, then she put her arms around his big head and cradled it. He reached up to cup her breasts and then kissed them through the sheer green wool.

"OK, Big Guy," she whispered. "We did it."

He put her on his lap and they held each other tight.

13

DARCY, ALL HER LIFE, had been afraid of grease fires.

"They just springs up at you. That's why I keep salt next to the stove," she explained to Trina and Barry, who were helping to prepare macaroni and cheese and salad, the day's lunch. In another part of the big bright room, Charles, picking at a guitar before a circle of children, sang "Days of Wine and Roses." Trina thought he sounded like Perry Como.

"If you don't got salt you can use baking soda to smoffer the fire. Just as good. We always keeps it near the stove. Don't we do that, Sybila?" she asked her sister, hoping to get a validation but getting nothing back but silence from the woman who was busy stirring a pudding.

"Hey, Darcy," called Barry. "Did you ever hear of spontaneous combustion?"

She shook her head. "No. I never heard about it. What is that?"

"It's a very rare thing," Barry explained. "Somebody'll be walking along, fine and dandy, maybe coming home from the grocery, carrying applesauce or canned pineapple, and then poof! That very same person turns into a fireball. No rhyme, no reason, just total incineration. And no one knows why it happens."

Darcy stared at him and shook her head. "You sure do know a lot."

"He's making it up," said Trina. She didn't like to see him tease Darcy, even though she knew it was hard to resist.

"There's still nothin' scares me more'n a grease fire," Darcy continued. "Once my mama had a grease fire and she had to take this here wool blanket—a good one too—and throw it over the fire to smoffer it. Didn't she, Sybila?"

"She did," Sybila replied, stirring the pudding.

"Weren't no one braver than my mama," Darcy said, mostly to herself. "She was good, through and through."

"Better'n any of you," Sybila cried, without looking at them. "You all is nothin' compared with my mama."

"Shut your mouth now, you," Darcy warned.

Barry and Trina looked at each other. From the time Trina had first come to the Center, she had seen Sybila go from a silent withdrawn person to an increasingly hostile one. Sometimes she wondered if she should talk to Loretta about it or

Charles. She wondered if they didn't notice and why they wouldn't notice. The questions confused her and nagged at her as she set the table for lunch.

"Now listen," said Barry, coming up behind her with the napkins. "What I am about to tell you cannot be told to a single living soul."

She turned to look at him. Was he sick? He could be, she thought. "What?" she whispered.

He looked around. "I'm going to be a clown," he said. "Barry Berringer. Games. Riddles. Sleight-of-hand. I put up a card at the Y and I've already gotten my first assignment."

"You're kidding," she said, feeling relieved.

"Saturday is my big day. A townhouse on Ninety-second. Fifteen three-year-olds. I've never been this nervous in my entire life. My audition for Carnegie was nothing compared to this. Playing at the Public was a lark."

"So what are you doing it for?"

"The betterment of mankind," he shot back. "What do you think I'm doing it for? Money! I need money!"

"You sound desperate."

"I am! I'm sick and tired of being poor. Dirt-poor. I didn't grow up poor—I'm not used to it. My parents always had things like Carr's biscuits in the house."

"Is there a lot of money in being a clown?" she asked gently.

"Not at first," he acknowledged. "But I was reading in *Our Town* about this guy named Reuben who started out doing parties in people's homes and then he rented space on Broadway and now he just bought a brownstone on West Eighty-eighth that he's making into a huge party facility. I figure if I work hard and save . . ."

He trailed off. She gave him an encouraging pat on the arm. "It sounds very ambitious. Go with it, Barry."

Charles looked up from the guitar. "Are we ready?" he asked Trina. She nodded. "Come, everyone," he said. "Lunch."

Everyone ate lunch together at the Center. It was part of the tradition. And always, weather permitting, a hot meal. The activity around food preparation was meant to simulate a home environment, and the children were encouraged to enter the kitchen area and help out if they wished. One day a month was kids' day to cook, and there were things that were fun to prepare, like meatloaf and grilled cheese and such. As they ate lunch, Trina never failed to be impressed by the children, their orderliness and their fine concern for one another. They were supremely competent children. They knew how to cut their food into manageable squares. They knew how to use utensils. From the earliest ages, they knew how to drink from a cup. Most important, they knew how to take care of themselves. That's what good group care did: it taught children how to take care of themselves. As Loretta always told them, in their staff meetings, what they were doing was breaking up the oh-so-sacred mother-child dyad. And, by so doing, they were securing freedom and health for the children.

After a few bites, Hildy, who was as skinny as a stringbean or, as Trina's grandmother would have said, a *lukshen* noodle, pushed her plate away. "Can I go?" she asked Charles.

"No. We all sit at the table until lunch is over."

She thought a minute. She was the kind of kid you could see the wheels turn around in her head. "Can I help Sybila in the kitchen?" she asked.

Charles and Trina exchanged a look. She, among them all, was their ruination. She was smart and tough and hardly seemed to need them.

"All right," said Charles, excusing her.

Hildy loved the kitchen. In her house, the kitchen was pretty. The walls were yellow and there was a picture of red flowers and a picture of the sun and a picture of a clown she had drawn with her crayon. In the morning she drank orange juice there and her mommy drank coffee. Coffee was hot. When she tasted it once she burned her mouth on it. Her mommy didn't cook on the stove. They had a microwave. Her mommy liked Chinese food. She liked dumplings.

She stood in back of Sybila and watched her. Her elbows were fast and dark and sharp. She liked Sybila. She was scared of Sybila. Once Sybila gave her a diamond from her hat. She liked Sybila's dresses. They were very soft. Sometimes they had shiny flowers on them. Today she didn't have shiny flowers. Something white was wrapped around her head. She was holding a spoon. A big spoon. The big spoon was going around and around in the pot.

"Sybila?"

Sybila turned around. There was no smile.

"What are you doing?"

Sybila stared at her. She had yellow eyes. "None your business."

She was making a mean face. "You're making a mean face," Hildy said, feeling that bubble feeling that was funny and that made her cry.

"No I ain't," Sybila said. "All of it in your imagination."

"No. You're bad."

"Don't never say it to me. Never!"

She wanted to go away from there but she couldn't. The bubble broke. She started to cry. Then she saw the pudding spoon and then she screamed even though she wasn't supposed to.

The first call was to Liv Sloan, chairperson of the board. "She's in a meeting," her secretary told Charles.

"It's urgent," said Charles. "Please ask her to call me back immediately."

As soon as the client—a horrible filthy-rich old widow—had left, Liv got on the phone. Charles was not the sort of person who used the word "urgent" idly, she was quite sure. "What happened?" she said, prepared for the worst.

"There's been an incident," said Charles.

Her intelligent mind considered the word. *Incident*. It ruled out death. Death was not an incident. It ruled out accident. An incident was not an accident; an accident was not an incident. An incident implied some sort of malfeasance or some sort of abuse. She immediately thought of that day-care center in California, with its slaughtered rabbits and terrified abused children. She trusted and hoped that this was not how the word "incident" was being used here.

"Tell me what's happened," she said calmly. Whatever it was, she didn't want to throw fat on the fire with premature anxiety.

Slowly, carefully, with great detail, Charles told her the whole story. How Hildy went into the kitchen to help Sybila. How suddenly there was a howl and, for a long time, inconsolable crying while they tried to get the story out of Hildy. How they found the bruise on Hildy's ear. How Sybila would say nothing. And how, when they questioned Sybila, she wound up running out of the Center, with Darcy in pursuit. Then Loretta called Julie to tell her what had happened and Julie absolutely freaked, went berserk, told them that she was taking Hildy out of the Center—she'd been there all her life—and bringing charges not only against Sybila but against the Center as well.

"Should we be taking her seriously?" Liv asked.

"I think so," Charles replied. "She's a very serious type. I don't think I've ever seen her more upset. I don't think I've ever seen *anyone* more upset."

"It *is* upsetting," Liv allowed.

"Julie also has an enormous guilt complex about Hildy. With something really unfortunate like this happening, she'll want a trial, sentencing, and punishment. Close it up and seal it away."

She could relate to that, Liv thought. It was one of the reasons why she had become an attorney. The neatness of it. The fact that things meant what they meant or, better yet, that what you were aiming for was the entrapment of meaning in language. That and the money. No, that was glib. And she wasn't a glib sort of person. Sam was glib—he was other things as well, but he certainly could be glib. His writing suffered from his glibness. There was too much style, too much artifice; there wasn't enough feeling. She suggested as much to him once—gently—but he took it very badly. What do you want me to do? he demanded. Bleed all over the paper? She didn't offer him much criticism after that. He found her too literal. She *was* literal. She liked to find the base truth, the essence, of any given situation.

"We'd better have a meeting tonight," she said. "I'll call the others."

"OK," said Charles. "Let me know."

The members of the board were Felice Winston, Patrick McIver, and Bill Dowell. It was arranged for them to meet, with the teachers and Julie, at the Winstons' apartment at eight.

When Liv arrived, just before eight, Olivier was still up and bouncing off the walls. He was a very bouncing-off-the-walls kind of kid. Liv didn't know Felice or Frank very well—Felice traveled a good deal, as spokesperson for several national products, Lipton tea, Liv thought she recalled, and maybe Sunshine or Keebler or one of those, and Frank was a technician of some kind for one of the networks— but once, in the playground, Felice had talked her ear off about how hard it was to keep Olivier under control and what a problem it was his being the only black child at the Center. Certainly, thought Liv, the incident with Sybila wasn't going to help.

"Olivier, stop it or you're going into your room!" Felice cried to her son, who was chanting a rock song unnecessarily loudly. "What can I get you?" she asked Liv.

"Nothing, thanks," Liv said, staring at Felice's brilliantly colored, beautifully textured robe that looked like it came from somewhere like Senegal. She was quite a beautiful woman, thought Liv, and carried herself in an imposing but graceful manner. "That's a beautiful robe."

"Yes, isn't it?" Felice replied. "Thank you. It was handcrafted by members of the Xhosa tribe." She fingered the robe as she spoke. "I like to wear African garments around the house. I believe it's useful for Olivier."

Olivier, who was winding up a wind-up car, didn't seem like the sort of boy who was particularly interested in textiles, Liv thought.

"I've also gotten interested in African cooking," Felice continued. "It's a far more sophisticated and subtle cuisine than you might expect."

Liv glanced at her watch. It was three minutes past eight and no one else had yet arrived. This was annoying. She wanted to be home with Freya and Aaron. Her breasts hurt. Every night, before Freya went to sleep, she nursed her. This was, Liv realized, some sort of compensation for being unavailable during the day. But then some compensation was better than no compensation. She took her mothering very seriously. She took everything very seriously. That's why she was successful. Sam took nothing very seriously. He was a joker. But how he could make the kids laugh. He'd play puppets with Aaron, in the funniest voices, until Aaron was gulping for breath between laughs. She didn't have that kind of gift. She couldn't make the children laugh that way. But she could give them milk and put bread on their table.

"Bedtime, O," said Felice, taking her son by his hand. "Will you excuse us?"

Felice and "O" were gone quite awhile, and she could hear some screaming and then silence again. She looked around. Everything tasteful and probably more expensive than it needed to be. She supposed she shouldn't count other people's money. Sam always said it was one of her worst habits. But money was very important to her. She suspected that Frank and Felice lived well above their means. The materials were so showy. Chrome, brass, bronzed mirrors, laminated wicker in subtropical colors. It was not the sort of environment in which she felt at home. But then again, Liv never had any black friends. It wasn't that she didn't want any. She had grown up in a small town in Westchester—Pleasantville— where her father was an orthodontist. There were no blacks in Pleasantville who were there for any reason but to clean Pleasantville. Indeed, it was, to a large extent, that cleaning that made Pleasantville pleasant. Actually, she was very pleased that Aaron—and now Freya—would grow up with black friends whose mothers wore African robes in their homes.

"Bedtime is impossible," said Felice with an apologetic smile as she came back, sat down, and lit up a Tiparillo.

"In our home too," said Liv. "It's strange. I can't ever remember putting my parents through that."

"Nor I. Times have changed," said Felice.

At 8:10 the doorbell rang. It was Patrick McIver and Bill Dowell. The teachers came moments later. Loretta had on a black coat and a red felt cloche. She looked like something out of a bad gangster movie, thought Liv. Heavily armed.

"So it's only Julie we're waiting for?" asked Loretta, decloaking and settling in.

"Only Julie."

Ten minutes later the doorbell rang. Julie was breathless but impeccably dressed. She spent a fortune—had to, she said—on her wardrobe. Liv remembered that Julie had once told her she had a bootmaker.

"Sorry I'm late," said Julie, running a hand through her hair. All of her gestures were manic; it was one of the reasons why Liv could never get close to her. Liv recognized herself to be a slower-than-normal person who squinted and who had small tolerance for the highly theatrical sort of personality.

Wine and tea were poured. Felice, in her robe, which sounded heavy as she walked around the room offering nuts, took her hostessing very seriously. Liv waited for her to sit down.

"As you all know," Liv began, "we're here because of a very unusual and very troubling situation which arose today at the Center and which involved Sybila and Hildy. Loretta, would you please review it for us?"

Loretta told the story, making it short and blunt, trying to contain it. "I have, of course, already discharged Sybila of her responsibilities," she concluded. "We cannot give second chances to any member of the staff who strikes a child."

"That's good to know," said Julie sarcastically.

Liv watched Loretta and Julie square off. Fasten your seat belts, she thought to herself.

"Why'd she do it?" Patrick asked, popping peanuts into his mouth. "Anyone have a clue?"

"No. We couldn't get the whole story out of Hildy or Sybila," said Charles.

"Because she's a lunatic," said Julie, pulling out a Parliament, "which is why I have to see to it that she's put away."

"Come on," said Loretta. "I don't think there's enough there to 'put her away.' Do you?"

Julie gave her a hard look. "I think you're playing with our kids' lives."

There was a stunned silence. Liv caught Trina, who seemed to be breathing shallowly. She tended to hide behind Loretta's skirts, but tonight Loretta was having the skirts pulled right out from under her.

"Whoa. Let's go a little slow here," said Patrick.

The great glad-hander, thought Liv. All right—one per group. Necessary, she supposed.

"Loretta, can you provide us with some details about Sybila's background?" asked Bill Dowell.

"Sybila has worked as a cook for twelve years," said Loretta, pulling her legs under her, trying to make herself look cozy. "She has worked for a rectory. She has worked in high-school cafeterias. She worked in the cafeteria at the McBurney Y."

"What else?" Bill pressed.

Loretta shook her head. "She is deeply religious. And she lives with Darcy." She looked around at all of them. "She has a history of psychological problems."

"Now we're getting to it," said Julie, inhaling deeply.

"Sybila has been diagnosed as a victim of lead poisoning," said Charles. "She can function on an everyday level. But the damage is there."

"Her mother used to lock her in the apartment while she went to work," Loretta said. "She used to eat the lead paint. I thought, and part of me still likes to think, that she was worth giving a chance to."

"At the expense of our children's safety?" Julie cried.

"She had no history whatsoever of any violence," said Loretta. "She never seemed a violent person before today."

Liv saw the look of doubt pass over Trina. "Other opinions?" she solicited.

There was another moment of silence. "She scared the bejesus out of Caitlin," Patrick said. "Come to think of it, she scared the bejesus out of me."

"I don't think she was in control," Trina said in a tiny whisper. "Today it just seemed to come over her. Darcy told me that Sybila feels her God is deserting her."

"Poor woman," said Loretta, who had her own deeply religious streak and for whom there was nothing worse than the idea of God's desertion.

"Poor Hildy," said Julie sternly, keeping it on course.

"Ladies and gentlemen," said Felice, standing imperially in her robe, "we are talking about the death and destruction of a black woman. What it means to us individually is some kind of sadness. What it means to the Center is a cultural loss."

Liv wasn't quite sure what she meant, but she kept her mouth shut. Julie didn't. "Felice, I hear you, but my kid's got a swollen ear tonight. Tomorrow I'm taking her to an audiologist to see if there's been any damage. If there is, I'm going to have to look for a way to cover my costs."

The threat of action was on the table now.

"Your daughter has been part of our family since she was seven months old!" Loretta cried, tears in her eyes.

Julie shook her head. "Sorry, Loretta. You've been getting lax." She turned to the other parents. "I'm convinced the Center is a dangerous place."

"You can't deal with the fact that life intruded on your little girl," Loretta said. "You're so full of crazy guilt because you're away all day and all night that you think if you put her in some kind of hermetic environment noboby'll blame you for—"

"Cut it!" Julie snapped. "I won't be case-studied by you, Loretta. You're wrong and you're screwing up and you're liable!"

Loretta was the first to leave. She shot up, pulled her cloak around her, and strode toward the door. "Do what you want," she said. Turning to the others, she announced, "I'm washing my hands of this. We can write Hildy off—I don't want her back under these conditions. Craziness I cannot deal with."

The door slammed and Julie was the next to get up. "I warned you," she said. And then she was gone.

There was another deep silence. Liv didn't know what to say. If she had a gavel, she'd bang it.

"We're talking here about the death of a black woman," Felice repeated, drawing her robe around her.

Charles caught up with Julie in the street. He had to run after her, calling her name. Her legs were long and she was fast, but he was faster.

"Julie!"

She gave up. She stood there on the corner, almost panting, and turned slowly. "What?" she demanded, clearly out of patience.

"I want to talk to you."

"I have nothing to talk about. I'm all talked out."

"Please," he said, staring at her. There were times when he could turn on a special light in his eyes, and he could see her looking into them. "Coffee?"

They found a nice little spot for coffee. Every block in their once-decaying neighborhood now had a nice little spot for coffee. She ordered cappuccino; he ordered his American and black. He suspected it would be a long night.

"Don't try to change my mind," warned Julie, pulling out another Parliament. "You're wasting your time."

"Don't worry about my time," he said. "I'm not nearly as covetous of my time as you are."

She took in a long fiery drag. "What is this? National 'Get Julie' Day? If it is, you can go fuck yourself."

"Very nice," he said. "Tell me," he asked, lightly fingering the edge of the table. "What are you going to tell Hildy?"

"There are plenty of other day-care centers. The Center is not the only—"

He held up his hand, just as he did with the children. "I'm sure of that," he said, "but that's not what I asked you. I asked you what you were going to tell Hildy."

She sighed with elaborate impatience. "I don't understand what you're asking me," she said.

"Because you don't want to understand," he replied. "It's simple. Once again: what are you going to tell her?"

She stabbed out the cigarette. "I will tell her that it was a bad place. She understands the concept of good and bad."

"She understands everything," Charles said. "And what will you tell her when she wants to know why Mama kept her in a 'bad' place as long as she did?"

"I'll cross that bridge when I come to it."

"You've come to it, Julie."

She stared at him. She looked very pale, almost white. "I'll tell her I made a mistake, OK? 'Mama' made a mistake."

"No," Charles said with mock horror. "Not Mama! Not Mama, who believes that people never make mistakes."

"Fuck off, OK?" said Julie, her face pinched with anger.

"People make mistakes—"

"No!" She got up, threw down some money on the table. God forbid she shouldn't pay her own way. Then she went out the door, her heels exploding like gunshot.

He followed her out of the coffee shop. He wasn't going to let her get away tonight. She ignored him for a block and then she wheeled around and he could see, from the bone-tautness of her face, that she had lost it, her most precious thing, her control.

"What do you want?" she hissed. Her catlike qualities, always there, were amplified by her rage. She looked like she could pounce on him, claws unsheathed, but, if anything, it made him feel doggy and excited.

"I don't want you doing this," he said. "You've got too much at stake. I don't want you blowing it out of anger. I don't want you doing that to Hildy."

"Don't you worry yourself about Hildy, OK? I can take care of Hildy."

"I'm sure you can. She will not go hungry—"

"Listen, just stop following me," she warned.

"You can't do it alone, Julie. Hildy needs us. You can't let the whole bunch of us just disappear from her life, as if we were wiped out by some plague or typhoon or something."

She stared at him, her face that awful dead white, and then the blood came back into it, a flush, as she covered her mouth with her hands, gripping her jaw, doing anything she could to forestall the tears, but they wouldn't be forestalled. They came and she shook her head, as though she could shake them away.

"Let me take you home," he said, taking her arm.

"No. I don't need you to."

"Stop talking about what you need and don't need. I know there's nobody in the world you and your daughter *need*. But if there's just a bit of extra room, I'd like to get in."

She stared at him. He made his eyes do the thing with the lights. They got into a cab. He couldn't afford cabs as a matter of routine, but every now and then . . .

When they got into her apartment—her beautiful, thoroughly feminine apartment which, by virtue of its thorough femininity, could seem brutally Amazonian at certain times—Julie got a full report from her babysitter, an old Latin woman named Flora who doubled, some days, as her cleaning woman. He joined Julie when she went to look in on Hildy. The swelling at her ear was down considerably; it seemed not to be such a damaging blow after all.

"Do you want some coffee?" Julie asked when they went back into the living room.

"No," he said. "How about a brandy?"

She had—surprise—the good stuff. Courvoisier. Very superior old pale. He watched her pour it slowly, carefully, into two very fine crystal brandy snifters. Then she sat down opposite him, on one of the two suede sofas that seemed to be remarkably free of stains. She tucked her legs under her. She was wearing some kind of oversize futuristic Japanese garment that billowed out like a parachute beneath her.

"OK," she said, looking directly at him. "You're right. I don't want you all to disappear from Hildy's life."

"Thanks," he said, sipping from the cognac.

"So? What am I going to do?"

"You're going to do nothing. The situation has been resolved. Sybila is gone. The board will discuss any other precautions or contingencies that need to be taken."

She took out a cigarette, lit it as he watched. "Don't tell me I smoke too much," she warned.

"I don't have to," he said—directly, playfully—"you already know."

"What about Loretta?" Julie said. "I was practically excommunicated."

Charles shrugged. "Loretta blows off. You will go out to lunch, the two of you will have a drink, you will make up."

"Who'll pay?"

"Come on, cookie," he said, putting his feet up on the coffee table. "Life's too short."

She blew several perfect smoke rings and then grinned. "You think you're pretty hot stuff, don't you?"

He grinned back. "What do you mean? Don't you know—I've been trying to tell you for a long time—I'm the fantasy of the eighties. Mr. Sensitivity. Mr. Touchy-Feely."

She gave him a profoundly searching look. "You're unreadable."

He felt his tom-tom going. This was music to his ears. He hadn't been with a woman for a long time, and even longer since he was with a woman he really cared about. Now, tonight, he would be with this woman.

"Charles?" she said, her voice suddenly thin, almost hollow.

"What?"

"What do you want? This whole business. I can't understand you—"

"I'm easy to understand," he interrupted. "I'm amazingly simple. That's why I seem so hard to read."

"You're simple," she said. "Right."

His grin grew into a smile. He was wild about her: she was full of juice. She needed a man—which he was—and then she would be spectacular.

"You don't know anything about me," she said.

"I know plenty about you."

"No, you don't. There are things about me I've never told anyone . . ."

Secrets, huh? You want to tell secrets? But that's not what he wanted to talk about.

"Do you like men?" he asked.

"Oh, please."

"Do you?"

"Charles . . ."

"Do you like men?" he said slowly. With incredible fluidity, he slid over to her couch. He touched her dark hair, which was his favorite part of her, so far that is. "I think you do."

She looked at him and then her face sort of crumpled. "This is idiotic. I haven't been with anyone in so long . . ."

"So what? It doesn't atrophy. Believe me."

She looked at him, and he at her, and losing no time he kissed her. "You don't even know me," she said. "Hardly anything about me . . ."

"Anything communicable?" he asked.

She looked shocked. "No!" She touched his face, sending knives into him. "You?"

"I'm clean."

There was a silence. "I believe you," she said, putting her fingers to his lips.

"Well, then," he said, leaning into her, ready to go.

14

"NO, YOU DIDN'T wake me," Trina told Darcy, early on a Saturday morning, and it was the truth. She always woke early. It was part of growing up on a farm—or an agricultural collective, which is what her father liked to call it. "What's the matter?" Trina asked.

"Oh, Trina," Darcy's voice came back to her over the phone. "I got to talk to somebody. I just got to."

It wasn't a great day for talking. Bill was picking her up at noon and she needed a bath. But she wasn't the kind to put off someone who needed something so bad.

"Wait an hour," Trina said. "Then come."

But Darcy couldn't wait. She came early, in the middle of the bath. Trina made wet tracks to the door. It didn't matter: she was never much for soaking in the tub.

"Trina," Darcy said, standing there in the doorway, dressed in an old, used peach velour jumpsuit, "I know it's early, but this is as low as I ever been . . ."

"Come in, Darcy," Trina said.

Darcy took four spoons of sugar in her coffee. She lifted the cup with both hands and sipped at it, as if she were a shipwreck survivor and this was consommé. Finally, when she'd had some toast, she was able to talk. Trina didn't want to rush her.

"I ain't seen my sister since yesterday," Darcy said, picking up crumbs with her moist fingertip.

"Not since the . . . incident?"

Darcy nodded. "She just disappeared into the city," she said, taking off her glasses, which were sweaty, and using her napkin to wipe them. "She done this before. Once she been gone two months and I found her livin' in one of them hotels."

Trina took sips from the maté tea. "Have you thought about calling the police?" she asked.

Darcy laughed at the idea. "The police is goin' to spend a lot of time lookin' for my sister? Don' fool youself."

They were quiet. Darcy buttered some more toast and chewed at it despairingly. Trina tried to think of some helpful words. "Listen, Darcy," she said, "maybe Sybila needs this time alone now. She's been through a lot and—"

"No," said Darcy firmly. "There ain't no time she meant to be alone. She weren't prepared in this world to be alone."

Who is? thought Trina. Darcy wasn't. Her sister was sick, damaged, dangerously bent. But it was her sister. The only blood she had in the world. Trina knew what that meant. They weren't so different, she and Darcy. They both had crazy sisters, except, in the end, Trina's turned out not to be.

"I don't know what made her do it. Lord God, that's as precious a child as you'll find. Hildy was her favorite! I swear to God, she loved that girl like the one she ain't never gonna have. Somethin' got into her head, like a seizing maybe, and she couldn't get no control over it. She wouldn't never do nothin' like that to a child or anyone else neither. She the gentlest kind, I swear."

Trina nodded. "I know, Darcy. But listen to me. Sybila's got problems. You know that. All kinds of problems. And most of them . . . well, you can't do anything about them."

She watched Darcy withdraw. She watched her face, usually so soft and so round, develop, in a spooky flash, the same hard planes that characterized Sybila. "I know all there ever was to know 'bout Sybila and her problems. There ain't a day gone by I don't got to think 'bout Sybila and her problems."

"But they're not your problems, Darcy," said Trina. "You just can't let your sister's problems take over your whole life."

There was a silence—an angry, charged silence—as Darcy stabbed at crumbs with her forefinger. She was a great big sloppy woman, Trina thought. When she walked, the ground shook and dishes clattered on the shelves and her emotions splashed all over the floor. Trina felt sorry for her. She used to be that way. She used to let it all hang out.

"I shouldna come here this morning," Darcy said.

"It's all right, Darcy. You needed someone to talk to and I was—"

"We ain't really friends," Darcy bluntly interrupted. "We just work together. I wanted to go see Charles, but he weren't around. He woulda known what to say."

Trina stared at her. "What do you think he'd say?" she asked.

"Easy," Darcy said, making thoughtful circles on the plate with her greasy finger. "He'd tell me to go find her. He'd say, 'Darcy'"—and she held up her hand and gentled her voice—"'go out into the city and find her.'"

There was a stillness in the room. "All right," Trina said at last, wanting to be done with it. "If that's what you want, then just go and do it."

The arrangement was for Bill to bring the boys to Louise for the weekend. This was unusual. Although their unwritten agreement specified a fifty-fifty time split, generally it came down, by mutual agreement, to something more like seventy-thirty. They would split evenly during the week, but most weekends it was Bill who wound up taking the children. Why? Because he wanted them and because Louise wanted him to have them. It was fine with him. He wouldn't have known what to do with his weekends if he didn't have the kids. With the kids there was baseball and soccer and football. In the winter there was skating and sledding. Next winter he would buy the boys cross-country skis and they could use them in Central Park or, some weekends, upstate. Some weekends he would take the boys fishing and, come summer, he thought maybe he'd even plan a trip to Nova Scotia or Maine, where they could really fish and hike and camp and be close to nature.

Weekends with the boys were very full. When it wasn't sports, they'd go see the blue whale at the Natural History Museum, or they'd go to the Bronx Zoo. They went to the Bronx Zoo a lot. Petey could already tell you that the capybara was the world's largest rodent. Once he took them to the Aquarium and they watched the seals being fed and had hot dogs on the boardwalk at Coney Island. At night, he'd run movies for them on the VCR. He had managed to collect an excellent library for the boys, and could select from two dozen classics such as *The Adventures of Robin Hood, Captains Courageous, The Jungle Book, Gunga Din,* and *The Thief of Baghdad.* He had to confess that it annoyed him when they expressed a preference for *The Dukes of Hazzard* over these immortal films.

Still, he couldn't imagine what he would do with his weekends if he didn't have the boys. Not having the boys—losing the boys—was his worst nightmare, his most horrible fear. A school bus stalled at the tracks; drunken drivers; asbestos poisoning; AIDS germs that Louise unwittingly brought home. The fear of his children dying was so intense, so profound, that to contemplate it would induce in him a real phsyical sickness, a tide of nausea cresting in his stomach.

Even this morning, as he set about getting things together for the boys' weekend with Louise, he felt some of that same deep nausea. He didn't like them out of range—that's when things could happen. The range he had set up for himself—in which he could feel comfortable—fortunately included their school and their day camp and their after-school programs. It did not, he had to confess, include weekends with Louise. What was it he was afraid of? That she would leave them in a store? That they would be taken from a shopping mall by some maniac who would commit unspeakable acts of violence against them? It wasn't a realistic fear. Louise was a responsible person; she never performed less than outstandingly at any task she was assigned. Moreover, he doubted if she had been anywhere near a shopping mall in the last decade. And yet . . . yet. It could happen. How? Why? *Because she didn't love them enough.* That's why he feared her. Her insufficient love for them would not only wound them emotionally, but could kill them.

He opened the fridge and took out some eggs, breaking them into a bowl and beating them.

(—Why is a cook cruel? Denny liked to ask him.

—I don't know. Why?

—'Cause he beats the eggs and whips the cream.)

He called the boys to the table and gave them their scrambled eggs. He watched them as they ate and tried to poke fights with each other.

"Now listen, boys," he said, when they finished, "it's almost time to go. I want you to get dressed very quickly. Clean clothes, understand?"

Today they had to look good; Louise would see any imperfections and she didn't want imperfections. She was taking them to her Aunt Pru's house in Ridgefield. Her mother was going too. A day in the country. Bill could not quite shake the irrational but very real feeling of hurt at being left out.

It didn't matter though. He would have his own day in the country. He was picking up Trina and driving up to the mountains. They'd find some nice little place for dinner, maybe get some trout. He had never spent the weekend with Trina. There had been nights, many nights by now, but the weekend . . . that was for the boys. Somehow Trina didn't feel right for the weekend.

She wanted so much from him. She wanted him to call her every night; she wanted him to see her every night he wasn't with the boys. Maybe one of the reasons he was with the boys so much was that he didn't want to be with Trina that much. He was afraid she would consume him. She had problems, deep problems. It scared him a little, her problems. They seemed so titanic—they seemed to have waves and she seemed to have waves. When he thought of her moods, he thought of the moon and tides and waves.

He looked at the clock. It was 9:15. Time to get going. He went to the boys' room and, as he knew he would, found them incompletely dressed. As he knew he would, he found himself belting their belts, straightening their socks, doing their shoes.

"I don't know why I have to do your shoes," he grumbled, on the floor, at their feet, in a compromised position. "That was the point, I thought, of getting you Velcro."

Then they were out the door—finally—and they managed to find a cab.

"Now remember," he told them, as they neared Riverside, "Aunt Pru and Grandma do not like to have noisy, obstreperous boys bouncing all over the place. And if your cousin Doro is there, I want you to be extra nice to her and to include her in your games, do you understand?"

They ignored him, playing with the hinged Plexiglas drawer that was there for collecting change.

"Do you hear me?" he demanded, stabbing each of them with his forefinger.

"Yes!" they cried together, disgusted with him.

He straightened them up in the elevator—their hair, their collars, their shirt-tails—and when Louise greeted them at the door, she was smiling her approval. He stole a look at her as she knelt down to kiss them, straighten their collars, smooth their hair. She was dressed girlishly, in a dirndl skirt and a simple white blouse. Her hair was pulled back and tied with a ribbon. She wore the little silver-and-onyx daisy earrings that he had given her on the occasion of some minor surgery. It made his heart beat faster to see her in those earrings, looking girlish, looking happy in the face of their family's ruination.

"Hi, Bill," she said, looking up at him, the tone of an afterthought.

"Hi."

"Mother's here," she said. "Mother!" she called.

Her mother came into the foyer. "Grandma!" the boys cried, rushing to hug her. She was an excellent grandmother, sane and sober and loving. She had been an excellent mother-in-law as well.

"Bill," she said, extending her hand and then kissing him on the cheek. He felt a strange quiver pass through him. He wanted to throw his arms around her, to hold her tightly, as tightly as he could. Consequently, he pulled away from her with some abruptness.

"Nice day for an outing," he said, with a strained smile.

"Isn't it?" Abigail replied. "I can't wait to get these boys out of the city," she said, touching their hair.

He felt a stab of pain enter him. He wanted to be the one to get these boys out of the city. But they were gone already. Even though they stood here next to him, they were gone from him. They knew the rules. They knew they had already been passed.

He helped them down with their things.

"Are you staying overnight?" he asked Louise.

She paused before answering, a moment too long. The suggestion of his intrusiveness had been planted. "Yes," she said. "We've been asked."

Abigail went to get the car. Bill stood with Louise and the boys while they waited, knowing he didn't have to.

"I packed Denny's medicine in his backpack," said Bill (Denny had an ear infection). "He's been difficult about taking it. They seem to have made it taste worse this time."

"We'll manage, won't we, Denny?" she said brightly, patting his head.

Denny looked at her adoringly. He wanted to shake his son, to tell him that there was only pain for him there, a one-way street of pain. Impulsively, he reached out and put his hand on his older son's well-made shoulder. His wife's hand was still on Denny's head. The laying-on of hands. They looked at each other. Then they saw Petey looking at them. Petey put his finger through Bill's belt loop.

"Why can't Daddy come with us?" he asked, in his lisping but still powerful voice.

He watched her as she looked away, touching the ribbon in her hair. "Daddy can't," he said, kneeling down and kissing his younger son's ineffably soft cheek.

"Oh, where's Mother?" Louise said.

The other boy came into his embrace. He kissed Denny's cheek, not so soft, the sculpted bone nearer to the surface. Abigail pulled up in her Saab.

"Come, boys!" Louise cried. "We've got to beat the traffic!"

They ran off, leaving him. Abigail waved and then the car pulled off.

He stayed there a moment, waiting until the car disappeared.

Why is the motorist cruel? he asked himself.

Because she beats the traffic, the answer came, resounding in his head.

She misted her wrists with toilet water. Carmel bought it for her in the duty-free shop the summer she went to Mexico. Trina liked the smell: old crushed roses, beaten-up roses, mixed with wine. She stood before the mirror and stared at herself; she had minutes to kill. She stared and she stared; she didn't know what she was looking for. Some sign that she had changed. But to what? She still didn't know where she was going. Yes, she did: she was going to the mountains.

He had mentioned Woodstock. As if it were a magic word. She didn't tell him that she knew all there was to know about Woodstock; that she had embroidered denim jackets and skirts there in a cold barn all winter long; and that there was nothing magic about it. Instead she kept her mouth shut.

The doorbell rang. She looked at herself once more in the mirror, then she opened the door and he stood there. He looked very clean; he had cut his hair. She thought of his hair—copper rings—on the floor of the barber shop. She kissed him, touched his cheek.

"It's a beautiful day," he said, taking her bag as they headed out. It was a very old bag, an ancient bag, made of carpet, and it had belonged to her grandmother. It was the only bag she had—the only bag she would ever want to have. She saw the way he looked at it, not saying anything.

He didn't really say much all the way up the West Side Highway. There was roadwork and then traffic and he was a nervous driver in those situations. But then they were over the bridge, with the river gleaming under them, things suddenly calmer, so she figured she might as well talk.

"Julie's keeping Hildy at the Center," she said. "Charles told me."

Bill nodded. "Makes sense." He slowed briefly, to let a car merge on. "She's a funny woman. Julie. She's so . . . determined."

"I don't blame her," said Trina. "It's her daughter. If I had a daughter and she was hurt, I'd do everything I could to make it right for her. But I wouldn't let it happen. I wouldn't let my daughter get hurt."

There was a silence. She had heard her own intensity; he had heard it too. She looked at Bill, who took his eyes off the road—just that much—to look at her. "I'd make her safe," she whispered.

They crossed the river at Poughkeepsie. The day was getting clearer and brighter, and she was feeling better but she wasn't feeling happy. She wondered if she would ever make "happy" with Bill. She couldn't see their future; there was no line to their future. In the past, she would have thrown the tarot but when she stopped believing in things, she gave up the cards.

She moved closer to him; she wanted him to put his arm around her while he held the steering wheel. Her father used to do that. When they were very small, she or her sister would sit between his legs in front of the steering wheel. Nobody wore seat belts those days. There were no laws.

After they went through New Paltz, he wanted to stay on back roads. She knew which ones were the good ones. She put him on the road that went through Rosendale, a pretty little run-down town along the river. "New Yorkers have been here," she said, seeing an upscale bakery with oversize croissants in the window. She thought of her town—Fleischmans—how it would never change. Only the old ones were there now, or Jews extremely orthodox. There were no croissants in Fleischmans, she would bet.

They drove through Rosendale, up toward Route 28, past ramshackle white houses that sold "HONEY" or "LAB PUPS." She had a fantasy—it lasted only a minute, or less than a minute—of Bill stopping the car, dashing into the house, hurrying back with a smile on his face and a black puppy with one brown ear, one blue eye, and she would name it Oddjob and it would be theirs together. But then they were beyond the house that sold "LAB PUPS" and there was nothing in her arms.

After that, they got on an even smaller road, all overhung with ash trees and beech. It was dark here: it was woods. She breathed in the dense close humusy smell that felt as much a part of her as the smell of her armpits or her hair when it hadn't been washed.

"Let's stop," she said, touching his arm, ready to beg if she had to.

"Where?" he said, even though there were so many places.

"There."

It was an indentation in the road. Others cars had stopped there. Other people had gotten out of their cars and plunged briefly into the woods, these woods which once were endless but were still deep enough to lose yourself in.

"I don't know," he said. "It's getting late. We ought to check in somewhere and then tomorrow we can—"

"Please, Bill," she said.

He brought the car to a stop. "OK," he said. "But just a little hike—just a few minutes."

She threw her arms around him, kissed him deeply. Then she leapt from the car. "Oh, Bill," she cried. "I've wanted to be here for so long now."

She saw, in his eyes, the reflection of her happiness. She put her arms out to him and he let her lead him. There were animal tracks, the onyxlike leavings of deer, fans of fern, a cluster of dead-white Indian pipe. She looked all around; she had to hold her breath. This was her place, she thought, as they moved deeper into the woods. And then, a few yards further on, she felt the overwhelming need to empty herself. "Watch, Bill," she whispered. She bent down and lifted her skirt; for a moment, in the stillness, the only sound was the sound of her own flow.

*   *   *

He sat in the spongy dark deep moss. This was a cool place, damp, with secrets; he had no idea how deep the woods went but they looked to go very deep. He could see the top of her head. There was a gold shaft of light that lit up her reddish-gold hair. Then she passed between two small trees and he could see more of her. She moved with a keen sense of purpose, gathering things quickly but with utter and remarkable quietude. Hunched over, splay-footed, she moved with the rhythm of one at home in her surroundings—an Indian crone perhaps or a fierce druidic herbalist.

They'd been here, in these woods, for an hour now. It was only supposed to have been for a few minutes. But he couldn't tear her away. She was like a dog off a leash. It was the strangest thing he'd ever seen: a transformation. He expected her to fly up into a tree at any moment. He had the uneasy feeling that she could bewitch him, and steal him away with her into the forest.

He put the feeling aside and lay back in the cool deep dark moss. It was soft enough to be a pillow. Wouldn't it make a fine pillow, he thought, if it were clipped and sewed into a sack?

He smiled at the notion. She was good for him, bringing him into nature this way. She could teach him to relax. God knows, he needed to relax. He drove himself with unreasonable intensity over things that were often truly insignificant. But then he had a history of serving harsh taskmasters. Now one of his purposes in life—one of his goals—was to break free of a past that had left him with the message that he wasn't good enough. Good enough for what? He had, after all, been to Harvard, and Harvard Business School, and had married the girl he loved, and had fathered two fine boys. But it wasn't good enough. There was never a time when he stopped telling himself he hadn't done well enough.

But, with Trina, it was different. She was so unlike the sort of people he knew. She seemed removed from the normal cycles. Not only was she not on the fast track, but she was on no track at all. She was some kind of hybrid, combining serenity and confusion.

He pulled up some moss and brought it to his nostrils. The earth smelled of rot, always a faint excrescence of rot. He closed his eyes, wanting to retreat into the furry darkness behind his eyelids. He lay that way for a while and then he became aware of a presence astride him—the absorption of sound—and he opened his eyes and there she was, her smile, and she sank down so that she was sitting on his upper legs, and she had pulled her skirt up, making an apron of it, and held in that apron a salad of wild greens and field onions.

"What have you got there?" he asked, encircling her waist with his hands. Her smallness delighted him. Louise was as thin as she, but very long, maybe even longer than Bill in her stocking feet.

"Lots of things," she said, unfolding her apron so that her wares cascaded onto his chest. "Mallow, orpine, cheeses, shepherd's purse . . ."

He grinned. "Interesting. But what do we do with it?"

She stared at him. "Eat it," she said. "It's food."

"Food for woodchucks. I kind of had my heart set on a Caesar salad."

She frowned. "That's what you go to expense-account joints for," she said. "Caesar salad for two. Surf and turf."

He reached up and ran his hand along her breast. "You makin' fun of me?" he challenged.

She took his hand and held it against her breast. "We're very different, aren't we, Bill?" she said, almost a whisper.

He looked at her. What should he say? "No," he replied, pulling her down to him.

He lay in the cool deep green moss. It felt better than anything had ever felt. It felt so good, he thought, there ought to be a law against it. But, as he was finally learning, so late in his life, there wasn't. He looked down and saw him in her mouth. She knew how—*baby*—she knew how. The moss oozed damp against the back of his neck. He scared the birds with his coming.

Afterward he put her in the crook of his arm. "How do you know that that stuff you picked isn't poisonous?"

She ran a finger around his nipple. "Because I studied it."

"What did you study it for?"

She rested on her elbow and looked down at him. "How come you're asking so many questions about it? You're making me feel like I'm weird."

He grinned again. "You *are* a little weird."

She reached down into the pile of greens that he had shaken off to the side and held up a long rank weedy thing. "Cheeses," she said.

"Ugh. Don't eat that. Even the name is disgusting."

"What's disgusting about it?"

"I don't know. It goes against the laws of nature. Cheese is what you make from milk and rennet."

She nibbled at the green. "It is in the nature of a law to be broken."

He stared at her. "Sometimes you remind me of a witch."

She stared back at him with her peculiar pond-green eyes. She didn't say anything for a long moment; she ran her fingers all through her hair. "That's an accusation women have always had to live with," she said at last. She gave him a hard look. "Isn't that the part of the world where your people come from? Where they burned and where they flogged and where they hung women for witches?"

He held his breath. There were bird sounds. A minty odor came up from the greens. He touched her cheek with the palm of his hand. She looked at him and then closed her eyes. She unbuttoned the buttons of her white blouse. Her breasts were free. Slightly the color of apricots. Her lovely breasts.

When again she opened her eyes, he saw them silvery with tears. "What did I do?" he said. She shook her head. He sat up; he folded his arms around her. "Don't," he whispered, putting kisses in her hair.

"Love me, Bill," she said.

He kissed her breasts. Rain began—lightly, like a whisper—and he sucked on her breasts. His mouth full with her breast was strange and almost amazing to him. He felt worried by it; hungry and full; tender; devouring.

"Love me," she said.

But the rain wouldn't stop. It just came down—more of it and more—until he stood and put out his hand for her and convinced her that she had to go.

The rain didn't last long. When it was over, they opened the windows of the car. The air smelled incredibly fresh and pure. They headed back along back roads—past brown fields, waiting to be green, and houses, well-kept or shot, and barns of grayed garnet or beetle-shell brown.

This was her country. He knew nothing of it. He didn't know where to go; he didn't know how to get there. But she knew it all. It was as if the roads were her veins. She was taking him home. He didn't know it. He thought they were headed to Woodstock. They would get a room there for the night; they would do the town. But there was time for that. Didn't he know it? There was all the time in the world.

"It's pretty here," he said. "What's it called?"

"Big Indian," she replied.

"Big Indian," he mocked, in a Big Indian's voice. "You know area well."

"Yes," she acknowledged, staring out the window, seeing how much she could remember. It was in that creek—the Esopus, swollen now—that she and her sister had gone with inner tubes. Big black inner tubes. You push yourself off and then it's down you go, down the river, and sometimes you're fast as trout, sometimes you're lily-pad slow. Often you're with your back to the river and you can't see where you're going and it's scary, it's very, very scary.

—*Katrina! Katrina!*

Phyllis was the scairdy-cat. She sobbed all the way down. It didn't make sense, why she was so scared. It was Trina who always got thrown. It was hips that kept you in the tube and Phyllis had the hips.

—*Help me, Katrina! Help me!*

But she didn't help her. She never helped her. Even in the end, when she was crying for help, she didn't help her and it was this that was the great crime of her life.

—Now listen. Don't say a word just listen. Something was wrong very wrong. Something Daddy did. Daddy did something very wrong, Trina, and you have to know it.

She didn't want to hear. Even as her sister lay there—on her deathbed. Go back into your sickness—*go.* But she couldn't not hear. It was too loud. Afterward, when everything was quiet, dead-quiet, she heard it better. It was like ringing in your ears—tinnitus—you heard it best in a silent room. She did everything she could not to hear. She stuffed cotton in her ears, cotton in her brain. She stuffed cotton in her pussy. But it was always there to be heard.

"How do you know it so well?" he asked.

She didn't know what he was talking about. She looked at him blankly.

"How do you know this area so well?" he said.

She shrugged. "I spent time here."

"So you know where we're going?" he said.

"Yeah," she replied. "I do."

Then they were north—just a little bit north. The sign on the road said Fleischmans. "What's that?" he asked. "Some kind of Jewish Catskill resort?"

She thought a moment. "Yeah," she said. "Some kind of Jewish Catskill resort."

She had him take a left, on Westcott Road, and then a right, down Old County 5. "You're taking me somewhere, aren't you?" he said, a sense of destination imposed upon him.

"Yes," she said.

"And it isn't a shortcut to Woodstock, is it?" he said, his tone half-accusatory.

"No," she replied. "It isn't a shortcut to anywhere."

Then they were at the grassy knoll where they used to play Mother, May I? and jumped rope. When there was a cow, this is where the cow would graze. For a while there was a little pony named Ginger. In the summer the field would be littered with steaming dung droppings and the blue flies shone in the wavy heat like metal filings and her dreams would grow maggoty.

All at once—or maybe it wasn't all at once; maybe it had started this morning or last night or the night before last or the night before that when she knew they would come here and she knew she would see these fields, and now, as they drove, the house, boarded over, buttercup-yellow, dead-buttercup yellow—all at once she felt a heavy emptiness spread through her. She needed to get out. "Bill," she said, touching his arm, the hair on his arm, "we have to stop, Bill."

"What's the matter?" he asked, sounding like he thought something very bad was happening and maybe it was, maybe it wasn't.

"I have to get out, Bill. Let me out."

He stopped the car. There was nobody else on the road; she didn't think there would be. He followed her, as she crossed the road. Without an explanation—without a word—she stepped over the stone-and-picket fence, into the wet March field.

"Trina?" he called.

She didn't answer him. She didn't care if he were part of this or not. She headed down the hill, toward the house, and only the sound of his footsteps told her that he would be part of it.

She moved quickly, but he caught up with her. His hand was on her arm, rougher than she ever expected him to be. "Tell me what's going on," he said.

She stared at him; she gave him a full moment. "There's nothing to tell," she said. "I'm home. This is my home."

She saw him look around. "This is your home?" he said. "There's nobody here."

She said nothing. She didn't have to answer him. She headed toward the house.

The hill was muddy; she stumbled and he held her by the elbow but then she pulled away from him again.

There were smells in the air. Mint again, wild thyme, and somewhere, remote, the smell of bacon. Her grandmother wouldn't come into the house for the smell of bacon. *It's not why your great-grandfather was put to death,* her grandmother would say, *so his granddaughter could cook bacon.* The smell of bacon and the smell of poultry. The smells and sounds of fowl roosting in the yard.

She was at the door. She rang the bell, the big farm bell, put there as if this were a ranch. When the bell rang, they'd come running from their chores to eat the Table Top pies Carmel left by the sink.

"What are we doing?" Bill asked, coming up behind her, but she didn't answer him. She didn't know what they were doing. She jiggled the front door, but there was a padlock on it and she didn't have the key.

"This is your house?" Bill asked her, maybe not believing what she had said before.

She turned to look at him. His face was worried. "It's nobody's house," she explained.

"You can't go in there," he said.

What was he talking about? Did he know how much of her was in there? All her secrets . . . they were all in there.

She went looking for some way to get in. Then she wondered why she was making it so hard. She took a rock and smashed a pane of glass in the kitchen door. She saw another window broken up above. She wondered if kids did it. She wondered if they took this for a ghost house.

"Well, I'm not sticking around for this," he said, but she didn't say anything and he didn't go anywhere. She was careful, as she stuck her hand past the jagged edges of the windowpane; she didn't want to get hurt. Then she opened the door and was in the big empty kitchen. The wallpaper, with its pattern of Dutch girls, was faded and greasy. The stove had a rusty black spider sitting on it. Wires reached like tentacles from an overhead light stripped of its fixture.

"How long has it been since anyone lived here?" he asked.

"A long time," she said. "My mother tried to sell it, but couldn't. We'd let it run down after my father died. Then she sold the land to the neighbors and moved into Kingston."

There was a silence. "It's a nice little farmhouse," he said.

"He built it himself, my father. With his own hands." She looked around the empty room. "He was very good with his hands."

She moved from the kitchen down the hallway. The air was thick with dust. In a corner of the hallway was a memory. She bent down. There was the *K*. There was the *A*. There was the *T*. *Katrina*. It was as far as she got with the little penknife her father had given her. Her mother beat the stuffing out of her.

Then they came to the bottom of the stairs. She turned to him. She put out her hand. "Come," she said. He looked unsure but she reached out and took his hand. The stairs groaned beneath their feet. Settling noises, she thought, but settling for what?

Then they were in the bedroom. Just as she remembered. The windows caught the light, so late in the day, and turned the room peach. He had known that when he built it. There were a lot of things he knew, and a lot of things he should have known.

"Why didn't you just tell me you wanted to come here?" he asked her.

"I don't know," she admitted.

He stood very close to her. He touched her hair. "Did something bad happen here?"

She looked at him and then she looked down at the floor. In this late light, the wood of the floor glowed a beautiful color, like honey. "Yes," she whispered, and that was all he needed to know now, that was all she was going to tell him.

"Then let's get out of here," he said. "You don't have to go back. I know that. That's something I've learned. You never have to go back. You never have to look at anything if you don't want to . . ."

But she wasn't hearing him. Everything he was saying was wrong. She had to go back. She had to look. She had left something behind and now she had to find it. "Bill," she said. He could help her find it. *Bill*. She moved against him. He didn't know what to do. Did she have to teach him everything? She took his hands and put them at her waist. She reached up and put her hand against the back of his neck and she pulled him forward, so that their lips were touching. There—that's how—and then this and this.

There was nowhere soft for them to be. But you didn't need a soft place. That was nothing but human folly. The animals did it where they stood and so should they, and so, when they sank down to the floor, it became a soft place for them. There, she said, in that soft place, there.

He began to moan first. She was intent on that. She went about it with all of her resources. And then, when he started, she found her ticket. She moaned too. And shuddered. And groaned. The way she used to hear the animals giving birth. For isn't that what she was doing? Giving birth. Something huge coming out of her. God. She held on to him—held on—and then came her scream—as he had never heard it before—and he thought it was her pleasure and maybe it was maybe it wasn't but whatever it was—whatever it was—it wouldn't stop until it tore off the roof, tore it right off, and sent it sailing up into the sky.

PART THREE

15

LOUISE HAD NO PATIENCE for mime. She simply had no tolerance for things left unsaid. Neither, she believed, did the children. And so she was surprised to see them sitting there, at David Poole's birthday party, seemingly rapt, as the entertainers, Trina and that fellow from the Center, postured before them in whiteface. The very sight of whiteface was enough to make her break into a rash. It reminded her of an evening, many years ago, when Bill took her to see *Children of Paradise. Les Enfants du Paradis,* he had called it and still did. A great French epic of the screen, made during the Occupation. It starred some great French actor—she couldn't remember his name—as a sort of Pierrot figure, running around Paris in whiteface. She had hated it—found it excruciatingly boring—and they had had a big fight about it. He had called her "rigid" and she had called him "silly." It was remarkable, she thought, how the appellations still fit.

She rose from where she was sitting, cross-legged, behind Petey, and went to the bar which the Pooles had thoughtfully set up for the parents. She poured herself a glass of red wine; it was one way of getting through a four-year-old's birthday party. Actually, she couldn't remember the last time she had been to one. They didn't really give them for the boys. It wasn't their style. Instead, they always tried to do something special for them. Last year, Bill took Denny to see *Big River* on Broadway and got him the original-cast album, and he took Petey to some kind of Sesame Street theme park outside Philadelphia. It was better than this nonsense, she thought, as she felt herself warmed by the wine.

She looked at the mimes flitting about at the other end of the living room. It was really a cavernous room, much bigger than theirs. It must have been fifty feet long. But it wasn't very well done, Louise thought. The furniture was too matching and there were children's drawings on the wall. Actually, the room reminded her of Nancy Poole—big and blank. Louise could never think of anything to say to her. As far as she knew, Nancy Poole had no career. The idea of a woman, in 1986, not having a career seemed nothing short of barbarous.

She took another sip of the wine. Petey turned around to look for her and she waved at him and he smiled and turned back. Why was he so insecure? she wondered. And Denny even worse. They were really such insecure children; sometimes it put her teeth on edge. In that respect, they took after Bill.

"One way to get through it, huh?" someone said to her, from behind. She turned; it was the big red-headed man who was the father of the little Down's-syndrome child. She felt terribly embarrassed—she couldn't remember his name. Something Irish, she thought.

"Yes," she said. "A glass of decent Bordeaux does the job nicely."

"I need something a little stronger," he said, pouring himself a bourbon.

"Help yourself," she said. "That's what it's here for."

"Kids look like they're loving it though, don't they?"

"I suppose."

"Me, I hate that mime stuff. That French guy . . . what's his name . . ."

"Marcel Marceau?"

"Yeah. Gives me the willies."

She couldn't help smiling a little. "It's an acquired taste."

"I need to acquire it about as much as I need to acquire shingles," he said, taking a deep sip of the bourbon. He stared at her. "You're Petey's mom, aren't you?"

"Yes. And you're . . ."

"Caitlin's father. Patrick McIver."

"Louise Strong Dowell," she said, as they shook hands. "Have you been at the Center long?" she asked.

"About a year."

She touched her high white brow. "I'm sorry. I rarely get over there. My work . . ."

"It's okay."

They stood silently for a moment, looking at the mimes. Trina and that fellow from the Center. What *was* his name? She didn't know anyone's name. "What's that fellow's name?" she whispered. "With Trina?"

"Barry, you mean?"

"Oh yes. Barry. I forget."

"How can you forget Barry?" he laughed. "It's like forgetting who Peter Pan is."

She looked at him, smiled slightly, and, glass of wine in hand, went to sit down again, cross-legged, behind Petey. Again, the great attentiveness of the children struck her and she couldn't understand it. She looked up at the stage—not really a stage, just a space, but a stage nonetheless—where Trina and Barry kept drawing an imaginary bucket from an imaginary well and the bucket must have had a hole in it. An imaginary hole. Some of the children giggled here and there, but laughter didn't seem the real point of it all. She wasn't sure what the real point of it was.

But they were rather good, Louise thought after a while. At least they moved with a certain sense of stage command and their timing didn't lag. But then she really didn't know about such things. She really didn't know what drove people onto a stage. She thought of herself as a scrupulously private person, with no interest in taking the spotlight, mask or no mask. Indeed, she found herself somewhat repelled by the childlike qualities of the performers. Trina and Barry. She wondered what could have led them into their work, this strange mash of diapers and baby oil and financial insolvency and whiteface. She tried to imagine a life focused on things like birthday parties and she could not. Even going to a child's birthday party was a substantial effort for her, and one which she would not have made if Bill had not begun to issue rumbling noises.

It was extraordinary to her that he had begun to do so. It had certainly been his habit—and the tenor of their relationship—for him not to do so. And yet he had told her, when she asked him if he could take Petey to David Poole's party, that he could not. She asked him why and he told her it was none of her business. It wasn't *his* day. It was *her* day. With great irritation, she told him that she would make other arrangements to have Petey taken to the party. And that's when he committed the outrage.

—Oh no you won't.

She didn't know what he was talking about—she truly didn't. What do you mean? she asked him. What are you talking about?

—I'm talking about *you*. *You're* bringing him to the party.

She had never felt so stupid in her life—she couldn't understand anything he was saying. And then, when she reminded herself that she could never *be* that stupid, she decided that it was he who was being so stupid and she felt an incredible surge of anger and contempt pass through her.

—There are certain things you *have* to do if you want to be a mother. You have to know who your children's friends are. You have to know their names. You have to know who their parents are. You have to show your face at their birthday parties every now and again.

—I don't *have* to do anything.

And then there was this long silence, palpably unpleasant, as they stared at each other until finally, in this low sure voice that she was wholly unfamiliar with, he told her that he wanted the children. He didn't want to share them. He wanted them to himself.

Which is how she came to be at David Poole's birthday party today, watching the cretinous whiteface antics of people she couldn't have cared less about. She wasn't going to hand over the children to him—was he insane? She couldn't imagine what he was thinking. And yet it was interesting—it made her feel that much better about Bill. This new lack of predictability was interesting, and she took him more seriously for a change. Actually, even though he didn't know it, his sudden assertiveness had made her stall on the business of getting a separation agreement together.

"Mommy, I'm thirsty," Petey whispered, turning around to her.

"Wait," she whispered back.

"No. Now."

She sighed and rose to her feet again. At least it was an opportunity to refill her wineglass. She got the apple juice for Petey and then she sat down again behind him, holding the cup as he took sips, lest he spill some on the Persian rug which must have been very expensive even if it didn't look very good at all. *And you have to hold his cup when he needs his cup held,* she thought, hearing Bill's voice as she watched Petey's look of intense concentration—the most serious concentration in the world—his little round pale face puckered with the effort of that concentration. Just then, she felt as pure a feeling of love for him as she had ever felt. It surprised her and she tried to analyze it, why it happened here, happened now. It didn't happen often; this she knew. It sometimes made her suffer to realize that it didn't happen often and she didn't know why it didn't happen often. Why? She wondered why. That question—that word: Why?—it gave her pleasure like nothing else. Even without the answer. Sometimes the question is better than the answer. She looked at her child, and at all the children in the room. Her child had been carried inside of her. She had felt him scale her ribs. There is no connection—no *contact*—more intimate in this world. She had had difficult births. She had a narrow pelvis and the children, as children will, had gotten themselves into contrary positions. But she had fought the C-section. Fought it tooth and nail. Bill didn't help. He stood by her side with little beads of sweat on his upper lip, on his brow. The children were born in August. Both children, at the very end of August. Labor Day, she thought, with a little smile. It was very hot. And Bill was very scared. It was because of him, she was convinced, that she was almost unable to deliver the babies through natural childbirth. He was a rotten coach. He wasn't even a very good cheerleader, which is what he had been when they first met at Harvard. He had forgotten all the moves. He wanted her to give in. He didn't want to see her suffer. If you don't want to see me suffer then get out, she had screamed, in her transition. You could scream whatever you wanted in your transition and nobody held it against you. So he stood beside her, queasily solicitous, like a waiter in a bad posh restaurant, everything but the tea towel draped over his forearm. It took over twenty hours each time. Her doctor worried about the fetus but she didn't. Don't, she screamed, as she felt the thing inside her swim inside her, riding closer and closer on the crest of each wave of pain. She knew it would come. It was her body and her body worked. *It works,* she screamed, as she was lost and then found again in an ecstasy of pain that no one but her could understand.

"Mommy," Petey whispered. "More."

She looked at him, feeling momentarily confused. "No," she said.

"Mommy, yes!"

"No," she hissed, "and stop asking or we'll leave."

He got a tight hurt expression on his face that she couldn't bear. She stood up, quickly, and removed herself from him. She didn't like it when he was this way. The demands, the selfishness—she didn't like it. As she made her way toward the back of the room, the sounds of laughter followed her. Turning, she saw the mimes onstage, flapping about like birds, great big ungainly ugly birds—marabous. She looked at one of the birds—who called herself Trina—and wondered what she was all about. A woman like a bird on a stage. Then—and this was strange—she saw Trina's eyes travel around the room and settle on her. Even from this far back, the eyes, green, looked peculiar in the white face and she felt chilly from having them light on her. *And you have to know their teachers and their teachers have to know you.* The laughter built as some of the children—the very demonstrative ones, like Hildy and the little Down's-syndrome girl—got up and made like birds too. Louise unlocked her gaze to look at Petey, but he wasn't laughing nor was he dancing. He wasn't doing any of the things the other children were doing, and she asked herself why.

*   *   *

Nancy and Sam were about to hand out goodie bags at the front door. All the children were waiting—Hildy, who had come with Molly and Michael; Olivier, brought by his father, who was better at keeping him in line than anybody else on this planet; fat little Martha, who was anticipating the candy with an avid expression; and Petey, who was the first to get one, diving into its contents.

"Not here, Petey," said Louise, trying to get his coat on him.

But he wasn't listening. The bags were rich, stuffed, valuable. Inside were Hershey's kisses and Tootsie Rolls and little plastic tops and long red plastic fingernails that you could put on your fingers to make you look ghoulish and miniature Rubik cubes that they were too young for and paper fans and little Slinkys. A treasure, and one that he intended to examine right here and now, so he sat down on the floor, one arm in his green Pacific Trail jacket, the other busy at work with all the nice crap.

"Stop it, Petey," his mother said. "Right now."

They never allowed him crap, Trina reminded herself, as she stood with Loretta at the door, about to go. They never got him good junk. They never gave him candy and they never let him watch television. They wanted him to be perfect and they wanted him to take care of himself. They wanted him to be like the best little houseplant in the whole world, that always looks good and smells nice and is healthy and growing without any care. But he wasn't playing along. He was mostly such a good little boy, but not now, not just right now, as he turned the goodie bag upside down and spread its contents all over the floor.

Trina watched as Louise went whiter than usual. She was such a white woman, Trina thought, such a mean white woman.

"Clean it up," she said in a whisper. "Now."

He cleaned it up—she had that sort of power—but with the maddening slowness of movement that kids bring to times of pressure, Louise helping him with an exaggerated attitude of assistance, and when the bag was refilled again, she took it from him, removed the candy, and handed it back to Nancy Poole.

"We won't be needing this, thank you," she said with a kind of smile. "And thank you for having us."

And then Petey started to cry. Trina wished he would howl, the way Aaron would have under the circumstances. But he didn't. He made a little mewling sound when he cried—a broken little mewling sound.

"OK. We're going now," said Louise tightly, a red stain creeping up her neck, Trina noted, with a sense of satisfaction. She shouldn't be so white. She *should* show the hot blood staining her neck, creeping up into her cheeks, and she did, and Trina was glad. She was glad, she thought, as she heard Petey's soft crying climbing the elevator cables and then, out on the street, the sounds of the heartbreak wafting through the open window. She wasn't the only witness, Trina thought; others had seen it and she was glad.

When everyone was gone, and only Sam was left, Nancy let David open the presents. There were so many of them—mostly junk, but tantalizing junk—and Sam had to face the task of quelling Aaron's jealous anger.

"It's not your birthday," Sam said in an overly rational voice. "It's not your day to get presents."

"Don't tell me!" Aaron cried, covering his ears.

"All right. We're going," Sam announced, getting up and reaching for his coat, but this only made Aaron shriek and so finally Sam had to scoop him up and remove him to another room to talk some sense into him.

"What's the matter with Aaron, Mommy?" asked David, who had started to bang at a cobbler's bench that someone had given him.

Nancy stared at David for a long moment that was filled with love. Her son was really such a fine person. Loretta always called him a "solid citizen" and that's what he was and she had to learn not to confuse "solid" with "stolid," not to think of him the way she thought of herself.

"He's unhappy, sweetie, because he wants what you have and he can't have it," she said simply.

"Because today's my day," David said, smashing the red peg on the cobbler's bench with his little wooden hammer.

"That's right."

"Where's Daddy?" he said, hammering at the yellow peg.

"Daddy's in Caracas," she replied. "It's very far away," she added.

In another few moments, Sam and Aaron returned. Aaron was much calmer—jovial almost—as he sat down to watch David play and wait his turn at the toys.

"Birthday parties will really bring out the beast," Sam said.

"What'd you do?" Nancy asked.

"I told him I would lose respect for him if he continued to act out," said Sam, deadpan.

She laughed. She realized that the wonderful thing about Sam was that he continually made her laugh. Justin never made her laugh. She didn't know if Justin himself could laugh any longer, let alone make her laugh. But then a shared sense of humor had never been a big part of their relationship. They shared other things—a sense of respect for each other's abilities, a sense of physical desire for each other. But that had changed—with the baby, with the *babies*—and it left a hole and neither of them had done anything to fill up the hole.

"You're funny," she said.

"Funny ha-ha or funny weird?"

She shrugged. "Both. You make me laugh."

"You make me hard," he whispered, so the children couldn't hear.

Her smile drowned in the look of fear that washed over her face. She got up quickly and went into the kitchen.

She was pulling meat out of the freezer when he walked into the kitchen. She had pulled the meat out too late, she realized, and she would have to broil it half-frozen and it was a shame.

"I'm sorry," he said, coming close to her.

"I'm not that sophisticated, Sam."

"Neither am I."

"I can't talk dirty with the kids sitting that close."

"I know," he said. "It was stupid."

"I don't know if I can talk dirty at all."

"You don't have to talk anything," he said. "Talk is cheap."

"There you go again," she said angrily. "I don't like it, Sam. I don't like it."

"Nancy, I'm sorry . . ."

"Talking dirty makes me *feel* dirty and I don't want to feel dirty. I want to feel something else."

"I'm sorry," he said. She stared at him. He looked apologetic. No, more—he looked abject. She had the impulse to hug him. She realized, almost with a sense of horror, that he was becoming too special to her and she didn't know what to do with that.

"I hate my life," she muttered.

"Oh, Nancy . . ."

"No, really. I hate it. It's so . . . *clogged*. I don't *do* anything. I hate my husband . . ."

"Then divorce him."

"Oh, easy for you to say. But what about you? You and Liv?"

"Nancy, it's not the same. I don't feel that way about Liv," he said. She heard the choked tone in his voice. It made her feel so angry and loving of him. "We have two children . . ."

"Oh, you have *two* children. I see."

"Stop."

She closed her eyes and shook her head. "What am I saying?" She laughed. "This other-woman speech and we haven't even made it yet—it's crazy. I'm sorry."

There was silence. Sam pushed a finger—or tried to—into the frozen piece of meat. A stupid gesture, she thought, but again one that made her ache in a way she hadn't ached for years.

"This just can't go on like this," she said bluntly. "We probably shouldn't see each other at all, under the circumstances. God knows, we surely must be the two most inept would-be adulterers of all time," she said, forcing a smile at the end.

"Hey. That sounds like something I'd say," he replied.

There was a silence between them; they could hear the sounds of the children. Negotiation—endless negotiation. It was amazing how, at this tender age, the Center was able to instill in them a skill for peaceful negotiation.

If you share I'll let you but it's mine special from home new for my birthday but I haven't got any toys here and you've got to share if you want me to come back . . .

"Listen to them," he said.

"No," she returned. She moved closer to him, making up her mind, putting her arms around him, kissing him. It took him a second to kiss her back but then he did, kissing her neck and her hair.

"You smell good."

Don't tell me I smell like the new-mown hay, she prayed, but he didn't.

"I don't believe you," he said.

"What?"

"That stuff. About the kids being that close."

Believe me, she thought, as she listened for them, making sure they were busy.

"Nancy."

"Sam," she said, pulling away, "I want this. I know that I want this."

He looked at her, his fingers digging into her soft shoulders, his teeth clenched. "Yes."

"Soon, Sam."

"OK."

"When?"

He thought a moment. "Wednesday?" he said.

She laughed first and then he did, seeing the humor in it.

"Don't ever let anyone tell you rabbit's a warm fur," said Loretta, hugging herself as she and Trina walked down Central Park West.

"I won't," Trina said. "Not that a lot of people are trying to."

"Beaver's warm. Seal. But not rabbit."

"I don't like furs anyway," said Trina. "You kill an animal, you skin it, you hang it in the closet, you put it into cold storage. The idea of a living thing ending up in cold storage doesn't sit right with me."

"We all wind up in cold storage," Loretta said dismissively. "Why's it so frigging cold anyway? It was warm just a few days ago. This is weather to make you sick."

"That's March." Trina shrugged.

"*Late* March," Loretta shot back. "And how come you've got an answer for everything today?"

Trina shrugged again. "I'm in a mood, I guess."

"What kind of mood? You made a big hit at the party."

"I hated that party," Trina said, sounding suddenly fierce.

"Oooh. You *are* in a bad mood. Come have coffee."

"No. I've got to get home."

"Yes," Loretta said, taking her by the arm. Loretta always had her way.

They wound up in a little coffeehouse on Amsterdam Avenue. Loretta ordered a buttermilk scone and coffee. Trina only wanted chamomile tea.

"That's why you're so thin," Loretta said. "You can say no to a scone. You know, I remember a time when you couldn't find a scone anywhere on the Upper West Side," she reminisced. "God, the neighborhood was great in those days. There were fish stores and notions stores. I used to make all my own clothes and most of Gregory's clothes too. There used to be a wonderful little yard-goods store on Broadway run by two little old Orthodox Jews who hated each other and would yell terrible things at each other and their goods were top quality and practically free."

"I didn't know you sewed," Trina said.

"Oh, sure. I should make you a dress sometime," Loretta said. "Green velvet, huh? But frankly," she said, "these days the fabric would cost so much it wouldn't be worth it. Everything's changing. This neighborhood—more stores than you can shake a stick at selling soaps shaped like hearts or soaps shaped like dicks but you can't buy a fillet of flounder anywhere. Hey—I heard this joke," she cried. "They opened a funeral parlor on Columbus Avenue and guess what they called it?"

Trina shrugged; she felt silly guessing.

"Death 'n Stuff."

Trina laughed a little in spite of herself, covering her mouth with her hand.

"Oh, look. The Great Stone Face crumbles," said Loretta. "So why'd you hate
the party?"

"I don't know," said Trina. "I just did."

The food came. The waitress set it down with a theatrical flourish.

"I don't know why I'm eating," said Loretta, buttering the scone. "I ate like a
pig at the party. It's just that I love food lately. I've decided I'm not going to
restrain myself. My body needs it. I'm going to be a big fat old lady. Like Simone
Signoret. She said she didn't give a damn and she ate all the *marrons glacés* she
wanted."

"And now she's dead."

"Yeah. But so are a lot of other people. I need some sweet things in my life. God
knows, I don't have a man to bring me any sweets."

Trina always wondered why she didn't. There were so many women in this city
who said they couldn't find a man. Trina didn't believe it. There was always some
man there, waiting for her, whenever she was ready.

"So you still haven't told me," said Loretta, drilling in, "why'd you hate the
party?"

Trina took a sip of the chamomile tea. It always reminded her of Peter Rabbit.
*His mother put him to bed, and made some chamomile tea; and she gave a dose of
it to Peter!* Was it strange to associate so much of the world with the things of
childhood? Yes, it was strange, she acknowledged; it was very, very strange. "It
always takes me a while, after I've performed, to come down. I don't like the
whole process. That's why I don't do it anymore."

Loretta gave a laugh that was a snort. "It's the only process I really like. When I
gave up acting, I gave up a function that I've never found a replacement for. It
was like losing a kidney."

"You think?" said Trina.

"All right, all right. But I never found anywhere else to put that kind of energy,"
Loretta said, buttering another section of scone. "To tell you the truth though, I
don't believe that's why you hated the party."

"You don't?" said Trina.

"No, I don't."

And she was right, of course. And of course that's why she was the big boss,
because she was right more of the time than anyone else. "I just felt bad," Trina
said. "I felt bad about Petey."

Loretta held aloft the morsel of scone. "I *hate* that woman," she said in a hoarse
whisper that could be heard throughout the shoebox restaurant. "She's as cold a
bitch as ever walked God's earth."

Trina felt a warm glow of satisfaction pass through her like a current, but
showed nothing. "She's involved in some very important research though, isn't
she? AIDS, I think."

"Fuck her research," Loretta snapped. "She's got AIDS of the heart. Or something worse. Blight. Canker."

"What do you know about her?" Trina asked quietly.

"Know? All I know is I never saw a mother like that. She gives career women a
bad name. Not that it has anything to do with career. Liv Sloan's got a career but
she's there for her children. Of course, with Sam available, she doesn't have to be

there the way she normally would, but if Sam was suddenly not there, she'd know how to take over. She wouldn't need a full-scale orientation. Look, Julie Nolan's as into her career as anyone, but she knows she has a kid. She knows that if her child loses a tooth, you put a goddamned quarter under the pillow. Louise Dowell wouldn't even notice if her kid lost a tooth."

"Do you really think you're being fair?" asked Trina, striving for an impartiality she felt none of. "After all, they say that scientific research makes demands that have to—"

"Oh, stop!" said Loretta in sheer disgust. "That's just a cover-up. She has nothing to give—that's what her problem is. I've known her—at least as much as you *can* know her—through two children. I know that she's as empty as a brown paper bag. It's Bill who keeps that family going and, frankly, he's not exactly playing with a full gourd either."

That hit Trina like a slap across the face. "What do you mean?" she said, trying to keep her voice casual.

"He's just not a person to feel comfortable with," Loretta replied, getting on to the remaining third of her scone. "He's so terribly devoted to the children and he's so terribly suffocating."

"I don't think that's true," said Trina, hating the relentless way Loretta went about buttering the pastry.

"Of course it's true. He's your classic passive-aggressive. He's a sufferer and a victim and he doesn't get any from his wife who treats him like shit and he's the one who has to move out and he puts so much onto the kids that he makes them nervous wrecks."

"They love him," she protested.

"Kid'll love anyone they're supposed to love," said Loretta. "They love their mother too, I'll bet."

How could they? Seeing Louise at the party today, Trina felt sick. To grow up with a mother like that—it was horrifying. Fast as a flash of lightning, she gave birth to a fantasy that grew to maturity in a matter of seconds: she would be the boys' mother. She would help them. She would rescue them.

"You look about a million miles away," said Loretta.

Trina shook her head.

"It's hard—I know. You look at those children and they're so good and so sweet and you think to yourself—how could they ever be anything less than that? But something inside you tells you that they will. Their mother is an ice maiden and their father's got a rod up despite all that goodness and—"

"Stop it!" Trina said. She didn't want to hear this about Bill. It was all wrong. Loretta was all wrong.

Loretta stared at her for a long moment. Trina looked at her, then looked away. Loretta took a sip of her coffee and then held the mug in her hands for warmth. "Don't tell me," Loretta muttered at last.

"Don't tell you what?" Trina said finally.

"I said: Don't tell me."

OK, thought Trina, looking into her tea, I won't tell you.

"You and Bill Dowell," said Loretta.

Trina said nothing.

"Oh God."

"Loretta, what am I supposed to say when you keep saying—"

"Oh God." Loretta pushed the mug away, into the center of the small bistro table. "You understand this is nuts? Madness. Insanity. You understand that, don't you, Trina?"

"I think you're overreacting, Loretta."

"Overreacting? You're sleeping with one of my parents and I'm overreacting?"

It was amazing, Trina thought, how quickly Loretta's long pale oval of a face could become red, flushed, transformed. It was even a little frightening. "They're separated," she said quietly.

"It's just not right," Loretta said, wiping her hands on the paper napkin. "It's a conflict of interest."

"I don't see it that way," Trina said.

"But I do!"

You fucked Charles, Trina thought. Everyone knows that. The real problem is you don't have anyone to fuck you now—that's the real problem, isn't it? But she didn't say anything. She held her tongue.

Loretta sat there staring at her. The one thing in the world she really hated— the one thing in the world she really couldn't stand—was having someone stare at her this way. She reached up to touch her hair, and Loretta saw the show of weakness and zoomed in again. "You're making a mistake," she said in gentled tones. "This is a very big mistake—the king of mistakes."

Trina looked down at her own big white knuckles. "I make those kinds of mistakes," she whispered. "You see, Loretta, that's what I meant, that first time, when I asked you if you didn't want to know something about me. About where I'd been and who I am and what kinds of mistakes I make."

Loretta shook her head. "I know one thing. You never made a Bill Dowell mistake before."

There was a look and then Trina gave one more little shrug of her shoulders. "I'm willing to take my chances."

16

SIBERIAN PEA. Tree of heaven. Nannyberry. Aaron's beard. Sam walked through the park with his field book, noting the tree and shrub species. He had become something of a self-taught naturalist. The trees, the shrubs, the birds—the bitterns and the ruddy ducks; the indigo buntings; the greater and lesser scaups— he wanted to put all of it into his book.

A year ago he had known none of this, and now he could almost qualify as an expert. He enjoyed being expert at something. Now, when he walked through the park with Aaron and Aaron said, Look at the flower! Sam could say, That's not a flower, son, that's a black haw.

—Did you say a black whore, Daddy?

Sometimes he cracked himself up, Sam thought, as he walked on.

It was a splendid day. Spring was fully entrenched. Flowers were everywhere: forsythia and cornelian cherry; mountain phlox and birch catkins. The ground was warm, giving up its odors of fertility; people were taking their dogs for long walks; and here he was, at his work, unencumbered by the cold.

After a while, he sat down on a bench in the Ramble, with the cup of coffee he had bought at the Boathouse. He opened his pad to begin, but first read the last paragraph from yesterday's installment.

It meant crossing the Great Lawn, and Junius had never crossed the Great Lawn. There were always boys with bats about, people jumping, people running, people doing odd things. Junius knew, deep in his grain, that there was danger in people doing odd things. But what choice did he have? Iris needed his help. He had no choice.

Not bad, thought Sam. He read it again and decided there were two gray areas. "Deep in his grain"—did he need that? No, he did not, and he crossed it out, thinking how easily solved that problem had been. Then, in that same sentence, he was disturbed by the construction "danger in people doing odd things." Was it danger *in*? Or danger *with*? Danger *from*? He tried out all possibilities and wound up leaving it as it was.

So. Now he was ready. To cross the Great Lawn. He looked up at the trees. What a miraculous place this was—how nicely it had grown in. Olmsted certainly knew what he was about. He had undertaken a big job and he had done it well. Sam supposed he could say the same about himself—the writing of a novel was, after all, a big job too—but it didn't really feel the same. There was not enough that was concrete; indeed, there was virtually nothing concrete. The only thing that was concrete about writing was success, and even that, in the end, proved profoundly abstract.

But making a park—that was real. A few years ago he had decided that he too wanted to make parks. Liv was supportive—inordinately supportive, Sam soon came to feel. It was as if she couldn't wait for him to leave behind his writing, although nothing overt was said. Quite the opposite.

—You can always keep writing. Look at Wallace Stevens—he sold insurance. And William Carlos Williams. And Michael Korda.

—Sure. And Korda even finds time to go horseback riding.

—You know what I mean, Sam.

Yes. He knew what she meant.

He took a course in drafting at the Bronx Botanical Gardens. If he was going to go for a degree in landscape architecture, which would mean two years in school but a fairly healthy job market when he got out, he might as well start with what was daunting to him.

He always considered himself a person of above average intelligence—way above average—but he had his areas of blindness, or perhaps some kind of minimal brain dysfunction. He was, for instance, useless when it came to following instructions on how to hook up a VCR. He was equally bad—in fact almost embarrassingly inferior to Aaron—when it came to assembling children's toys. He feared that this area of weakness would be underscored dramatically in Basic Drafting I, but he bit the bullet and dove right in.

It would be nice to report that his intrepidness paid off, but it did not. Right off there were too many tools—templates and T-bars and compasses and others whose names he had mercifully blocked. He wasn't good with tools. Nor did he have a neat hand. No matter how hard he tried, his drawings always looked like Rorschach tests. Every week he sat next to this guy from Pratt whose drawings were insufferably exquisite and his confidence just kept plummeting. The worst of it was that he could never get his lines to intersect at the right points. He was always off and he realized that one couldn't afford to be off because then your black willow tree would wind up right smack in the middle of your reflecting pool and that wouldn't do at all, not at all.

When he got a C in the course, he decided to terminate his career in landscape architecture.

—Sam, no. It's just one course. It's like giving up a career in psychology just because you didn't do well in statistics.

—That's exactly why I gave up a career in psychology.

It was just as well, he thought, after a while. Prior reports that the job market in landscape architecture was bullish proved misleading. And did he really want to spend his life picking out shrubbery for suburban banks? It was really just as well.

But you had to admire a guy like Olmsted, he thought, as he looked out at the exquisite Bank Rock Bridge that connected the Ramble to the land south of the Lake. Olmsted was a visionary. And Sam was not. He never fancied himself a visionary, but, as with all people who write, all creative people, all "artists," he liked to think that he had a spark of genius. When he was twenty-five, twenty-six years old, he believed he might prove his genius. At that time, he was having stories published in good places: *North American Review, Prism International*. The stories were very dark and sharp and cutting. He broke the rules in a way that twenty-five-year-old writers should break the rules. But perhaps he wasn't as willing or as able to break rules in his personal life. Ultimately, he opted for conventionality. And then, as the years went by, he subjected himself to sober scrutiny: Did he have a deeply conventional streak that inhibited him from realizing his goals as a writer? Had he been far too willing to marry and settle down? Not that he was really *that* willing—he'd put up a struggle of sorts. But after they were living together for a year, Liv went to work on him. Her parents, you see, were your typical provincial sorts. Liv insisted they have two phones in the apartment, and that Sam could never answer hers, lest Dr. and Mrs. Himmelfarb should think there was an m-a-n living with her.

—Fuck it. Tell them we're cohabiting. What are you afraid of?

—No, Sam. Dr. Alcan says that would be engaging them.

—Better you should engage them than you should engage me.

But, of course, she did engage him. His resistance broke down and then there was the very short engagement, complete with Corning broiler pans and Sunbeam toasters from the cousins, and then an August wedding in the Himmelfarb backyard, the caterer turning out fawncy omelets and California champagne because, in the words of Mrs. Himmelfarb, "if it's good enough for the President, it's good enough for us."

Well, at least they made money from it. Very good money indeed. By the time all the returns were in and counted, they were close to ten grand richer. At the time, it seemed enough for Sam to write his novel and for Liv to go to law school. Unfortunately—or maybe fortunately; who could say?—law school turned out better than the novel. The novel—it was called *Do You Believe in Magic?* and had to do with a professional magician released from a state asylum—was respectfully rejected by a dozen publishing houses. Scribner's saluted Sam's "ear for dialogue." Little, Brown addressed his "eye for characterization." Everyone had praise for his sensory faculties but nobody bought his book, for, along with the muted praise were allegations of "speciousness" and "something hollow at the core."

Something hollow at the core. For months after that, he fantasized about killing the editor who had offered that pearl. How? Very quickly, in the elevator at 666 Fifth Avenue, with an ice pick or, some days, piano wire.

—Sam, you just have to go on, honey. I know it's a blow but you can't just give up.

But who was she to talk? She had made Law Review in her second year. She was such a damned good student. And you could see how much she loved being a student. She grew her hair long, wore gold-rimmed glasses, jeans, sweatshirts. She had the time of her life, throwing herself into it, in that uniquely productive way she had.

As for him, he stopped believing in magic and started to panic, taking on too many bad writing jobs. All sorts of pseudonymous things, with naive young women getting fingered for the first time in exotic climes like Acapulco and Rio and Bali. But he was jocular about it all, and wryly self-deprecating, telling everyone that he was just out to make a little dough while he worked on something of his own. And he did work on something of his own. He sold *Grounder,* his dog novel, to Doubleday and then there was the film sale and he had his twenty-thousand-dollar check in hand, feeling very flush, with all their friends blinded by the stardust that had touched them.

But how long do you think that lasted? Not very long at all. A writer's block followed—a big one; not exactly the Empire State Building of writer's blocks but maybe the Woolworth Building. Lots of false starts; lots of bad writing. And then came Aaron, and the excuse to stay home and justify his existence with something other than writing while Liv made good in The Law and had that amazing paycheck every week, the most steady money they'd ever known.

You couldn't ever give up that kind of money, thought Sam, as he sipped his coffee. Sometimes they toyed with the idea of moving upstate, giving up the fast track and all, but they just couldn't give up that money. Maybe it was a mistake, thought Sam, as he watched a squirrel having an extended approach-avoidance encounter with him. *Play your cards right, buddy, and I'll put you in my book.* The squirrel stared at him and chattered. Nancy was so afraid of them; it was funny how, when someone was so afraid, they sensed it and jumped up at you, onto your lap, as they did that day. Poor Nancy.

But he mustn't sit here thinking about Nancy. This was his work time. Besides, he didn't know what to do about Nancy. He felt like a fool—this seduction, going on and on, both of them getting more worked up than was good for them. He just didn't know what to do.

He drained the coffee cup and stared at the page.

*		*		*

But what choice did he have? Iris needed his help. He had no choice.

There was no way around it: It was time for Junius to cross the Great Lawn. But what was going to happen? He had resisted outlining this novel. He was afraid an outline would make it stale. So it was as new and untested to him as to anyone.

Slowly, carefully, he crept out of his hole and began, in mincing steps, to cross the Great Lawn.

"Mincing" steps? He didn't want to make Junius look lavender. He changed "mincing" to "tentative." Good little Junius. What a brave little soul. And all for the love of a good woman.

He glanced at his watch. 2:25. Soon he would have to leave to meet Liv and Aaron at the carousel. And Freya—mustn't forget Freya. She was almost three months already. She was a little person, Liv kept reminding him.

Three months. Liv's maternity leave would soon be up. Time flies, he thought, the thought rustling about in his mind like dry leaves. She told everyone how happy she was being an at-home mother these past three months and how she wasn't looking forward to going back to work. He hated it when she said that. It was as if she were saying that if her husband were an adequate breadwinner, she wouldn't have to do what she did. Well, fuck that, he thought—fuck that on so many levels. For one thing, he had never made her any promises.

—I'm never going to take care of you. We're always going to take care of ourselves. We're always going to be aware that human lives can only merge so much and that essentially we're all alone for all time.

OK, she had replied. She had this damned ability to say OK. It was as though she didn't really believe him or listen to him. What she really believed was that he would take good care of her. And in some ways he did. He tried to make her happy. The two children, the support for her work, the way he held down the home—he had made so many things possible for her.

Did she value any of this? She went around telling people that "if only she could be a full-time mother." As if they didn't look at her and think: Who are you kidding? For she was not only ambitious but unconflicted about her ambition. Not that she was the sort of person who would stab someone in the back, but she had a sense of herself and her own accomplishments and she succeeded. She had been the valedictorian of her high-school class in Pleasantville. Her father, an unfulfilled optometrist who had always wanted to be an ophthalmologist, wanted her to be a doctor. But she didn't want to be a doctor. She went on to Radcliffe and majored in English and started her graduate studies at Yale, where she was planning on becoming the great authority on Mary Ann Evans, aka George Eliot, but she'd had this traumatic affair with a lechy professor there. The Great Chink in Olivia Himmelfarb's life. Then a breathless escape to New York City, and publishing, where everyone thought she was terrific and so did he. And she thought he was terrific. And so they got married. With fawncy omelets in the backyard.

Shit, he thought, checking the time. How did his days manage to evaporate the way they did? And this was his precious time. During Liv's maternity leave, he had been allowed to structure his time as he saw fit. And he should have had so many more pages to show for these three months. But he didn't. He didn't even want to count how many pages he had written, because there weren't enough, not nearly enough.

He felt bad. Not bad inside, although he felt that too, but just plain bad. A bad boy. He hadn't done his work. He spent too much time reading up on the trees and the shrubs and the birds—the cucumber magnolia and the myrtle warbler. He hadn't seen the forest for the trees. Maybe he just didn't like to work. Could he be that freakish thing, that aberration of nature: a man who didn't like to work? Like his father, who'd languished in a low-level civil-service job and wound up retiring at sixty-three to a room in the White Coral Sands Hotel in Margate, Florida.

He went back to his notebook, making himself write.

With tentative steps, he crossed the Great Lawn. The grass, in mid-spring, grew so fast and they hadn't cut it yet so it gave him good cover. As he made his way, he smelled something funny. A fruity smell he'd never encountered before. It came off a woman person lying down with her flesh to the sun. It was coconut oil, which he'd never smelled before, and he paused, his nose twitching, wanting to eat, but unable to find the thing that there was to eat. Finally, he pulled himself away from the intoxicating smell, remembering that Iris's life was in his hands.

He wished he had more coffee. He wished he could smoke. Nothing had replaced smoking for him. But how could he smoke? It wasn't fair to smoke when you had two children. But then, he thought, wasn't that again an example of that conventionality that had robbed him of his promise? To worry about others that way, when what he should be doing—finally—was to worry about himself. But he had never made that commitment to himself that an artist should make. He never had the guts.

He looked once again at his watch. It was time to go. They would be waiting for him at the carousel. Damn them, he thought, with exhaustion, as he rose and headed south.

"Mommy!"

Liv knelt down to let Aaron run into her arms. Only one more week of this, she thought, as she felt his damp little cheek against hers. Why was he so thin? Because he didn't eat. He only ate hot dogs and bread and applesauce. What had they done to make him such a fussy eater? And what had happened to make him run into her arms this way? He rarely showed this kind of spontaneous affection.

"How was his day?" she asked Trina as she helped him on with his coat.

"He had a good day," said Trina. "He spent a long time at the sand table. He loves the sand table."

Liv was so glad she could send her child to a place where they had a sand table. That was the thing about the Center—it seemed chaotic but it was actually very well-run. Loretta was awfully good when it came to materials; she always had the best things from Community Playthings and Childcraft and so forth. The best wooden blocks, the best wagons, the best sand tables. Of course, they paid through the nose for it. It cost them thirty-eight dollars a day to send Aaron to the Center. And then, in three more months, it would be time for Freya to start. Then they would be paying over seventy dollars a day on child care. The thought made Liv's stomach twist. She didn't like the idea of handing over seventy dollars a day, sand table or no sand table. Where would they find the money? She made a goodly sum, all right, but not that goodly. Sam had better sell his new novel. She wondered if people really wanted to read a book about a rabbit. Would she want to read a book about a rabbit if it weren't written by her husband?

She felt disloyal thinking these thoughts, but wouldn't deny them. Sometimes she wondered just how hard Sam really worked. When they worked together at Ernest Wesson Books, he never worked very hard at all. He always wanted to play—long, long lunches, with two or three drinks, and sometimes cutting out of the office for a movie or just a walk in the park. Everyone thought he was kind of brilliant—there wasn't a writer you could name that he didn't have some kind of passing familiarity with—and so he was indulged, like a gifted child. But ultimately, Liv believed, there is no substitute for work.

"Stop!" Aaron whimpered.

"Stop what?" she said.

He shook out of her grasp and then shook himself out of his coat.

"Aaron!"

But then she saw that his shirt sleeve had ridden up inside the coat—just the kind of thing that drove him crazy.

"Let me fix it," she said. "Stand still."

He stood still and she fixed it.

"You see," she said. "If only you would use your words . . ."

They headed out of the Center. She had the baby in the Snugli and Freya felt heavy, but she hadn't felt like taking the carriage out today. Yesterday, when she picked up Aaron with the carriage, he insisted on pushing it and had pushed it right into a parked car. Not good for Freya, not good for the car.

She was halfway down the block when she heard someone call her name. She turned around. There was Anna, pushing Molly in her stroller.

"Hi there," Liv called. "What are you doing here early?"

"Oh, I just got back from the ospital-hay," Anna said, as she caught up with her. It was necessary these days, if one were a friend of Anna's, and just about everyone was, to have a fairly good grasp of pig latin.

"Is everything OK?" Liv forced herself to ask.

"Oh, yeah. Yeah. Fine," said Anna. "I was going to go back to work but I figured, screw it, I was going to give myself a little reward. Pick up Molly and head to the park. Are you headed that way?"

"Yes. I'm meeting Sam at the carousel. Want to come?"

Anna thought a moment. "Well, I'll start out—see how far I get."

The park smelled fresh and good and sweet. The trees were fluffy with buds and new growth and people were out exercising.

"Look at that guy," Anna said, nodding toward a man doing warm-up exercises. Liv looked at him. He was about six-feet-three, bare-chested, in tiny shorts, with the body of a god.

"I see," Liv murmured.

"Let's go closer," Anna said.

"Oh, stop."

But Anna insisted and they made their way onto the cinder path that ringed the reservoir. After they had passed very close by, and were a respectable distance beyond, Anna turned to Liv and rolled her eyes. "His nipples are more erect than mine have ever been," she whispered.

"Oh, stop." Liv said, turning around to look. "Not than mine," she added.

"No fair. You're nursing." Anna stole another look and shook her head. "Do you realize how many hours a day he must exercise? Who has the time for it?"

"Not I. And not Sam," Liv said, smiling a little. "Sam's getting this wee little potbelly." Liv thought it was kind of cute actually, but when she teased him about it he got furious.

"Michael's not," Anna sighed. "He's like you—he doesn't put on an ounce. The rest of us mortals—we eat a slice of protein bread, we blow up."

"Oh, please. You look wonderful."

"Yeah, the wonderful thirty-day cancer diet."

There was an awful silence and then Anna touched Liv's arm. "I'm sorry. I don't know why I said that."

"That's okay," Liv said, managing a faint smile.

"How's the baby?" Anna said quickly, changing the subject that badly needed changing.

"A little dream," said Liv. "She's everything you-know-who was not. He screamed for three solid months. Strained at every diaper change. Twelve-minute naps from which he'd wake up screaming like a wild man. But she's so serene."

"Her Serene Highness, eh?" Anna smiled.

"Oh, yes. Our little princess," Liv said, looking down at her as she slept so peacefully on her chest. Why didn't Sam love her yet? It had been almost three months. He said he did, but she didn't think he did. Even with Aaron, who seemed to do everything he could in the beginning to make it difficult to love him, Sam showed this fierce devotion, this unassailable empathy.

"Look," Anna hissed. Liv looked: the Adonis was running past them. Every muscle in his body stood out in a kind of sculptured relief.

"Very nice," said Liv.

"Do you think we sound like two horny ladies of early middle age?" asked Anna.

"God. I hope not."

"I tell you, my little problem has not done wonders for our sex life," Anna admitted.

Liv hesitated. She wasn't the sort who generally discussed the intimate things of her life, but Anna was so open and she was so fond of Anna. "Pregnancy isn't exactly the great aphrodisiac either."

"It's like we forget about it. You think of all the things you have to do all day— dinner, laundry, work, phone calls, paying bills, putting the kid to bed, this and that and this and that, and then you get into bed at night and you're *exhausted*. All you want is to have someone give you a little back rub."

Anna stopped herself. She was open, but only up to a point. Liv rushed in.

"I know. It's really only if we go away for a weekend . . ."

"Yes. Exactly. Or if we blow a little dope."

"Well, yeah. But we haven't even done that in God knows how long. And of course we haven't gone away in ages."

"It's not as if we're not *capable* of having a good time together. Under the right circumstances, we can have a wonderful time together."

"I know," said Liv soberly. "It's just that the right circumstances rarely present themselves."

"Mommy never told us about this particular issue," Anna said, after a moment.

"Mommy never *cared* about this particular issue. At least my mommy didn't . . . I think," Liv said, with a little laugh.

Anna laughed along. "Well, at least we *care*."

They walked on a little further, the children eating bagels. "So when are you going back to work?" asked Anna.

"A week from Thursday," Liv said, feeling a flicker of something—loneliness, hollowness, she wasn't sure what.

"Are you ready?"

Liv shrugged. "At least I had three months. For a while there it looked pretty hairy. I thought they were going to draft me back for an emergency."

"Listen, I wish I had the kind of career you do. You should run back to your office. Freya will be fine."

Liv glanced at Anna. Given where Anna had been this past year, Liv wondered how she could say that. "And you've got Sam," Anna added. "You don't have to worry. It's the perfect setup."

They walked on just a bit further and then Anna came to a stop. "I'm kind of pooped," she said. "I guess I'll take a rain check on the carousel."

Liv tried not to stare at Anna, but she couldn't help it. Anna's fatigue had an undeniably ominous undertone, particularly when you remembered the dynamo she was six months ago. "All right," Liv said. "I'll call you. We'll make a date for the four of us."

"Oh, good," said Anna. "Bye-bye, Aaron."

Silence, of course.

"Aaron, Anna and Molly are leaving," Liv said.

He looked up. "'Bye," he muttered.

She sighed, waved, and pushed on.

He was waiting at the carousel. She was twenty minutes late. Only during her maternity leave was she unconcerned with punctuality. Otherwise she was crackerjack—shower and makeup in the blink of an eye; clothes out of the dry-cleaner bag; once-over with the lint brush; and then out the door. She would not be late for work.

When it came to his work, however, there was never any reluctance to shaking up his schedule. If Aaron was sick and unable to go to the Center, then it was Sam who got to stay home with him. And if the car went on the blink—it was Sam again. Good old reliable Sam. You can adjust your schedule, Sam, went the old song. *Oh, Sammmmm . . . you can adjust your schedule.*

The infuriating thing was that he needn't have stopped his work just when he did. He could have written another page in those twenty minutes. The fact was he needn't have agreed to meet her at the carousel in the first place. What did he need it for? But he felt guilty. Here she was, with the two kids, going to the carousel, and what if Aaron needed help getting on and off? What would she do with the baby? And she had been so happy when he suggested he meet her. It was spring, their first spring with the new baby, and the whole family would be doing something all together, and what could be nicer?

What could have been nicer was if she had been here on time. She was almost never this late. A flash of anxiety exploded behind his eyes. They were walking down Central Park West and a gypsy cab, racing a light, swerved to avoid a collision and jumped the curb, smashing into his family. They were all dead now, or dying en route to Roosevelt Hospital. Liv and the baby had been killed instantly; Aaron was in a coma, with massive brain damage. The hospital was trying to reach him right now but he didn't have an office with a phone like a normal person. His office was on a bench, in the park, with angry squirrels chattering at him over his lack of nuts.

Just then, he spotted them coming down the path. In a moment, his anxiety turned to anger and disgust. There was no excuse she could make that would be good enough.

"Where were you?" he demanded, when she was still ten yards away.

"I'm sorry," she called back. "Freya was hungry. I had to stop and feed her."

"Great," he said. "I've been waiting a half-hour."

"Sorry. I would have called but . . ."

She trailed off. *But you can't call a park bench.* Then he noticed Aaron, sucking his thumb in the stroller. A very nice picture of a three-year-old boy. "Aaron, get your thumb out of your mouth."

"Sam . . ."

He gave her a furious look. She had something to say about everything. She leaned down. "Aaron, do as Daddy says."

Aaron ignored them both. He had this uncanny and awful knack for doing the wrong thing at the wrong time, Sam thought. Sometimes he hated him—hated his own son. "Do you hear your mother?" said Sam, hearing himself but unable to stop. "Now get your thumb out of your mouth."

Aaron looked up at him. The thumb stayed in his mouth, and now his index finger covered his nose, almost entirely obscuring his face. Sam wanted to pick him up and slam him down. "If your thumb isn't out of your mouth by the time I count to three, there's no carousel. One . . . two—"

"Don't count, Daddy!" Aaron keened.

Sam stopped. Aaron took the thumb out of his mouth. Sam felt flushed. He saw Liv glaring at him. "Come, Aaron," she said, leading him by the hand through the gate.

Sam stood at the fence and watched his wife and son negotiating. Aaron wanted to ride in one of those seats that old ladies and handicapped people ride in, and Liv was urging him onto a horse. What a little pussy his son was sometimes, like now, as he watched him holding on to Liv's skirts. But she lifted him onto a horse—a black horse with a gold bit and flecks of white foam at the jaw—and he could see her murmuring encouragement.

Liv stood next to the horse that first ride with Aaron, white as a sheet, holding on for dear life. It wasn't as if this were the first time he had ever been on a horse, Sam thought with disgust. He had no lustiness, this son of his—he took after his mother. He was as smart as a whip and manipulative and cold—just like his mother. But then, just as soon as he thought these things, Sam hated himself for thinking them. How could he think such things? They weren't true. Don't think them, he told himself, as the carousel went around and around to the tune of "Tie a Yellow Ribbon."

When it was done, he saw Liv whisper once more to Aaron and then she left him there, tied onto the horse, looking scared but trying to look brave. That look of bravery was piercing, thought Sam, with a sudden ache of tenderness, but then Liv was coming toward him. She still waddled, he thought, but perhaps that had something to do with carrying a baby like a lump on her chest.

She stood next to him. Freya began to whimper and so she stood there shaking a little, hoping the motion would lull her back to sleep. "There, there, baby. There, there."

Where where? He didn't want to look at the baby. Her face, in her crying, was all red and wrinkled, like a sun-dried tomato. He looked instead at Aaron, who was holding on to the carousel horse as if it were a runaway stallion.

"You're not going to resolve the thumb-sucking that way," she said.

"Oh. Then you know how to resolve the thumb-sucking?" he returned.

"No, I don't," she replied. "All I know is that ordering him around is the worst possible thing."

"You know that, do you?"

"He'll start wetting his bed again."

"And I'll be responsible."

She stared at him, continuing to shimmy for the fretful Freya. "What's got into you now?" she said.

Now. The innocuous adverb carrying such force in the context of her remark. He looked at her and then turned away, waiting for Aaron to make his revolution and then, as he came into view, waving at him. Why was he looking so grave? Sam wondered. What was wrong with him now?

"OK. I'm sorry I was late," Liv said, after a deep breath. "I did my best but I guess it wasn't good enough."

"You were a half-hour late. That doesn't mean anything to you when it concerns *my* work, does it?"

"I think I have a very healthy respect for your work," she countered.

"Yeah," he muttered, wishing she would shut the baby up.

"And what does that mean?" she said, her mouth pursing just the way her mother's mouth pursed in an argument.

"You know what it means. Don't cross-examine me."

"You're really in a mood today, aren't you?" she said, her shimmy becoming more strained, almost jerky. "You tell me when I'm on the rag, but believe me, you're just as bad."

There was a silence and then Freya screamed. "What's the matter with her?" Sam said irritably.

"How the hell should I know?" Liv cried, trying to get her to take a pacifier. "Calm down, Freya. Though why she should calm down now, given the vibes, I don't know."

Sam turned to look at the carousel. There came Aaron, his posture showing no signs of relaxation. Sam waved. "Look at our fun-loving kid," he said, as Aaron passed from view.

"Get off his back today, will you?" Liv said.

He turned to look at her. He stared at her and, for a moment, hated everything about her: her hair, her skin, her pale eyes, the way her earlobes connected to her cheek. The terrible thing was he couldn't understand why he felt this way. "Fuck you," he said.

She looked up at him, her face altered by the shock. They didn't have much of that sort of language in their house, not since the children anyway. He watched as her eyes glistened with the beginning of tears. A regret collected inside of him, like a huge bubble, and he had to fight to keep it down.

"Why don't you just go?" she said, in that thin voice she sometimes got. "I mean, who asked you to come today? You *volunteered*. And I thought we'd have a nice time of it but I should have known better, given the way you've been."

"The way *I've* been? How have I been?" he demanded.

"You've been a *prick*," she said, stopping her shimmying altogether and letting the baby cry.

Sam stared at her. There was this awful music, "Cherry Pink and Apple Blossom White," on the calliope. He turned and saw Aaron coming around. He waved. She waved. Until Aaron was out of view.

What was there to say? He didn't like fighting. He didn't like fighting because he always had the need to win a fight and he'd do anything, say anything, to come out on top. She wasn't like that—funny for a lawyer, but she wasn't. She'd fold— and cry—and take days or even weeks to get over it. He knew at once, the bubble growing inside him, that he was in this for the long haul now. "Maybe I've got a reason," he said.

"Oh, I'm sure you do. Lots of them. All sorts of terrible insensitive things I've done to your tender ego . . ."

"That's right. You've hit the nail on the head. You live in your little dream world. Miss Streets and Company at work, then Mother Earth on maternity leave, and don't give a flying fuck for what *my* needs are, what *my* life is all about . . ."

"Oh, I'm sick of it," she cried, covering her eyes. "Ever since I got pregnant— I'm just sick of it."

"That's right. Cry. That's always useful."

Aaron came round again. Sam waved. So did she. He saw her wave, even with the tears. What the hell were they waving for? And Aaron had begun to crumple, his face all red with his own set of tears. Why was he crying? Had they forgotten to wave last time around? Why the fuck was he crying? Did he see his mother crying? Sam felt a panic or something—the bubble bursting—and he rushed through the gate and jumped onto the carousel, moving with effort toward Aaron, whose wails he could hear now in the clamor of the calliope. It was so strange to move this way, through this unpeopled carousel, the ground beneath him undulating, as if he were moving through water or in a dream. He had dreamed it, hadn't he? What he had done just now, with Liv. What he was about to do. What was he about to do? He didn't want to think about it, but he knew. He knew what he had to do. He needed something new in his life. He had made the decision. "Aaron!" he called, as he came closer, and why was he crying so piteously? He pulled himself up onto the horse, behind his son, and pressed his legs closely, tightly, around his son's hips, and put his right arm around his son's waist and felt the broken pump, as he pressed his lips against his son's thin unlovely hair. "Now, now," he said. "It's almost over." As they made this last revolution, he saw Liv watching them but this time, for some reason, she didn't wave.

When it was done, he helped Aaron down and then Aaron ran on ahead of him, through the gate, throwing himself at Liv, his arms around her legs, burying his face against her.

"You don't have to go ever again," she said, as she patted his head, and Sam couldn't help thinking that it was the wrong thing to say to a kid like that.

"What scared you?" he asked, but Aaron was too far gone to answer.

He and Liv looked at each other. He frowned. "I'll take the kids home," she said. "You can go work."

He nodded. "I won't be home too late," he said.

"Whenever," she replied, as she took Aaron's hand and headed west.

He stood by the carousel for a few moments until they were out of sight. The large bubble inside of him seemed to grow bigger, leaching out into his arms with a kind of anginal discomfort. He would have been alarmed, if he hadn't known what to do for it.

There was a telephone booth not far away. And he had a quarter. Certain things he felt nostalgic for, he thought, as he dialed, like the ten-cent phone call.

"Hello?"

"Nancy, it's me—Sam."

"Oh, Sam. Hi."

Oh-Sam-Hi. He felt scared and giddily romantic—a feeling he hadn't felt in years, in a lifetime. "What are you doing right now?"

"Right now? I'm cleaning wax off a carpet."

"Really."

"Yes, really. Do you know how to do it?"

"Uh, no."

"You put a piece of paper towel over the wax and then you apply a warm iron to the paper towel, drawing the wax up into it."

"Oh, Jesus. You're making me hot."

"There are lots of little secrets I know. Household hints and all sorts of things."

"Where's David?" he asked.

"At Olivier's."

"And Justin?"

"Lucerne."

"Good old successful Justin. Can I come over?"

"Yes. Please."

He took a cab there. He almost never took cabs. The cabdriver had on some kind of Arabic music that made Sam think of belly dancers.

When he got up to her apartment, she opened the door and he looked at her and thought she was beautiful. She was wearing an old Cornell sweatshirt and jeans. Her hair was pulled back and tied with one of those cheap plastic-ball things. He could sense the movement of her breasts even under the capacious sweatshirt.

He didn't say a word. She closed the door and he pulled her into his arms for a kiss. They embraced like that for several long moments, as he touched her breasts, first through the sweatshirt and then reaching beneath it, feeling her silken flesh in his hands and feeling his bubble not quite disappear but become encased, encapsulated, inside a bigger bubble of new sensation.

"Sam," she whispered.

He kissed her soft neck; he squeezed her soft breasts.

"Let's not feel guilty, Sam," she said. "Let's not."

OK, he told himself, let's not, as she led him into the bedroom.

17

"GOOD MORNING, ladies and gentlemen," Abigail Strong said from the stage of the Soames School auditorium. "Today we are pleased to present the third and fourth forms in their production of *Jake and Honeybunch,* a musical based on folk tales of the American Negro. We request that flash attachments not be used during the performance. Thank you."

The houselights dimmed. Bill Dowell glanced at Louise, who was sitting beside him in a red felt hat and red kidskin gloves. The Red Guard, Bill couldn't help thinking.

"This is the story of Jake and Honeybunch, a farmer and his mule," narrated Debra Reynolds, Denny's classmate, a real "American Negro," whose solid frame and stentorian voice brought to mind a seven-year-old Barbara Jordan. The chorus, dressed in floor-length white robes, like the cast of *The Green Pastures,* began to sing "The Ballad of Jake and Honeybunch," while two very serious little boys banged out rhythm on snare drums. The spotlight hit the star—Dennis Dowell, dressed in overalls and ragged flannel shirt, playing Jake to the Honeybunch of his best friend, Alistair Craig, whose father was very high up with Morgan Stanley.

"Honeybunch," Denny began, in a quavering falsetto not so far removed from his customary falsetto, "what are we going to do? It hasn't rained in two months. A powerful dryness is upon us."

Children onstage often sound like drunken Indians, thought Bill, but it was only a fleeting intellectualization. What he really felt was this enormous pride and pleasure. He himself had always enjoyed performing—first his musical career, then the cheerleading—and now his son was showing himself to be a natural performer too. Denny's usual shyness seemed not an issue on the stage, and he captured attention with his fine-bred handsomeness, his well-made form.

"We got to find a solution, Honeybunch, or else . . ."

Or else. The big pause. Everyone waited, but the next line was not forthcoming. Denny was frozen. Bill glanced at Louise, who stared straight ahead. Couldn't she see what was going on?

"He's forgotten his lines," Bill whispered.

She said nothing, but he noticed how tightly she held her red gloves. He looked back at the frozen stage. *Or else Sugar Mountain will be ruined,* he wanted to shout. Did Louise know Denny's next line? he wondered. No. That was too much to ask. It was enough she was here today. Never before had she done this sort of thing, taking time out from her work to see her son in a show. That was one way the separation had changed her, he thought, as she turned to him finally, and whispered, "Why doesn't he say it?"

"He will," Bill promised. "Don't worry."

She put a hand over her eyes. "They're just letting him suffer."

But then the music teacher, Mrs. Oliphant, called up his cue in a voice everyone could hear. "We got to find a solution, Honeybunch, or else Sugar Mountain will be ruined," Denny said rousingly, his arm around the mule, the audience bursting into applause.

Bill turned to Louise. You see? he wanted to tell her, pleased as always that he had kept his promise, but it was too easy to say I told you so and so he said nothing.

She leaned down to give Denny a kiss. "You were wonderful, Denny," Louise said. "Really."

"I forgot," Denny murmured, his thin white arm around her back.

"Yes, you did," she acknowledged, "but it doesn't matter."

Bill waited for the exchange to end and then knelt down beside his son, bringing him into his arms for a giant hug. Unlike his own father, who had instituted hand-shaking so early in the game, Bill would never stop hugging his sons. "Wow," he said, smoothing down Denny's cowlick that was the same cowlick Bill had had as a child and that even today would reemerge if his hair were barbered incorrectly. "You were something else, buddy."

Denny's shyness came down suddenly, like a final curtain, and he squirmed in Bill's arms.

"Hey, you," said Bill scoldingly, "can't you stand hearing good things about yourself?"

"He wants to get back to his classmates," Louise said. "Don't you, Denny?"

Denny nodded and Bill let him go. "See you tomorrow," Bill called after him. Suddenly he felt something strange—a sadness. Tomorrow seemed so far away. He looked at Louise. She was working her way in, wasn't she? They didn't care about him as much as they used to; their mommy was new and shiny and special.

"Wasn't our Denny a show all by himself?" said Abigail as she approached them. She was wearing a silk dress designed with numbers and letters in primary colors. He couldn't imagine where she had found it.

"Yes," Louise concurred. "He was very good."

"Celia Oliphant tells me he's the most enthusiastic performer she's had in years," Abigail continued. "I'm sure that some will make accusations of nepotism but it's clear to me he deserved to be the star."

Louise and Bill exchanged amused smiles as Abigail went on to greet the other parents.

"The proud grandmother," said Bill.

"She never cared about *my* stage career nearly as much as her grandson's," Louise said archly.

"I never knew you had a stage career."

"Oh, yes. I played Priscilla Alden in fourth grade at Brearley," she told him. "I thought I was divinely chaste and noble in the part."

"I'm sure you were."

They walked out together. It was breezy and she pulled on a red glove.

"I really wish it would get warmer," she said. "It's cool for this time of year."

"It will."

They walked on for a moment, not saying anything. "Are you going back to the office?" she asked.

"Yes," he said. "Why?"

She pulled on the other red glove. He could tell they were very fine, with tiny pearl buttons along the cuffs. "I thought perhaps we could have coffee."

"Coffee?"

Her lips puckered into a small, mischievous smile. "Yes. Coffee."

They went to Sarabeth's Kitchen in the Hotel Wales. It was a tearoom sort of operation, much favored by affluent young matrons, some in expensive jogging suits. Bill and Louise sat at a window table—very pretty, cloth napkins in a floral print, and a Gerbera daisy in a bud vase.

"This is lovely," said Louise, who seemed unusually animated.

"It *is* nice, isn't it? Much nicer than the hotel. One wonders why they don't do a real refurbishment, given the location."

"Because people don't always maximize their opportunities," she explained.

They both ordered pumpkin muffins and coffee and Louise lit up a cigarette.

"You're not smoking more than usual these days, I hope."

"No," she puffed. "Well, maybe a little."

"Oh, Louise . . ."

"I've been under a great deal of stress, Bill," she said, taking deeper puffs.

"Work?"

She rolled her eyes. "And you always accuse *me* of having work on the brain. I was thinking, actually, about our separation."

There was a pause. A baby, in an old Silver Cross carriage as big as a compact car, began to whimper. Bill looked down at the stainless-steel cutlery. The yeasty smell of baking coffee cake made the air seem thick. "It's what you wanted, isn't it?" he said finally.

She poked a long nail into her muffin. "You make it sound so premeditated. As if I had this life plan, with Separation as Step One, and here we are and everything's just dandy."

"Well, let's face it—you're not exactly the capricious type," he said, with a slight smile.

She smiled a little herself. "No, I'm not," she agreed. She took a sip of coffee. "Mmmnh. Good coffee."

"You should watch your coffee consumption," he told her. "You know what it does to you."

"I've almost given it up altogether," she said. Her lips parted slightly; they were dry and she licked them. "Doctor's orders."

He waited for more, but it wasn't coming. "What do you mean?"

"I didn't want to tell you . . ."

"Louise . . ."

"I had a lump."

A lump. She was absolutely phobic about cancer. He remembered a night when she had become hysterical, absolutely hysterical, about blood in her stool and he had to slap her—incredible, like in the movies, but it worked. "Why didn't you tell me?"

"I didn't want to involve you . . ."

"How could I not be involved? You're the mother of my children."

She smiled a little at that and then got rid of the smile. "It didn't seem fair," she said soberly. "Anyway, it turned out to be a lot of nothing. A little cyst. I felt so silly. But the point of the whole story is that there seems to be a link between caffeine and cystic conditions, so—"

"So you're sitting here drinking coffee," he interrupted, his face becoming very stern.

"Oh, stop it," she laughed. "One cup."

He watched her as she sipped. The hat was rather becoming to her after all, he thought. But then why was he surprised? She wasn't a beautiful woman or even a pretty one, but she knew how to put herself together. And she was pretty to him, he thought, with a sudden raw tenderness. "It does sound as though you've been under a lot of strain," he said.

"Don't even ask. How's your work?" she inquired brightly, changing the subject.

"Fine," he replied, breaking off a chunk of muffin but then just letting it sit there. "Actually, you'll never guess who's coming to see me about funding this afternoon."

"You're right," she said. "I'll never guess."

"An emissary from the Center. Loretta got it in mind that she should get some money to study mainstreaming."

"Mainstreaming?" Louise said. "That sounds like something you do with a needle."

"Hardly. For the uninitiated," he explained, "it means putting handicapped children in with normal children."

"Such as the little Down's-syndrome child?"

"Yes. Caitlin McIver. And now Loretta's planning on taking in some other children with disabilities."

"Is she trained to do that?" Louise demanded.

"She needs no special license," said Bill. "And she does have adequate credentials."

Louise shrugged. "It's so like her—biting off more than she can chew. Are you going to give her money?"

"No, no. Conflict of interest. But I'll see if I can point her in the right direction." He sipped his coffee. "And how's your work?"

She grimaced. "That's the other thing. Oh, Bill—I can't tell you what it's like working on this AIDS thing. It's so scary. I wake up at night feeling as if I'm inside this terrible nightmare . . ."

Then why are you doing it? he thought. "Maybe it isn't the smartest thing," he ventured. "The children . . ."

"Oh, God. Not that again," she cried. "You don't just *catch* this thing, for God's sake. You don't just look at the virus and up it jumps into your sinuses. And I don't prick myself with needles either, thank you."

He felt ashamed, and angry that she was making him feel ashamed. She must have sensed his anger for she reached over, surprisingly, uncharacteristically, to pat his hand. "Don't worry, Bill," she said gently. "I'm not making any mistakes. Do you think I could ever forgive myself if I made a mistake where the children were concerned?"

Or if you made a mistake period, he thought, but didn't say it because her hand was still on his hand.

"It's not the personal risk—which is minimal—that gives me the willies," she said, removing her hand, going back to the coffee and a second cigarette. "It's the big picture. It's what life on this planet could become because of AIDS."

He was worried about her. She seemed very tired and very strained and she was a highly strung person to start out with. It wasn't good, what he was seeing.

"The case load is doubling and redoubling," she said urgently. "And we know so little. God, Bill—we know so little."

"Calm down, Louise," he said. "Please calm down."

She looked at him and then looked around. A waiter was calling into the kitchen for more fruit butter. "It's a very grave situation, Bill," she said finally.

"I know it is," he replied. "Listen, the Foundation is funding its share of AIDS research. I know what the score is."

"You don't know what the score is!" she cried. "What we're seeing here is more than frightening, more than tragic. We're talking about something that could potentially be devastating . . . ruinous."

There was a silence. The sun streamed through the window. There were the sounds of cutlery touching glass and pot lids crashing in the kitchen. He didn't know what the point of this lunch was. He didn't know what it accomplished other than to confuse, to obfuscate.

"It's getting rather late," he said, glancing at his watch.

"You've hardly touched your muffin."

"I think, ultimately, that pumpkins are best left to pies."

"No. They're wonderful," she protested. "They're so moist."

He got the waitress and took care of the check. It was an odd circumstance. He wondered how other separated couples handled money when they went out together. Fortunately, he thought, as he got his change, it wasn't a lot of money at issue.

He helped her on with her coat. It was that army-green greatcoat she bought two or three years ago at a Banana-Republic store. He remembered it well. Afterward, they spent an hour or so in the travel bookshop downstairs. Those were the days when they had very big plans—it was their hobby then to plot the itineraries of great exotic journeys. Down the Nile. Down the Amazon. Patagonia. Tasmania. The Aleutians. By skiff, by dhow, by felucca. He recalled now, with a sort of fondness, how she had claimed infectious diseases as her special bailiwick, steeping herself in the epidemiology of strange malaises like kala-azar or Chagas' disease. "This one they call the kissing disease," he recalled her saying, as if it were yesterday, "because the bug affixes itself to one's lips." She needn't have done all that work, he thought, smoothing the shoulders of the coat, for they had never gotten any further than St. Maarten, with Denny, in desperation one winter when they were fighting and losing a battle against strep.

"Share a cab?" she asked as they stood at Madison and Ninety-second.

He shook his head. "I'm going to walk," he said. "It's the only exercise I get."

"You should do more."

"There's a lot I should do and don't."

"I'd walk with you," she said, "but I haven't the time, I'm afraid."

"Oh. Well," he shrugged. "Another time."

They looked at each other and managed to smile.

"That was nice," she said.

"Yes."

"Shall we do it again?"

He thought a moment. "Why not?"

For another moment they just stood there. They were standing in front of a toy store that had a big bubble-blowing bear as a sidewalk display, and every few seconds a stream of bubbles would issue from the bear and sail up to burst against them. She stepped forward, close to him, and put her arms around him and pressed her cheek against his. They were the same height. She had always been able to wear his clothes—his shirts and his sweaters and sometimes even his slacks. "Bill," she whispered. "Bill."

Before Bill even had the chance to say anything, Louise turned to enter a standing cab.

"Rockefeller University," she told the cabdriver.

"I didn't know they had one," he said.

"Sixty-sixth and York."

As the cab turned on Ninety-second, she began to experience a siege of physical sensations that she could not explain. Her mouth went alarmingly dry; her head began to pound; her extremities grew cold almost to the point of numbness; and she had that peculiar unsettling feeling of being poised above an abyss, a feeling that customarily served as prelude to her very occasional bouts with fever. She hoped it wasn't a virus. She couldn't afford to be sick—she simply couldn't afford it. But certainly this was why she had been feeling so strange all day. Bill must have thought she was a lunatic; she certainly had acted like one. Why had she done that at the end? It had made him so uncomfortable; she could feel the discomfort running through his bones. Then why had she done it? Because she had wanted to. Was that so inexcusable? They had been married for such a long time; they had had children together. When such a thing was ending, you could not expect it to end cleanly. There were always loose strings dangling and if you pulled a string you might find there was no end and the whole thing might unravel. It was so different with her lover. When he told her that he was accepting a position in Denmark so that his wife could be near her ailing mother, she didn't mourn. Oh, she was sad, yes, but the sadness, she assured herself, was bound to pass. But with Bill—this was a lifetime she was bidding good-bye. Was she really prepared to do that? Say good-bye to the concept of an intact family? It wasn't fair to her children, nor to Bill, nor, she now was coming to feel, to herself.

The physical sensations intensified, and then she realized she was probably very sick and should be going home. But she didn't want to be sick and she didn't want to go home. She was very scared. The cab was going too fast and she was so tired and she had to find a cure or the world would end and she didn't know what she wanted and she couldn't let go of Bill and her head hurt and she thought perhaps she loved him after all and her mouth was dry and she worried for the children and her extremities were shockingly cold.

She caught a glimpse of her reflection in the rearview mirror. It was fear, she told herself. She was in the grip of fear. But this was wrong, she thought—very, very wrong. There was no purpose to the fear; it served nothing and it must end. It must end and things must get better.

The cab came to a stop in front of the University. She stuffed some money into the little tray and got out. For a moment she felt wobbly, as if she had landed after a very long flight in a land with a different climate. But then, with a sense of relief and an almost trembling attack of joy, she looked around and saw that she had, in fact, landed in a lush and private green place she knew very well. It was, she would be the first to admit, a strange vision of Paradise, but then, she would have to ask, who knew what Paradise was? She walked across the green quad, toward her office, feeling much better about everything, quite sure, in her heart, that everything would turn out for the best.

By the time he reached his office, Bill had had enough of walking. He looked at his reflection in the plate-glass window of 355 Fifth Avenue and thought his coat was too long and his hair needed to be cut. His hair always needed to be cut. It grew like something in the jungle.

In the john, he gave himself a more careful look in the mirror. Before long he would be forty and this astonished him. It was a mistake, he told himself, a clerical error. He was too young to be forty. He was really twenty-six.

Where was the age in his face? It was hard to find. He had no lines, no wrinkles. Sometimes he liked to think he had the secret of perpetual youth but he didn't. No one did. The age was there. The skin, although unlined, had thickened, coarsened, lost its first blush or even its second. The whites of his eyes were not altogether clear. They had just the faintest soiled look, like the whites of hard-boiled eggs handled by someone who had just read the New York *Times*.

Sitting down at his desk, he glanced at the clock. It was nearly two-thirty. Almost time for Loretta. Although he admired Loretta, he wasn't at all looking forward to his meeting with her. Ever since he had become entangled with Trina, he felt ill-at-ease with people from the Center. The entanglement was confusing him more and more. He was fond of Trina, but he wasn't sure he understood her. She wasn't the sort of person he would have met if it hadn't been for the Center. They never really seemed in synch; he never really knew what was on her mind. When she was hungry he wasn't. When he was tired she wasn't. Often, when he said something, she stared at him as if she couldn't make out his words. Even the sex . . . it wasn't what it had been. He had come to feel that her sexual needs were abnormal, symptomatic of emotional problems that he had always, on some level, sensed she had but that now, knowing her as he did, he knew to be manifold. He knew that some very bad things had happened in her past. He knew also that she was working toward telling him what they were. What she didn't know—what he hadn't yet told her—was that he didn't want to know all of it.

The biggest problem he had with Trina was that she still felt like a stranger to him. He glanced at the picture on his desk. It was an eight-by-ten of him and Louise and the boys on vacation in Rhode Island. His mother had a home there; he could go whenever he wanted, with enough notice that is. He had never removed that picture from his desk—why should he? Through it all—in the beginning and in the middle, if in fact they were now in the middle, and even, when and if it came, at the end—he wouldn't cut Louise out of the picture. There were moments of rancor and moments of bitterness but there was no *real* rancor, no *real* bitterness. Most men and women, he was convinced, had a person in their life who was the matrix of their personal growth and history. Louise was undeniably that person in his life. He had given her the best years of his life, the time-honored plaint went, but it was true—the best years. Perhaps what diluted his bitterness was the knowledge that he, in turn, had been given hers as well.

He sat a moment and then, at precisely two-thirty, there was a knock at the door and Bill's secretary admitted Loretta. He was surprised by her punctuality and also by her outfit, which was plum-colored and tailored and very professional-looking. She always struck him as one of those large women with long hair preordained to wear caftans, muumuus, and other forms of tents, but today she was in that good wool suit, with heels, and her hair pulled back.

"Loretta," he said, extending his hand, "this is a treat."

"Bill," she replied, gripping his hand in a firm shake, "the pleasure is mine."

They sat down. He offered her coffee or tea; she took tea. "So," he said, "here you are."

"So," she replied, with a smile, "here I am." She crossed her legs. "First let me say, Bill, that I haven't come to the Pendleton Foundation for a handout," she began, jumping right in. "I know that with you on the board of the Center that would be a conflict of interest. But I have come to feel that the Center is doing something very special, not just with the mainstreaming but generally speaking."

He pressed his fingertips together and leaned back in his chair.

"Let me make myself clear," she said. "Ten years ago I came to realize that I was living in a city of working couples and that there would be a growing need for day care of the highest order. I set out to meet that need, Bill, and I think I have. Not that I found an idea whose time had come and yelled Eureka! and got rich—hardly; you know what I make—but I did build up something from scratch and I'm proud of it. I think it's a great prototype and I think we deserve money or grants or whatever to help make it work even better."

She sat back in her chair. It was quite a speech, thought Bill, as he smiled at her. "I couldn't agree with you more, Loretta. Now what we have to work out is a plan to help you get it."

"Why shouldn't I get it?" she demanded. "Look at all those things that get funded—the ones that Proxmire gives awards to. Studying musical ability in chinchillas and all that crap."

"That's science, Loretta," Bill pointed out, amused. "What you have to do is convince people that day care really matters."

She let out a snort. "No easy task. People still think of day care as some kind of glorified babysitting."

She was an interesting woman, a compelling woman. She had that quality that one associated with certain women of distinction—Margaret Sanger, Sister

Kenny, the suffragists. A quality of mission. So much so that the mission over-shadowed the life, which was, in fact, a life full of mistakes, big and little messes, but that didn't matter. Her life had a largeness to it, which was exactly what his life did not have, Bill reflected soberly.

"I've spent all these years just trying to keep things going," she said. "All the administrative problems, the managerial headaches—you know what that is—but now I have the feeling that the thing's bigger than I am. I want money to write up a study on it. I want to tell people what the experience of shared child-rearing could mean to this society."

"That sounds fine, Loretta," said Bill sincerely. "Really splendid. But if we want to make a go of it we'll have to get down to work and put our heads together."

She grinned. "That's the best invitation I've had in ages."

They spent another half-hour or so with Bill giving her names, which she wrote down in a precise hand in a lined notebook. Then, when the time ran out, he walked her to the elevator.

"Hey," she said. "This job you have—giving away money—it isn't bad work, is it?"

"It's not as easy as it looks," he said. "There are always a lot of hands grabbing at you."

They were silent then, as they waited for the elevator. He wondered why it always took so long. Then he saw her looking at him. "Everything under control with the kids and all?" she asked.

"I think so," he said. "Thank you for asking."

"It's hard on children," she said, putting on her sunglasses.

"It is."

"But they're such good ones, those two."

"They are, aren't they?"

"Sometimes though, the good ones can be too good," she said. "And then there are problems."

There was a moment before he spoke. "I'd like to talk to you about that some-time," he said.

"Anytime. Just come by."

The elevator door opened.

"Thanks so much, Bill," she said.

He watched as she got on and as the elevator door closed. Then he walked back to his desk. He felt very tired. What was she suggesting? That the children were having problems? Of course they were having problems. Everyone had problems.

Just then the phone rang. He wasn't in the mood to talk; he wished the phone would disappear. He let it ring twice and then he picked up; Dorothy, his secre-tary, got annoyed if he didn't answer his own phone when he was around. "Hello?" he managed.

"Hi. It's me."

Me.

"Bill?"

"Hi."

"Are you OK?" Trina asked. "You sound funny."

"Do I?" he said.

"Listen, I've only got a minute but I wanted to see about tonight."

Tonight. He had forgotten tonight. He didn't know what tonight was. "Tonight?" he said.

There was silence on the other end and then she spoke. "Yes. Tonight," she replied. "The time. The place."

He thought for a second. "Victor's?"

"Uh-uh. I used to wait tables there."

He looked out the window. He could see a woman in the office building across from him drying her hair with a blow-dryer.

"Chinese?" she suggested.

"OK."

They made a time and they made a place.

"Well then," she said, sounding far away, "I'll see you later."

"Yes," he murmured, looking from the woman drying her hair to the woman in the picture on his desk.

She waited in front of the Happy Plum. She wondered about the name. These days they gave Chinese restaurants real weird names. In the old days they just used to call them Wong's or Lee's or whatever, but now they had to get fancy.

At 7:20, twenty minutes late, he came rushing into view. His coat was open and flying behind him. He must have expected her to be angry but she wasn't.

"It's OK," she said as he apologized.

"I couldn't get away. I got a couple of calls and—"

"It's OK."

They looked at each other. "You should have gone in, gotten a drink . . ."

"I don't drink."

"Some tea or something."

"I wanted the air," she explained.

She took his arm and they went inside. The maître d' acted like he knew Bill, but of course he didn't. They were seated next to the fish tank, which had some kind of golden catfish swimming in it.

"Close your eyes and make believe you're at the Aquarium," he cracked.

She closed her eyes.

"OK," he said. "What do you see?"

"Walruses," she replied. "Making love."

"On that note . . ."

She laughed. She felt good. "I want a lot of food," she said.

"Ah. A woman of appetites."

"Hot stuff. Steamed dumplings. Lots of garlic."

"*Lots* of garlic?" he said, giving her one of those wry, over-the-spectacles look, except he didn't wear spectacles.

"OK. Skip the garlic."

They ordered more food than they probably needed but she didn't care. She was so hungry. He didn't seem to be. He ordered a Scotch and sipped it slowly. She asked him about Loretta's visit and he told her. She had the funny feeling when he was telling her that he didn't really want to tell her. Sometimes she felt he didn't like to talk to her very much.

"How was Denny's show?" she asked, after a silence. They were eating cold sesame noodles, not so easy with chopsticks, and she kept a napkin in her fist, ready to wipe away the drips.

"Very sweet," he said. "'A musical based on folk tales of the American Negro.'" He laughed a little and she wasn't sure why, but she smiled. "Denny was fine. He forgot his lines, but redeemed himself with his singing."

She watched him use the chopsticks. He was good at it. "Was your wife there?"

He looked up. He seemed surprised by the question. "Yes," he said. "It was history in the making. Louise Strong Dowell, in person at one of these things."

"Did she like it?" Trina asked.

"Did she like it," Bill repeated. "It's hard to tell. She's either making a genuine effort or else she's putting on a very good show. Or maybe it's a little bit of both. Whatever it is, I think she's managing to convince the boys, and I suppose that's good."

"You do?"

"Oh yes. They *should* get something from Louise—I think they deserve that much, don't you?"

They ate in silence for the next few minutes. She looked above his head at the catfish in the garishly lit tank, the tilted castle, the chest of buried treasure.

"Still," he said, "she *was* there. I think, in her own way, she's trying. I just wonder how the boys will do when she fails. Of course," he said, with a tone that was almost admiration, "she's not the kind of woman who generally fails at what she undertakes."

The catfish pressed up against the glass and almost seemed to grin at her. "Petey was in bad shape today," she said, bluntly, for effect.

He held his chopsticks aloft in the air, like batons or maybe wands. "What do you mean?"

He got this little worried look on his face sometimes that made her want to hurt him. When she felt that feeling coming on, she took a deep breath. In, out. But the air was close—the odor of cooking grease. "We were all doing clay," she told him. "Plasticine, actually," she added, although she supposed that didn't matter. "Anyway, Olivier and David started acting up and waving around these snakes they had made and I had to kind of get tough with them and then all of a sudden Petey, who'd been so quiet and working so nicely, like he always does, started throwing his clay on the ground and stamping on it and when I asked him what happened he just kept apologizing. It was funny," she concluded.

There was a long moment of silence. She was able to hear the high-pitched whines and growls of Chinese being spoken in the kitchen. He stared at her and she began to feel hot. Maybe it was the food, she thought—the MSG.

"That's it?" he said.

"What?"

"The whole story?"

She looked away from the catfish and shrugged. "Yeah."

"You know, you don't always use the right words," he said, sounding angry or far away or different.

She acted like she didn't know what he meant. "What do you mean?" she said.

"You say 'funny.' It was funny, you say. When what you mean is that it was 'strange' or 'peculiar' or 'alarming' or 'destructive' or 'symptomatic.' But you say 'funny.' You ought to start using the right words."

She acted like she couldn't understand what he was saying. "I'm sorry," she murmured, with another little shrug, and he nodded, bringing the chopsticks artfully to his lips.

As they walked back to her place, she tried to think of ways that would make him feel better or happier. He fell into a mood after she told him about Petey. He wasn't one of those people who fell into moods a lot, but when he did they were deep and she wasn't sure if she could get him out of it.

As they passed a phone booth, he stopped and said he wanted to call the kids to say good night. For a moment, she watched him as he stood there, but then she looked away, not wanting to intrude on his privacy.

A man who looked as peddlers must have looked a century ago—Italian, dark heavy mustache, crumpled fedora—was selling toys right beside her. One of the toys was a small rubber octopus you threw against glass. He demonstrated it for her against the window of the Chemical Bank. With some kind of built-in sticki-ness, the octopus managed to hold on to the glass and slowly, almost as if alive, slithered down the sheer wall. She thought it was cute and she bought two of them for more money than they were worth.

"Everything OK?" she asked when he got off the phone.

"Fine," he replied and nothing more.

When they got back to her apartment, she put on some Bach—she had gone out and bought it, so she would have it for him—and made tea for them and some nice English cookies she had found in the supermarket. She was trying to make things nice, the way he liked it.

They sat next to each other on the sofa. After a while, she put her hand on the back of his neck and began to rub him there. He didn't say anything at first, and she rubbed harder. She had strong hands.

"You're tense," she said.

"Who? Me?"

"Yes, you are. Come on. Let me give you a massage."

He shook his head. "I've never liked them. I'm very ticklish. I always start laughing . . ."

"You can laugh during one of my massages—it's OK. I won't take it person-ally."

She finally convinced him. He took off his shirt and his pants and she went to get some massage oil from her medicine cabinet. It smelled mostly of rosemary.

"Now just relax," she said.

She was very good at it. She had lived in Woodstock in the days when massage was right up there with bread and shelter on people's minds.

"That was good," he said finally.

"I'm glad you liked it."

"Where'd you learn to do that?"

"From my swami."

"He taught you well."

"I'm a good learner."

They looked at each other and she lay down beside him. "God, I'm tired," he said, but she didn't listen to him. She took his hands and placed them on her breasts. Then, in a little voice, she told him what to do. And, after a moment's hesitation, he did as he was told. She wondered, as she drifted off to sleep, if he would always do as he was told.

When she awoke, from that fast deep sleep that comes, she saw him staring at her.

"What's the matter?" she asked.

He didn't say anything. Just shrugged a little. He seemed sad. Maybe it was just that sadness that comes afterward, but whatever it was she hated to see him like this.

"Look," she said, springing up, moving across the room to get her bag, glad to be naked.

"What?" he asked.

She reached into her bag and pulled out the two rubber octopuses. "Mert and Gert," she said, grinning as she opened her fist to present her surprise to him.

One was red and the other royal blue. He grinned a little too. "Cute," he said. "Very cute. What do they do?"

"Just watch," she replied. There was a long mirror on the inside of her closet door and she threw them against the mirror. She watched Bill as he watched them tiptoe down.

"What will they think of next?" he said.

"You try."

He threw them against the mirror. They did just as well this time, although now you could see that they left a sticky residue on the glass that could be hard to clean off.

"Very cute," he repeated. "Mert and Gert?"

"Ozzie and Harriet." She grinned.

"Dwight and Mamie."

"Ron and Nancy," she giggled, feeling a full-blown case of the giggles coming on.

They continued to watch the careful downward progress but then, all of a sudden, the red one moved faster than the blue one and put its sticky arms all over the blue one and pulled it off the glass and they fell together to the floor in a heap.

"Oh well," she shrugged, still giggling.

"Bill and Trina," he said quietly, not looking at her.

She giggled again but then she stopped. It was time for him to go, he said, as he rose and went after his clothes.

18

THE AMAZING THING was that Darcy looked happy. Charles hadn't seen her looking happy for so long now. Not that she complained or made things difficult for anybody. She wouldn't do that. It wasn't for her to do that. Her job was to help others. That's what kept her going. She was there for the children—that was her life.

But she looked happy now, didn't she? As she sat there, one pew away from him, on the day of her sister's salvation and deliverance, her face was almost transformed. All in yellow, with a white straw hat, she turned to smile at him.

"She looks good, doesn't she?" Trina whispered.

"Yes," said Charles, glad to see her smile but saddened by the state of her teeth.

It was a poor Pentecostal church—the Chapel of Salvation and Deliverance, on 121st Street—and there weren't enough prayer books to go around so he and Trina shared one. Trina's fingers, at the dark corner of the Bible, were short and bitten, he noticed.

"I have accepted Jesus Christ and committed my life to Him," intoned the reverend, a portly black man with a rolling wave of light gray hair and a voice that could rumble or quiver at will. "I have let my sinner's life burn out like ash."

Amen, brother. Charles saw Darcy nodding, her back and neck thick and powerful-looking.

"No sin that I have committed is too great for His understanding," shouted the reverend. "His compassion would cover the oceans like a lid and fill up the chasms and the gorges."

And another round of amens. Out of the corner of his eye he could see Loretta, sitting beside Darcy, the word formed on her lips. Loretta was a believer. The way she told it, she had rediscovered the faith ten years ago when her mother developed myasthenia gravis. Today they could do more for it but, at the time, it drove Loretta into religion.

"It is through our tribulations that we must enter into the kingdom of God," cried the reverend, whose name was Salt and who could have been thirty or sixty, he had that kind of smooth fat face.

Charles looked back at Darcy. She was holding Sybila's hand. Sybila was dressed nicely too. She was wearing a light wool lavender coat, the kind that you saw on little black girls at Easter. Why she was wearing a coat in June was another question altogether, but Darcy had gone to town, doing up her sister's hair in tight braids, putting her into a decent pair of shoes, buying her a carnation corsage. It must have taken all Darcy's money.

—I can't believe she's back. She been wanderin' the streets. Can you imagine? With the filth out there? Then there she is—at the door—and I think I seen a ghost. But it ain't a ghost. It's her. She got tears streamin' down her cheeks and she says, Everythin' I done is wrong and I says to myself, Almighty God just don't let her done somethin' terrible and I says, What you done? And she says, I didn't love Him but now I do.

And that's why they were here today, because Sybila had found Him and now was going to be born again. She sat there, her face composed. It was a handsome face when it was in repose. Heavy brows and high cheekbones. Charles wished her better luck this time around.

"And Paul said to the Philippians, 'I look upon everything as loss compared with the overwhelming gain of knowing Christ Jesus my Lord. For His sake I did in fact suffer the loss of everything, but I considered it mere garbage compared with being able to win Christ."

Mere garbage? Had Paul really said that? Charles didn't know—he couldn't say.

He really knew very little. It had been so long since he had been in a church. Probably the last time was his sister's wedding and that was sixteen, seventeen years ago. A big church wedding in the Good Shepherd Cathedral, Winnetka, Illinois. He was twenty-one, twenty-two years old. Sometimes he wished he had a picture of himself from that time. He remembered feeling very handsome. It was a formal wedding, in the morning. The men wore cutaways. His hair was very long then—that was the style of the day—and he didn't always keep it as clean as he should have, but that morning he had washed it and it was thick and shiny and reddish-brown, like a fox's pelt, and he had a beard then, neatly trimmed for the occasion, and he could remember looking in the mirror and thinking: Hell, man. Don't you look good?

"For pride, brothers and sisters, is a spiritual cancer that will gnaw away at our skins and then at our muscle and then at our bones until we take the only medicine that will stave off the pain and the misery . . ."

And the wedding was everything a wedding should be. His parents were happy that day, not knowing that in time their son would ruin everything, not knowing that each of them would die in such bad pain before their rightful time. They had filled the church with stephanotis. There was always enough money to do things like that. His father was one of the most successful insurance brokers on the North Shore. And his mother's family, who had been in the bottling business, had done well by them too.

That day his sister was marrying Lieutenant Brian Beltran of the United States Navy. He was a communications specialist who would one day work for Panasonic. There were lots of young men in uniform, which didn't sit well with Charles, just then developing his political conscience at the University of Chicago, but there were, as well, lots of beautiful girls. There was a girl there—his sister's classmate from Lake Forest College—half-Chinese and what was her name? Something immensely pretty. A flower name, he seemed to recall. Poppy or Holly or Ivy—something like that. And they made eyes at each other all day long and by the time there was dancing he was carrying around a hard one and she made a beeline for him and they danced close and slow together. It was the summer, he remembered, that "Close to You" had just come out and all the bands were picking up on it as the perfect wedding song and everyone wanted to hear it again and again and he danced again and again with that girl with the pretty name and the next day he took her to the beach even though it was foggy or maybe because it was foggy, so foggy you couldn't see two feet in front of your nose, and they did it under a towel.

"Charles."

He looked up. Everyone was standing and singing.

> *O sinner man, how can it be?*
> *Wheel in the middle of the wheel.*
> *If you don't serve God, you can't serve me,*
> *Wheel in the middle of the wheel.*

As he stood, he could hear Darcy's voice sailing above everyone else's. She was singing like a mighty angel today. He wished he were listening to her somewhere else; he didn't want to be in a church today. He wasn't sure why. It wasn't as if he had bad associations with church. Just the opposite—as a boy, he had always liked church. He liked the smells. He liked the walk home. He liked Sunday dinner. The Easter ham. Just a few months ago, when he made Easter eggs with the kids, he felt that same pang. The tradition of it—the remembrance of when he had been part of a tradition—it gave him this pain. This pain in his heart.

> *Well, don't you know it's praying time*
> *Wheel in the middle of the wheel;*
> *Lay down your way and go to God,*
> *Wheel in the middle of the wheel.*

He listened very carefully and then started to sing. He had a good voice: he had sung in the boys' choir. It was one thing to sing, he told himself, but he wouldn't take Communion. He would excuse himself and wait out on the street. Every man had to do what he thought was right. He wondered if Julie had ever had Hildy baptized. He must remember to ask her, he thought, as the singing filled up his head.

There must have been enough food for twenty. Tuna salad and cottage-cheese salad and three-bean salad and potato salad and deviled eggs and deviled ham and banana bread and a towering angel-food cake with coconut icing.

"I didn't do a thing," said Loretta, hands held up in protest. "Darcy did all the cooking. I just loaned out the space."

Charles stood at the table, plate in hand, and tried to decide.

"Now you better eat," cried Darcy, coming up behind him. "Did you ever see such a bag of bones?" She pinched Charles's side—or tried to. There was nothing to pinch. He was as skinny now as he had been as a boy. "I swear," said Darcy. "holdin' on to you would be like holdin' on to a lead pipe."

She exploded with laughter, shaking all over, head to foot. Jelly belly, thought Charles, looking up to see Loretta staring at him with a faint smile. He smiled back—a little—and turned his attention to the food, helping himself to some of everything. The fact was he liked to eat, even if he never put on weight.

"I'm just so proud of my sister!" Darcy cried, out of nowhere, giving Sybila a hug, which Sybila received but did not return. "Loretta, ain't you proud of her?" Darcy demanded.

Charles looked to Loretta. No matter what, Loretta would not allow Darcy's sister back into the Center and that was how it should be. She had abused a child and there were no second chances after that. These days, with all the day-care scandals, you couldn't play it too safe.

"I think it's just terrific," Loretta said, throwing an arm around Darcy. "And I think you're terrific."

They gave each other a big kiss, a big hug. And when you were hugged by Darcy, you knew it. As they broke away, Darcy, shaky from all the emotion, staggered backward and knocked into the edge of the table. A coffeepot was sitting there and Charles reached out to try to keep it from spilling but he wasn't quick enough. The coffeepot tipped over onto him, soaking his pants and splattering painfully onto his left forearm.

"Oh Lord!" Darcy started to scream. "Oh Lord!"

The burning wet fabric was scalding him. He dropped his pants right there. Luckily he had done a laundry last night and had on clean underwear. "Sorry," he murmured.

Sybila moved gravely from the room but Loretta and Darcy and Trina stood there watching him. He had never felt more exposed in his life, not even when he used to walk nude through the women's dorm at the University of Wisconsin.

"Come on," said Trina, taking him by the elbow. "We're going to put some cold water on it."

"Oh, Charles," Darcy moaned, wringing her hands. "Let me put some butter on it."

"No," said Loretta. "No butter. It's not done that way anymore. Trina's right."

"Oh Lord," Darcy cried. "Just when you think everything's going good . . ."

He went with Trina to the bathroom. It was a great big bathroom, all done in yellow and turquoise tile. There was a glass sliding door to the tub, etched with a scallop-shell design. Loretta and her husband had started to put money into the place when he was raking it in as a stockbroker during the go-go years. But then it all fell apart—the market, the marriage—and now Loretta was sitting on this jumbo two-bedroom, waiting for the building to go co-op so she could borrow the money from a rich aunt in Hartford and buy herself a piece of the rock.

"It's really red," said Trina, examining the arm, which Charles held under the icy spray.

"Yeah. But it doesn't hurt."

"Yet."

"Poor Darcy. It's going to ruin her day."

"It sort of had to happen, didn't it?" said Trina, after a moment.

"What do you mean?"

She shrugged. "How are your legs?" she asked.

"OK. Once I got the pants off."

"I thought Sybila was going to have kittens," Trina said, bursting into giggles.

"Stop."

"No, really. And Darcy and Loretta?—free show." She looked up at him. The giggles stopped and she smiled. "You've got nice legs."

He looked at her. She seemed so small sitting there. "Thanks."

"I've been waiting for the warm weather to see you in shorts but here we are—sneak preview." She put the cold washcloth to his red kneecap. "I bet you used to run track, huh?"

He smiled, letting the shower cool his red-hot skin.

"Did you?"

"Hurdles," he admitted.

"You're kidding."

"Why would I be kidding?"

She shook her head. "It's just that I love hurdles. I love to watch it. I can never figure out how it's done."

"What do you mean?"

"You know, like how you can jump when you're running like that . . ."

"It's not hard. Sort of like walking and chewing gum."

"Hey, you're teasing me. What I'm talking about is the coordination. It's a beautiful thing to watch."

"I was always a fast kid," he said. "You know the scene in every lousy movie about some kid who grows up to become a great man and races the Union Pacific across the wheatfields? I was that kid. Except it was a commuter train and subdivided land and I didn't grow up to become a great man."

"Who says you didn't?" she shot right back.

He stared at her. Over the pelting sounds of the shower he could hear the sounds of Darcy's remorse. *Just when you think everything's going good . . .*

"What are you going to wear home?" she asked.

He shrugged. "A bathrobe?"

"Oh, now. Wouldn't that be a pretty sight? Your sexy legs sticking out of one of Loretta's bathrobes."

He took his arm out of the spray. "I think I'm cured."

"Let me see."

She examined his arm in a professional manner. "You keep it under," she instructed. "It's going to get all blistery if you don't."

"You have a degree in emergency medicine maybe?"

"When I was a kid, I only wanted to become a nurse," she said, putting the washcloth to the other knee. "I devoured those nurse stories. Cherry Ames was my alter ego."

"So what happened to your adolescent aspirations?"

"I got a job as a candy-striper at Our Lady of Perpetual Care Hospital in Saugerties. There was this bitch nun who had it in for me from day one and got me off the path for good."

"A bitch nun?" he asked, wry again. She struck him in a funny way, almost making him laugh.

"Yeah," she said. "Somehow she couldn't reconcile Christ-killer with candy-striper. So I decided instead to become an actress."

There was a silence and then he took his arms out of the spray. "I really think I'm OK now."

"OK," she agreed, staring at his long thin arms. "You're one of those what-do-you-call-its, aren't you?" she said.

Lapsed Christians? Political fugitives? He didn't know what she meant and he didn't want to guess. "Yeah. I'm one of those what-do-you-call-its."

"I mean those people who never put on weight. A body type," she said, flushing slightly.

"Oh. You mean an ectomorph."

She nodded.

"Yeah. I guess I am."

"I'm the opposite. What's that?"

"An endormorph."

"Yeah. That's me."

"No, you're not," he said, drying his arms. "You're a mesomorph. In the middle. It's the best thing to be."

She gave him a crooked little smile. "Aw. You're just saying that."

"I think we'd better go back to the party," he suggested.

She sat there for a moment. "Before anyone gets suspicious, huh?"

"Yeah," he said, after a moment. "Before anyone gets suspicious."

*   *   *

Darcy made a memory book for the occasion. Everyone had to write something in it.

"For Sybila," Charles wrote, with an uneasy feeling as he watched the woman rocking in the rocking chair, broodingly silent. "We are as much as we see. Faith is sight and knowledge. The hands only serve the eyes."

He signed his name. If nothing else, he knew his Thoreau. You didn't go through a life like his and not know your Thoreau.

"Congratulations," he said to Sybila as he reached out to shake her hand. By now he had on a pair of Loretta's gym shorts so it was all right.

"You going?" asked Darcy.

"Yep."

"Take some food."

"No, no. I'm stuffed."

"For later."

"Her mother was an Ethiopian Jew," cracked Loretta through the haze of smoke that surrounded her whenever she was away from the children.

"On that note," he said, with a wave.

"'Bye, Charles," Trina called.

"Good-bye, everyone."

Down on the street, he was relieved to find it warm enough for shorts. He looked at his watch. Four o'clock. He promised Julie he would be over by four-thirty. She needed his help putting up some shelves. He was glad to help her, to show off the fact that he was good with his tools, good with his hands.

He walked slowly up West End Avenue. In a D'Agostino shopping bag he carried his soiled pants. He felt a little funny because he was wearing workboots instead of sneakers with the shorts and it looked strange and clunky. Although he never much cared about clothes, lately he had been trying to dress a little better when he was with Julie, keeping his shirts clean and ironed and his shoes shined. She noticed things like that. She herself was immaculately groomed.

As he walked, he was struck by how warm it was. On the one hand that made him feel good—the body responds involuntarily to the warmth—but, on the other hand, it made him feel less than good. The change of seasons was difficult for him now. Time was passing, and he wasn't sure how to get a hold of it. Soon it would be summer. That meant taking the children, each day, to the park. That meant the vast heat of a New York July and the children irritable at naptime and he without air-conditioning, his head next to the cheap little fan bought at Good Will, and then August, with the crazies on the street, and the garbage turning putrescent in a matter of hours, and the Center closed for two weeks and his having to make a few extra bucks as a counselor at a summer camp in Riverdale, bone-tired and facing, in the relentless heat of late summer, the wreckage that he, the Golden Boy from the Gold Coast, had made of his life.

But this was crazy. Mindless self-pity. Inexcusable whining. Life was a matter of decisions, good ones and bad ones. He had made a decision and the decision had become history.

The time?

September 1969.

The place?

Milwaukee, Wisconsin.
The situation?
Nixon's saturation bombing of Southeast Asia.
And so was set the stage for his contribution to history, Charles thought, walking now with less speed up the avenue. He couldn't just stand by and watch, could he? And so he had made his decision. All through those broiling late-summer weeks he planned an action with Philip Coulter, an explosives expert who had left behind a trail of craters in Kansas City, Chicago, St. Louis. "The Manassas Mauler," the papers called him and they called him that too, having that summer rejected everything of the zeitgeist but sports and Breyer's ice cream. Coulter liked Big Ben clocks. He bought them cheap at Montgomery Ward's and combined them with blasting caps and nitro. On September 22, 1969, Charles placed one in an empty paint can and, dressed in paint-spattered Sweet-Orrs, carried the bomb into the third-floor men's room of the Selective Service headquarters, removed the bomb from the paint can, and installed it in the paper-towel dispenser. The third-floor men's room was, generally, underfrequented and he was in and out of the building in six minutes flat.

There was no doubt about it: Coulter made a damned good bomb. It was scheduled to go off at ten-thirty that night and it did. Nothing wrong with that bomb. Only thing wrong was their timing. According to their information, the janitor was supposed to be on the second floor at ten-thirty. But the janitor, it later came out, had an asthmatic wife whom he had taken to the emergency room that afternoon and so he was behind schedule.

Curtis "Sonny" Walker. Moved up from Memphis in 1949. Seven children. An asthmatic wife. Twelve years in his current job. The bomb had blown up in his face. The bomb had blown up in their faces. Suddenly they were murderers and, what's more, suddenly they were stupid murderers.

He had made a mistake—a very terrible mistake—and he couldn't afford to make any others. What he had done could not be undone. The question was what should he do? He was faced with the most difficult decisions of his life. He was twenty-two years old. He had to weigh his options. How could he serve better? In prison, maintaining the struggle from behind bars, or underground, with a free-dom of sorts? He opted to go underground, assuring himself that he had made the decision rather than the decision having been made for him.

Since then—for what, by now, represented most of his adult life—he had lived underground. Subterranean. His vision dying. Living by a sense of smell. He had let most of his contacts die out. What he had created for himself was not so much a solitary life, but a life in solitary. He was responsible for the death of an innocent man, a crime for which he had to pay dearly, and all these years he had inflicted a punishment on himself that he tried, at every juncture, to make as severe as possible. Now, after all these years, dared he to think that perhaps he had repaid some of his debt?

—Only the interest, buddy. Only the interest.

He took a deep breath and jogged the one block west to Riverside. It was one of the few places in New York City that he genuinely liked. It was quiet here and for one who had grown up in quiet, verdant surroundings, the absence of loud noises was a premium and a blessing. There was a kind of splendor to where Julie lived.

The river flowed past all her windows, sparkling on sunny days, and with the windows open in the warm weather, you could almost hear river noises. There were times, he thought, when he was liking her apartment far too much. There were times when he found himself liking her too much. Or loving her too much. He wasn't sure how much he actually liked her. Suddenly his feet felt heavy in the workboots and he stopped jogging. He walked the rest of the way to her building.

He took the elevator to the fifteenth floor and rang the doorbell. There was no response and he rang it again and then again. Finally she opened up and stood there, in a long man's shirt, white, and paint-spattered jeans and pink Reeboks. She looked like an ad for whatever an at-home successful young woman uses or thinks about: bran cereal or Scotchguard or IRAs.

They kissed hello. Not a passionate kiss, Charles noted, but then Julie could be stingy.

"Look at you," she said, stepping back.

"It's warm out," he said. "Have you been out?"

"Uh-uh. I don't go out on Sundays. Strictly coffee, croissants, and the Sunday paper."

He stepped further into the apartment. The river, past the open windows, was sparkling today. "Hildy!" he called.

"She's out," said Julie.

"Where?"

"Heller Norman took the kids over to a fair. Cathedral of St. John the Divine."

He poured some coffee from the thermos sitting on a little marble-topped ice-cream table. "Any more croissants?"

"All gone," she said. "Sorry."

They looked at each other for a minute. Then she began to do some kind of balletic exercise, her long legs gracefully extended and then raised to hip level.

"What are you doing?" he asked.

"Exercise."

He nodded.

"I was in the middle when you came in."

"Go ahead," he said, sipping the coffee as he toured around the living room. He noticed on the bookshelves a photograph he'd never noticed before. A woman and a girl. He looked at it very carefully.

She exercised for a long while, maybe twenty minutes. She usually exercised twice a day, once at home and once at the gym. She was thinking about buying an expensive piece of home gym apparatus. When she was done, her hair was tousled. She took a rubber band and made it into a ponytail.

"Now you really look like a dancer," he said. "Were you ever?"

"No."

He pointed to the photograph. "Who's this?" he asked.

"Me and my mother," she said, through some ancillary stretching exercises.

"Where was it taken?" he asked.

"Riverhead," she groaned.

"Long Island?"

"Yes."

"That's way out, isn't it?"

"Yes."

It was like pulling teeth. "Is that where you were born?"

She stopped the stretching and sighed; she shook her head and shoulders a little. "We lived there after my father died."

"How old were you when he died?"

"Eight."

He looked at the photo; the girl was long and stringy, like Hildy, and the woman had a kind look. "What's your mother's name?"

"Hildegard," she said, after a moment. "Hildy's named for her. She was German." She extended a long leg and caressed it. "A German war bride. After my father died, we left Boston and moved to Riverhead, where she had a cousin. She gave facials and massages in people's homes." She put her leg down and stared at him. "Will you help me with the shelves now? You promised."

Subject closed, he thought. "Sure," he said. "I always keep my promises."

She showed him the shelves. They were those plastic-coated wire ones, cut to order. "I'm redoing my closet."

"Why don't you just get rid of some clothes?" he asked but she didn't answer him.

They went into the bedroom. Her bed—a fine old four-poster she had found up in Maine, worth a fortune, usually covered with a lace duvet—was piled high with all her clothes. He wondered where they would make love today.

"A child could do this," he ragged her, as he got together everything he needed, the screwdriver and the level and the screws. "I'm surprised you're not handy."

"Why are you surprised?" she asked.

"I don't know. You're so capable at most things."

"The hell I am." She sat back and watched him. "I learned long ago that the key to success—at least, *my* success—was concentration. I'm lousy when it comes to diversifying."

"I don't know. Careerist, mother, lover . . ." He gave her a roguish smile. "Doesn't sound too bad to me."

She ignored the joke. He watched her long fingers work at freeing the screws and anchors from their little cellophane pouches.

It wouldn't take very long to put up the shelf, he thought. As he worked, he listened to WQXR. They were having an all-Schubert program.

"Shall I make some coffee?"

"I don't care."

"So why are you wearing such an odd outfit, may I ask?" she asked, after some silence.

There was something tight in her voice; it troubled him. "It's a long story."

"That's all right. I've got all afternoon."

"Darcy was giving a lunch," he said, grunting a little as he screwed in the screws. "For her sister. Today Sybila was born again. She was baptized in the Chapel of Salvation and Deliverance. I went. So did Trina and Loretta. And then Darcy brought food to Loretta's."

"Is that why you're dressed that way? Was it a mass baptism?"

"Some coffee spilled on me. I took off my pants and Loretta lent me these."

She laughed. "You've got it in the shoulders and Loretta's got it in the hips. It's called nature."

He stared at her. She was being a bitch today. He had seen flashes of it before but he told himself not to be troubled by it. She was a busy woman under a lot of pressure; she didn't always mean what she said. "You're right," he said. "Loretta's got hips. Big hips but nice hips."

"Sounds like you know firsthand," she said, hugging her legs.

He shrugged and set the next screw in place. "What got you going on these closets?"

"Oh, don't change the subject," she said playfully but not too playfully. "You're a slippery character, you know that? Every time I'm about to find out something about you, you change the subject."

"That could be kind of irritating," he acknowledged mildly, making a show of concentrating on the third screw.

"OK. Let's have it. Did you screw Loretta or not?"

He touched the point of the screwdriver against his palm. In prison they sharpened these and used them as knives. "Whether I did or not has nothing to do with anyone but me," he said quietly.

Her lips arched down into a frown and she gave him a hard look. "Do you know there are all kinds of stories circulating about you?"

"Is that so?" he said, sounding bored, or trying to sound bored.

"Yeah. That's so. Everyone has a different theory about the elusive Charles. Some people think he used to be a junkie. Some people speculate that he's a fugitive. One of those sixties radicals who went underground and never came up."

Oh, one of *those* sixties radicals. Was she describing some kind of freak, some nearly extinct species for which she had no more compassion or regard than your average turn-of-the-century milliner had for the passenger pigeon? He gripped the screwdriver with excessive force. "Don't believe everything you hear," he said, looking away from her.

"I'm not hearing anything," she snapped. "At least not from you."

He stopped screwing and emerged from the closet. "You want to know all about me," he said. "But I don't think you're going to like what you hear—that's the problem."

"Try me."

"OK. I'll try you," he said, standing over her now, forcing himself to sound calm. "I'm from Winnetka, Illinois. From 1965 to 1968 I attended the University of Chicago. When I started I was your typical ambitious, politically aware young man of the sixties. Charles Tucker was my name; political science was my game. I planned on going to law school. Had my heart set on the ACLU. I was going to change the system from within."

She grinned a little.

"What's so funny?" he asked, pouncing on her.

"Nothing."

"You grinned."

"I don't know," she said. "It was such a long time ago, that kind of thinking."

"Only yesterday," he said, holding tight to the screwdriver. "Then came the sixty-eight convention. You remember that, don't you?"

"Yes," she said, frowning more deeply so that suddenly there were two sharp creases above the bridge of her nose. "I remember that."

"You weren't there, were you? I don't remember your face."

"No, I wasn't there."

"Watching it on TV?"

"Yes," she returned, tight-lipped.

"Well, I was one of those who got their brains scrambled on a nightstick. You remember—it's when you got up to adjust the color."

She looked like she was thinking of something to say. Her mouth kind of curled up but she kept it shut and for that he gave her credit. "After that I began to get more and more confused," he continued. "I discovered acid. Did you ever try it?"

"What is this?" she said. "Show-your-old-battle-wounds time?"

"You asked me questions," he said with a self-righteous tone that he used freely despite the fact that most of what he was saying was a lie. "I don't know how many trips I must have taken. It scrambled my brain even more. I wound up in weird places—Omaha, for a year, on a farm; Albuquerque; San Jose. Odd jobs. Shoveling manure. Picking beets. Working in a ward. Somehow I made my way east. It took a long time to come back but the kids helped. And here I am."

She stared at him. "End of story?"

"End of story. I'm sorry to report that I'm just one of your run-of-the-mill sixties casualties. Nothing glamorous."

She looked at him and then looked down at the floor. She hugged her legs again. "I could never understand all that," she said softly. "People throwing it away like that."

"We didn't throw it away, Julie. We lost it."

She looked up at him again. He could tell, from her expression, that she could understand losing things even less. "I suppose it would be belaboring the point to suggest that we are very, very different."

"Don't worry about it," he said. He put down the screwdriver and took her hand in his. "Don't you know we've all got about eight or nine lives stuffed inside of us?"

"Not me," she said, with a kind of harsh pride. "I'm the same person now I've always been."

He sat down next to her. The realization that what she was saying was the truth, the absolute truth, struck him as poignant. He felt sorry for her, and sorry for himself because he was about to lose her and he didn't want to lose anything else. "Let's make love," he said, touching her cheek.

For a moment she said nothing and then she shook her head. "No, Charles. We can't. Hildy will be home any minute," she said. "Heller Norman's dropping her off before five."

He drew back. "I don't understand. We wasted all this time. You should have said something . . ."

She shrugged. "I didn't know it was a fair-trade situation. You put up my shelves, I put out."

"Is that what you call it?"

"Oh, stop. There'll be other times."

As she said it, both of them saw the words hang there malevolently. "We could have put the shelves up while Hildy was here," he said.

"It's so hard to get anything done with her underfoot," she said, standing. "You know that."

Quickly he rose. With a kind of ache—a childish kind, like a child's ache for something sweet—he put his arms around her. He felt her resistance but he undid the buttons of her white man's shirt and then he had her naked breasts in his hands. Small freckled breasts, immensely beautiful. He went at them with a kind of hunger that scared him, but not enough to stop.

"Charles. Please . . ."

He needed it so bad. He felt something gathering in his throat as he sucked at her breasts.

"Stop," she whispered.

He didn't want to hear her. He held on more tightly still.

"Stop!" she cried. "Stop it!"

He froze. He didn't want to look up because he felt he had done something very bad, but then he did look up and saw that her eyes were squeezed shut and her hands were balled up into fists. "I don't want to be confused," she said, mostly to herself. "I don't want to be confused."

She repeated it like a litany. He felt . . . He didn't know what he felt. "So," he said dryly, not knowing how else to sound, "you don't want to be confused."

She stared at him. Then, furiously, she shook her head. "I don't understand you," she said, spacing out the words.

Then the doorbell rang.

"You see?" she said, the question almost tearstained.

Quickly she pulled herself together and he followed her to the door. It was Hildy, with Heller and Martha. She was carrying a purple balloon. "Charles!" she cried.

He knelt down and Hildy ran into his arms.

"How did it go?" Julie asked Heller.

"Great," said Heller. "Hi, Charles."

"Hi, Heller."

"Charles was just helping me put up some shelves," Julie explained.

"Yes," he said, standing up. "Nothing to it. Well, I've got to run."

"No, stay," pleaded Hildy.

Charles turned to look at his favorite little girl.

"Charles has to go now, sweetie," said Julie, gripping her daughter's shoulders.

"Yes," he said, reaching out to touch Hildy's bright red hair and then turning to go.

It wasn't until he was out on the street that he realized he'd left behind the D'Ag Bag with his dirty pants in it, but he didn't have the heart, just then, to go back and get them.

He went straight home and lay down and took a nap, but then, when nighttime came, he didn't think he could stand to be in his apartment any longer. He got up, threw on a pair of pants and a T-shirt. He headed downstairs to make a call. He had always liked the idea of not having a phone.

"Hello?"

He was so glad she was home. "Trina, it's me—Charles."

"Hi."

There was a tiny point of silence. "It got blistery," he said.

"You see? I told you."

He touched his forefinger to the chrome plate where a telephone number had been scratched. "What are you doing?"

"Nothing. Reading."

"What are you reading?"

"The Diary of Anne Frank."

"Can I come by?"

And then another tiny point of silence. "Sure," she said.

He'd never been in her apartment before. He was surprised by it: the spaciousness, the daisies in a mason jar, the cat.

"You live like a regular person," he said, looking around.

"That surprises you?"

"Yeah."

She filled up the kettle. "And you don't?"

"Oh, no," he said. There was a bowl full of sourballs. He started to unwrap one and then wondered what he was doing. "I live in a little rathole."

She put the kettle on the stove. "When I came to New York, you could get a place like this. Anyone could. Even a waitress."

"If it goes co-op, you'll make a pile."

"Shit," she said with a laugh, rolling her eyes. "Listen to us. Talking real estate. Who do we think we're fooling?"

He felt the strangest feeling. It was almost as if he had always known her, and always would know her. The kettle whistled. He felt so close to her now, as though they shared skin or chewed food for each other. "They don't want people like us," he said.

"Who doesn't?" she said, pouring the water.

"The city. They want rich people. Rich people who know where they're going."

"Well, they've got us," she said, with a stubbornness that made him smile. "Tea?"

"Yeah. Real strong."

"But of course. A man's cup," she teased.

The tea smelled like apricots.

"It's apricot tea," she explained.

"It's good."

They sipped the tea.

"I didn't even look at your arm," she said.

He held it out for her to see. There was the tiniest of blisters, small as a seed pearl.

"That doesn't look so bad," she said.

"It hurts."

"You can take it."

"I don't know," he said, shaking his head. "It doesn't get easier."

"What can I do?" she asked, after a moment. "To make it better."

He stared at her. "I don't know."

"You've got to know," she said, sitting down on one of the ladderback chairs, stirring honey into her tea. "If you don't know, I can't help."

He looked around the room. There were watercolors on the walls. "I guess I'd just like to talk."

"Just?" she said.

He tried to smile but it didn't form. "I could tell you all my secrets."

She stood up and pushed her chair right next to his. He reached out for her hand and, closing his eyes, put her knuckle against his lips. She patted his hair—silver hair—patted it.

"You won't tell," he said—a joke—but then he said, "You won't."

"You know me," she whispered.

"And I think, when I'm done, I'd like to sleep here tonight."

"Yes," she said, patting his hair.

"The floor would be fine."

"I've got a sleeping bag," she said.

He touched her cheek and then, before going on, sipped the hot, strong tea.

19

THE FIRST SIGN of it was so slight that she paid it no attention. But when she urinated again, Corinne couldn't help but notice that there was a pinkish tinge to the water. She thought it must have been something she ate. Lately she had been drinking a lot of cranberry juice and certainly that might tint one's urine. But then, a little later, there was a distinct stain in her underpants. Her knees turned to jelly as she got up from the toilet and headed into the bedroom. It was silly, she knew, but she kept her legs pressed tightly together as if that in some way might forestall whatever was happening.

She dialed the doctor's office.

"Dr. Waterman, please," she said. "This is Corinne McIver and it's urgent."

"Can you tell me please what the problem is, Mrs. McIver?" returned the kind, firm voice.

"I'm staining. At least I think I am."

"What week are you in?"

"The eleventh."

"The eleventh," the voice returned. "The doctor will get back to you in—"

"No, you don't understand," she heard herself blurt out. "I'm staining. Listen," she said, deliberately now, "I'm very high-risk."

"Yes, I know," said the kind voice. "The doctor will be back to you within five minutes."

Corinne hung up the phone. *Very high-risk.* It was such a strange, funny way to think about herself. She didn't like to think of herself that way. She liked to think of herself as being very strong. Inside that very small body was a strong person waiting to get out.

The phone rang and she lunged at it, her insides churning.

"Yes?"

"Corinne?"

"Yes?"

"Hi. It's Liv Sloan."

"Oh. Liv."

"Did I wake you?"

"No, no."

"I'm just calling about the raffle tickets. I'm your raffle monitor."

"Liv, I can't really talk right now . . ."

"Are you okay?"

"Yes. Fine. I'm just waiting for a call. Can I get back to you?"

"Sure."

"Tonight?"

"Fine."

She hung up, feeling totally rattled. At least she hadn't told everybody that she was pregnant. She had only told Anna and Anna could keep a secret. The thing she wouldn't be able to endure was everyone's pity. Thank God, she thought, she hadn't told her mother, who would berate her for having even tried again. Thank God she hadn't told Caitlin.

The phone rang. She picked it up. "Hello?"

"Corinne? It's Michael Waterman. What's going on?"

She gave him the details; she described everything that had come out of her body.

"Well," he said, when she had concluded, "it sounds like something we should look into."

As she headed downtown in a cab, she made arrangements in her mind. Caitlin was at the Center until three and, after that, she could ask Anna or Charles to take her. As for Patrick, she would call him when she needed to, not before. There was no point in calling him early; he'd only go crazy in his not-so-quiet way, rattling off question after question.

—Now let me get this straight, Doc. You're telling me that in the eleventh week of pregnancy there's nothing you can do? With all the stuff I read in the *Times*? All that neonatal surgery? What about if she stays flat on her back for the rest of the pregnancy? Around-the-clock nurses? What about that? Money isn't an issue.

The questions, the questions. The hard sell. Get to know your product. Show the other guy how much you care. And then talk money. Because it all boils down to money, doesn't it? Except you're not going to buy yourself out of this one, Patrick McIver.

—Just tell me what it costs. They haven't invented the deal that couldn't be made.

Oh but they have, Paddy old boy, she thought, leaning back in her seat, feeling the bitter seepage. You bet your sweet bippy they have.

She sat in bed watching *I Love Lucy*. It was one of her favorites. The one where Lucy goes to ballet class and gets her leg stuck in the barre. God, she was funny, Corinne thought, laughing a little and then turning it off. If she didn't watch out, she would lose her mind.

She wasn't used to being in bed. It wasn't something she enjoyed. Staying in bed for several months was some people's idea of heaven, but it wasn't hers. Particularly not with Patrick around. He had been home with her since Monday and it was taking its toll. He had never missed three days of work before. For the last three days, they had been interviewing housekeepers, but so far all of them had been wrong, just plain wrong. She wouldn't leave Caitlin in the care of someone who was wrong. Patrick would just have to take off from work, even if it killed him.

His response had been to turn the apartment into a busy hive. The phone rang constantly; there were messengers in and out; and yesterday he even had some of his underlings over for a meeting. He trooped them into the bedroom, to pay their respects, and she sat there, in the stupid fluffy pink bed jacket he'd bought her for some cyst or other, and smiled.

Oh well.

He was trying to do his best. She had to give him that. He'd even gone shopping. He had taken it upon himself, hadn't even heralded it with an announcement. Simply went down to the Sloan's and came back with the things he felt he could handle on his own and that were supposed to meet her prenatal needs: Pop-Tarts, corn toasties, and Maypo.

—Maypo?

—Isn't it something? he said cheerfully. I didn't even think they made it anymore.

She didn't know why he felt he had to be so cheerful. It got on her nerves. The fact was he was ricocheting off the walls. He kept bouncing this pink Spalding. She'd look at him and she'd see the six-year-old boy he must have been. His mother had seven of them—four girls and three boys. God only knows how she did it. The whole pack of them were these wild-spirited things, slipping from sweet to surly without warning. But his mother knew how to handle them. She was a devoutly religious woman who enjoyed an off-color joke. That combination—it pleased Corinne. Unfortunately, she developed diabetes at sixty and didn't know how to lay off the Social Tea biscuits and so had lost a leg and eighty-five percent of her vision. If she had been in good shape, Corinne would have asked her to help out.

—Well, what about your mother?

Uh-uh. Only as a last resort, she told Patrick. The fact is she would rather have a drunken Haitian with TB. Well, no—make that a drunken Haitian. First off, her mother didn't even know she was pregnant so there'd be two or three days of rebuke and recrimination.

—First you freeze me out, then you call for the rescue squad. Isn't that just swell?

After that, there'd be the criticism about her trying again.

—There's more to life than the biological, darlin'. When do you think you're going to learn that?

She felt herself begin to ooze even at the thought of it.

"Need anything?" Patrick asked cheerfully, sticking his head in.

A chocolate Pop-Tart maybe? "No. Thanks. I'm fine."

"Soda?"

"No."

He sat down on the bed and looked at the TV listings. "There's something called *The Little Foxes* on Showtime. Bette Davis. Herbert Marshall . . ."

Something called *The Little Foxes*. He knew nothing. The only thing he knew, thank God, was how to make money. She couldn't imagine what it would be like having a child like Caitlin without money. "When did it start?" she asked.

"Nine-thirty."

She sighed. "Put it on."

The Hubbards were already deeply in battle but it didn't matter; she'd seen the movie enough times before.

"Sure you don't want anything?"

"No," she said, unsmilingly.

The phone rang. He leaned down to kiss her forehead and then went to get it, to make some more money. He really was doing his best. By tomorrow, they'd have a woman and then things would return to normal. Caitlin would be a little confused about why Mommy was staying in bed, but it would work out somehow. It had to.

The movie was over by eleven-thirty. The doorbell rang twenty minutes later. It was the woman here for the interview. Twenty minutes late. Corinne felt her heart sink at this first trouble sign. Lateness was a lousy trait when one of your responsibilities involved picking up a child somewhere.

"So?" he asked, when the interview was over and the woman was gone. "Didn't meet your standards?"

"*My* standards," she said, as she fluffed up the pillows.

"Yeah," he said, still trying his damnedest to sound cheerful. "If it were up to me, I'd hire one of them. Give it a try."

"Sure. What do we have to lose?"

"OK, OK," he said, making a big show of backing off. "Mama knows best."

You're damned straight. "Anyway," she said, "I've got coverage for tomorrow. Heller Norman'll bring Caitlin in the morning and in the afternoon Mrs. Montgomery's coming to clean and then Darcy will bring Caitlin home and stay till you get back."

"When did you work all that out?" he asked.

"While you were out buying Pop-Tarts," she said, unable to resist.

"So you mean I should go back to work?" he said, doing his best to sound skeptical but looking for all the world like someone who'd just gotten paroled.

"Yes," she said. "You should go back to work. And I've decided to ask my mother to come for a while after all. Until we get set up with someone."

There was a silence. She knew that he knew he was supposed to protest, but she also knew that he wouldn't. "If you think that's the answer," he finally said.

"It's one answer," she replied, turning on the TV again.

It was three o'clock and Patrick was at the Center. The fact that he was rarely there, coupled with the fact that he was the biggest of the daddies with the reddest hair and the loudest laugh, meant that he was soon surrounded by kids.

"Visiting royalty," said Loretta, who was already starting the day's cleanup.

"That's me. Roll out the red carpet," he replied as he gathered Caitlin's things.

"*La niña es un poco loco hoy día,*" Loretta said, indicating Caitlin.

Loco? "What do you mean?" he asked.

"Very wound-up. *Mucho attenzione.*"

Why was she speaking this dumb patois? If he wanted to hear dumb patois, he could hire a lady for a lot less *per diem* than he paid to the Center. "She's not used to having to be careful around Mommy," he said.

"Of course," she replied. "I just thought you should know."

He got Caitlin into the stroller and headed toward the park. It was a beautiful day and he wanted to keep her outside this afternoon, both for the fresh air and to keep her away from Corinne, who needed the rest. At Corinne's suggestion, he brought with him a cinnamon-raisin bagel and Caitlin was happy with it. What did they do, before the Hebrews took over and there were bagels everywhere?

"Good?" he asked.

She nodded.

He pushed the stroller into the park. It was so splendid today you almost felt glad to be alive. There were these big bushes covered with some kind of fleecy white flower that smelled of his childhood. Summer was coming.

They entered the playground. As he sat down on a bench in the shade, he realized that this was the first time he had ever been in the playground on a weekday afternoon and it felt weird. As he undid the belt on the stroller, he fancied that everyone was looking at him. He felt large and awkward. He looked down at his knuckles and they seemed enormous, like billiard balls. When he freed Caitlin, she wanted uppie on his lap and while she sat there, eating the rest of the bagel, he was sure they were looking at him, the mothers and the nannies and the children. Some of the mothers smiled at him and he smiled back, feeling like an ox. He looked at his watch. It was only three-thirty.

"Why don't you go play?" he suggested.

She shook her head.

"You want to swing?"

"Yes," she said, jumping down and pulling him by the hand.

She loved to be pushed on the swing. She could sit there all day. She threw her head back and watched the sky. It was one place where she could keep her mouth open.

"More!" she cried.

That meant harder. He pushed harder. He wondered why she liked it as much as she did. Maybe it had to do with some kind of excess physical energy, the way a schizophrenic might rock. Or did it have to do with being a child and just liking to swing? It was that kind of question—the kind for which he had no good answer—that got him all bollixed up.

"OK," he said, "here we go. Up into the sky."

Caitlin squealed and the squeal played on him like a bow across strings. He loved to hear that happy sound from her. She had, in fact, all the earmarks of a happy child, but then how happy could she be? He didn't trust her happiness, nor his own.

"Watch out for the stars! Watch out for the moon!"

Again she squealed. He knew what buttons to push. He knew this little girl of his. He wondered what would happen when the new one came. *If* the new one came. He wondered if he could keep on giving Caitlin the kind of love and attention she needed.

—She'll have a sibling. Like any other child. And she'll make an adjustment like any other child.

But she wasn't like any other child. That's what Corinne didn't seem to realize. And what would they say to her—how would they explain it—when her little brother or sister outstripped her at everything? What kind of adjustment would she make then?

"Hello there, McIvers! Hi!"

He stopped pushing the swing and turned to see who was calling. For a second—a crazy second—he felt a flush of shame, being caught this way, in the playground, in the afternoon. Utter craziness, he thought, shaking his head, as he spotted Nancy Poole and David.

"Hi!" he called. "Great day, huh?"

"Super," Nancy said, bringing the stroller to a halt. Patrick watched David take off, shimmying up a chain-link rope. He was physically very advanced for his age.

"There he goes," said Nancy. "Run wild, run free."

Patrick looked at her and smiled. She was a lot of woman. Built big. She reminded him of the dairy queens he used to lust after at William McAdoo High School. "He's a fine healthy boy," Patrick agreed.

She looked at him and he looked back at her, seeing, or thinking he saw, something in her face that made him darken. "Yes," she said. "He is."

He went back to pushing the swing. "More, Daddy!" Caitlin demanded, so he pushed her harder. She wasn't afraid to go high, he noted, with a fierce admiration.

"How is Corinne?" Nancy asked.

"All right. Holding her own."

"God, she's got guts."

He turned to look at her. "Yeah."

"I'm sure she's going to pull through this," Nancy said.

He nodded.

"I went through the same thing with David. Confined to bed."

"You did?" he asked, genuinely surprised.

She smiled a little. "Yeah. Fragile little me."

He smiled. He had never really spoken to her before. Just hellos and stuff.

"Thirsty," Caitlin announced.

Damn. He hadn't brought any drink with him. Talk about stupid. "When we get home," he said, knowing full well that the tactic wasn't going to work.

"Now, Daddy," she began to whine.

"I've got juice," Nancy said, going into her bag.

"No, that's all right . . ."

"Here," she said. She pulled out a six-pack of Heart's Delight apricot nectar and pulled one off for Caitlin. Patrick took Caitlin down from the swing and handed her the can, watching her drink it down. "More," she said.

"No," he said strictly, "there's no more."

"Here," Nancy said, handing him another. He hesitated. "It's *OK*," she insisted.

Caitlin drank it down as fast as the first and, when she was finished, she returned the empty to him and ran off to join David.

"There's a lot to think about, isn't there?" he said. "Juice, snack . . ."

"There sure is," she replied—but not coyly, not smugly.

"You know, it's funny being here," he said. "In the afternoon, this way."

"How so?"

He shrugged. "The only man."

"Like the rooster in the henhouse?" she grinned.

He smiled again, but then he frowned. "Christ, I don't know how some men can come here all the time. Let the wife go off to work to hang out here with the dirty diapers and the . . ." He stopped himself. "But you're going to think I'm a sexist pig."

"No, I won't."

"Yes, you will."

"You're entitled to your beliefs."

"Well, maybe I am." He looked around, to find Caitlin, but he didn't see her right off. It made him more nervous than it should. "You take a guy like Sam Sloan. I can't figure it. I mean, I know he's a nice guy and all—smart—but what the hell's he doing here? I just can't figure it out."

"Well, different strokes . . ."

"Bull," he said and he saw her look up at him, her eyes widened slightly.

"There's two sides to every story," she said equably.

He stared at her. "No, there aren't. There's a right way and a wrong way. You believe that, don't you?"

She stared at him.

"Don't you?" he pressed.

"I guess so," she said at last, not quite looking him in the eye.

"Glad to hear it," he replied, closing. "Now I better locate that gal of mine."

All the way back from the park, his words echoed in her mind. *There's a right way and a wrong way.* How had she forgotten something that simple? It had taken someone like McIver to remind her. He wasn't a New Yorker and neither was she. Nancy had lived in New York for more than ten years, but she had never become a New Yorker. She didn't care about the things New Yorkers cared about. She didn't care about clothes or fancy food or co-op conversions. She didn't care about money. Justin made so much money it was obscene, but nobody was worth that much money. She knew that if she didn't have Justin around, she'd be forced to earn her own money and she knew, too, that she could do it. Even though she hadn't held a job in four years, she had not yet become one of those women who were frightened by the prospect of making their own way. She was as smart as she needed to be. When she and Justin had taken courses together at Cornell, she had topped him every inch of the way. So there. The bastard. Thought he could just go off and have a life of his own, become a phantom to his wife and son. Well, she'd had enough of it. Finally, she'd had enough.

She could go back to the farm with David until she got on her feet again. Go back to school. Get an MBA and a nice job in New Jersey. Princeton, maybe. Johnson & Johnson. There was no stigma when a woman her age went back to school. And David would have a wonderful time on the farm. He'd learn to milk a cow, birth a calf.

There was always the possibility that Justin would make things hard for her, but she didn't think he would. The worst thing that could happen to Justin would be to get custody of David. David hardly knew him. Three-quarters of the time Justin was off somewhere making a deal and when he was home, more often than not he'd be flat on his back with the wet heating pad, nursing the lower-back pain that didn't get nursed when he was off on his peregrinations.

You see—she knew things. Words like "peregrinations."

But, if he decided to, he could make life very hard for her. She didn't have a job. She didn't have a career. If he went after custody, he could put up quite a fight, particularly with all that money behind him. All that money. Sometimes she wished he had never started to make that money. Then maybe they'd be a happy family. But who was she kidding? The reason why she had picked him out of the crowd in the first place was that he had money—or, more accurately, ambition—written all over him.

Those were the days when she liked ambitious men. Hyperkinetic Jewish hustlers. What an odd acquired taste, she thought. She would have been better off learning to like brains in black butter.

Now she'd gone full-circle. From hyperkinetic Jewish hustlers to laid-back Jewish househusbands. If Justin ever found out about Sam, he could get custody. She had no dirt on Justin. She wondered, if she put someone on his tail, if there was dirt to be found. He certainly wasn't getting his physical release with her. Maybe he had a girl in every port. Caracas/London/Buenos Aires. All those places he went to make money. Did they rub him and oil him like a pasha in those foreign climes? Did they bring him eunuchs with jasmined buttocks? She didn't know the man anymore. She didn't know what he liked or didn't like. She didn't know where or how he wanted to be touched, what he wanted in his mouth. He was a total stranger whose familiarity jarred her.

"Mommy, I'm hungry," David said.

She looked in the stroller bag for a rice cracker. As she handed him one, the sky began to darken. Here it was, about to rain, when the sky had been so clear only a moment ago, and she couldn't understand it.

"We better hurry," she said.

The raindrops were as big as grapes and pelted them hard. She ran but the rain was too much so she took refuge under an awning. She used to think a spring shower was a romantic thing, but now she didn't know what a romantic thing was. It clearly wasn't the thing she had with Sam.

Sometimes getting something is less satisfying than wanting it, she reflected as she stood beneath the awning. Like a Dove bar. She'd heard so much about Dove bars—how they were hand-dipped in Belgian chocolate, how the ice cream was nearly all butterfat. In the beginning, when she first heard about them, she searched everywhere for one. In the beginning, you could only buy them from a vendor but she could never find a vendor. Finally, they came to the supermarket and she was able to buy one and it was good. Really, it was very, very good. But it wasn't good enough and she hated herself for having cared that much about it.

Same with Sam. She knew it was kind of degrading comparing Sam to a Dove bar but also kind of apt. Getting him wasn't as good as wanting him. Not that there was anything disappointing about him technically or in terms of his performance—the cut of his jib, the warp of his woof. His jib and his woof were just fine. But in the aftermath, it had all seemed very clearly a mistake. As they lay side by side in the bed, there was the smell—bitter almonds—of their error.

—That was nice.

—Yes.

He had dressed quickly and she hadn't discouraged him from doing so. The bitter smell . . . it pervaded the room. They weren't going to be each other's answers. All that seduction, the tight quarters, the lingering touches—it was simply a place to put their energies. That was the thing about Sam and herself—they were so alike. The realization came to her as she watched him get dressed: They weren't connected by any greater or lesser passion but by the fact that they were both chronically underemployed. If it hadn't been so funny, she thought then, as she thought now, she would have laughed.

"Mommy. It stopped."

She looked up. He was right. There was no rainbow but the rain had stopped. Impulsively she knelt down and hugged him. Her little man. As long as he was in her life she'd never be alone.

"Let's go home," she said, knowing what she had to do, wondering if she would do it.

"She hasn't stopped complaining since she got here," Corinne whispered to Patrick, in the dark, at the end of yet another endless day. "She walked in the door and complained about the plane trip, the trip from the airport, and the trip up in the elevator."

"So what else is new? That's your mother."

"I must be crazy. Really. I'd better go have my head examined . . ."

"Stop working yourself up into a lather," he cautioned. "It's a limited run."

"Easy for you to say. You'll be away all day and, I have a hunch, most nights."

"Would I do that to you?"

"Oh, come on," she snorted.

"How about getting to sleep?" he said. "I've got an eight-o'clock meeting tomorrow morning."

"You see?" she said, vindicated, as he rolled over and presented her with his endless expanse of back.

In the morning, as they breakfasted together, Rose complained about the diet margarine. "Here I am, sixty-eight years old, and suddenly I'm supposed to give up pure creamery butter."

"Patrick has a high cholesterol count," Corinne explained.

"It's red meat that does it, not butter. Has Patrick stopped eating red meat?" Rose asked belligerently.

"We'll buy you some butter, OK?" Corinne sighed. "Let's see if there's a movie on," she suggested. Her mother, thank God, was a movie freak.

Rose stared at the TV for a few moments. *"Hello, Frisco, Hello,"* she announced, in the clipped decisive tone of a game-show contestant. She had total recall of every film she had ever seen and could identify just about anything within ten frames.

"Let's find something else," Corinne said. "I'm not up for Betty Grable this morning."

"That's Alice Faye, dummy," Rose said, settling in. "This is the one where she sings 'You'll Never Know.'"

You never will, will you? Corinne thought, sinking back against the pillows.

She must have slept for hours. When she awoke it was one o'clock. Rose had set a lunch tray beside the bed and was herself asleep, having drifted off over a Cynthia Freeman novel. Corinne looked at the tray and didn't recognize any of the food. There was American cheese on white bread and sweet pickle slices. Corinne couldn't understand it and had to go to the bathroom.

"Mother?" she called. "Mother!"

Rose awoke in the sloppy way aging people do. "What?"

"I'm sorry. I need the bedpan."

"Jesus, I thought the house was on fire."

She did her business—her mother's phrase—and turned to the lunch tray. "Where did all this food come from?" she asked.

"I went to the store while you were out. You didn't have a thing to eat in the house."

"What are you talking about? There's cheese and bread . . ."

"I've got better things to do than to start slicing up my own cheese, and your bread tastes like sawdust."

Corinne sighed. She didn't want to think about the provisions Rose had laid in. Swiss Knight, Velveeta, olive loaf, Post Toasties. Poor Patrick. Poor Caitlin. Poor Corinne.

"Eat up," Rose said, a cross between a nurse and a prison matron.

As Corinne picked at her lunch, Rose went to make some business calls. Rose's other self, Aunt Shirley, also a divorcée whom Rose had known for forty years and whom she had taken into the business twenty years ago, was one of those people who have a magnetic pull for problems and Rose would be a while straightening her out. With Rose out of sight, Corinne had the impulse, which she had thought long since buried, to ball up her lunch and hide it in the pillowcase. But she knew Rose would find it. She had found it when Corinne was nine and she would find it when Corinne was thirty-nine.

"That Shirley," Rose chuckled, upon her return, as she settled down in the bedside chair. "She couldn't find her way out of a paper bag."

"But she's good with people," Corinne pointed out, as she always did.

"Mmmnh," Rose said noncommittally, arranging the ottoman.

And you're not.

"How did Caitlin seem this morning?" asked Corinne.

"Fine," said Rose, pulling out her needlepoint cigarette case. "What are you worried about? You think she can't cope with the fact that Mama's out of commission for a while?"

"Yes. I think that might be a difficult concept for a three-year-old to grasp," Corinne replied defensively.

"Any three-year-old?" Rose asked, as she lit up.

"Yes. Any three-year-old," Corinne said, feeling that steel rod of anger rise up in her like a hydraulic lift.

"Well, I hate to disappoint you," Rose said, "but she seemed A-OK. Acted like it was a big treat to have Grandma taking her to the Center."

Corinne wasn't surprised. Rose was good with Caitlin. Rose treated everyone in the world the same way. Grocers, butchers, delivery boys, maids, employees, daughters, salesmen, sons-in-law, doctors, dentists, janitors, granddaughters. There was no differentiation. For Caitlin, that was like a day in the country. Even though Caitlin didn't know the facts about herself, Corinne was sure she had some sense of being different. A lot of people tried to act as though she were the same as everyone else, but it didn't work. And here came the Genesee Express, treating this little girl, for better or worse, as though she were *exactly* like everybody else.

"You want some tea?" Rose asked.

"No thanks."

"Tell me if you do. I'm at your beck and call," she said, more than a touch wryly.

"I will."

Rose took in another lung-filler. "Why are you doing that to yourself?" Corinne asked in disgust.

"'Cause I like it," Rose replied. "Anyway, look who's talking. She's flat on her back, like a beetle who can't turn over, and she's giving me helpful health tips. That's a hot one."

"OK, Mother."

"Frankly, why anyone would *choose* to get into a situation like yours . . ."

"I didn't *choose* it. For God's sake."

"Didn't you two whiz kids ever hear of adoption?"

"I'm having this baby, goddammit!" Corinne cried.

There was a silence. "OK, OK," said Rose. "You're going to rupture something if you keep it up."

Corinne sighed—something she did a lot of around Rose. "Find a movie, will you?" she said.

With a grunt, Rose got up and flicked on the TV. She stared at it for thirty seconds. *"Chicken Every Sunday.* Dan Dailey and Celeste Holm."

"Even I could have told you that," Corinne muttered, lying through her teeth.

An hour later, as Rose sat engrossed in the less-than-engrossing climax of the film, the doorbell rang.

"Shit. Who the hell could that be at a time like this?" Rose grumbled as she stomped to the door.

"Yeah?" she demanded, opening up.

"Uh, hello. I'm Anna Diamond."

"Who?"

"Anna Diamond," Anna said, unprepared for this. "I just thought I'd stop by to see how Corinne is doing."

"Oh. Well, come on in."

Anna followed the woman back into the bedroom. "Hi, Corinne," she called.

"Anna. What a nice surprise."

"Well, it's over," Rose said glumly, as the cast of characters rolled. "I guess I'll go see about dinner."

Corinne waited until she was out of earshot. "Thank you for coming," she said, very gratefully.

"Here," said Anna, handing her a package.

"Oh, you shouldn't have."

"It's nothing. Really," Anna emphasized. "Nothing."

It was Gummy Bears. "Oh, how cute," Corinne said.

"How do you feel?" Anna asked.

"Oh, fine."

Anna gave her a look. Corinne never complained. It wasn't healthy. "So that's your mother."

"Yes, that's her," Corinne said, picking out a green Gummy Bear.

"Been driving you batty?" Anna said, diving right in.

Corinne looked up in surprise. "Yes," she admitted. "Yes."

"A thousand yeses."

"A million."

"What can I do to help?" Anna asked.

"Find me Mary Poppins," Corinne replied.

Anna laughed. "Just hire someone."

"That's what Patrick keeps telling me," Corinne said, unable to suppress her annoyance. "But how can I just hire someone for a child like Caitlin?"

"She'll handle it, Corinne. The important thing now is for you to get back on your feet. And aggravation is your worst enemy."

Corinne chewed on the Gummy Bear for a few moments. "You don't know what a major thing it is for my mother to come in like this. She's not the maternal type. I'm very touched."

"You're also going nuts."

Corinne nodded. "I saw a woman from Guyana who was actually very sweet."

"Hire her."

"I'll sleep on it," she said. "Anyway, how are you?"

"Fine. Just fine," Anna assured her.

They chatted for another few minutes and then it was time to go to the Center.

"Thanks so much for coming, Anna," Corinne said.

"I'll come again soon."

Anna said good-bye to Corinne's mother, who was watching TV in the kitchen, and then headed downstairs. Poor Corinne, she thought. To be confined to bed that way—what torture. Why didn't bodies work the way they were supposed to? You reached thirty-five and suddenly things began to fall apart. Suddenly you were struck in the face by human frailty. There was no getting around it. Everywhere you looked you saw it.

But Corinne would be all right, Anna decided as she made her way down Central Park West. Corinne was a fighter. And so was she. That's why they were friends. They were so different, but they had certain things in common. Neither of them would give up. Neither of them would spend a lot of time feeling sorry for herself. Both of them knew how important it was to win the fight.

Suddenly, as she walked along, thinking these thoughts, she became aware of a cool breeze in the air, almost a chill. She stopped to belt her raincoat. Standing there, in front of the Eldorado, she caught her reflection in the plate-glass lobby door. Look—how thin she had become—she who had never been thin.

PART FOUR

20

IT WAS AUGUST and the city was quiet. Anyone who could afford the time or the money to get away had already done so. To the seashore, and sand castles, beach-plum jelly and bayberries, children with their ears pressed to shells. Or the mountains, trillium and lady's slippers, the turning-up of worms, swimming to the float, fields of fireflies.

"Do you remember summer when we were kids?" Trina asked Charles as they walked through Central Park on this empty hot Sunday afternoon.

"I remember."

"It wasn't anything like this," she said, shaking her head. "It went on forever and there were no plans. You just went out the door in the morning and in the door at night. Simple as that."

"Nothing was ever as simple as that," said Charles, stopping for a moment. He was lugging a heavy shopping bag, filled with food, and had to change hands.

"Are you OK?" she asked. "We don't have to go all the way."

"I'm fine," he said.

He wanted to show her the Conservatory Garden. She wasn't a big one for formal gardens, but she didn't want to disappoint him. Lately they had been spending time together on the weekends. Bill had taken the boys up to Rhode Island for the two weeks that the Center was closed and Julie and Hildy were on a big razzle-dazzle vacation at a resort in Steamboat Springs, Colorado. Everyone was away.

"Is it much further?" Trina asked.

"I don't think so." He looked around. "Can't be more than half a mile."

"I'm worried about you. You could throw out your back."

"Don't worry about me," he said.

But she did. Ever since he had told her his story she had wanted to protect him. Wanted to be his shield. The thought of him in danger scared her through and through. Just last night she had a terrible dream where he was being whipped by soldiers in these weird hats, like fezzes. She woke up screaming, all in a sweat. She hadn't done that in years, not since Phyllis died.

For weeks now he kept coming in and out of her thoughts. Over and over again she replayed that night he told her his secrets. They were up until three, four in the morning. She made them chamomile tea, with lots of honey in it. A tonic for the nerves, she promised as he kept on talking, spilling everything. Finally she rolled out a sleeping bag for him and found an extra pillow. They lay in the dark for a while, just the sound of their breathing. Then she called out to him.

—Charles?

—Yes?

—Come here.

He came to her bed. It was such a nice bed. It had belonged to her paternal grandmother whom she had never known. Oak. All carved in a tulip design. Plenty big for two. He was just in his underwear. Underpants and a sleeveless undershirt. His legs and arms were so long and thin but strong too. His skin had a kind of glow. He got into bed beside her. She was wearing an old flannel nightgown printed with violets. There was just enough light in the room for her to see him. All around was darkness.

—It's cold on the floor.

She took his hand. She wasn't sure what she felt. She had so much feeling for him. She folded herself against him, felt his long hard body next to hers. I won't let anyone hurt you, she thought—maybe even whispered—and then they were asleep, just like that, touching all through the night, just touching. After that, they were like such good friends. And she was glad they hadn't gone any further. After all, it was harder to find a friend than a lover.

"There it is," he said. "Just over the hill."

They entered the Conservatory Garden, which, even more than the rest of the park, was strangely deserted.

"It's like the day after around here," she said.

"Yeah. Nice, isn't it?"

"It's so quiet."

"It's always quiet here. Mostly old ladies use it. They appreciate the symmetry of the paths and the plantings."

She looked around. "It's sort of nice," she said as they sat down on a bench. "If you go in for formal gardens."

"You don't?"

"Uh-uh."

"How come?"

She shrugged. "Just a nature girl, I guess."

"There was a boy," he began to sing. *"A very strange enchanted boy . . ."*

She looked at him. "What's that?"

"'Nature Boy,'" he said. "Nat King Cole. You know." He began to sing again. "Da da da da da da da da da da da da. *The greatest thing you'll ever learn is just to love and be loved in return."*

She stared at him for a moment. "Before my time," she said.

"Mine too. How old are you?"

She put a hand to her breastbone. "A lady never tells her age," she drawled. "Thirty-five. Old, huh?"

He shook his head. "About what I thought. Seasoned."

"Old," she corrected. "And the pity is I haven't done anything with my life."

"Come on," he said. "It's too hot for self-recrimination."

"But I haven't. I was supposed to be an actress. I was good."

"I'm sure you were."

"But I never learned the trick of self-promotion."

"That's important for an actress."

"For anyone."

He looked at her. "Do you want to eat?"

She shrugged. "A little."

He pulled out a container from the shopping bag and opened it up.

"What's that?" she asked.

"Baba ganoush." He found the pita and handed her one.

"Mmmnh. Good. What else have you got in there?"

"Lots of stuff. Cheese, olives, dried fruit . . ."

"I can't believe you. You must have spent a fortune."

"I owed you," he said.

She stopped chewing. "I hate that kind of talk. You don't owe me anything."

"Oh, yes I do," he said quietly. "I owe you a lot."

"Anyway," she said, after a moment, "I gave it up. I told myself I wasn't going to make it as an actress."

"You still could."

"Oh sure. Character parts," she laughed. "No. That's closed." She shook her head. "I really haven't done enough with my life. I've missed out on so many things."

"Such as?" he said, scooping up some more spread.

"A baby."

He looked up, surprised.

"What's the matter?" she asked. "Don't think I'm the maternal type?"

"I just never heard it before."

"There's a lot from me you haven't heard," she said, licking her fingers. "This is really good. What's in it?"

"Eggplant," he said. "You never had it before?"

She shook her head. "I served it but I never ate it."

"Let's move to the grass," he suggested.

She looked around. "Not here," she said. "I'd feel like I'm trespassing."

They headed out of the Conservatory Garden and up a knoll to a quiet spot, all to themselves, beneath a plane tree.

"Didn't like it, huh?" he asked.

"The baba ganoush?"

"No. The garden. You looked like a caged bird in there."

"I'm very sensitive that way." She stretched out on the blanket. "Oh, this is nice," she said. "Listen to the quiet."

"Yeah," he said, playing with a dandelion puff. "Blow," he said, turning to her and then wincing.

"What's the matter?"

"My shoulder."

"You see," she said, sitting up. "I told you."

"Never say I told you so."

"Lie down."

He lay down and she straddled his back. Her hands went to work.

"Hey. You are good."

"I could make a living from this," she said. "I'm that good. There," she said. "There's the knot."

"Ow."

"Hold on. There," she said. "It's easing up."

She went on massaging him. It would be better with oil, she thought.

"Does Bill Dowell like this?" he asked.

She stared down at his back. He had a line of four small brown moles, like a highway legend. She didn't know how to respond to the question—angry or honest. "Not much," she said, choosing one.

"How come?"

There was a silence. Charles was her friend. Maybe the best one she ever had. Better than Barry. She loved Barry but he was too busy being a clown to help her. "He's not a sensuous man," she said at last. "What about Julie?"

"Julie's not a sensuous man either," he joked.

"Come on. Seriously."

He thought a moment. "She likes to be touched," he said quietly.

She nodded, even though he couldn't see her. "Women do," she said philosophically. She slapped his back. "You're through." She reached into the bag for a peach. "Want one?"

"OK."

She tossed him a peach and then lay down beside him. "This isn't so bad, is it?" she said.

"No. Not bad at all."

"Beats all that sand."

"You said it."

"And this way we don't get cancer," she said, biting into her peach. The juice ran out of the corners of her mouth and she wiped them off with the back of her hand. "We should have brought a radio."

"You're right," he said, looking up at the clouds.

She looked up too, to see what he was looking at. "Cumulus," she said.

"Very good. Go to the head of the class."

"I never did," she admitted, with a grin. "I was never very good at school." She ran her hand through the grass. "I bet you were."

"Oh, yeah. Mr. All-Around here."

"And I bet you had a perfect childhood."

"You said it. Green lawns, clean limbs, twilight baseball . . . everything perfect."

"That's what I always wanted," she said. "Still do a little."

"Forget it," he said, shaking his head. "Believe me, you can never overcome the curse of a perfect childhood."

"Well, that's one curse I'll never have to worry about," she said. The cumulus clouds looked close enough to touch. "We never had it easy. For starters there was never enough money. Of course, we weren't supposed to have a lot of money—that would have been wrong—but there was never *enough* money. You were supposed to live off the land, and even though he was a pretty good farmer—"

"Who?"

"My father. He was a pretty good farmer." She stopped for a moment, letting the clouds roll by. Cumulus. In school she used to call them cucumber clouds. "Isn't there anything to drink?" she asked.

"There's wine."

"OK."

He poured her some wine. She was very thirsty. Wet your whistle, she thought, wishing it were colder. "But it's not enough to be a pretty good farmer," she continued. "You've got to be a great farmer. And even if you're a great farmer there's too much goes wrong. Lighting, hail, drought. But I'm sure you know all about that."

"Didn't he?"

"No." She shook her head. "No. You see, he was a street fighter—always thought he could win. But he always lost. One thing after the other. Kept coming up, kept getting his head bashed in. For a while he raised mushrooms—did pretty well with it—and when that ended came poultry." She shuddered to make her point. "I hate fowl. Hated it then, hate it now."

"You don't eat chicken?"

"I wouldn't eat a chicken if I were starving. Dirty birds. Dirty stupid birds. Come down with every disease in the book. It got so my father was tearing out his hair."

"Did you ever read 'The Egg'?" he asked. "It's a story by Sherwood Anderson."

"No. I missed that one."

"It's all about a man driven to madness by poultry farming."

She thought about that for a while. "Well, I don't know if he went crazy or not but he kept getting angrier and angrier."

"What did he do?"

"Drank. Mostly. Got into fights. Sometimes he beat us up a little."

"You?"

"Yeah. Me. But just a little. He had a belt from the Army."

He poured some more wine. "And your mother?"

She laughed. "Uh-uh. No way. Carmel would've put a boning knife through him. We were one thing—she could live with that—but he didn't dare lay a hand on her."

"So what did you do?"

She shrugged. "Hid. At least I did, anyway. Phyllis could take it more. But then . . ."

She stopped herself.

"Tell me," said Charles.

She looked up at the clouds. They were like cotton swabbing, all around her. She turned to stare at him. "Then he liked to make up," she said.

There was a silence. Funny how silent it could get here in the middle of New

York City, but then that was August. "I never knew it," she said, not knowing why she was going on, but having to. "Phyllis never said anything. But then—when she got sick—he was already gone. She had aplastic anemia. Ever hear of it?"

He nodded.

"The bone marrow goes out of commission. She was working in this porcelain factory. We think that's where she got all messed up. All those chemicals."

"Was it investigated?"

She shrugged. "We never got it together for that. You see, when she was dying, all this other. . . stuff came out." She looked at him. She had the urge, so strong, to touch him, but she held back. "In the end, we took care of her at home. She was all . . . faded. You know how something looks when it's been sucked out by a spider?"

"Trina . . ."

"That's how she looked. Not a lot of pain though, so that was good. Some days she could talk real well. Carmel wasn't around much. She already had the hobby shop. Mostly it was me and her. I was waiting tables at the American Charcuterie then. Did you know it? In the CBS building. Big place—big lunch business. All the low-level CBS types. In the evening I was playing in a show down on Hudson Street. *The Sign in Sidney Brustein's Window*. I left the show. I left the job." She ran her hand through the grass at her side. "We used to sit out back—it was just getting warm. I used to make real lemonade. Fresh-squeezed. You should've seen how much sugar she put in hers." She smiled a little. "I guess she figured it didn't matter."

There was another silence. He poured some more wine—truth serum, Trina thought. She took a long drink of it, warmer still. "Some days she talked and talked. One day she was having this dream. I woke her up. She looked at me for a minute. Like she didn't know who I was. Then she told me the whole story. Like it just came spilling out. How it went on for two years, and how he used to cry afterward, and hold her head between his hands, covering her ears."

She fell quiet again. This time he took her hand. "Trina."

"I didn't believe her. I thought it was the sickness. All those white blood cells—gone to her brain. Even after she died, I still didn't believe her. Two years went by and I started to get crazier and crazier. You see, I couldn't put it out of my mind. I started to believe her. When I told Carmel, she freaked. Oh God, Charles," she laughed. "You should've seen her. She's shorter than I am—five feet—but she thinks she's Mighty Joe Young. She starts slapping me. Like she really wants to hurt me. And she does."

She sat up. There was a dandelion puff at her feet and she pulled it out of the ground. Softly, she blew it, watching the seeds travel nowhere to write home about. "I never told anyone. Once I almost told Bill, but then I didn't." She turned to stare at him. "I don't know why I told you."

He looked at her for a long moment and then reached up to touch her cheek. "You trust me," he said.

She put a hand over his hand and closed her eyes.

"Don't eat that," Julie said.

"Why?" asked Hildy. She was holding a piece of bacon in her hand.

"Because bacon is terribly, terribly fatty and very bad for you."

Hildy popped it into her mouth, swallowing it in nearly one gulp.

"All right," said Julie, lifting her third cup of coffee to her lips and looking out the picture window.

The view from the Thunderbird Restaurant, located mid-mountain in Steamboat Springs, was breathtaking. And the food, for what it was, was quite good, very fresh although heavy. Eggs, bacon, biscuits and gravy—who ate like that anymore? She had given up eating like that when she moved from her mother's house. And just as well. Her mother died prematurely of arteriosclerosis. She loved fatty food and paid the piper.

"So," said Julie, "how do you like those mountains?"

"Fine," said Hildy.

"Those are the Rockies, darling. The Rockies."

Hildy played with her placemat.

"Stop that," said Julie. "Or we'll have to leave the restaurant."

Hildy stopped.

Julie fished in her purse for a cigarette. This was the first real trip they had taken together and Julie had wanted to make it perfect. She looked across the table at Hildy, who was wearing a purple jumpsuit. Purple offset her reddish hair, and there were purple ribbons tying up her pigtails. She was wearing a cap with the word "Steamboat" emblazoned above the brim and around her neck she had on a necklace of tiny turquoise beads.

"Do you want some more milk?" Julie asked.

"Uh-uh."

There was a silence as the view loomed beyond the window. "Penny for your thoughts," Julie said. Hildy looked confused and Julie smiled. "What are you thinking?"

Hildy gingerly jabbed her palm with the tines of her fork.

"Stop that," said Julie.

"When can we swim?" Hildy asked.

Julie sighed. "You were in the pool all day yesterday."

"I want to go today."

"If it was just swimming you wanted, we could have gone to Montauk and saved ourselves a lot of money." She put out her cigarette; somehow, in this clean air, it seemed wrong to smoke. "We have to see the sights, ducky. Go on a hike. Breathe that mountain air."

Hildy looked down at the tabletop, which was heavily burled and heavily polyurethaned. "Why do we have to do what you want?" she said.

Julie gave her a long examining look. She was a startlingly articulate child—always had been. Of course, all of the children at the Center were so, perhaps because they had been engaged in social intercourse at so young an age. But Hildy, because she was so exposed to the world of adults, was even more so. Indeed, thought Julie, she was rather *too* articulate for her age. "Is that what you really think?" asked Julie, trying to keep the recrimination from her voice. "Do you really think I planned and saved for this vacation for *my* benefit alone? Think about it, Hildy," she suggested.

After their lunch, they took the lift up Quickdraw Trail. The trails here all had

Western names: Flintlock, Tomahawk, High Noon. They caught the lift to the top of the mountain.

"Isn't it beautiful?" Julie cried. She had been here to ski several times before, and loved the town's frontier friendliness, its relaxed, almost raffish way of life that was so much a contrast to what she had back home.

Hildy said nothing, but held tightly to Julie's hand. Julie looked down at the small white hand encased in her own large hand. She had very large but gracefully formed hands. She was a big woman. She didn't mind that. It was difficult, growing up, to always be towering over the heads of the boys in her class. But now she didn't mind a bit towering over the boys. She dressed to maximize her height. High boots from Maxime, black and brown, every other year.

"I'm scared," said Hildy, as they went gliding high above the aspen trees.

"Now stop that," Julie chided gently, as Hildy gripped her hand. It felt good, she thought, looking down at the little hand, to see Hildy needing her this way. She was such a strong and resilient child. She almost never expressed fears or worries.

When they got to the top, they jumped off together and began to giggle. It was a dizzying panorama. Everywhere you looked were snow-capped peaks and in the valley below was Steamboat Springs, as nestled, sleepy, and magical as Brigadoon.

At first, it seemed there was no one else at the summit. The mountain was all theirs. She wasn't surprised—in the summer the entire area was merely a shadow of its other self—but then she heard voices. And then, a moment later, she saw a man and two boys hiking over the ridge.

"Look," said Hildy, her eyes widening.

"I see."

The man, spotting them, gave a friendly wave. Julie smiled back. He was tall, maybe forty-five, a trifle overweight through the middle, shaggy blond-gray hair, yellow shades. His sons—at least that's what she took them for—were copies of him, except that their hair was pure blond and there was no middle-age spread.

"Some sight, isn't it?" the man said as he approached. She could see, as he came closer, that there was some labor to his breathing.

"Spectacular," she agreed. "Did you climb up?"

"Yes, ma'am," he said proudly.

Ma'am. He was probably a dentist from Westchester who was trying to sound like Marshal Dillon. How she hated that sort of thing. "Tough climb?" she asked.

"Manageable." He turned to the boys. "What do you say, guys?"

They offered goofy laughs and then turned, scrambling up some rocks. Hildy ran after them. "Careful," Julie called. "Careful!"

"It's okay," the man said. "They'll watch her. They're real responsible around little ones."

"How old are they?"

"Russ is twelve and Sam's nine." He looked at her and smiled broadly. "I'm Ben Dove," he said, extending his hand.

"Julie Nolan."

"Are you a hiker?"

"Not really." She looked around to check on Hildy. "We took the lift."

He nodded. "It's nice in the summer. Whereabouts you from?"

Whereabouts. "New York," she said. "Manhattan. And you?" *Larchmont?*

"Oklahoma City," he said, squinting into the sun. "Not all that far," he added, turning to fix her with his relentlessly amiable grin.

"Oh," she said. "Oil wells?" she asked, a mocking lilt to her voice.

"Not a one," he said good-humoredly. "I'm a radiologist."

"Oh. It's *Doctor* Dove," she replied with a little smile. "Now that sounds like something out of a children's book."

"It does sort of, doesn't it?" he admitted.

She looked around and didn't see Hildy. "Hildy?" She rose and headed up the ridge. "Hildy!" she cried. One of the boys—the older one—popped his head up from behind a rock. "She's okay," he said. "She's with us."

"Stay where I can see you, Hildy," Julie called.

"Russ is real responsible," Dr. Dove reminded her. "He babysits a lot and hasn't lost one yet," he laughed.

Until the first one. "Yes, well—we are very high up."

"I guess living in New York City, you like to keep her in sight," he said.

"Everyone should," she replied. "Most abductions occur in quote-unquote 'safe' suburbs."

"Yeah," he said, "but you've got to give the kids some leash, don't you think?"

"She's only four," said Julie.

"She looks like a real sweetie," he said. He squinted into the sun again and rocked back on his heels. "Where are you staying?"

"Sheraton Village," she said.

"Us too. Been here long?"

"Two days. Yesterday she was in the pool all day long," said Julie. "Today we decided on this little hike. There's so much to do. I want to take her riding. Hot-air ballooning."

"Don't forget rafting on the Yampa," he said. "And Ragner's."

"What's that?"

"You've never been? It's this great Scandinavian restaurant."

"Isn't that a contradiction in terms?" she shot back.

He grinned. "You're a real New Yorker, aren't you?"

"Am I?" She shrugged. "I'd better find Hildy."

She headed up the ridge again, toward the scrambling sound on the rocks. She thought of a condor swooping down, and away, with her child.

"Why don't we get the kids together for a swim later on? Back at the Sheraton?" he called after her.

"Oh," she said. "Well, possibly. Let's see how the day goes."

He nodded. "Is it just the two of you?"

She turned to look at him. "Yes."

He nodded again. "I'm divorced." A quick smile. "This is my big time every year with the boys. They live in Houston with their mom. She married into NASA. Hard to compete with that, huh?"

She smiled a little. Zinging in and out of her mind was a passive little fantasy of Hildy falling off the mountain while she stood here talking to this radiologist.

"I'd be honored if you and your daughter would join us at Ragner's tonight," he said.

Ma'am. If he had a hat, he'd have tipped it.

"Thank you. That sounds lovely," Julie said, "but we're seeing some old friends tonight."

The scrambling sound. "Hildy?" she called, turning up the ridge. When she got to the top, she could see Hildy and the two boys working on a kind of stone column, piling stone upon stone. It was already about two feet high.

"Look, Mommy!" Hildy cried, with animation.

"Yes, dear," said Julie. "I see."

One of the boys—the younger—looked at Julie with great seriousness. "How old is she?" he demanded.

"Just four," said Julie, with a swell of pride, laying a hand on Hildy's head.

"She balances *good* for four," he said.

"Come on, guys," Dr. Dove said, as he caught up with them. "We had our pit stop. Now let's pull it out."

The boys picked up their rucksacks.

"Don't go," Hildy pleaded.

"Well, little one," said Dr. Dove, kneeling down to her, "your mom and I made plans to see you at the pool later on. How's that sound?"

Hildy smiled a little and he patted her head. She and Julie watched them head down the path. They were tall boys, just like their father.

"I want to swim," Hildy said, her voice just beginning to whine.

"Not now," said Julie.

"I want to swim!"

"Just hold on. We're doing this now," Julie replied. "Anyway that's not where those boys are going now if that's what you're thinking."

"Will they be there later?"

"We'll see," said Julie.

"I want them to be."

Julie bent down and placed her hands on Hildy's shoulders. "Those are big boys, darling," she said. "When you see them at the pool they'll be busy doing all sorts of other things. Don't expect them to play with you."

Hildy looked crushed. Julie sighed and took her by the hand, leading her over to the observation deck. "Now isn't this beautiful?" she declared. It really was. She was so glad she had decided to get off the East Coast for a change. Clear her head. Between Hildy and the Center and her work and Charles, her head had become more cluttered than she should ever allow it to be. When she got home, she'd make a point of keeping it clear. The thing with Charles—it was just pure foolishness. A physical attraction—that's all. How could she ever make a life with a man like that, a man without ambitions, without direction?

"Here," she said, handing Hildy a stone. "Throw it over."

Hildy looked at the stone and then threw it as far as she could, which wasn't very far but far enough. It made her smile as little.

"If it was winter you wouldn't be able to do that," said Julie.

"Why?"

"Because you'd have an avalanche. That's when great big drifts of snow come down and bury everything in their path."

Julie watched the wheels turning as Hildy digested this.

"But in the summer you can do it. You can do pretty much whatever you want up here. You can be queen of the mountain. Look," she said, now that they had the summit to themselves. "It's all yours. To do whatever you want with. Go ahead, baby—do it! This is your chance."

The rock went sailing over the side. Julie and Hildy held hands, following it until they could see it no longer.

On a clear day you could see Block Island, and it was a clear day. So far they had been very lucky with the weather, thought Bill. August could be a tricky month, but somehow, in this year of his adversity, special favor had been granted him.

He rearranged the blanket to shade the cooler he had brought down to the beach. In a way, he regretted the age of the cooler. It made things altogether too easy. When he was a child, he would come to this beach and when his session had ended, he would pad back to the cottage and there would be his jelly sandwich and his glass of milk. In the afternoon, there would be bike riding and, some days, berry picking and crabbing in Quonochontaug Pond. Everything was ordered and all orders were followed. Now things were entirely different. The boys, accustomed to snacking, insisted on bringing Cokes to the beach. Bill, in the grip of a nostalgia that ran wild up here, went out of his way to make sure it was the "classic" variety.

He looked across the expanse of white-sand beach and beyond, to the ocean. Sometimes he felt as if his body only really came alive on that first immersion during this yearly pilgrimage. The tingle . . . and the rush. He saw it in the children too. It was like a baptism for them, or a rebirth. They shed the year's share of city soot that invisibly caked their skin and took on a glow, an ease that was denied them fifty weeks a year. He watched them now, a distance away. They were working side by side on a sand castle. Working *together*. Miracle of miracles. Oh yes, their fraternity was securely established—in almost any situation, their eyes traveled until they sighted each other, and there was certainly a sense of responsibility toward each other. But as for real camaraderie—that was reserved solely for the summer sojourn.

Lately he had thought a good deal about living up here. In his line of work, relocation was a distinct possibility. He could probably find something in Providence. Buy a nice little house, get the boys set up in a good school, impose an order on his life and theirs. There were cousins and aunts and uncles nearby. He was sure the boys would be happy here after the initial adjustment.

In order to give it to them, he would have to fight Louise. She was not ready for them to be removed to Rhode Island. He didn't understand why she was not. It would simplify matters. He wasn't saying she didn't have something to give them. Indeed, she had some very special things to give them. But those very special gifts could just as well be distributed two days a month as fifteen. No, the reason for the negotiation and renegotiation of their agreement was that she didn't want him to have more than she had. This was her nature. She was competitive; she was tenacious. She had set out to achieve, and achieve she did. And it was strange: although this streak of hers had essentially ruined their life together, he almost loved her for it. She was clearly a superior person.

And Trina was not. The sad truth, but the whole truth and nothing but the truth. He wasn't talking about natural gifts—one could tell she was a person who harbored wellsprings of tenderness and intuition. Rather, he was talking about what she had accomplished in her life. The answer was disturbingly little, and this made her very needy. The truth—the whole truth—was that she was searching for her identity through someone else's identity and this Bill could not abide.

He looked across the beach once more and saw that the castle was growing. They were such competent children; there was so much they were able to do. Denny was the castle-builder of the two. He was something of a dreamy child. He loved costume and fantasy. His favorite place in the world was the Medieval Hall at the Metropolitan Museum, and lately Bill had introduced him as well to the Cloisters. Petey, on the other hand, was a pragmatist. The great pleasure for him, even at this tender age, was museums of natural history or science and technology; the flight deck of the *Intrepid;* knobs, levers, and pulleys. Bill hoped the disparity of their personalities would evolve into a rare sort of complementariness and that they would become twenty-first-century Wright Brothers, inventing whatever needed to be invented.

As Bill tried to imagine what might still need inventing, the boys came tripping across the sand to him, looking more like sandpipers than inventors. "We're thirsty," Denny declared.

"We want soda," Petey clarified.

"You do, do you?" Bill said. "What's the magic word?"

"Please," said Petey.

"Abracadabra," said Denny, who laughed at his own joke and repeated it until his brother laughed.

"Oh. Wise guy," said Bill, poker-faced. He reached into the cooler and pulled out a single can. "This one's for you," he said, handing it to Petey, who looked a little guilty.

"Oh, please," cried Denny, mock-abjectly, hands raised in an exaggerated gesture of supplication. "Puh-leasse!"

"OK, OK," said Bill, fishing out another Coke, suppressing a smile.

They were good boys. Such good boys. Going through all of this with so few complaints, so little whining. He would make it up to them. All he needed was a little more time. Surely he and Louise could achieve some kind of détente. It wasn't as if she hated him. After all—when she had kissed him that day—wasn't she telling him that he was still very special to her? Indeed, that she still loved him in her fashion?

"I'm going in," Denny announced.

"Me too," said Petey.

"Be careful," Bill said. He would keep an eye on them from the beach, of course, and Petey didn't go in above his knees, but he had to impress on them that the ocean was a dangerous place.

"We will," Denny promised, as they ran off.

But the sad thing, thought Bill, rearranging the blanket over the cooler, was that they had such high hopes. And yet that's always the sad thing, isn't it? Still, when he and Louise were just starting out together, contemplating the family they were about to make, the future seemed unbridled.

—We don't need a whole lot of money. That's not the kind of people we are.

We're too good to fall into the trap. We'll have our work and our family. Anything else can take a back seat.

But the fact was that they weren't too good and they did fall into the traps. Particularly the money trap—is there anyone who cannot fall into it? Particularly in New York City, where the money slips through one's fingers with the most alarming speed? The first of the month becomes a torture chamber—crucible for the worst fights—and you lose all that nice distance you have the rest of the time when you can joke about being downwardly mobile.

It was in that respect that he had failed her. He should have made three times the money he did. With his educational and cultural background—there was no excuse. To inflict money anxieties on a woman as highly strung as Louise was grossly insensitive. He had promised to take care of her and—by reasons of his own insecurity, inertia, self-doubt—he had not.

"Daddy," said Petey, running up the beach, "there's jellyfish."

He received his son on the blanket. His little body was cold. Of course that was a value up here, to be unflinchingly chilled in the face of the elements, but he felt, nonetheless, the need to wrap a towel around his son's shoulders. "They're harmless," he said. "They can't hurt you."

"But once you said . . ."

"No, no. That was in Florida. That was something different. The Portuguese man-of-war. Remember?"

"But they hurt."

"No. You're confused," he said. He pulled Petey onto his lap. His body was warming. His skin felt so warm and smooth. He kissed the back of his neck. Salt. Bill remembered when the boys were babies—Petey particularly, because Petey had been the plump one. He remembered how he would nuzzle against his neck, in that soft warm plumpness, rewarded by gurgles of pleasure. It's such a sensuous thing to hold a baby. The smell—sweet—and the cooing sounds, the incredible lilylike skin. He missed that—the sensuousness—he missed it. "They don't hurt. I promise you. Would I let you go in if you could get hurt?"

Petey thought about that for a moment—too long a moment, thought Bill with a dry amusement.

"Come on," Bill said. "Be brave. Let's go."

He rose, lifting Petey onto his shoulders. Soon it would be time to go back to the cottage. Mother was a dragon if they were late for meals.

"Tomorrow morning, we'll have to get up early and go look in the tidal pools," he said.

"What's that?" asked Petey.

"It's the water left behind when the tide pulls out. The tide's a kind of rising and falling of the ocean," he said, realizing that Petey didn't know what a tide was.

"The ocean falls?" asked Petey.

"Well, no. Not *falls* exactly," said Bill, realizing that that could be a scary concept. "More that it changes its *level*. Sometimes it's up, sometimes it's down. And that all depends on the moon. But don't ask me why."

"Why?"

"You asked me why!" Bill cried in the loony voice of *Sesame Street*'s Grover, making Petey laugh. "I don't know why. Just nature. But when the tide pulls the water out, pools are left behind and there's all kinds of marine life in them: crabs and snails; shrimp; barnacles; sea urchins. It's fun to see what you can find."

"What else?" Petey asked.

"Well," said Bill, thinking, "we haven't found any bottle glass yet, have we?"

"What's that?"

"That's really pretty stuff. It's pieces of broken bottles and jars, and these pieces get tossed around in the ocean and all the tossing and the sand and stuff rubs them and rubs them until the sharp edges disappear and everything is all smooth. Mostly you find green or brown bottle glass. But sometimes you get a bright blue piece or a purple one even."

"I want it," Petey said.

"Tomorrow," Bill replied. "Tomorrow we get up very, very early and go beach-combing."

He felt Petey's hands playing with his hair. It was such a nice feeling. Walking along this beach, secluded, quiet, one of the nicest places one could be in August, his son on his shoulders, playing with his hair . . .

"Where's Denny?" said Petey.

He looked up and down the beach. He looked out at the ocean. Nothing. Blue. He froze. Then ran. Petey's arms around his neck. He threw him down. Heard him cry.

"Denny!"

A roar.

He ran along the beach.

"Denny!"

Denny Denny. He ran into the water. Denny. Where was Denny? God. Where? God. He swam. There. Far out. Pulled east. On the water small far Denny.

"Denny!"

Oh God the water too strong too strong God like an animal God a bear a bull Denny don't Denny please don't God please I'll be good God I'll be good I'll never do it again God please.

"Denny!"

Where was he God where was he I'll do anything God I'll be good God he's so young God Mama help him God help me I'm closer God please please God.

"Denny! Swim! Denny!"

A roar.

I can do it God I'm so close God don't let him God how I've suffered God I've suffered God help me God.

"Denny."

Reaching out for him. Contact. Pulling him close against him. Faster. Oh God. Mama. Make me faster. Kick kick frog swim fish kick. Faster. Water too strong God. Everywhere arms.

"OK OK OK."

Kick now kick. Kick now. Again. Now. There. Beach. Sand.

"Don't die. Mama. Don't die."

He put his mouth to his son's mouth. He breathed out. God. Anything God anything. Again. Vomit. Yes God. Yes. "Denny! Denny!" Breathing. Coughing. Yes! Yes! Yes!

"Daddy."

"God!" he heard himself crying in a kind of exaltation, as he wrapped his breathing boy in his arms.

They stayed in the park until twilight.

"One day I'd like to sleep in the park," said Trina, as they gathered their things.

"Unwise," returned Charles.

"I bet a lot of people do it," she said.

"A lot of people do a lot of things," he said, heading up the hill.

They walked back to her apartment. The streets were littered and the sky seemed unwilling to darken beyond the soft waning of the twilight. A woman was bathing herself in the street with a bucket.

"What are you going to do tomorrow?" he asked.

She shrugged. "I don't know. I told Barry I'd help him sew some costumes."

"He's really making a go of it, isn't he?"

"I guess," she said.

"I give him credit," Charles said dryly. "He had the foresight to see that there was money to be made in the clown business."

She nodded. "That's Barry. All his life there was a successful person struggling to get out."

They walked on. "Tomorrow, we've got a field trip," said Charles, after a while. "I'm taking all of the Bobolinks to the Bronx Zoo."

"The Bobolinks?"

"That's how the camp is divided up. Bobolinks, Orioles, Wrens, Larks . . ."

"Got it."

He glanced at the storefront up ahead. "You want some ice cream?"

"Uh-uh."

They walked on. Every now and then, as if by accident, they would brush against each other.

"You really shouldn't have stayed in the city," Charles said. "Should have gone somewhere."

"Where should I have gone?" she said.

"The ocean?"

"Oh sure. The Hamptons. On five dollars a day," she laughed.

"It just seems a shame to be in the city in August."

"I like it," she confessed. "It's a good place to do nothing."

When they got to her apartment, it was a hotbox even though the windows were open and the shades had been drawn. She turned on the fan.

"God," she said, standing in front of the fan, feeling it on her damp white cotton blouse. "It's brutal."

She went to the kitchen to get a bowl of water. She set it down in front of the fan.

"What's that for?" he asked.

"To cool the air," she explained.

He gave her a look.

"My grandmother swore by it. Want some iced tea?"

"OK."

She put lots of lemon in it. When he wasn't looking, she ran a lemon half across the back of her neck and on her temples.

"Here," she said, handing him the glass.

She watched him sip the tea. He looked hot and thoughtful and she wanted to touch him. "You don't use sugar, do you?" she said.

"White death," he replied.

"I use a lot. Three spoons. I hope you don't think less of me for it," she said, straight-faced.

He smiled. "You're pretty funny sometimes."

"Funny-funny or funny-weird?"

"Both. But I meant funny-funny. That always surprises me about you."

"Why? Because I seem stupid?"

He stared at her. "In a way. A space cadet," he said. "You know how to use that, don't you? But it's so far from what you really are."

"It's not so far," she said. She put down the glass of iced tea. "You see, after that . . . thing I told you about . . ."

"Your sister."

"Yes." She looked down at the floor for a moment. The cat was there, staring at her, waiting for something. "After that I said, Let's just turn off here, OK? And then I was like Sleeping Beauty. Waiting for the right person to wake me up."

"Did you find him?" Charles asked, feeling the air from the fan.

She stared at him and then she stood up, came over to him. She sat down on his lap. "I know it's hot," she whispered.

His arm came up to encircle her waist. Slowly—maybe it was the heat, maybe the odd long shadows in the room—he put a hand to her breast. As he touched her, she felt something melt in this heat.

He rose with her, carrying her in his arms. She had her arms around his neck, feeling the rivulets of sweat down his back. He carried her to the sofa and laid her down, arranging her there, like a sick child, with a tenderness that made her close her eyes.

Then he was undoing her sneakers. She started to say something but she couldn't get the words out. What would she say? I love you I need you Make love to me I want you. Why? He had her shoes off. His hands were firm on the soles of her feet. She was putting herself in his hands.

Her eyes closed. Her fingers in his hair. She had told him everything there was to tell. He worked on her feet and then he moved up and made circles on her temples. Then he was kissing her. She pulled him onto her, feeling his weight and his length, pressed down beneath him. She ran her hands through his thick gray hair and down his back. She wrapped her legs around him; they kissed so deeply. Then he pulled away, out of her grasp, and smiled down at her and stroked her hair.

"Charles," she murmured.

He undid the buttons of her blouse and the buttons on her pants. He undressed her. He was good at dressing and undressing people, she thought. His stock in trade. He rolled down her underpants. She closed her eyes again. The whir of the fan, the imaginary breeze off the water. The danger of the water so close to the fan. In high school Darla Goetz had been killed when a fan fell into her bath. Oh, Charles. He was doing slow things to her nipples. She pressed him against her nipples. Opened her eyes. Look how anyone sucking a breast becomes again a child. She closed her eyes. The whir of the fan, the cat's meow, the thick scent of marigold on the fire escape. His mouth on her belly. Her fingers in his hair. Holding him. Then pushing him. Then—a moment—and she sucked in her breath, held it. Oh, what was he doing? She pressed her thighs against his ears. Arched her back. Stop, but he wouldn't. A keening noise and it wouldn't stop. Kept going. Out the window.

Then it was like she slept. He was gone and then he came back. He found a washcloth and washed her with cool water. Well water. He was naked now. Look how beautiful. As he leaned down, to plug in the fan closer, she could see his balls through his ass. Touched herself. His body lean, furry down by the belly, and his penis long and thin, hard now when he turned, straight up. He put the bowl of water in front of the fan, lay down beside her.

"I slept?" she asked.

"Yes," he said, running the washcloth across her breasts, down her back.

"How long?"

"Oh, hours." He grinned. "Hours and hours."

"It's so hot," she said, pressed against him.

"Yes."

"I don't think I can stand it."

"Oh yes. You can."

"No," she said. "I'm melting. Really. I'm melting."

He kissed her. She threw a leg over him. Next time she would search every bit of him, but now . . . now . . . She braced herself against the sofa and he moved into her. As tightly as she could she held him. His back slick with sweat. Held him so tight. He couldn't slip away.

Oh, she said, taking no time. She heard him cry out—the pain, joy, everything. Charles. Baby. She closed her eyes, made two fists, and let herself fall.

21

"GOOD MORNING, Mrs. Diamond? . . ."

That's Ms. Diamond to you.

"I'm Gertrude Slade of Reach for Recovery," said the attractive silver-haired woman, positioned in the doorway.

Bully for you.

"It is the aim of our organization to visit every woman who has undergone—"

"Listen," Anna interrupted. "I'm not up for this, OK? Not today."

Gertrude Slade's blue-veined hands formed a steeple. "That's a perfectly normal reaction," she said gently, "but before long, you'll want to—"

"Please!" Anna cried. "Please."

The color drained from the woman's face. Maybe this was her maiden outing, thought Anna—and wouldn't it be just her luck to get someone on her maiden outing? "I know I'm perfectly normal," Anna said. "Except for this one little thing." She licked her lips; her mouth seemed always to be dry. "Could you maybe come back another day? If it's not too much trouble?"

"Of course," said the woman. "Good luck to you, dear," she added, as she withdrew from the doorway.

Anna looked out the window. The East River sparkled in the sun—as best the East River could sparkle. Thanks to Rose Mead's influence, she had gotten a room with a river view.

But after a while she even tired of the river view and went back to staring at the ceiling. There was a crack there. *A crack in the ceiling had the habit/Of sometimes looking like a rabbit.* One of the last things she had done on Sunday morning before she left for the hospital was to read *Madeline* to Molly. It had been Anna's favorite book from her childhood and now it was Molly's. Before there was feminism, before there were women's caucuses, before there were anatomically correct dolls and Fisher-Price speculums, there was smart, plucky little Madeline, who was not afraid of mice, who loved winter, snow, and ice, and who underwent major surgery with such aplomb that she had all of her peers aching to go under the knife too. She set a standard to which Anna still aspired, even now, as she lay in her bed at New York Hospital, trying to digest the fact that four days ago she had her left breast and some axillary lymph nodes removed.

She turned her head to the right. To her left was the bandage, and a drain with some awful yellow fluid being pulled out of her. To her right was something nicer: an enormous pink plush bunny rabbit with a note that read "All our love and faith in your speedy recovery. The McIvers." Sure it was corny and sure it was tacky but Anna loved it all the same. At night, in the dark, she could see it sitting there, huge and benign, and she felt safer for it. There was something to be said, at this particular time, for soft cuddly things and warm, bright colors.

Everyone else had sent flowers. Sam and Liv. The Pooles. "Your friends at the Center." Her Uncle Morris, who had made a killing in the imitation-diamond jewelry market, sent an enormous acrid bouquet of football mums, spray-painted red, yellow, and aqua. Although she supposed it was thoughtful of him, it made her feel like a Mafia chieftain lying in state. She wished he had sent money instead. Maybe, she thought, somewhere down the line, they could hit him up for a loan, but then she remembered her cousin Sherry, who was going through Uncle Morris's money trying to get her *nouvelle* Jewish catering service off the ground, and, with a bitterness that filled her entirely, Anna saw her own chances dwindle.

How would they survive? If she lived—and since the lymph was clear, the odds were eighty percent in her favor—how would they survive? The effect on their lives—the pain; the fear; the cost—how would they survive? Michael's mother died of abdominal cancer when he was twelve. And although he hadn't brought it up and probably never would, she could see, in his eyes, that he thought life was playing a bad joke on him. But I'm not a bad joke, Michael. I'm serious . . . altogether serious.

She turned back once more to the plush pink rabbit. Boo. That's what she called him. Don't ask why. It came to her, like that, in a haze of Demerol. Wait until Molly sees it. And all those Mylar helium balloons that her friend Elaine had sent—wait until Molly sees them. And wait until she saw Molly. But don't jump on me, Molly. Don't jump on Mommy, baby.

The first time around they'd gone for the conservative approach. Now you have to understand that there is a confusion in terms for the layman when you talk about breast surgery. "Conservative," in this context, means "to conserve." And "radical" surgery—wherein the breast is removed and sometimes the nodes and the pectoral muscle—is really the more "conservative," i.e. "establishment," method. She had had the lumpectomy but, finally, it was not enough. Or, maybe, not finally. There was no telling what she was in for from here on in.

Boo. Suddenly she was crying. These days it happened that way—suddenly. Well, at least she never had large breasts. And at least Michael had never been what you'd call a breast man. Maybe, if she was lucky, he would turn out to be a scar man, she thought, hearing herself cry, hoping that someone would come in to witness it.

And someone did. Her mother. Arms laden with magazines. Rushing to her bedside.

"Anna! What is it? Tell me."

"Oh, it's nothing," Anna replied, wiping away the tears.

"Tell me," her mother insisted.

"It's nothing," Anna said. "My time of the month," she shrugged.

She thought it was a good joke but her mother didn't laugh. So maybe it wasn't a good joke. It was her fucking prerogative to make a lousy joke, wasn't it? She stared at her mother—frosted hair, immaculately groomed, double-breasted—and wanted to pick a really good fight.

But her mother wasn't taking the bait. Not today anyway. And that, more than anything, made her feel ill. Because, in the past, the healthy past, her mother always took the bait, even when the bait wasn't there.

"I brought you some magazines," Faye said.

"Thanks."

Her mother made as if to hand her the magazines, but then thought better of it. The arm, the arm. She started reading off the titles. "*Redbook. Ladies' Home Journal. McCall's* . . . didn't you tell me you had an article coming up in *McCall's*?"

"*Mademoiselle*," Anna corrected. She wrote service pieces every now and then. Having odd talents for writing, crafts, and hobbyism, Anna had forged some kind of hectic career out of merging them all. "In October. 'How to Make a Bikini Out of Washcloths,'" she murmured, the words like something from another planet or from some other life altogether.

"*Savvy. Ms.*," her mother continued. "*New Woman* . . ."

"That's me," Anna quipped.

Her mother paused but, again, didn't address it. You could see, though, that the lines of her face had already deepened measurably. She put down the magazines. "Anyway," she said, "they're here. If you want them."

"Thanks," Anna said. She was behaving very badly, not at all like Madeline, and she didn't feel good about it. "I'll get to them today."

"There's no rush," her mother said.

"Oh yes," Anna replied. "Pretty soon it'll be time for me to get back to work . . ."

"Oh, Anna. Please. Don't push it."

"I'm not *pushing* it, Mother. All I said was—"

"You have to give yourself a chance to recover. I know you. Little Miss *Spilkes*—that's what we used to call you."

The Yiddish equivalent of Little Miss Ants-in-the-Pants—yes, that's what they always used to call her. "For your information, Mother, I have a career. My income is not inconsequential to us."

"I told you, Anna," Faye said firmly. "Daddy and I have already discussed it and we want to lend you and Michael—"

"Forget it!" Anna cried. "Number one, we don't want to borrow and number two, you don't have it to lend."

"What do you mean? What are you talking about?" Faye countered. "You know everything about our personal finances, may I ask?"

"If you have so much money sitting around, then why haven't you ever bought a dryer?" Anna challenged. "Why do you still hang your wet laundry in the bathroom?"

"Oh, Anna. Really," her mother said, with a sound that was in between a snort and a laugh. "I can't believe what I'm hearing."

"Mother, please," said Anna. "I thank you and Michael thanks you but we will manage."

"How?" Faye demanded. "You won't be able to work for at least several months . . ."

"I'll work tomorrow. Tomorrow morning I will take notes for an article."

"Oh, yes?" Faye returned and Anna could see, with much satisfaction, that her mother was finally taking the bait. "And on what will you be writing, may I ask?"

"'How to Make a Prosthesis Out of Washcloths,'" Anna shot back, on a manic wave of anger that felt better than anything she'd felt in days but that only lasted for a second.

The room became very quiet. Anna looked at her mother. Her face very red. Her lips pursed. Her earlobes, old and elongated, from too many years of wearing heavy gold earrings. Funny, thought Anna, how she had never noticed that before. She looked away, unable to bear it. "Sorry," Anna said dully.

There was silence.

"I *said* I'm *sorry.*"

"I want to help," Faye whispered.

Then let me do this, Anna wanted to say. Just let me be a bitch.

"Do you want me to leave?" asked Faye.

"No," Anna replied, quickly.

Faye looked in her bag for something. A breath mint was Anna's guess.

"You remember Dr. Kittenplan?" Anna said.

Faye looked at her. There was a lump in her cheek. She must have found the mint, Anna decided. Or else it was cancer. "Whatever made you think of him?" asked Faye.

"Every year he used to take a full set of X rays," Anna said. "Didn't he?"

Faye continued to stare at her. "I suppose so . . ."

"You know, they don't do that anymore," Anna said. "Not as a matter of routine."

"Well," said Faye, after a moment, "that's the way they did it then."

"I know," said Anna. "I understand that. But the other thing is—what I'm wondering—he never used a blanket, did he?"

"A blanket?" asked her mother, confused. "You don't mean a napkin?"

"No. Not a napkin." *If I meant a napkin, I'd say a napkin.* "I mean a blanket. A lead blanket. For protection against the X rays."

There was a long moment. "I don't know," said her mother.

"Why?" Anna asked forthrightly. "Why don't you know?"

"I don't know," Faye repeated. "I mean, it isn't something that we asked about then and even if it was—"

"But it was X rays!" Anna cried. "Don't you understand? It was X rays! Couldn't you anticipate what it would mean to have a full set of X rays every year, every goddamn year, without even a goddamn lead blanket to protect you?"

"Dr. Kittenplan was an excellent dentist!" her mother insisted, her voice trembling, her face flushed, tears finally welling up in her eyes. "Everyone used him. Everyone! He did research!"

Anna nodded. "That's all well and good," she said. "But he was careless, wasn't he? He was careless and now I'm suffering for it."

She watched her mother try to say something, but it was taking too long. Anna closed her eyes and pulled the cool white sheet up to her neck.

She must have slept. She did a lot of that. Fading in and out of sleep. Just then the door opened and in walked her husband. As always, these days, he was carrying flowers and, for a change, chocolates.

"Hi there," he said, giving her a kiss.

"Hi," she said, her voice little-girlish, as it became now and then, without warning, these days. "You're late."

"Traffic," he said.

She watched him as he set down his parcels. He looked very good today—natty—in a light gray tropical wool suit with a pink silk tie.

"Here," he said, filling the vase and placing it by her bedside. "Anemones."

One of the better things about marriage was living with someone who knew you didn't like your flowers painted. "They're lovely," she said.

He opened the box of chocolates. A Perugina assortment. She helped herself to one and so did he. She liked soft centers; he liked nuts. The secret of their marriage. What was disgusting though was that he would eat exactly one. Was that why she got cancer? Because she ate too many sweets, drank too much coffee, took too many aspirin, and, before Molly, smoked too many Parliaments? But it wasn't fair. She wasn't a cancer personality. She was messy and disorganized and cheerfully neurotic. If anyone was a cancer personality, it was Michael. He was the tense, rigid one, hard on himself, driven. Weren't those the characteristics of a cancer personality? And yet here she was—bandages and drains—and there he was, in his natty Alan Flusser suit.

"Delicious," she said, at last, the chocolate feeling all wrong as it went down.

"You're looking well," he said, sitting down in the chair beside the bed.

"You think so?" Her response sounded innocent enough, but already an edge was creeping in. Why was he sitting in the chair next to the bed? She had asked him more than once to sit on the bed itself.

"Definitely," he said, examining a scuff on his black shoe. "Your color has improved."

"All the way up to ashen, eh?"

He smiled. "No, no. I'd say you're actually heading into the pink. And from there it's just a stone's throw to rosy."

He'd always made a big deal of her fabled rosy complexion. Which, of course, she herself had always hated, thinking she favored a beet.

"How do you feel?" he asked, looking up from the scuff.

"The same," she said. "Maybe a little better," she added, to be plucky.

"Everyone's called. Everyone wants to know how they can help. Tonight we're invited to Liv and Sam's for dinner."

"Oh. That's nice," said Anna, feeling a bolt of pure envy pass through her. The idea of Michael and Molly out visiting without her made her feel empty. If she died—and there was a twenty-percent chance of it, or at least that's what they told her—he'd waste no time finding a new wife. A healthy one this time. How could he not? A man alone with a little girl—who would blame him? And not just for Molly's sake. For Michael too. He was a man who should be married. It would be bad for him to live alone. But don't let Molly call anyone else "Mommy." Please, Michael. Not that.

"So I'll be over a little later tonight," he continued, "after I get Molly home. Mrs. Sullivan will stay with her until I—"

"Michael," she said, wanting to tell him that thing right now, while there was still time.

"Yes?"

"Come sit by me on the bed."

He came up onto the bed, but kept one foot on the floor. Just like they used to do in the movies back in the days of censorship, she thought. The Hays Office. They made Fred MacMurray, in pajamas, keep one foot on the floor while he was in bed with Claudette Colbert. "All the way," she whispered.

He climbed up all the way. Both feet off the floor. He sat there, feet dangling, looking kind of silly, and, for a moment, he was her child. Yes. It wasn't so odd, she thought. Sometimes it happens like that between married people. One becomes the child, the other the parent. Then it changes. Then it goes away and then it comes back again. She took his hand and kissed it. He lay down next to her, on her good side, and they were quiet together for a long while.

"How's Molly?" she finally asked.

"OK, I think."

"My mother's bringing her by?"

He looked at his watch. "In fifteen minutes."

They had arranged to have Molly downstairs so that Anna could wave to her. They had been doing all sorts of things to compensate for Anna's absence—just as they did when Michael went on business trips.

"You're sure she's okay?" Anna asked.

"She seems to be," Michael said thoughtfully. "Although for the last few days she's been having a lot of accidents."

"Pee accidents?"

"No, no . . ."

"Not BMs?" Anna said, in dread.

"Get your mind out of the toilet, girl," he said, and she smiled a little, and laced her fingers through his. "I mean juice accidents. I mean fishsticks-on-the-floor accidents."

"Oh," she said. "You mean attention-getting accidents."

"Or anger-venting accidents. She wants her mommy back," he said. "No two ways about it."

"Michael," she began, but then, as before she got no further.

"What?" he said.

"I don't ever want her to call anyone else Mommy," she said, in a rush, so it was done.

She held on to him, but, for a time, he seemed so far away. "Michael?"

"I'm here," he said, his voice funny.

She closed her eyes. When she opened them, and there was no telling how long they had been closed, he was standing over her. Her mouth was very dry and he poured water for her from the Styrofoam pitcher.

"Drink this," he said, as though it were a cure.

She could feel the water fall all the way down—a deep dry well.

"Can you walk to the window now?"

She looked at him through the dull red haze that hurt.

"I'll help you," he said.

She got out of bed and held on to him as he led her to the window. It was a sunny day, she noticed. Maybe she had noticed it before. It was hard to remember, because of the sleeping, what was today, what was yesterday.

She looked down at the little strip of park that ran along the street and there she saw Molly. She was wearing red overalls and holding her grandmother's hand. Her hair, somehow, was in pigtails.

"Molly," she called, waving with her right hand, feeling her arms ache with the desire to hold her.

Whether Molly actually saw her or not she might never know, but she was waving, as she must have been instructed to do. "Up here, honey," Anna cried, but there was too much distance and, after another moment, Anna turned. "I'm tired, Michael."

"OK," he said, offering his arm.

She held on to him as they walked slowly back to the bed, and wondered if she felt different to him.

"Come on, Molly," Michael said gently. "Do what you have to do."

But Molly didn't seem to hear him. She was playing with the toilet-paper dispenser as she sat on the pot in the first-floor men's room of the Metropolitan Museum of Art. Sometimes, when he watched her like this, he couldn't really believe he was a father. Molly was an accident—conceived while Anna was using her supposedly 99% effective diaphragm—and Michael had been opposed to having her. They weren't ready; they weren't far enough along in their careers; they didn't have enough money. But Anna, who thought Molly was a miracle, her "one-percent baby," wore him down. Under the circumstances, however, Michael hadn't behaved the way expectant fathers are supposed to behave. He lost weight instead of gaining; he didn't photograph Anna in Madonna poses; and he didn't put his hand to Anna's stomach and wonder whether this was a hand or a foot he was feeling. In fact, he was a little nauseated by the whole process, seeing the fetus as a kind of invasion, a parasite. He tried to keep this attitude to himself but finally, toward the end, it came out. Anna had asked him one time too many to touch her stomach.

—You keep asking me to touch your stomach.

—So? What's wrong with that?

—It's just that you keep asking me and I don't want to and I can't say that.

—But you just did, Michael. You just did.

He would never forget her look of surprise and hurt. His poor Anna. What had he done to her?

"Where does it go, Daddy?" Molly suddenly asked.

"Where does what go, honey?" he replied, pulled from his reverie.

"The poop."

"Oh. Well, it goes down pipes and into sewers."

After she was done—and it took a long while—he took her by the hand and led her out onto the floor, through the Egyptian rooms and out onto the street. It was hot and sticky outside and he took her for ice cream. It was one way of getting through a summer day in the city, he thought. That was the other thing about the . . . thing. They had planned to spend a month in Sag Harbor. Michael's friend Polly Gorton had gone to Barcelona and was letting them rent her cottage for the cost of covering her expenses. It was a great little house, weathered shingle, window boxes planted with red geraniums and blue lobelias, close to the ocean. What a good time they would have had there. Poor Molly. She was spending the whole summer in the city. It wasn't fair. A child should not be trapped in New York City for the summer. All kids should have some part of the summer when they can just run out-of-doors, walk barefoot in the grass, catch fireflies. The thought of her having to wait a whole other year to have any of that filled him with sadness.

"Hey, there, ice-cream face," he whispered, and she grinned at him.

They took the crosstown bus to Sam and Liv's. He felt funny going there tonight. In a way, it was almost a betrayal. Going upstairs in the elevator, he didn't know why he had said yes. He supposed it was because he wanted a few hours that were untainted, and now, realizing how futile that was, he felt stupid and guilty and hesitated before ringing the bell.

"Coming!"

The door opened and Sam stood there, the baby in his arms, and Aaron, looking fretful, affixed to Sam's leg.

"Welcome to Bide-a-Wee," said Sam.

As they went in, Michael glanced around. The place looked a mess, as usual. Sam and Liv were the worst housekeepers he knew. When you went to the bathroom in their apartment, you habitually encountered a wastebasket that overflowed with used cotton balls, cotton swabs, Band-Aid wrappers, denuded toilet-paper rolls, discarded coupons, broken crayons, hanks of human hair, and assorted unidentifiables that you didn't want to wonder about too long. Whenever he paid a visit there, Michael, who was scrupulously clean and whose idea of relaxation involved prowling with a Dustbuster, had to restrain himself from going at their sinks with the Comet.

"We're a little behind schedule," said Sam. "Actually I'm covered with shit."

Michael stared at him, particularly his shirt. "You certainly are."

"Freya exploded on me. Direct salvo to the midsection. I was about to change her diaper, looked away for a second, and then—whammo! Torpedo run! Did you ever have that happen to you?"

"Uh-uh."

"Believe me, Michael," he said gravely. "It's not what you want to have happen to you. Excuse me a second while I clean up, will you?"

"Please," said Michael.

"And you do mean please," said Sam, returning to the bedroom.

Molly ran down the hallway with Aaron, into his room. They were very good friends, even though they occasionally liked to torture each other. Michael wouldn't be at all surprised to see one of them come shrieking out of Aaron's room at any moment, streaming with tears, but then again they might actually play for half an hour without any disturbance at all.

"There we are," said Sam, as he came back in. "Clean as a whistle. Sorry about that."

"Hey. Listen," Michael said. "It happens."

With Freya on his hip, Sam went to the kitchen cabinet and pulled out a bottle of Jack Daniels. "Have one?" he asked.

Michael didn't usually drink hard liquor, but if ever there was a day for it—a week for it—this was it. "Sure," he said. "With a lot of water."

"Listen," Sam said, as he poured, "as it turns out, Liv's working tonight. Emergency deposition."

"Oh," said Michael, feeling awkward. "We could go out for dinner . . ."

"Don't worry about it," Sam said. "I got a Chirping Chicken." He handed Michael his drink and sat down across from him, in an armchair that had laundry drying on it. "How's Anna?"

"She's OK," Michael said.

He waited for Sam to say something. *Tough break. What a gal. If you need anything . . .* "Santé," said Sam, lifting his glass, and they drank.

"Liv's beside herself with remorse," Sam said. "She really wanted to be here tonight."

"Tell her not to worry about it, will you?"

"She's been working like a bitch lately," Sam said. The baby began to fret and he put her across his lap, jiggling her up and down. Michael thought he was jiggling her perhaps a little too hard. In any case, she wasn't quieting down. "She's like this all day," Sam said, sipping from the bourbon. "She takes catnaps. Twenty minutes at a time. Then wakes up screaming."

How can you stand it? Michael wanted to ask. "Is she teething?"

"Who knows?" Sam shrugged. "You can always say a kid is teething, right? I let her cry a lot," he confessed. "I've got to. If I didn't she'd become totally dependent. Can you hold her for a minute?" Sam said, handing her to him.

"Sure."

"I'll put dinner on the plates," he said, as he headed into the kitchen.

Michael arranged Freya on his lap. She took one look at him, her lower lip began to tremble, her face screwing up, and then she let out a howl.

"Don't worry about it," Sam called. "It's just something she does—don't take it personally. Just walk with her a little."

He walked with her. At first, she screamed an awful, gagging, retching kind of scream but, after a few minutes, she settled down a little. "There, there," he said. She fell into a kind of little mewing sound, and he patted her back. Molly, thank God, had been an easy baby, slept a lot, smiled when she was awake, smiled when she was cutting teeth. It was a blessed thing that she had been that way, ill-prepared as he was for fatherhood. He hadn't been very well-prepared for being a husband either. He wasn't the kind of person who was easily prepared for life's passages. When he was feeling hard on himself, which was often enough, he would describe himself as "weak," "frightened," "incapable." He saw life as a constant testing of his mettle, and he had always been the kind of kid who threw up before tests.

"How's she doing?" Sam asked, crossing the room with plates of chicken for the kids.

"Better," Michael said.

"Good work, Bauer," Sam called as he headed down the hallway toward Aaron's room.

Michael, feeling more confident, jollied her up a bit. She stared at him, with a pained watchfulness, getting ready for another attack. "OK. OK," he whispered.

"How's it going?" Sam asked, crossing back through the living room again.

"So far, so good," Michael replied.

Sam set out their chicken and potato salad on paper plates, and poured them each some more bourbon. "I'll take her back," he said, reaching out his arms for her.

Michael returned her. Almost immediately, Freya began a piteous screaming. Christ, Michael thought—did he beat her or something?

"Come on, Pieface," Sam said, with an unpleasant smile. "It's only Daddy."

Altogether, over the course of dinner, Sam must have had four bourbons. Michael had two and felt looped. Through it all, Freya kept on crying as Sam held her in every imaginable position. "I'm throwing in the towel," he announced, toward dessert. "I've decided to find a full-time job."

"Really?" said Michael. "But what about your book?"

"What about it?" Sam said, holding Freya under the arms and swinging her lightly while she whimpered. "I couldn't possibly get any less writing done on a full-time job."

"What will you do?" Michael asked.

Sam shrugged. "Publishing. Magazines. Escort service. Something in which I can use my verbal and communicative skills."

"Well," said Michael, "I guess it's not such a bad idea. All things considered."

"It's a great idea," Sam said. "There's going to be a lot of changes around here. Long overdue." The baby pulled up her legs and let out a huge amount of wind. "Delicate lass, isn't she? Paul Bunyan couldn't cut the farts she does." But it didn't seem to help. Still she writhed. "OK," Sam said. "Into your crib."

He disappeared for a moment. Michael covered his face with his hands. He was so very tired. Amid soul-wrenching screams and sobs, Sam returned to the table. "She'll go on like that for a while. But it's the best thing for her, I'm convinced. Either that or she'll bust a gut."

"Listen, Sam," said Michael. "Have you spoken to your pediatrician? Maybe he'd have some ideas . . ."

"What's he going to tell me?" Sam said. "She doesn't like the vibes here—that's the problem. Her mother's gone all day and half the night and Daddy is the bogeyman she's stuck with. Don't you think I know why she's crying? Because we're chained together here. The Defiant Ones. Getting along like oil and water."

There was a silence. Jesus, Michael thought. It wasn't as though he and Sam were even such close friends. Michael wished he could leave right now, but how could he?

Sam pushed away his plate and lit a cigarette. "Don't smoke, do you?" he said.

"No," Michael replied.

"I'm sorry," Sam said, blowing smoke at the ceiling. "It's not like you needed this tonight, eh?"

"That's okay," said Michael, not knowing what else he could say.

Sam took another puff, held it for a long while, blew it out. "When?" he said.

"What?" Michael asked.

He shook his head wearily. "When did it get so fucking hard?" he wanted to know, thick-tongued but undeniably lucid.

Michael stared at him. He felt, suddenly, a lot of things: empathy, contempt, other feelings that didn't have names. My wife has cancer. My wife is in pain. My wife could die and I could be left with a motherless child. My wife, who is the one who takes care of me and loves me and brings me out of myself and gives me a happy life, is in mortal danger. So don't come crying to me about your problems when you don't even realize how much you have. You jerk. You asshole. You bum. "It's been that way for a while, don't you think?" Michael said finally.

Sam shook his head. "Uh-uh. No. All of a sudden. Just like that."

There was a silence. "I've got to go," Michael said, after a moment.

Sam nodded.

Michael gathered up their things. After some time persuading Molly that it was time to go, he finally made it to the door. Sam, having rescued Freya from the crib, stood there as before, with the baby crying and Aaron holding on to his leg.

"Thanks," Michael said, not quite looking him in the eye, as he turned to leave.

A few days later, it was time for Anna to come home. Faye stayed with Molly while Michael drove to the hospital with his father-in-law, Fred Diamond, in Fred's new baby-blue Buick LeSabre.

"It's the custom touches I like," Fred said. "The adjustable steering wheel. The courtesy lighting."

Michael stared at the window. Anna was coming home.

"Can I stand here?" asked Fred, when they got to the hospital.

"Yes," Michael said. "They'll let you stand."

"If they chase me, I'll circle around."

"They won't chase you," Michael replied. He was fond of Anna's father, a kind man who had, two years ago, sold his interest in the Stride Rite children's shoe store he owned with his brother Leo and who now, in his retirement, was voluptuously engaged in the study of Talmud. But Fred had this fear of driving in the borough of Manhattan that was now, at this particular moment, difficult for Michael to tolerate. "Don't let them chase you," Michael cautioned.

"If they chase me, I'll circle," Fred said, looking drawn.

The fact was Fred was always circling. To speak with Fred was to engage in a dialogue of an unsettling circular configuration. He was a self-effacing man who liked his wife and daughter to make the decisions. Michael sometimes harbored the deeply disturbing notion that Anna had looked for a man like her father and had found one. "All right," Michael said. "We'll wait for you here."

He had to be patient with Fred, he thought, as he took the elevator to the seventh floor. It wasn't easy to see your daughter go through something like this. Not after all the time you spend telling a daughter that nothing's going to hurt her.

—Trust me, honey. Daddy won't let anyone or anything hurt you.

And she does trust you and it's all a lie. Before she's through, she'll get splinters and sunburns and tonsilitis. And sometimes, as it happened with Molly, she'll crack open her head horsing around and wind up in the emergency room, with stitches. And sometimes—without warning—even worse things might happen. So why the lies and why, oh why, do they believe you so readily and so wrong-headedly, over and over again?

"'Morning," said one of the nurses as he reached the floor.

"Good morning," he returned briskly.

The nurses liked him. Why not? He was one of the good husbands. They saw how he came every day, with flowers, and now here he was, carrying a shopping bag with personal items, purposeful and steady, come to retrieve his wife.

He approached the room with a curiously light step. Suddenly nothing was real to him. He saw himself, with the shopping bag, in the reflection of a chrome-plated broom-closet door, and he wondered who that was and what he was doing here, with the shoes, the red canvas espadrilles, in the Charivari shopping bag.

As he walked through the door, the sun, off the river, sent a corona through the room and she stood in the middle of it. He thought of those life-after-death stories—people floating toward a great warming light—and he squinted. She looked very nice. A nurse must have helped her dress.

"Hi," she whispered.

He felt his throat close. Be strong, he told himself. He moved toward her. "Hi."

She stared at him. Her face was different. There was a shadow beneath her jaw. "I'm ready."

"I brought you your shoes," he said.

She looked down and so did he. She was barefoot. He knelt, removing the shoes from the bag. Gently he lifted each foot and placed them in the red shoes. He'd done this for her when she was pregnant with Molly and it had been difficult for her to bend.

"Thank you," she said as he rose.

He reached out to touch her cheek and then, there, the shadow. She cried, as he knew she would, but when he let her into his arms and held her against him, it seemed all right.

"Your father's waiting downstairs," he said.

"He must be a wreck," she sniffed. "He's always afraid they're going to chase him."

"He is," Michael acknowledged as he gathered up her things.

The nurse brought the wheelchair. They left the flowers and an ugly little cactus that the florist had made to look, with beads and pipe cleaners, like Speedy Gonzalez or whatever. He took the brace of Mylar helium balloons for Molly and then they thanked everyone and headed downstairs. Fred was there, looking nervous. She got into the car, kissed him hello. It was a hot day. August. The temperature had been sitting at ninety-five for a week now.

Fred drove up Park Avenue as though it were lined with eggs. There was one pothole he missed and Michael saw Anna wince. He looked out the window. They would get through this, he told himself. Yes, they would. Because that's what life is—getting through things. He reached out for Anna's hand and held it in his lap.

When they pulled up in front of their building, Faye and Molly were waiting outside. One of their neighbors, an aging character actor named George Gold, had a parrot named Cicely whom he aired on summer days and Molly, entranced by it, hardly noticed at first when Michael and Anna emerged from the car.

"Look, Molly," Faye said. "Look who's here."

Molly turned to look. They could see the doubt on her face. Michael pulled one of the balloons loose from the bunch and gave it to Anna to give to Molly.

"Here, sweetie," said Anna, as Faye went to the car to give Fred instructions.

"It's silver, Mommy," Molly said as she reached for it.

But something got messed up—some signal or other—and the balloon passed into the gulf, floating up, out of reach, quick, like a jet, high. The look of doubt spread on Molly's face and she began to wail.

"No, honey," Anna said. "There's more. Lots more."

"I don't want my balloon to fly away!" Molly screamed.

"Honey . . ."

"I don't want my balloon to fly away! I don't want my balloon to fly away! I don't want my balloon to fly away!"

Michael scooped her up. As he held her, Anna showered her with kisses. "Mommy's home," he heard her whisper into Molly's ear. "And I'm not going away anymore."

With great care, they made their way inside.

22

IT WAS THE TUESDAY after Labor Day and everyone was back at work. Everyone except Nancy. Unless, that is, you regarded homemaking as work, but she didn't. She spoke not of her work but of her chores. This morning it had been her chore to bring David to the Center. It was a chore she happened to enjoy, particularly when she saw how excited he was to be back among his friends after the holiday separation. He was really such a sweetie, open and affectionate. But wasn't it boys like David—sweet, open, towheaded boys—who were in the worst danger of being snatched from suburban shopping malls? The question—the fear—hung there, in the morning, like a dark and heavy drape. If she remained in Manhattan, chances were slim that she would find herself in a Montgomery Ward's or a Sears or a J. C. Penney's before David grew old enough to defend himself. But if she were to go back to the farm, that's just where he would wind up—her little boy, in mortal danger, and all because of her.

She pulled the sheet over her head in the bed to which she had returned just after taking David to the Center. This was her future. Sheets over the head. Excessive eating. Masturbating in the early afternoon. At least, she thought, with a vestige of self-respect, she never turned on the soaps.

Was there anything emptier or more desolate than being a housewife in a house where your husband cared nothing about you? The question, self-pitying as it was, was also rooted in an undeniable reality, for she had just endured an August that had driven home the point of their lovelessness, driven it right through her heart like a stake.

They had rented a house in Robin's Rest on Fire Island. Robin's Rest was . . . what? A hamlet? Not even. A cluster of houses sprinkled on the sand. Theirs was a particularly expensive sprinkle, ten thousand for the month, right smack on the ocean, all glass, the beach at their feet. Not that she had much use for the beach. Being as fair as she was, she burned easily. But Justin had an oily skin. Thick, oily, Levantine. Which, to some degree, was what had allowed him to become an investment banker in the first place, she ventured to say.

For David, Robin's Rest should have been paradise, an endless and immaculate sandbox without cars. The trouble was he didn't have a happy mommy with him. Oh, she did all the happy-mommy things—combed the beach for shells; poked at horseshoe crabs in the bay; tossed a beach ball back and forth in the heat of the day—but she wasn't fooling anyone. Every afternoon, sure as the tides, she developed a blinding tension headache, the band of pain coiling and constricting around her skull like an iron python, and then she'd be no good at all. Then she'd send David outside to scratch idly in the sand, or put him in front of the TV regardless of what was on—*The Partridge Family; The Brady Bunch*—she didn't care.

She had spent months anticipating the family vacation that might somehow—magically—right everything that was wrong. But then suddenly, in early August, Something Very Big came Justin's way. Something to do with a refinery in Brazil—she wasn't quite sure, only half-listening to what he told her.

—Haven't you made enough money this year? she had asked him as he packed, carefully placing his things in the ostrich-skin T. Anthony carryall by which he swore. He was so proud of his travel accouterments. *Elegant but tough.* The precise epitaph he'd like to see written on his tombstone, which she too would like to see written, the sooner the better.

—You don't seem to understand, Justin. You have a family. You have a son. You have a responsibility to your son.

—No, Nancy. *You* don't seem to understand. My responsibility to my son is to ensure his financial future.

—What about his emotional future, you fucking asshole?

—As far as I can see, there's nothing wrong with him emotionally. But then again you've only had him for just shy of four years, haven't you?

It amazed her, as she sat there, watching him lovingly pack his custom-made Addison on Madison shirts, how deeply and abidingly she hated him. But what amazed her even more was that she had once loved him. She had, hadn't she? In Ithaca, those years, when she had run her hands over his smooth brown flesh . . .

Tentatively, tenderly, she touched herself. And it wasn't even early afternoon. What did she want? She thought of Sam, tried to remember something of Sam. She thought of the fur on his chest, which she had never much liked in a man before, and the scratch of his dark heavy beard, and the way his erection curved up, like a bow, something she'd never seen before.

He had been a good lover. If one could, in fact, be a good lover laboring under a burden of guilt such as he was carrying. As soon as they had gone into the bedroom and closed the shades and taken off their clothes, the awful cheesy stink of guilt went up. It wasn't until he was out of the house and she opened the windows and uncapped the jars of potpourri and fried onions on the burner that the smell began to diminish and she could breathe again.

Because he loved his wife and told her as much after he came into her, uttering a series of small mournful gasps.

—We've been together thirteen years.

—It's been fourteen for me and Justin.

—Liv's a wonderful person. She's a wonderful wife and a wonderful mother and a wonderful lawyer.

—So what's less than wonderful about her?

—Nothing. It's all my fault.

At that point, as she recalled, he paused before continuing.

—I mean, if there's anything, it's not intentional. It's just that she's very . . . focused. And that's kind of hard for me sometimes, because I'm not.

—Focused? You mean, as in driven?

—No, no. She's not driven. She's really a good person. A caring person. And I really do love her.

—So I hear.

—You've got to understand. It's not like with you and your husband.

—I understand (she said). I understand.

She sat up in bed, reached for the brush on her night table, brushed her hair. Her hair was so thick, if you brushed it a dozen times, it almost seemed to increase in thickness twofold. The Head of Hair That Conquered Cleveland. She looked at herself in the mirror. She was thirty-seven years old and her breasts, heavy as they were, had not yet sagged. She couldn't imagine why they had not. She never exercised. At one point, Justin brought home for her a Victoria Principal exercise video he'd bought at close-out. She suggested to him that it was entirely appropriate to close out Victoria Principal. She thought Victoria Principal had the face of a mean toy dog. Nancy didn't think of herself as being fat, because she wasn't fat—she was large-boned and that was the truth—but one of her legs was probably thicker than Principal's waist. She hated Justin for doing that and was glad for one more reason to hate him. Maybe, she thought, she was too much woman for him.

She stood up and walked to the mirror. She stared at herself. Identifying marks: kidney-shaped light tan freckle on left breast. Inverted right nipple. Appendectomy scar of faded coral. Varicosity on right calf. There she was. Ninety percent water. Ribonucleic acid. Simple and complex sugars. She squeezed her eyes shut.

—If you go away now, don't expect me to be here when you get back.

—Nancy . . .

—I mean it. I can't do this to David. I'm serious.

—Hey, first you call me a fucking asshole and then you issue threats and ultimatums. I don't know what's the matter with you.

—But you are a fucking asshole, Justin. You are.

And yet here she was. Waiting for him. His secretary—Deanne, of the Andrews & Alcott suits and the designer opticals—called to tell her he'd be home the day after tomorrow. She had the feeling he'd be carting an emerald. Somehow he seemed to know when she was at the breaking point and somehow he seemed to care a little bit. She didn't know what that was about. Maybe it was about fourteen years. Or maybe it was about the fact that at heart he was essentially a Good Jewish Boy. After all, he hadn't wanted anything more than to make money. That wasn't so bad, was it?

And yet here she remained. Waiting for him. Move your ass, girl. She turned sideways. Big soft flour-white ass. She touched her ass with both hands, lifting it slightly to the angle she would have liked it to be at. Here she was, waiting for the straw that broke the camel's back, except there wasn't any straw and, if anything, she was closer to a cow than a camel. It was time to do something. You're too young to die, she told herself, releasing the lobes of her ass and watching them fall down.

With a sense of calm that was unexpected, unexplained but somehow not entirely unfamiliar, she went to the closet and got down a suitcase.

The doorbell rang and Sam made a last effort to jolly up Freya, but she was beyond jollying. "Don't scare the babysitter," he warned her as he admitted Desiree, an aspiring actress, into their unkempt lair.

"She's very unhappy," Sam explained, depositing Freya into her arms.

"My poor pumpkin," Desiree cooed to her fretful charge.

"She really needs a nap," said Sam. "I tried, but nothing worked. I fed her. I rocked her. I even hummed the love theme from *The Godfather,* which usually does the trick."

"She'll nap for Desiree, won't you sweetheart?"

And indeed, Sam noted, Freya began to settle down. Maybe she just liked young women with spiked hair. "What are you auditioning for?" Sam asked, seeing the playscript under her arm.

"Oh, this is for my class. *The Crucible*," she said. "Do you know it?"

"Do I know it? I *live* it," Sam cracked.

He left them laughing and headed downstairs, onto his bike, which was chained at the curbside, and over to the park. It was only one day after Labor Day but Sam was struck by how quickly an autumnal feeling had infected the air. There was a palpable sense of depopulation in the park, a wistful postdiluvian ambience of scattered debris and exhausted resources, as if the park were not a park at all but a kind of emptied lunar fairground.

He pulled up to a bench—his bench—and just sat there for a moment. The quiet in the park was faintly eerie and almost thrilling, coming as it did upon the heels of his daughter's screaming. It wasn't right, he told himself, that she should be so unhappy so young. But he tried not to think about it. This was his time to think of nothing but his novel. Untitled Novel by Sam Sloan. *Under the Chinese Scholar Tree. The Horse-Chestnut Bough. Mariner's Gate.* He had thrown out more titles than he had thrown out used Pampers. The fact that he had not yet hit upon a great title—*For Whom the Bell Tolls; Of Time and the River; And Quiet Flows the Don*—disturbed him. Was it some innate flaw of the book that had prevented a great title from announcing itself? Then again, don't all great novels have great titles by virtue of the fact that they identify greatness? And why was he sitting here thinking about this just now when it was his time to write and he could just as well ponder these cosmic issues during the dishwashing or pot-scrubbing parts of the day?

He turned to the last of yesterday's installment:

> In the warm sand beneath the alder tree, Junius placed Iris on the spring bed of birch catkins and surveyed her wound. It was a fearsome thing, deep, black-red, curling into livid frays at the edges. He couldn't imagine how she would survive and daren't think what he would do if she didn't.

Daren't? There were times, writing this book, when he didn't know where things came from and wished they hadn't come uninvited. He must be scrupulous in avoiding an Englishy syntax that had characterized anthropomorphic writing since Beatrix Potter.

> He couldn't imagine how she would survive and he didn't dare think what he would do if she didn't.

And now he had the "didn't" redundancy and that was no good at all.

> He couldn't imagine how she would survive and he didn't dare think what he would do if she failed to.

He thought about it for a moment. Even worse. He began to feel a slight edge of anxiety, which could easily become a torrent if he let it. He wan't good. That was his problem. He was no fucking good.

> He didn't see how she could survive and what would he do if she didn't?

Oh Jesus. It was only getting worse. He was really screwing it up now. Because he couldn't even handle the syntax, he was losing the nuances of meaning. Here he was, at a pivotal point in the novel, and he couldn't even string simple sentences together. Crossing the Great Lawn, Iris, the white rat, had been injured, perhaps mortally, by a boy's slingshot—the big scene of the novel, and he was blowing it. He tried again.

> How could she survive and, if she didn't, what would he do?

He put that up against the original and decided that, for now, he could live with it. After all, he had no other choice.

> Carefully Junius applied a poultice of crushed raspberry leaves, quivering as he did so, imagining that wound thronged with maggots, as it would surely be in another day's time, if his medicine didn't work.

He read over this sentence two or three times and decided finally that it was a good sentence and that he should be commended for it. Although he wondered if the "carefully" was really necessary. After all, how else would he apply the poultice? He wouldn't throw it across the room at her, would he? But perhaps he was being too exacting. His aim, after all, was to finish the draft, sell it, and make whatever corrections an editor deemed necessary. It was not productive for him to sit here obsessing over every comma and period. And so, with a deep sigh, he willed himself to begin the day's writing.

As Junius mashed the comfrey leaves for the soothing tea he was making, he thought of the look of pain and surprise that had crossed Iris's face upon her injury.

He stopped. He almost wished he didn't have to read it—that it was composed in disappearing ink and would vanish without a trace—but it wasn't and it wouldn't. The paragraph stared up at him, almost winking, and he felt the knife edge of anxiety again. *Upon her injury?* What was this? A state trooper's accident report? When had his writing become this graceless, this clumsy? He was losing it, right here, before his very eyes, and he didn't know what to do about it.

The problem was his inability to concentrate and over this he had no control. How could he be expected to nurse along an extended thought when he was being constantly barraged by the exhausting exigencies of a domestic situation that he, in his folly, had constructed for himself? He understood now how Sylvia Plath had come to end it all, in that English winter, with the croupy children, and the low-grade infections and the inviting gas burner. Not that he had such suicidal tendencies—no, he liked the taste of chocolate too much—but he had, at last, an understanding of what it meant to be trapped. That was the thing, and the pity was that he needn't have set himself up for it. There were other ways to go about it.

—Look at Wallace Stevens. He sold insurance.

He wanted to punch Liv out whenever she said that. All those people who think art is perfectly fine and meritorious as long as you combine it with a little underwriting. Look at Nathanael West, he always returned—a night clerk at a fleabag hotel. Look at Melville—a customs inspector.

But he couldn't say she was wrong, could he? The fact was he could have carved out more for himself. He needn't have painted himself into a corner this way, having to prove himself a genius or else show himself a fool. That wasn't very good planning, was it? Nothing he did was very good planning. Leaving publishing when he did. Having children when he did. The thing with Nancy. He wished that hadn't happened altogether. What had it accomplished? Now, with Nancy, there was distance, each of them feeling ashamed, and ashamed of feeling ashamed. And with Liv, there was the onus of the unspoken word. For all the vicissitudes of their marriage—and their vicissitudes had vicissitudes—keeping secrets had never been their game.

He looked back to his page and put pen to paper:

To see that look of pain touch the one he loved was for Junius a thing of almost incalculable despair. He had never loved before. He couldn't remember ever knowing his mother or his father, his brothers or his sisters. He was all alone in the large world, until, that is, he had met Iris. And now he was in danger of losing her, forever.

Ah, he thought. That was good. He felt a kind of release come over him and he put down his pen and closed his eyes.

After that, he wasn't able to write very much more and what he wrote wasn't very good. Finally, it was time to go and he got on the bike and pedaled off to the Center. As he pedaled, the wind whipped his face and he imagined himself taking off, levitating, like the boys in *E.T.* Wouldn't that be nice, he thought, but then again there were so many things that would be nice.

When he got to the Center, Aaron ran over to him and threw his arms around Sam's neck.

"Hey, buddy," Sam whispered, hugging him back. "Now that's a good hello," he added, wondering what provoked it. "Let's get you a rice cracker, OK?"

With transitional object in hand, they left the Center. As Sam settled Aaron into the bike seat, he noticed Nancy up ahead walking hand-in-hand with David. He thought about whether he wanted her to see him or not, and then he felt silly even making an issue out of it.

"Hi," he said, pedaling up beside her.

When she turned to look at him, he could see that her face looked worn. Her hair, pulled back with two tortoiseshell barrettes, was unruly, almost a mop. She had on a nondescript green linen dress, which was strange in itself, because she almost always wore pants.

"Hi, Sam," she said, not quite looking him in the eye but then, these past weeks, he had grown used to that.

"Where are you headed?" he asked, the clicking of the bike chain about the only noise on the street.

"Here," she said, coming up beside a beige Volkswagen Jetta.

"Is this your car?" asked Sam, aware that there was something fundamentally funny about the question, as if the only part of her that she had kept private from him was the year and make of her vehicle.

"That's it," she said. "Justin always wanted to get a BMW or a Mercedes," she added, finally looking squarely at him. "Something expensive and German. I persuaded him to settle for something moderate and German."

"I suppose that's an accomplishment, in its own way," Sam allowed.

She shrugged. "What does it matter? Now he'll get what he wants."

Sam stared at her. "What are you doing?"

She stared back at him. Then she turned to the kids. "Boys, go into the playground for a minute," she said, pointing to a crummy little public-school playground that she had never before allowed them to investigate. The boys didn't need to be asked twice. They ran, and Nancy and Sam watched them alight on the seesaw.

"I made my decision," she said. "A few hours ago. I'm leaving."

Sam folded his arms across his chest. "Does he know?"

"Uh-uh. Actually you're the first to know." She set down her large cordovan handbag on the hood of the beige Jetta. "He's still in São Paulo. Due back Thursday. At least that's what his office tells me."

"What's he doing in São Paulo?" Sam asked.

She smiled. "That's what I love about you, Sam," she said. "You don't realize that men like Justin go off every day to places like São Paulo or Caracas or Brussels or Osaka to do business. Because that's where the oil or the copper or the aluminum or the tungsten or the bat guano is. And you can make money from those things. Lots of money."

Sam looked a little crestfallen. "Are you trying to make fun of me?"

She put a finger to her lips and shook her head. "Oh, no, Sam. I would never do that."

"How can you just walk out?" he asked.

"That's what I know how to do," she said. "I mean, I know you're not supposed to be the one to leave because that's abandonment or whatever but I don't care. I've had it with this bullshit. I'm unhappy, Sam, and my kid's suffering, and I'm walking."

"Where are you going?" he asked.

"Home," she said. "Home to Broadway."

He looked at her, confused.

"Broadway, New Jersey," she explained. "It's a tiny little agricultural community in Hunterdon County. Last censused population approximately four hundred and fifty. No murders, no rapes. No fancy restaurants where you can get four different kinds of mushroom but you can't buy a lamb chop. No little boutiques where you can buy weird Japanese clothing for three-year-olds . . . shall I go on?"

"Broadway, huh?" he said, managing a small grin.

"Broadway. Well, you know Broadway—*your* Broadway—was originally a place to drive the sheep and the goats so I guess it's not that weird, right?"

The grin widened into a smile. "You know, suddenly you're almost as funny as I am."

She thought about that for a moment. "I guess you rubbed off on me. So to speak."

They looked across at the kids, who were hanging over the swings.

"Have you told David?"

She shook her head. "As far as he knows he's just going to visit Grandpa. He loves his grandpa. And Gramps. That's what he calls my grandfather, who's ninety-one years old and what they used to call spry."

"What am I going to tell Aaron? Your just disappearing like this."

She looked past him, checking on the boys, and then she looked back at him. "I'm sorry about that, Sam. I wish . . . tell him not to blame David," she said. "Tell him it's all my fault."

He hesitated for a moment but then he put his arms around her, not caring who saw. "Don't worry," he said. "This is good. Yeah. It's very, very good."

She felt him patting her thick head of hair and then, after a moment, she pulled away. "You've got to get your house in order, Sam," she said, full of words. "You've got something and you can't afford to lose it. You know, Sam, if you take a lawn and you've got only thirty percent good turf and the rest is really bad, really shit, all crabgrass and goose grass and hawkweed, and if you take good care of that thirty percent it'll come back, it'll drive out the bad seventy percent, Sam, and you'll have this beautiful lawn, this emerald-green lawn." She looked up at him. "Does that sound really stupid?"

"No," he said, after a moment. "It's good to know. Because, you see, I've never had a lawn. Probably never will."

"Sam, if I thought there was even ten percent that was good in my marriage I would have stuck it out."

"But there wasn't."

"No. It was bad. All the way through."

He took her hand. "I'm sorry," he said.

She waited a moment and then she called the boys. "David! Aaron!" she called. "Time to go!" She turned to Sam. "We'll make sure the boys stay in touch," she said, in a fever of last-minute promises. "Aaron can come out to the farm. He'll be our little Fresh Air kid. It'll be great . . ."

"We'll see," Sam allowed, as the boys came running.

"Come on, David," said Nancy, unlocking the door of the Jetta.

"Is this your car?" Aaron asked, taking it all in.

"Yes," David replied.

"I didn't know," Aaron told him.

Nancy looked at Sam and they laughed a little. Then, quickly, she got behind the wheel and pulled out, leaving behind a space for some lucky person.

OLIVIA H. SLOAN. NOTARY PUBLIC.

She still derived a kind of perverse enjoyment every time she wielded her official stamp. She liked the accouterments of her job, even if she didn't like the hours.

Suddenly there was a knock at her door and, with a reflex that she had to admit was pretty shameful, she began straightening her papers. "Come in," she called.

It was Jessie Lund, a first-year associate out of Northwestern who looked like Jane Pauley. "I've got the Manchester material," Jessie said brightly.

"That was quick," Liv said, pleased. Jessie was definitely overzealous, but there were worse things in the world than eagerness and nothing quite so bad as procrastination.

"I had a bit of a problem with Miss Lovejoy," Jessie began, naming the law librarian, but Liv held up a hand. "Never has there been such a misnomer," said Liv. "Miss Lovejoy was poured with the foundation thirty-seven years ago. She's a fact of life around here."

The two women smiled at each other. *Working women,* Liv thought, as she looked over the material. After a moment, she became aware of Jessie looking at the photograph on her desk. "Are these your kids?" she asked, with a smile.

"Yes."

"Oh, aren't they adorable? I just love children," Jessie admitted.

And baby ducks, stuffed animals, and Red Skelton, Liv thought, but then she realized that just because she was tired didn't give her the right to be bitchy. "Well," said Liv. "You must meet them sometime. Aaron comes in every now and then. Plays with the paper clips and gets Oreos out of Sy Fischman's cookie jar. He thinks a law firm is a place where people get to eat Oreos."

Jessie laughed, but then grew serious. "I think it's amazing," she said.

"What?"

"How you can combine a career and a family," Jessie said earnestly. "That's one of the things I worry about. If I felt that I had to give up a personal life for Comley, Wizan, then . . ."

She stopped herself. What had started out as simple sycophancy had suddenly turned dangerously confessional. But this is how the girl will learn tact, thought Liv, so let me be good about it. "I'm afraid I haven't any tried-and-true lessons, Jessie," said Liv. "All I can say is it's very hard work but it can be done. And should be done. Now, let's look at the Manchester material."

The rest of the day passed by quickly enough. She avoided any major or minor pitfalls and by 7:10 she was out on Vanderbilt Avenue and found a cab right off. The taxi got her uptown by 7:28. Before she went up, she stopped at the Koreans' for some grapefruit—one of the things in life that kept her going—and some ice cream for Sam. He loved Ben and Jerry's mint chocolate chip. As she opened the door, in the brief moment before they saw her, she felt, as always, slightly the stranger. Sam was playing Memory with Aaron, and Freya was in the swing.

"Hi," she called.

"Hi," returned Sam and Aaron—the men in her life, who didn't rush to the door to greet her. But then why should they? she thought, honest with herself, always honest with herself, as she crossed the room to distribute kisses to all. "Looks like a good game," she said, noting with relief that Sam was letting Aaron win. This was important to Aaron, who didn't like to lose. In that respect, she thought, he was very much like his mother. She too didn't like to lose, and she wouldn't.

She freed a slightly glazed-looking Freya from the swing, in which she was traveling back and forth with metronomic regularity. "Bunny," she whispered. There was a flicker of a smile—but just a flicker. Would Freya be able to pick her out of a crowd?

(What are you worrying about her picking you out of a crowd for? Sam would ask. Name a situation in which she would *have* to pick you out of a crowd.)

All that stuff about bonding . . . for what? She had been scrupulous about not allowing anything to come between her and Freya during nursing. For that half-hour or forty minutes, it was all Freya. Freya would suck and stare up at her and smile, and Liv would smile back. That was what they called bonding. But it seemed that there had to be a certain amount of maintenance and the sorry fact was that she couldn't provide that kind of maintenance on her schedule.

"Come, Bunny," she said. "Mommy has to change."

She set Freya on the bed while she slipped out of her workclothes. Off went the tailored suit, the Anne Klein blouse, the pantyhose, the calfskin spectator pumps. On went the No Nukes T-shirt and the faded denim overalls: her beloved mufti. Then she carried Freya into the kitchen, where she found a vanilla yogurt and some leftover salad in the fridge. She had become what was designated by cultural observers of modern Yuppies as a "grazer." That is, she ate here and there, when the mood struck her, of a diet almost exclusively composed of grains, cheese, vegetables, and fruit.

"What did you guys have for dinner?" she asked, sitting down beside them.

"Hamburgers," said Sam, trying to decide which Memory card to turn over.

"Wrong, Daddy!" Aaron cried gleefully, clapping his hands.

"Listen here. It is unnecessary and unsportsmanlike to applaud every time I make a mistake," said Sam.

"My turn," Aaron blithely replied.

Liv held Freya closely and picked at the salad, which had wilted almost, but not quite, to the point of utter sogginess.

"Did you all have a good day?" Liv asked them.

"Pretty good," Sam said. "How about you?"

"Oh, pretty good. No major disasters."

The boys concentrated on their game. Freya clung to Liv's overalls, playing with a brass button.

After a while, it was time for the children to go to bed. Liv lay with Aaron, in his bed, reading him *Bread and Jam for Frances*. "So you see," she said instructively to her son, as they reached the conclusion, "Frances finally tried something besides bread and jam and she liked what she tried and you might like it if you tried things too."

He curled up against her. "I don't want to, Mommy," he said in a tiny voice.

She stared at him. He was so pale and small—really a puny child, as she had been. She kissed his slightly damp temple and the crown of his head and his nose. "All right," she said, realizing that it was perhaps unnecessary for her to be instructive this late in the day. She started to sing.

> *I love Paris in the springtime,*
> *I love Paris in the fall . . .*

"Don't sing, Mommy," Aaron whispered.

"All right, luv," she whispered back, respecting his need to be contrary.

Soon he was asleep. She lay there examining him. He really was so thin. She hoped his constitution was strong. She hoped he'd never get sick. If anything ever happened to him, she couldn't live. She shut her eyes, trying to shut out the thought but also, in a strange way, entering deeper into the thought, with a curious kind of pleasure in the pain, such as one derives from nursing an ache in one's gum, and then the next thing she knew Sam's hand was on her shoulder, shaking her, but ever so gently. She often fell asleep putting the children to bed, so she knew, right off, what had happened.

"I fell asleep," she said, as he gave her a hand up. "Is Freya. . . ?"

"Out like a light."

They went into the living room. The apartment seemed so cozy and quiet. They often told each other how there was no better or more peaceful feeling than knowing that your children were safely asleep in their beds.

"Did Aaron have a good day?" she asked, as they sat down together on the couch.

"Fine. They took them to the park. Played under the sprinklers."

"Oh, good. It was such a hot day." She looked at him, straightening her glasses. "How did the writing go today?" she asked, a little tentatively, not wanting him to think that she was pressing for an accounting, but neither did she want to feel that her husband's work was off-limits to her.

"Good," he said and they left it at that.

She got up to make tea and when she came back he told her. "Nancy Poole left her husband," he said.

She put a hand to her breast. It was one of her dainty, ladylike gestures, passed down through the ages, and she used it reflexively to greet any news that surprised or shocked her. "When?" she asked.

"Today. She picked up David at the Center and got into their car and headed out to New Jersey, to her father's farm. She has a VW Jetta."

"Her father has a farm?"

"Oh yeah. You didn't know that? She used to be a full-fledged dairy maid."

She stared at Sam. She knew he had a friendship with her. The boys were very close and Sam and Nancy often spent time together in the playground. She herself didn't really know Nancy that well, but she always thought she seemed nice enough. It had always seemed to her very nice that Sam had this friendship. Sam's situation could be so isolating, and Liv thought it was really very nice indeed that the isolation was not complete. "She just walked out on him?" Liv asked. "Just like that?"

"So it seems . . ."

"She shouldn't have," Liv replied. "She's letting herself in for a whole mess of problems that way."

"She knows that," Sam said, with what struck Liv as an excessive emphasis.

"Well, if she knows it, then why did she—?

"Because she doesn't care," he returned. "She wants to get out, no matter what price she has to pay."

Liv couldn't help laughing a little. "Come now, Sam. Such phrases sound very good on television, but they don't really have much to do with reality."

"Don't condescend to me, Liv, OK?" Sam shot back.

She waited a moment before replying. "I'm sorry," she said. "I didn't mean to. It's just that you don't enter into a divorce situation the way you would an elopement. Particularly not with a man like Justin Poole. There are community-property issues, there are custody issues. You don't conduct yourself like a schoolgirl who's—"

"She was sick to death of it!" Sam said. "That's it. The bottom line. Can't you understand that?"

They watched each other. They weren't sure what was happening, nor did they know how to control it. "Well," she said finally, with a briskness that disguised nothing, "we really don't have to fight Nancy Poole's fights, do we?"

"No," he said. "We really don't." He looked up at the ceiling and then, frankly, back at her. "God knows we have enough of our own, we don't have to go borrowing from anyone."

There was a long moment, as he waited for her response, and then she managed a small smile. "Neither a borrower nor a lender be," she said, with an odd primness that she hated but that always emerged when she was nervous.

Then there was another long moment and the air seemed almost to buzz.

"I told Aaron," he said.

"What did you tell him?"

"That David was going away for a while. I don't think it quite sank in."

"Poor Aaron," she said, shaking her head.

"Poor David."

The buzz seemed to grow in intensity as they sat there beside each other on the couch.

"I bought some ice cream," she said. "Mint chocolate chip."

"Ben and Jerry's?"

"Of course." She got up, smiling slightly. "I'll go dish it out."

She went into the kitchen and got out two dishes and two spoons and the ice-cream scoop. Her hands were shaking but she tried not to focus on it as she went to get the ice cream from the freezer. But she couldn't find it in the freezer. How odd. She looked again, pushing aside the unidentified packages of meat that probably weren't even good anymore, but it wasn't there. Odd. She must have forgotten to put the ice cream in the freezer when she got home. How stupid of her. How idiotic. With a sinking feeling, she went to the front table in the hall and, sure enough, found the carton of ice cream still in its brown paper bag. It had totally melted and the pale green pool was spreading on the slate-topped dry sink and she didn't know what to do about it. She stood there, frozen, looking at the spreading melted ice cream. She needed to get a sponge or some paper towels but she couldn't move. She watched it spread, malevolently, and her shaking intensified. How odd and how sad, how even poignant it was, she thought, to see her little pleasant surprise turn out this way, the $2.49 thrown out just as good as if she'd flushed it down the drain, and now nothing for Sam's dessert and Sam so liking his dessert even though his little potbelly hardly needed it. But why deny yourself a sweetness in life? Sam always said, and she wondered if any of it could be salvaged. She stood there wondering, and when Sam came to find her, she looked at him, afraid, as though she had made an awful mess, but then hadn't she made an awful mess? she thought, shaking uncontrollably now.

"What's the matter?" he said.

She didn't say anything but it didn't take him long to see what the problem was.

"I'll get a sponge," he said.

She stood there, unable to move, and watched him as he returned with the sponge and went at the mess. It took two trips to the sink to rinse out the sponge but then it was all gone and that was the glory of slate, she thought. If it had been a wood veneer they would have had to have it refinished.

"Anyone want to lick a sponge?" he asked, with a grin that flickered on and off.

"I'm sorry," she murmured.

"Oh, forget it . . ."

"I'm sorry."

He stood there, looking at her. "You're shaking," he said.

"I'm sorry."

"Don't be sorry," he said. "You've got nothing to be sorry about."

"I'm sorry . . ."

"No. *I'm* sorry. OK? *I'm* sorry."

"No . . ."

"Everything I've done, Liv. I'm sorry. I'm so sorry. I didn't mean to hurt you . . ."

"No, Sam," she said, moving toward him. "Don't say it."

He shook his head. "I didn't mean to hurt you. I didn't ever want to . . ."

She put a hand to his lips. "Don't. Whatever it is, I don't want to hear it. I don't care, Sam. I don't care."

He put his arms around her and she was shaking in his arms and he couldn't stand it. He kissed her, on the lips and on the neck, but the shaking got worse. So he took her by the hand and led her into the bedroom. The bed was unmade. He hadn't gotten around to making it. Half-empty bottles of club soda sat on the night tables. The blinds were crooked. Everything was a mess. He threw off two or three toys from the bed and then they sat down. She took off her glasses and squinted. He realized, so late in the game, that every time they made love she never really saw that well.

"I love you," he said, embracing her.

She pressed her cheek against his.

"No matter what, I love you."

"I know," she said.

They held each other for a long time. Then he got up and she watched him, with fuzzy edges, as he went to lock the door.

When they got to Broadway, the first thing she noticed was that the town now had a video shop. A post office and a liquor store and a video shop. Broadway Lights. Nancy was pretty sure that it was owned by Jules and Merle Bonnier, who owned the liquor store and were plenty smart when it came to knowing what Broadway wanted.

She turned onto Old Diamond Highway and drove on, beneath the thick and magnificent canopy of still-unblighted elm trees. "Some of these trees are over two hundred years old, David," she said, but he was half-asleep.

As she pulled up to the farm, she saw her father on his knees on the front lawn, gluing a chair in the twilight. He could do anything with his hands. He even knew how to knit. The only thing Justin could do with his hands was dial a phone, she thought with a scorn that she recognized as being juvenile but that she didn't yet feel like giving up.

She beeped the horn and her father looked up. His face turned into a smile. He rose a little too slowly but then came bounding over to the car.

"Well, look at you," he called. "Look at you."

She jumped out of the car and headed into his arms.

"Oh, my," he said. "Look at you." He peered into the car. "Where's my boy?"

"He's sleeping, Dad."

He carried David into the house. Just as they got him into bed, David opened his eyes and then his grandfather's face turned into a smile all over again. Nancy hugged herself as her father said, "Look at my boy. Will you just look at him?"

"Is Gramps asleep?" she asked, as they all headed downstairs to the kitchen.

"Long gone, honey," her father said. "You'll see him in the A.M."

She helped her father set out cheese sandwiches and milk. She tried not to get too sentimental about cheese sandwiches and milk, but she couldn't help it.

"Why didn't you tell me you were coming?" he said. "I'd have had dinner for you."

"We wanted to surprise you," she explained.

They stayed up very late. She didn't tell him anything. She wanted everything about this evening to be good and it was. When David fell asleep again, they brought him up to his room and negotiated him into bed without a hitch. Then they went downstairs again and had Lorna Doones and peaches.

"Everything OK, honey?" asked her father, scrutinizing her.

"Fine, Dad."

"Your husband still the King of Wall Street?"

"Still king, Dad."

They sat there for a minute, eating the cookies.

"Who owns the video shop?" she asked. "Jules and Merle?"

"Who else?" he grumped.

"Broadway Lights."

They laughed.

"You want one?" she asked.

"What?"

"A VCR."

He waved it away. "Regular old TV's still all right with me. I like that *Murder, She Wrote*. You ever watch it?"

She shook her head.

"You should."

They talked some more, and then it was time to go to bed. She didn't want to keep him up so late that he'd have a hard time tomorrow. She didn't want to make anything hard for him. He gave her the linens and she kissed him good night. When she found herself in her room, she almost felt dizzy for a minute. Her room. Pink and green. Wallpaper of cabbage roses. She got down on her knees by the white iron bed and remembered how she used to say her prayers except she didn't have any prayers now. There was a three-quarters moon in the sky and the sound of owls. That was enough.

She fell right asleep but in the middle of the night, or what felt like the middle of the night, she awoke. She lay still for a while and then she pulled on her robe and went to check on David. Then, thinking better of it but unable to stop herself, she tiptoed into her father's room. She stood at the foot of his bed and watched him, in that sheet of moonlight, sleeping, old.

"Daddy?"

He woke right up. The way he always did. He reached for his glasses. She got into bed beside him. "Cold," she said. He patted her back. "I left Justin."

He nodded.

"For good," she added, lest he misunderstand.

"Are you sure?"

"Yes, Daddy. I'm sure."

"OK, honey," he whispered.

She snuggled against him. "I'm sorry, Daddy."

"Oh, now. You just get to sleep."

She slept and so did he. After a while, she woke up again and crept silently out of his bed and back to her own. She shouldn't have awakened him that way, she thought, as she hugged her pillow and fell back into sleep again.

In the morning, Gramps went with them to the barn. David wanted to milk the cow and Gramps wanted to show him how to do it.

"Just keep talking to her," Gramps told David.

"What should I say?" David whispered.

"Well, you could say, 'Nice Brownie,'" Gramps suggested. "'Good old girl.'"

"Nice Brownie," David said, squeezing the swollen udder. "Good old girl," he added shyly, and then, after a while, the milk hit the bucket.

"Got to take my medicine," Gramps announced. Although he acted otherwise, he liked the schedule of medicine-taking. He hobbled back to the house and left Nancy and David alone in the big barn. The barn swallows flew overhead. When David tired, Nancy took over and finished up the bucket. Then they sat together in the hay.

"Gramps says Brownie's going to have a baby," David said, as he played with her ring.

"Yes," she said. "A calf."

"Gramps said I could see it born."

"That'll be nice."

"When are we going home?"

"Not for a long while."

"Why?"

"Because," she said, "Daddy and I need some time away from each other."

"Why?"

"Because," she said, "we don't agree on a lot of things these days. But," she added, with a hug, "what we do agree on is how much we love you."

He molded into her. As they sat there, so quiet, a mouse ran in front of them. "Look," she whispered. The mouse ran behind the wheel of an old wagon, stayed there for a minute, then came out again and disappeared to another corner of the barn.

"Come," she whispered.

She took him by the hand and led him to the mouse place. She pulled aside some hay from behind the wagon wheel and uncovered the nest, with five little pink babies in it. The babies groped torturously and she felt her heart racing.

"Those are babies," she explained. "Mouse babies."

He leaned forward on his elbows, his face inches away from the babies. As he studied them, she felt a release, a kind of deep, calm letdown. She lowered herself to the straw so that she was next to him and she watched him watch the babies. Chances were the cat, a prize mouser, would have them by the end of the day. But he didn't have to know that, she thought, as she reached out to touch his hair just the color of the straw, and, then again, who knew? Maybe they'd be lucky.

23

SHE'D HEARD OF WOMEN who gave birth without ever having realized they were pregnant. One day, maybe while they were watching Donahue or painting their toenails Maiden Blush, the head crowned and they were mothers. Usually they were big fat women whose bulk disguised the extra weight. Always though they were stupid: it was a prerequisite of the condition. But Trina wasn't fat and she wasn't that stupid and she never painted her toenails. She knew exactly what was happening to her.

Her breasts gave it away, getting all swollen and tender, like they sometimes did when she got her period, except she wasn't getting her period. All her life she'd been regular as clockwork except for those times she was pregnant. She hadn't expected to get pregnant again—they told her after the third abortion that she shouldn't expect miracles—but all the signs were there and she felt something inside of her, the tiny egg, she really did, the way the princess felt the pea. So she got herself one of those home pregnancy kits and now, this morning, she waited for the sludge-dark ring to appear and sure enough it did.

She stared at the thing for a long time and then she flushed it down the toilet. Then she took a shower and washed her hair. And then, all clean, she looked at herself in the mirror, studying her breasts. Already they were much larger—no doubt about it.

She threw on her baggy pink overalls and headed up to the Center. The summer was just a memory now. Schoolchildren were lined up at the bus stops and men and women, hurrying off to work, were dressed in darker colors. As she walked, she caught glimpses of herself in store windows and thought she looked large. Maybe it was the overalls, which she had bought two sizes too big at a rummage sale. They'd be plenty big enough even if she carried full term, she thought, but then, as she left behind her reflection, she wondered what the hell she was talking about.

When she got to the Center, she found Darcy already at the morning cleaning, whacking at things with her dustcloth, muttering, her lower lip pushed out, curled up, fierce-looking.

"'Morning," said Trina, but Darcy shot daggers at her. "What's the matter?" she said, in no mood for this but feeling she had to ask.

Darcy gave her a slow burn. "You want to know what's the matter? I run myself ragged for this place and that's the thanks I get."

"What happened?"

"It ain't what happen," Darcy replied, whacking at the toys on the toy shelves so that they clattered. "It's what *ain't* happen. I thought we was suppose to be like a family," she cried. "That's what Loretta always say, ain't it? One big family. Well, if you're family and somebody in your family get sick or make a mistake or something, you don't just throw 'em out in the street, do you?"

Stranger things have happened, Trina thought, but that's not what she said. "What are you driving at?"

"What I'm *drivin'* at," said Darcy, in a mocking tone Trina had never heard from her before, "is my sister."

Darcy's anger made her massive and Trina was careful not to make any wrong moves. "What's the matter with Sybila?"

"There ain't nothin' the matter with Sybila!" Darcy cried. "That's the point! She right as the rain. Better'n she ever be!"

"Then I don't get it," Trina said, putting a light on under the kettle.

"You don't get what?" Darcy demanded.

"I don't get what you're talking about," Trina said sharply, having had her fill.

Darcy stared at her. It was the moment when she would either fold or reach out and snap Trina in two. "I'm talkin' about loyalty," she said, folding. "I'm talkin' about what's fair and what ain't. I know what Sybila done," she said, twisting the dustcloth around her hand like the handkerchief of a Victorian lady in a big courtroom scene. "And I know it's the problems and they never goin' to go away. But she better'n she ever be. It's God, Trina. God done it."

Good old God, Trina thought, waiting for the water to boil.

"I told Loretta," Darcy continued. "I told her how God saved Sybila. You know that, Trina. You was there at the baptism. Loretta too. I told her how she had to take Sybila back, that we didn't have no money sometime, even for the grocery or medicine. Some people in my shoes—they'd steal the Center blind—but not me. Hungry as I be I don't steal here or nowheres else. Even though everybody what sends their kids here is rich. Makin' more money one week than you or me is ever likely to see in our life."

"Darcy," Trina said, fed up with it but trying to make herself sound gentle, "Loretta's got her policies. You know she can't hire back Sybila or anyone else who's ever abused a child . . ."

"Abused? Abused?"

"Yes," Trina said firmly. "Abused. Your sister struck Hildy. Struck her hard enough to leave welts. She's never going to get hired back."

Darcy sagged. The dustcloth hung straight down from her arm, gray, like Spanish moss. "It just don't seem fair," she murmured.

Darcy looked so sorrowful and lost standing there; Trina had to say something. "What about the church?" she suggested. "Can't she work for the church? She's a good cook. Couldn't she work as a cook in a rectory or something?"

Darcy shrugged and the shrug turned into a great shudder that shook her from the top down. Trina could see that it was all pretty hopeless. Darcy would do nothing. She would wait for Charles or Loretta to make it all better. Except Charles and Loretta couldn't make it all better, not for Darcy, not for anyone.

The teakettle finally began to whistle and Trina turned off the flame. "Listen," she said, as she poured, "even in a family there are rules. And when rules get broken, people get hurt. It's done, Darcy. It's history. If it's money you need, ask for money. But don't ask for the impossible."

Darcy looked up at her, from behind her cheap, thick eyeglasses. "Easy for you," she returned, in a last fierce burst. "People like you—always got everything handed to you."

Trina could have laughed, but figured she had better not. Instead she poured the tea.

All day long, Trina thought of what she was carrying inside of her and wondered if anyone could tell. There was a time in her life when she believed she could see auras. Pregnant women, she once believed, possessed soft pink auras, like clouds. Of course in time she became convinced that it was all hallucination, leftovers from old peyote trips, and that she had no magical faculties and that she couldn't see anything anyone else could not see. But that didn't mean that there weren't such people out there who had that power—maybe even people she knew.

That afternoon, when they took the children to the park, she kept looking at her reflection in car windows, to see if she could spot something special.

"What are you doing?" Charles finally asked her.

She shrugged. "Nothing," she said, not even caring that he looked at her funny. He'd been looking at her funny a lot lately. In the beginning, when they made love, she felt so close to him. She felt that it had all come together. But it never all comes together, does it? Almost as soon as she started to feel close to him, he started to pull away from her. That's the way it always went. Men were always afraid of the way she was, the way she could feel so deeply. She thought— she could have sworn—he was different. But he wasn't. In spite of all his wrinkles, he was the same.

"Are you OK?" he asked, staring at her.

"Never better," she said, walking on ahead.

As they walked, Darcy, still in her own black mood, began to sing, turning a favorite song into a dirge.

> *Mary Mack,*
> *Dressed in black,*
> *Silver buttons all down her*
> *back.*
> *Hi-lo,*
> *Tipsy toe,*
> *She broke her needle*
> *And she can't sew.*

The song made her feel chilly, or maybe it was a real chill in the air, a late-September chill. She held Hildy with one hand and Petey with the other and that made her feel a little better. There was such sweetness in these children; she couldn't figure out where it had come from. It couldn't have come from Bill or Louise or Julie Nolan. In the beginning, she thought Bill was the sweetest man who ever lived. She used to watch him with the boys and wish she could have had him for a father. But now she knew he wasn't what she thought he was. Inside he was cold. Maybe he wasn't such a great father after all. Maybe he never really allowed his wife to get close to the boys. Or maybe he deliberately picked a woman, an unnatural woman, who didn't want to get close to her children. And Julie Nolan—she was cut from the same cloth. She had done to Charles what Bill had done to her. She had made Charles fall in love with her and then she had turned away. Trina couldn't understand people like that, and people like that couldn't understand her. And Charles—she thought Charles was her kind of people but maybe no one was her kind of people. Maybe she was one of a kind.

When they neared the corner, Trina held more tightly to their hands. "We wait for the green, not in between," she whispered, "and then we look both ways."

They hurried across Central Park West. It was a windy day and as they entered the park she felt again that cold touch of autumn and wondered if the children were dressed warmly enough. Soon the leaves would fall and everything would turn brown. Soon it would be a year that she had been at the Center. The time was going too quickly. As the children ran on ahead, she lightly touched her belly.

> *Mary Mack,*
> *Dressed in black,*
> *Silver buttons all down her*
> *back.*

Then she had this empty feeling inside and if she heard the song one second longer she would scream. She started to run and the children screamed, in surprise and delight, running alongside her, and she wondered if she could lose it that way, running so hard, and if she lost it that way, then maybe that's the way it was supposed to be but when she got to the bench in the playground and collapsed, breathing so hard, she could still feel the tiny egg hanging on, really she could, like a survivor hanging on to a floating stick of wood, in the tossing turning ocean, and she was so proud of it, this life inside her, this survivor.

The kids went over to the slide and she sat on the bench watching them, her fingers on her belly, wondering what she would do. As she saw Charles herding the others into the playground, she cupped her belly more protectively, as if he might do something to take it away from her.

"Looks like it might rain," he said, as he came to sit beside her, and she glanced at the sky, which was filling up with long gray furry-looking clouds, like squirrels' tails.

"Yeah," she said. Together they looked up at the clouds, and, seeing his face, beautiful in profile, she remembered why she had felt this love for him. She couldn't help it—she wanted it back, the way it was for that brief time—and she put her hand on his leg and stroked his thigh. He looked down and sternly shook his head. "Darcy might be watching," he said.

She took her hand away and placed it flat against her belly. She watched him pull out the workings of a hand-rolled cigarette. This was something new, she thought. A few weeks ago he had started up again, but never in front of the children. Now she watched him, with the Zig Zags and the tobacco and the kind of rolling machine she hadn't laid eyes on in years.

"What are you doing?" she asked.

"Rolling a cigarette."

"In front of the kids?"

He shrugged. "So they'll learn that people do stupid things to themselves."

He lit the bulging cigarette and inhaled three times in rapid succession to get it going, as if it were a joint. "If you're going to smoke," she said, "wouldn't it be easier to just buy a pack?"

He looked at her. "Whoever said easier was better?" he grinned.

Then they were quiet for a while, watching the kids. Hildy and Olivier started a pushing fight. Olivier was bigger than Hildy, but Hildy was tough. When she got into a fight, she made herself feral, baring her teeth, showing her claws. "I'd better get over there before one of them puts out an eye," said Charles, and she watched him walk over to them, watching his long lean body that once made her ache . . . that now made her ache. She touched her belly. What would he say if she told him? Every other time she had told a man, it was like a Chinese fire drill—up on the feet, pacing the room, smacking the forehead, lighting up cigarettes, a stiff drink. She had to laugh. What did they think might happen when they put their stupid little wee-wees where they didn't belong? She thought of those unborn babies. She hadn't cried for them. They hadn't seemed like life to her. They were just something that comes alive, like maggots or toadstools. Those times she had cried not for the fetuses, but for herself, and then she didn't even cry that much for herself, only enough to cleanse the system. But this time it felt different and she couldn't even say why.

She put a hand on either side of her belly, the way she'd seen women do in the late, heavy months of pregnancy. She had always wanted to have a baby growing inside of her. She had always wanted to know that feeling. It was all the stuff that came after birth that she worried about. She always worried that she wouldn't have enough love for a baby. Let's face it: she didn't have a great track record when it came to giving people what they needed.

"Those two are going to fill the Garden one of these years," Charles said, returning from his peacemaking.

"Did she bite him?"

"Didn't get a chance. But would have. He'd be carrying around her teeth marks for a week." He smiled a little. "She's so damned tough, that Hildy. Wonder where she gets it from."

Maybe he just liked tough women, she thought. She looked down at herself. She wasn't tough. She never had been and she never would be. She could maybe use a hatpin, but not much more. "You think just because she bites she's tough?" Trina said.

Charles nodded. "Julie's raising her tough. For better or for worse," he qualified. "I'm not bringing a value judgment to it."

She let loose a sniggering sort of laugh. "When did you ever not bring a value judgment to something?"

He looked at her, as though suddenly he was struck by the fact that something was wrong. Smart guy, she thought.

"Are you sure you're OK?" he asked.

She shrugged. How could she be sure? All she knew was that she had this sour feeling inside of her now—but then that could be the pregnancy. It was hell on a woman's system.

Hildy came running over, her arms folded high on her chest, like a real little battleax.

"What's the matter?" Charles asked, reaching out to put his hands on her hips, or where her hips would have been if she'd had hips.

"Olivier!" she cried, furious, abject, vengeful all at once.

"What's he done now?" Charles asked, suppressing a smile.

"He keeps showing me his feet!" Hildy said, her teeth baring involuntarily.

"He keeps showing you his feet?" Charles repeated, trying to get the charge correct.

"Yes!" she screamed. "And I don't want to see them!"

Charles pulled her onto his lap and she began to cry. "Now, now," he said, patting her hair. "Don't let him get your goat."

"What goat?" she sobbed.

He laughed a little. "A word to the wise—never use idiomatic expressions with kids," he told Trina.

The tone of instruction made her feel like a stranger. But not as much as seeing him kiss the crown of Hildy's head, so gentle. It wasn't that she begrudged Hildy the kiss. It was just that she wondered if Charles would ever love his own child that way. Again she touched her belly even though, truth to tell, she didn't know just where to touch.

*   *   *

Every couple of months they had what Loretta liked to refer to as the "town meeting" and tonight there was one called for eight. It was Trina's job to go over to the A&P to buy the sodas and the Entenmann's pastries. She particularly liked the chocolate-chip cake and the marble loaf.

"Did you get enough?" Loretta demanded, as Trina returned.

"Is this enough?" replied Trina, handing her the shopping bags.

"We really should bake," Loretta sighed, unpacking the cakes to set them out on plates with doilies. "It's so much cheaper and so much better."

"And so much more work," Trina pointed out.

Loretta always had these grand plans—improving the Center, improving herself, improving everyone around her. Maybe that's how she drove her son away. All her talk about building and baking, regrouting and retiling, spackling and sifting—it could drive anyone away. And the truth of it was that Loretta never really got much done. She wasn't any good at organization and she gave off too many mixed messages.

"You shouldn't have bought all chocolate," Loretta said peevishly. "Not everyone likes chocolate."

"Wrong. *Everyone* likes chocolate," Trina returned.

They hadn't been getting along well. Ever since she had told Loretta about Bill Dowell, Loretta had been acting funny toward her. Looked at her funny, as if to say, Why you? Imagine if she knew about Charles. Charles never liked to talk about Loretta. Trina thought he was afraid of her, as if maybe Loretta were out to get him, and maybe she was.

"I just don't understand," Loretta said, in that same aggravated tone. "You should have bought a pound cake or a coffee cake or something."

Trina knew that Loretta got nervous over these things, like they were board meetings or whatever, but this was crazy. "I think you're worrying about something that doesn't need to be worried about," she said, the voice of reason.

Loretta gave her a long look. "You don't know the half of what I've got to worry about," she said. "Town meeting means a lot. It's an opportunity to show that I've got a cohesive staff here, not just a bunch of ragtag . . ."

She stopped herself. There was a silence. "You want me to go out and buy a nice pound cake I'll go out and buy a nice pound cake," Trina said.

"Forget it," Loretta said, picking crumbs off the doilies.

Soon people started coming. Trina stayed in the kitchen, pretending to be busy with the cake, and listened to Loretta at the door. "Welcome, welcome," she heard her saying. Trina concentrated on making neat slices, and as she did so, Charles slipped into the kitchen, carrying jugs of red wine.

"What got into her?" he said. "She just chewed my head off for being ten minutes late."

"She's kind of wound up," Trina said, sounding like she was justifying Loretta when that was the last thing on her mind. "This is her big opportunity to show she's got a cohesive staff," she added, as further explanation.

"Good luck to her," he cracked, gathering the paper cups and heading back into the group.

When the meeting started, the first order of business was fund-raising, for the Center's financial situation was always precarious.

"What about a bake sale?" Heller Norman suggested.

"I think we need something a little more far-reaching," said Julie, who was always so commanding and articulate at these things. "Perhaps we could incorporate a bake sale as part of a larger fund-raising event, such as a bazaar."

Sam Sloan shook his head. "You're not going to knock out the deficit with cake sales and rummage sales. Who the hell's going to cough up real money for used Oshkosh overalls with formula stains all over them or the 200-piece Return of the Jedi jigsaw puzzle with 197 pieces?"

"I don't know, Sam," said Loretta. "If it's all part and parcel of a big event, a carnival, or a street fair or whatever . . ."

"Personally I'm sick of street fairs," Sam said. "If I see one more kid with a painted face walking around the neighborhood, I'm moving."

Everyone laughed, but then quickly grew serious again. "What about a raffle?" suggested Bill. "A lot of us work for corporations or organizations that might be willing to contribute something."

"Sure," said Patrick, blowing out smoke. "I can get my guys to throw in fifteen minutes' free phone time."

"Well, I don't see why a raffle can't be part of a big carnival day," Liv Sloan said. "Sort of the *pièce de résistance*."

"As it were." Sam grinned.

"We've got some good ideas here," Loretta said enthusiastically. "What we need is a recording secretary. Charles? How about you?"

Everyone looked at Charles. Trina looked at Charles. Sitting there, smoking his cigarette. "Yes, ma'am," he said. "I'd be honored to be your recording secretary."

Trina saw Loretta give him a smile that was like a pat on the head, and he smiled back at her. Trina felt sick to her stomach, which is the way a woman in her first trimester often feels.

"I think what we have to do," said Liv, "is draw up committees . . ."

Trina didn't make an announcement or anything. She just got up, went out through the kitchen, and into the yard. The air was surprisingly cold, although she didn't know why she should be surprised. She took deep deep breaths, trying to fill up her lungs with air, the way the massage guru had once taught her. Too bad he was such a selfish bastard—he knew a lot of good tricks.

She stayed in the yard for a long time. She might have spent the night if Loretta hadn't come after her.

"What are you doing out here?" Loretta said.

"Nothing."

"Nothing? It's not time to do nothing," Loretta said sternly. "We've got a town meeting going on in there."

And I'm out of town, she thought to herself, but didn't say it. "I don't feel too well," she said instead, an excuse she could use for the next nine months if she chose to.

"It's always something with you, isn't it?" Loretta said bluntly.

"What do you want me to do?" Trina said, suddenly worn out. "Tell me what you want me to do."

Loretta stared at her, bit her lip, shook her head. "Why are you doing this to me?"

Trina half-shut her eyes and looked beyond Loretta to the stone cherub that ruled the courtyard. Loretta thought she was her mother. But she already had a mother. "Doing *what* to you?"

"I don't know, Trina," Loretta said, with more head-shaking. "I thought we were friends."

You're a control freak, she wanted to shout, but didn't. "We *are* friends. Of course we're friends."

Loretta touched her knuckles to her temples, showing off the awful headache Trina had given her. "You think I'm deaf, dumb, and blind, don't you?" she said in a strained voice. "I know what's happening. You're getting it on with Charles is what's happening."

Trina didn't speak; sometimes it was best not to. She didn't know how Loretta knew. Maybe she knew everything, Trina thought, with a kind of awe.

"You're running through this place like a brushfire, aren't you, Trina?" Loretta said, in a tone of composed confrontation.

Trina pulled on her hair. "You make me sound like Cleopatra or something," she said.

Loretta looked at her for a long moment. "Trina, Trina," she said. She reached out to brush the hair away from Trina's eyes. "I don't blame you," she said soberly. "It's Charles. Listen, I know. I fell into the same trap."

Trina just stood there, letting Loretta fuss with her hair.

"I tried to warn you but you wouldn't listen. Had to learn the hard way. But enough's enough," Loretta said. "I've been telling myself that for God knows how long, but I haven't done anything about it and that's my fault." She sighed again—she was good at sighing. "It's hard for me. You can't imagine how hard. The thing with Sybila—I was sick for weeks over it. So you can just imagine what it will be like with Charles . . ."

What was she talking about? Trina wondered. Suddenly it was all going too fast, and Trina needed to slow it down. "Don't blame Charles," she said. "It's not Charles's fault."

Loretta stopped the fussing with Trina's hair and gave her a long probing look. "Of course it is," she said. "He's a very seductive person. None of us have been immune to him. But don't worry," she said. "Everything's going to be all right." She put her arm through Trina's. "Now I want you to come back in with me and stop mooning around. You've got a job to do," she said. "Are you coming?"

Trina didn't know if she were coming or going, but, after a moment, she nodded.

"Good," said Loretta, taking her by the hand and leading her back inside.

She was setting out more sugar and cream when suddenly Bill Dowell was next to her. She didn't know whether it was because he wanted to talk to her or because she was next to the coffee urn and he wanted more coffee. "Cake?" she offered, feeling awkward, using the first prop she could find, and then hating herself for the false hospitality.

"No thanks," he said. "I abjure desserts during the week."

Abjure. He always liked to use words that made her feel ignorant, she thought angrily as he looked at her and smiled, his lips thin and pale. "How have you been?" he asked.

She considered the question. "Never better."

"You look well," he said.

"So do you."

"You didn't have to say that," he replied, with his smile.

"I know I didn't."

The smile vanished. "Did you have a good vacation?" he asked.

She shrugged. "Hot. I stayed in the city."

He nodded.

"But you didn't, did you?"

"No. I had the boys up to Rhode Island."

"Oh. Nice."

"They say you can't go home again but I prove them wrong every summer." His crinkly smile returned. "At least I *think* I prove them wrong."

She studied him. It was funny how everything she had once valued about him—his smile, his thin bones, his hair the color of copper wire—now made her angry. Here he was, talking to her as if there had never been anything between them, and she hated him for it, she could kill him for it. "How's your wife?" she asked, folding her arms across her chest.

He flushed and his eyebrows elevated. "Louise is fine. Thank you," he said. "Terribly busy, of course. As always," he added. "Seems their team may be close to a major breakthrough in the AIDS thing."

"So then she'll be famous," said Trina.

"Well, I don't know about *famous* . . ."

"Sure," said Trina. "She'll be famous as can be. Everybody will know her and she'll have honors coming out of the kazoo."

"Trina . . ."

"Excuse me," she said, brushing past him, resisting the impulse to knock him over.

As she moved closer to the center of the room—the center of the Center—she felt her heart pounding but then maybe it was the room itself that was pounding. She wasn't doing well. She realized this. She'd been here before and she knew it—this feeling, no good, inside of her—and when she saw Loretta looking at her she felt like shaking a fist but instead she sort of twirled around the room, very gracefully and discreetly, almost a dance, and yet so discreet that no one but she would know it was a dance. She danced over to where Charles and Julie were making chitchat and she stopped in front of them.

"Oh, hi, Trina," Julie said pleasantly.

"Oh, hi, Julie," she returned. She looked at Charles. "What are you two talking about?"

"Hildy," said Charles. "Hildy and Olivier."

"Oh," said Trina. "Hildy and Olivier." She nodded profoundly. "They don't get along," she said. "All wrong together."

"So I hear," said Julie.

"But the funny thing is you always find them close by each other," Trina pointed out. "That's the funny thing. Why do you think two people who are all wrong for each other can't stay away from each other?"

There was a moment of silence. "Human nature, I guess," Julie said, pleasantly again but also a little guarded now.

"Human nature. Bingo. Go to the head of the class," Trina said and Julie's smile became fixed on her lips. "No wonder you make so much money," said Trina. "You're smart and smart people make money."

"Trina . . ."

She looked at Charles. He was the second man in ten minutes to say *Trina* that way and she hated that too. "What?" she whispered. *"What?"*

Julie put down her drink. "It's getting late for me," she confessed, with a polite yawn. "Time to say good night, I'm afraid."

They watched her walk off, through the room, and then Charles turned to Trina. "What the hell was that all about?"

"I don't know," she said, starting to move away, but he put out a hand to restrain her.

"Would you mind telling me what's going on?" he asked, very calm even though he was in a rage. And now she hated that part of him that she had always valued: that calm, that rotten counterfeit calm.

She pulled away from him and rushed through the crowded room. She could see Loretta looking at her, and Darcy, and Sam and Liv, Michael, Patrick, all of them, but she didn't care. Then she was out on the street and it was cool. The best, coolest night since last spring. She held the tips of her collar up, like little white wings, and let the breeze reach into her blouse.

"Trina!"

She walked faster. It was so stupid, the way he was calling her. What did he want? She wished he would go away, that they would all go away, and she would be left alone, as she had been in the beginning, sitting alone on a park bench, no one telling her what to do.

"Trina!" he called, harsh, as though she were a child, a child acting up, and when he reached her, he put his hand on her shoulder and brought her to a stop. She didn't turn to face him, so he came all the way around, put his hands on her shoulders, stared at her. "Hey," he said, in the calm voice. "Would you like to tell me what's happening?"

She shook her head. "You know what's happening."

"I do?"

"Yes. You do."

He removed his hands from her shoulders, ran a hand up, down, around his jaw and cheeks, as if he were feeling a beard that had once been there. Maybe in Illinois or Oregon or Albuquerque he had had a beard, she thought.

"You like her better than me, don't you?" Trina said.

He laughed—a laugh of amazement—and his eyes widened. "You're serious, aren't you?"

"You like her better than me because she's cruel to you," Trina said, "and you like that."

"I don't believe this . . . ."

"You like that," she said. "Just like Bill Dowell. That's OK," she told him, reasonably, "but what I've got to figure out is why men like that are the ones I get involved with."

"Listen, Trina," said Charles, the calm gone, looking angry and unhappy, "we need to talk. Something got confused along the way. This is not what I—"

"Save it," she said, in a whisper.

He reached out to take her hand. "Trina, I don't want what we have to get messed up. We're *friends*, Trina. We're the best of friends. It's more important to me than anything else. It's extraordinary."

She looked at his hand in hers. The cool breeze and the half-moon and the rustle of the leaves off the ginkgo tree all worked together and made her able to breathe. She folded her free hand over the hand that was holding her right hand. He didn't know everything, she thought, but he wasn't entirely wrong. She looked up at him. She didn't know what it was—couldn't give it a name—but something made her feel close to him again. "Loretta's letting you go," she whispered.

He peered down at her. "What?"

"I said Loretta's letting you go."

He took back his hand. "How do you know?"

"She told me."

He looked shaken and she didn't know what to say. "Listen, you can get another job. There's plenty of places for someone like you. They're always looking for men for this kind of work and you've got experience and . . ."

He shook his head. She stopped talking. He looked up at the moon. "God," he whispered.

She looked up to where she thought he was looking. It was a night where she could discern even the dark side of the moon. Such a night, she thought. "What do you want me to do?" she said. "Tell me what you want me to do." But he just kept shaking his head. There was nothing more to say. She walked off and this time he didn't try to stop her.

She carried her carpetbag through the Kingston bus station. The bag was bigger than she needed, but it was the only bag she had. As she walked through the station, a young man in jeans and tam-o'-shanter offered to carry it for her but she thanked him anyway. The bag had been her grandmother's and she wasn't about to let anyone else carry it. Her grandmother—Leah Spitzer Horowitz—claimed to have brought the bag over on the boat with her, from Riga, to carry all her worldly goods, her sausages and her chocolate and her photographs, a Bible and a wig, carnelian and marcasite jewelry. But Trina's mother said Leah was such a liar she didn't even know when she was lying and that she had bought the bag from a peddler on Allen Street.

"Where to?" asked the driver of the one waiting cab. He was a middle-aged sandy-haired hippie with a heavy gold earring in his left ear.

"Moorehouse Street," she said, placing the carpetbag on the seat and then sliding in next to it. "One-seventeen Moorehouse Street."

He took off with screaming wheels. She thought he looked familiar.

"Where you coming from?" he asked.

"New York City," she said.

"The Big Apple. Went down there in August. Seen Dustin Hoffman walking down Fifth Avenue."

"How did he look?"

"Short, man. Coulda eaten out of my armpit."

She looked out the window. The lawns were neat and so were the hedges, and the houses, for the most part, were in good repair. She closed her eyes. She hadn't gotten enough sleep last night. The driver put on a Grateful Dead tape too loud and began singing along. I've known a million guys like this, she thought, so tired, wishing she could lay her head on the carpetbag.

In another minute, they were at 117 Moorehouse Street. The house was stucco, the color of lichen, with late hydrangeas in bloom. She paid the driver and headed up the walk. She rang the bell and entered.

The air struck her with its sharp, tingly smell. Two parts alcohol and disinfectant, one part blood. The nurse, who was wearing a Hands Across America button, asked for her name.

"Katrina Dunbar," she said.

"Dunbar, Katrina."

"You've got my file."

The nurse jotted down something. "Have a seat, please."

She sat down on an orange vinyl chair. Every color in the room was bright—orange, aqua, sunflower yellow—and her eyes hurt from it all. She sat there, with the carpetbag between her legs, and stared at the other waiting woman, who was maybe fifty, quite heavy, in a lilac pantsuit. Trina guessed they weren't here for the same reasons. The only thing the same about them was they were here alone.

The last time she had been here she had also come alone. She hadn't wanted to tell the massage guru that she was pregnant. He would have wanted her to keep it. He didn't believe in killing anything; nobody did then. He would have wanted to be at the delivery, brewing herbal infusions so that the infant would have something good to smell.

"We'd like to get a urine specimen from you," said the nurse, handing a bottle to Trina, who went into the bathroom with it. As she sat on the toilet, she studied the walls of the bathroom, which were covered with woodcuts of mothers and children.

It took her a while to pee into the bottle. She'd never been a big one for peeing on command. Never was a big one for doing anything on command. Maybe that was her problem. When at last she relaxed and let go, the stream filled the jar and made her realize she had had to go all along. She put the jar on the sink, wondering if she were giving them more than they wanted.

She was in no hurry to go back out, so she spent some time looking at herself in the mirror, but that wasn't much fun either. The thing she hated most about her face was her pale red eyelashes. Sometimes she looked so washed-out, like an albino, and then her features became rabbity and she'd stare at herself in the mirror in wonder at how ugly she was.

Today she felt so ugly and deformed. She'd gotten the worst from each of her parents. Her mother's short thick hands. Her father's pale eyelashes and rabbity nose and mouth. Her mother's freckles. Phyllis had gotten all the good parts. Or, she should say, almost all the good parts.

She pulled her dress up above her breasts and stood sideways to the mirror, studying her reflection. There was, without doubt, a puffiness there. Overnight the fertilized egg had collected cells to it. Determined to grow, it was working every minute. Inside her was this growing thing, this life, and she was in charge of it. She had been given the job of growing this life. But now, in another few moments, she would be seeing someone about getting rid of it.

She sat down on the toilet again and placed her hands on her stomach and thought and thought until her head ached. It wasn't unnatural, what she was doing. In nature there were plenty of animals who destroyed their young. She had even witnessed it once—a gerbil eating her babies. Holding the little pink things in her paws and eating them. It was maybe the worst thing Trina had ever seen. She just couldn't understand it. It wasn't unnatural but it was wrong. She wondered then—as she wondered now—if any animals not held in confinement would eat their young that way.

Suddenly, as she sat there in the room with the woodcuts and the mirror, she knew she couldn't do what she had come here to do. She knew, sure as she knew her name, that the thing would haunt her. For the rest of her life she would hear that tiny ghost like a mosquito in her ear and at night she would see the ghost flying around her room, its minute white light casting disproportionate shadows, and every time she saw it, and she would see it all the time, she would feel this pain in her heart.

She stood up and looked in the mirror. There, like an unfolding flower, she saw her rare pink aura. This time she wouldn't let herself be convinced that she didn't see it. She took up her carpetbag and left the bathroom.

"I'm going," she told the nurse.

"But the doctor will see you in—"

"I'm going," she said quickly, hurrying out the door before anyone could stop her.

There were no cabs and she had to wait a long time for a bus but finally it came and took her over by Old Albany Road. Then she walked the ten blocks or more, down quiet streets lined with linden trees, at last coming to Carmel's Treasure Trove.

She walked past the white picket fence and up the path to the little shingled house. It was too small, the house, almost miniature, and weird, more like a cookie tin than a place where a human being might live. Trina bet that the kids in the neighborhood thought it was a witch who lived there. The shop was dark and there was a sign in the window that said CLOSED, which Trina couldn't understand. She made her way past shrubs and peered through one window and then another, surveying the dark interior with its baskets of beads and shells, feathers and ribbons, scraps of lace and shards of horn and bits of amber. It was just the kind of place where a witch might live.

She went around back and rang the bell but there was no answer, so she decided to wait, settling herself on the old swing that she recognized from the farm. Wherever Carmel was, there were always things like swings and cuckoo clocks and whirligigs.

It had been two years since she'd seen her mother, she thought, swinging in the swing, and two years since they'd spoken. The last time had been right in there, in the kitchen. From the swing, Trina could see into the kitchen. It was Carmel's showpiece, all done up in buttercup yellow and Persian blue. In the window were glass shelves lined with dozens of old juice glasses, hand-painted with oranges and lemons and limes, and lining the shelves were platters and cookie jars painted with more oranges. Trina never understood why her mother had such a thing for citrus. Maybe, in another life, she'd been a sailor and had the scurvy to worry about.

She closed her eyes then and just let the swing carry her back and forth. It was a strange place, that kitchen, for the kind of battle they had had two years ago. She remembered her mother covering her ears, the way she had come to see Hildy or Molly or Aaron do, shouting, "I don't want to hear it. I don't want to hear it."

—But you're going to hear it.

It was the wrong place to have a screaming, crying fight. The noise bounced off the walls like something crazy. But it had to be done.

—You're a liar. Always were, always will be.

—I'm not lying. It happened. Do you hear me? *It happened.*

—Liar! Liar!

Stick your head in fire. She opened her eyes. It was so quiet here. The quiet scared her and she had the impulse to take the carpetbag and run but something held her back.

As she sat on the porch she remembered how hungry she was. It had been hours since she'd eaten anything, which wasn't right, given the circumstances. Down the steps was a vegetable garden; there were still some cherry tomatoes left and wild, tattered fans of horseradish. She walked down the steps and helped herself to a handful of the cherry tomatoes; then she went back to the swing and waited some more.

It was late in the afternoon when she finally heard footsteps coming along the path. She stopped the swing from swinging and felt herself get all tight inside. Then she saw her mother rounding the corner, hurrying along, eyes down. She always walked with her eyes down, as if she were looking for money.

Hello, she wanted to say but she couldn't speak. Her mouth was dry as old leather. She rose and let the squeak of the swing announce her.

Carmel looked up. She was a small woman with a large head and her head was framed with a garland of brass curls that was topped with a blue straw hat. She stared at Trina until a huge honeybee, big enough for a queen, zoomed by and made her blink.

"How long have you been here?" Carmel asked, with an accent on the "you" that made it sound like something to be gotten rid of.

"A long time," Trina said. "The shop was closed," she added.

"What did you think?" said Carmel, shifting the large blue leather pocketbook from one hand to the other.

Trina just stared at her, waiting for more, until Carmel finally shook her head contemptuously. "Don't you even know what day it is?"

Trina shook her head. She couldn't remember if it was Tuesday or Wednesday or Thursday.

"It's Yom Kippur," Carmel said, hurrying past her to open the door.

Yom Kippur? She hadn't known. How could she know? Who was there to tell her?

"I've been in *shul* all day," Carmel said. As she entered, she turned to Trina. "You coming in?"

Trina nodded, after a moment.

She watched her mother move around the kitchen, setting down her hat and gloves and bag, straightening a picture, picking off a yellowed leaf from a kangaroo vine that was growing out of an old coffee grinder. She went through the kitchen like a White Tornado, Trina thought, and always had.

"You want tea?" asked Carmel, putting on the kettle. It was a big copper kettle, shaped like a beehive, dented but shining.

"OK," Trina said, realizing now that Carmel must be fasting and that she wasn't going to be offered anything else.

"I permit myself a cup of tea," said Carmel, as if she were being challenged. "Otherwise I get a migraine."

"Since when do you go to *shul?*" asked Trina.

Carmel shrugged—a jerky gesture, as if she were getting rid of an itch—and put the teacups on the table.

"Can I use the bathroom?" Trina asked.

Carmel looked at her for a minute and then shrugged again.

The bathroom, right off the kitchen, had remained unchanged. The same rosebud soaps were sitting in the same pink handblown brandy snifter, and there seemed even to be the same number of them. There was the same kind of toilet paper—lavender and gold fleurs-de-lis on a field of white—and the same guest towels—white, very starched, with tiny embroidered violets, too delicate to use. For a second, she had the urge to take something, as a sort of souvenir, but she resisted and left the bathroom as it was, coming back into the kitchen to the piercing sound of the teakettle's whistle.

She sat down at the marble-topped ice-cream table and watched her mother dunk the teabag first in one and then in the other teacup.

"You still like it so dark?" Carmel asked.

"Yes. Dark as I can get it."

Her mother dropped the bag into the cup and pushed it toward Trina. Then, alternately blowing and slurping, Carmel brought the steaming tea into her mouth, and then, with a grunt of pure satisfaction, she set the teacup down, put a tissue to her lips, and then stuck the tissue up the sleeve of her dress, for ready access. "So," she said, giving Trina a long hard look, "are you coming or going or what?"

"Or what," whispered Trina, moving the teabag around to get the most out of it.

Carmel nodded, verifying what she had heard. "You're still using that old carpetbag, eh?"

"Uh-huh."

"She bought it down on Allen Street. Ninety years ago if it's a day," said Carmel, who never liked to call her mother anything but "she."

Trina took a sip of tea and it was good. Her eyes wandered around the kitchen and caught the flicker of the *yahrzeit* candles by the kitchen sink. Her mother saw where her eyes had wandered and when Trina looked back at her, Carmel was staring with defiance.

"How's the store?" asked Trina, looking away.

"I can't complain," Carmel said, knocking marble. "People got more time these days to pursue a hobby."

Then again there was the silence. "So? You still trying to be an actress?" her mother asked, making an effort to keep her voice under control.

Trina shook her head.

"What then?"

Trina shrugged. "I get by."

"Cleaning other people's toilets?" Carmel snapped, her heavy dark eyebrows coming together like fighting caterpillars.

Trina said nothing. She sipped the tea and watched the sun in the west illuminate the juice glasses. Every now and then, Carmel gave out a grunt, of satisfaction or despair, it was hard to tell which. "I'm going back to *shul,*" she finally announced, rising and setting her teacup in the sink.

Trina watched her as she put on her hat and her gloves.

"It's *yiskor,*" her mother explained, righting the hat in the reflective window of the wall oven.

Prayers for the Dead. Trina set down the teacup and felt for her bag beneath the table.

Her mother went into the bathroom. While she was gone, Trina washed out the teacups. As she stood at the sink, she watched the *yahrzeit* candles flicker, their small flames casting large shadows that would play all afternoon on the white splashboard until they ended at sundown.

When she turned, there was her mother, standing like a bulldog in the ugly blue rayon dress with the orange poppies blowing across it, and it was clear she had been watching her. "Do you want to come?" her mother asked, her voice like a hammer.

Trina shook her head and her mother shrugged. But then somehow, as her mother marched down the driveway, Trina was following her out to the car, the 1983 Monza, metal-green like the eye of a fly, her bag in hand.

The air in the *shul* was like a closet—close; camphorated; too many old woolen coats pulled out at once from storage for the holidays—and she had a hard time getting a deep breath. Mostly the *shul* was filled with old people who, as they *dovened,* moved back and forth and from side to side, stretching and pulling together, like a giant wakening animal, and she stayed in the back, holding on to the carpetbag, listening to them beg forgiveness, even her mother, who never liked to ask anything of anyone.

For the sin which we have committed before thee by folly of the mouth;
For the sin which we have committed before thee by unclean lips.

There was a buzz in the *shul,* a low mournful busy sound, like that of bees working on the hottest day of summer, and she could see her mother hunched, legs astride, feet splayed, the veins in her neck and arms distended with the effort of her prayer, something for which she never before had the time or the appetite, but which now spewed out of her mouth loud and fast and furious, like the curses and insults she used to throw at the poultry with their feed.

And for the sin which we have committed before thee with wanton looks;
And for the sin which we have committed before thee with confusion of mind.

Her mother turned to look at her, her blue straw hat like a helmet on her head that would never fall off or even move, no matter how much she rocked back and forth, side to side. They looked at each other, and then Trina had to look away.

O my God, before I was formed I was nothing worth, and now that I have been formed I am but as though I had not been formed. Dust am I in my life; how much more so in my death.

Down to the ground she looked. She felt funny. Hot and sick. The life inside her was filling her up so that there wasn't room for anything else. Weak she felt and dizzy and she wondered what she was doing. Everything was going so fast. She knew nothing. She had no name and no face. Her thumbs had no prints. She smelled of nothing but water. You couldn't remember her face any more than you could remember a rock in an empty lot or a bolt of dust beneath a cot or a cow lying in a field or a root pounded by native women at the edge of a jungle. Her head ached and when she reached up to touch her scalp she felt the scrap of black lace that she had pinned there so she could enter the House of God. She hadn't been in the House of God in a lifetime and here she was now, and she couldn't breathe, the catarrh of the old people's prayers pushing out all the good air.

Remember us unto life, O King, who delightest in life,
And seal us in the book of life, for thine own sake, O living God.

And then the pounding again. Old men, old women, pounding their chests, beating their breasts. The time had come; another year had passed and the Book of Life was closing. The old men and the old women pleaded, pounding their chests, beating their breasts, in words she couldn't understand. Seal us in the Book of Life, O King. *O King.* And she looked at her mother and her mother looked at her, her mother's face large, gray, dented, bruised, and then her mother turned around and beat her breast with her pale blue fist. It was then that Trina came down the aisle, leaving behind the bag, and slipped in beside her, as her mother went on beating her breast, beating it louder than anyone, showing God how much she wanted to be included in the Book of Life, and showing Trina that wanting it was nothing to be ashamed of.

26

THE BUS ALWAYS took longer on the way back. Maybe it was because you were leaving behind the green, heading into places that were crowded and dirty and had nothing to recommend them. Whatever the reason, she didn't want to look out the window, and so, all the way from Kingston to Newburgh, Trina watched the teenage boy in the next seat work out strategies on a magnetic chessboard. Then, the rest of the trip in, from Newburgh to the city, she had an herbalist from Goshen going on and on, her talk laced with words that Trina once knew from some other place, some other time. Words like borage and lovage and horehound. Hyssop and sweet cicely. Lamb's ear and bee balm.

She finally fell asleep, midway through the Lincoln Tunnel. When the bus pulled into Port Authority, she woke and felt as though she had been asleep for hours rather than minutes. The herbalist slept too—a profoundly deep sleep, as if induced by magic poppies. It took some doing to awaken her, but when Trina finally managed, the woman was grateful and, in parting, wished Trina luck and happiness in her life.

Then she was on the corner of Forty-second and Eighth, waiting for the Number Ten bus, the carpetbag held tightly in her hand, trying not to catch anyone's eye but there was *Hey babe* and *Hey babe* and whistles and catcalls and men with peacock feathers in their hat brims and finally she had to look. That was her problem: she always had to look. She watched a pair of girls in the stairwell of the Hotel Freedom, shivering in their short leather skirts, their hair like briars of copper and steel, rhinestone-studded gloves on their hands. They had the wild, ruthless faces of huntresses and as Trina stared one of them touched her tit and smiled while the other laughed. Then Trina looked away, in a blush that convinced them they had caught her at her secret and made them giggle even more when what they had really seen was her staring into the face of something that had come too close and that was nothing to laugh about.

As the bus took her up Eighth Avenue, she counted the whores and the pimps, the beggars, the cripples, the pushers and the pushed. Carmel didn't understand why she had to go back and Trina hadn't known what to tell her. They had spent four days together. They weren't four warm/wonderful days but it was something. They didn't talk very much. She helped out in the store, running her fingers through the baskets of beads, like a trader on the old caravan route, when in fact there was precious little activity and if they got any customers at all they had to count themselves lucky. Every day Carmel would close up the shop at noon and keep it closed until two-thirty, as if they were in Italy, and they would go around back to the kitchen and set out a big dairy lunch—cottage cheese and muenster, tuna fish, health salad. It would take them a long time to eat it, mostly in silence, and Trina never felt so hungry, nor did she ever feel so full. She never ate so much butter, nor had so much cream in her coffee, nor took so many cubes of sugar.

Over the cake—and there was always cake, and always the same kind of bad packaged stuff on which she was raised—Carmel talked about the business, and how she was going to sell the property, and how she was going to retire to Florida.

—You? Retire?

—Why not? I deserve some goodies, don't I?

She didn't argue with her. Instead of arguing, she helped Carmel lay down new linoleum in the vestibule and hang sky-blue Swiss-dot curtains over the shop windows.

—When I decide to sell, I want everything to look its best.

—I thought you decided already.

—I did, I did.

Then, when the time came and she told Carmel she was going, Carmel sat there, over the head of cabbage she was shredding, and told Trina she had no more sense than the cabbage did. You could make a better life here than down there, said Carmel. Here you could make a decent life. *Oh yeah?* thought Trina.

Like you did? But she didn't say anything because it wasn't the time to say anything. It was the time to keep her mouth shut and see if the two of them could give it another go.

All the way in the car, en route to the bus station, Trina thought of telling her about the baby.

—Hey. You want to hear something?

—Sure. Why not.

—You're going to be a grandmother.

—Right.

—No, really. You are.

(And then a long long look.)

—*Mazel tov.* Do you at least know who the father is?

Which is why she didn't say anything about the baby.

They got to the station early. Carmel bought them Hershey bars and coffee and when that was finished, she reached into her big blue leather handbag and pulled out money. A crisp green bill. Fifty dollars.

—What are you doing?

—Take it.

—Hey. Stop.

—Just take it.

The bill was newly minted, crisp as a lettuce leaf, and Carmel must have loved it a lot because new crisp money had always been one of her favorite things, but in a gesture of abandon she folded it and then folded it again and reached over to stuff it into Trina's bag.

—Buy yourself something.

—Come on.

—I said buy yourself something.

Then it was 4:04 and time to board. *See you,* they said. Carmel stood there while the bus was pulling out. In the cranberry-colored jumpsuit with all the zippers—too many zippers for a woman her age—she looked thick through the middle and her face was big and round and gray, the nose and lips coarsened with age, and it was strange, thought Trina, looking at her this way, like looking at yourself through a warped mirror, everything a distortion but still the truth, and she waved all the way out of the bus station, even past the point where her mother could see her.

Now, not really so very far away but feeling very far away, she looked out the window of the Number Ten bus and saw she was near her stop. Getting off at Ninety-second Street, she set down the carpetbag on the sidewalk, took a deep breath, then picked it up again and headed down the street. When she got into her apartment, she found it quiet, still, and empty. The bloodleaf, which needed frequent watering, was dead on the windowsill. The cat was gone, as she figured it would be. It had left through the window, up the fire escape in search of food. She suspected it would come back, but even if it didn't, she didn't care. She looked around to see what had been stolen and, to her surprise, found everything just where she had left it.

She went to listen to her messages. She wasn't sure why she had a phone machine. If she hadn't once tried to be an actress, she wouldn't have had it. It seemed a weird thing to have as she sat there, eating an old orange from the crisper bin, the floating, disembodied voices coming at her.

Trina, it's Charles. Wednesday night. I'll try you again later.

Trina, it's Charles. I want to talk with you. I'll call again later.

Trina, it's Charles. Where are you?

She felt Charles's voice touching her, nudging her. She stopped eating the orange and listened to the next message.

Katrina? It's Barry. Give me a call, *ja*?

Then the buzz. Then another. Hang-ups. Then another.

This is Loretta at 9:15 on Thursday. You're not here and you haven't called in. Please let us know what's happening.

She turned off the machine. She didn't want voices coming at her. She put on her slippers and went down to get the mail. There were three pieces: a letter from her state senator; a menu from a Chinese takeout; and a letter with her name hand-printed on the envelope. She didn't know whose handwriting it was and when she opened it, as she got back into the apartment, and discovered it was from Charles, she thought how funny it was that she hadn't recognized his writing.

"Dearest Trina," it began, and quickly she put it down, away from her, on the hall table, where she didn't have to see it. She walked straight away from it and opened the window and let in some air. She didn't have to read the letter, she told herself, but then, moments later, when she came back to it, she felt stupid for imagining that she could have let it go unread.

I wanted to talk to you, but I don't know where you are. It's late Saturday afternoon as I write this, nearly dusk. And you've been gone since Wednesday night.

She sat down on the floor. Her legs were weak. Somehow the letter was fluttering in her hands.

It's still not clear to me what happened Wednesday night, and I've thought of nothing else. You said things to me that made me angry but that I now recognize to be the truth. But then what else could I expect from you? You are always true. That is your very special magic, Trina.

But I'm not a magician, she thought, furious that he shouldn't know that. I haven't got the wands or the silk scarves or the flying doves. I'm just a person. An ordinary person.

We were lovers, but that was of no extra consequence to me. What we were—what we are—and shall always remain—is the rarest of friends. I think I know no one better than I know you. Surely, as I am now, no one knows me as you do.

She had to stop again. She felt as though she were inside something dry and empty and tight—a hollowed-out, dusty acorn. She closed her eyes—squeezed them tight shut—but then she had to open them again.

You said I liked to be punished. That was a bold thing to say, but you're always bold. You're the boldest person I know. Bold and brave. And true. And I'm not. I wanted you to see that. And now that you've seen it, there's nothing else to know about me.

The words were hurting her. She hated the words, but she kept on reading.

I couldn't stay any longer. Too many bad feelings. Loretta, Julie—they didn't want me around. Do you know that classic story "It's a Good Life?" They made it into a *Twilight Zone*. About this omnipotent kid who wishes people into the cornfield? That's what they wanted, Loretta and Julie—to wish me into the cornfield.

She had to read that part over three times. Once to understand, twice to understand, the third time to understand.

You said I like to be punished. Maybe you're right and maybe you're not. Maybe what you meant is that I recognize and accept the condition of my life. What's done cannot be undone. I am given some time and then I am told to move on. That's what I am doing, Trina: I am moving on.

She kept reading and rereading those words, the blunt sound of her heartbeat filling the room.

But we're not going to be apart from each other, Trina. I will always be thinking of you. I will always be carrying a piece of you within me.

Like I'm carrying a piece of you within me? she thought, thinking the joke good enough for a laugh, but she didn't laugh.

You're so much better than you realize, Trina. I had to tell you that. It's essential that you learn that about yourself. You've come through everything life has thrown at you and you've stayed a child. Did I ever tell you about the time Hildy and I were in the park and she saw this woman who was a dwarf? You know our Hildy—says everything on her mind, never minces her words. And so she marches right over to the woman and in her bright, cordial way she says, "You never grew up." There I am, standing there, sweating bullets as they say, but don't worry, here's the happy ending. The woman smiled. "No, dear," she said. "I never did." And that's our happy ending, Trina. You never did either. And you mustn't. Don't ever grow up. That's your power, Trina. I love you, child. May the Force be with you.

Forever yours,
Charles

She put down the letter. She couldn't get over how beautiful it was, and how wrong. Everything in it was all wrong. He didn't know who she was. Didn't have a clue. She wasn't the person he was talking about. That must be some other person, she thought, as she put the letter back into its envelope and then, safe away, in a drawer.

She got to the Center by lunchtime, figuring they could always use an extra hand at lunchtime and that they'd be happy to see her. She figured wrong. Even

Barry, who was her friend and who was the first to see her, acted like he didn't want to know her.

"Well, well, well. Look who's here. Straight from her latest personal-appearance tour," he said as she entered the kitchen. "Captivating a nation, titillating a hemisphere . . . Mistress of illusions . . . Now you see her, now you don't . . . the one and only Katrina Dunbar."

He began to applaud and she shook her head. "Stop it," she said. He stopped it. "What are you doing here?" she asked him.

"Subbing for you—the Jimmy Hoffa of the day-care set."

She looked at him in his pert white apron. He seemed so small and silly, liable to blow away. "I haven't been gone that long," she said.

"Sure you have. Listen, toots, virtually nobody is remembered after four days. Washington, perhaps. Lincoln. Moses and Mohammed, and then you start stretching it. So don't let anybody ever convince you to take a vacation, Katrina."

She came over to the counter where he was slicing carrots. "Need some help?"

"No. And don't let Loretta catch you here."

She picked up a knife and started to slice the carrots into sticks. No one was going to stop her.

"Where were you?" Barry asked.

"Kingston," she replied, as she drew the knife down into the heart of the root.

"Your ancestral home?"

"I went to visit my mother."

"And how is the dear?"

"She's alive."

"You're so weird," he said.

She kept at the work, not looking up. She couldn't see him shaking his head, but she had the feeling that's what he was doing. "First you disappear, then Charles. You should have seen Loretta. It's like you guys were Bonnie and Clyde and she was a U.S. marshal. I thought she was going to have kittens."

"If anyone could," Trina murmured, dumping the carrot sticks into the big mixing bowl.

That made Barry laugh and she realized she had won the first battle, even if it wasn't a very hard one to win, but then she heard Loretta's strong fast step.

"La Stupenda," Barry whispered. "Do you want I should hide you in the broom closet?"

Loretta entered the kitchen, carrying a pile of towels, and then the two of them were looking at each other.

"The prodigal daughter returns," said Barry, trying to break the tension but fueling it instead.

"Where have you been?" Loretta said, setting down the towels.

For a moment Trina just stared at the laundry. It was amazing how clean Loretta could get it.

"Are you going to answer me?"

"Home," said Trina.

"Home?" Loretta returned, arching her eyebrow, which she could do so theatrically. "Family crisis?"

Trina wanted to shrug, but she shrugged too much. "I guess."

"You guess?" Loretta replied. "Doesn't sound like much of an emergency to me. You might have called."

"I'm sorry."

"We were desperately shorthanded. Fortunately, Barry was able to help us out."

Barry pushed a finger into his cheek, making a dimple like a child star's, and smiling inanely until Loretta shot him a look that made the smile vanish.

"I'm sorry," Trina said again, reaching out to help with the towels, but Loretta pulled them away from her.

"I think I'm going to make my calls now," said Barry, mincing pointedly from the room.

They were left alone. She couldn't stand the way Loretta was looking at her. What had she done that was so terrible? "Stop," she whispered.

"Stop what?" Loretta said furiously. "I don't understand you. It's as if you don't expect consequences from your actions."

Trina shook her head. "I had to get away."

"Of course. You and Charles. Off you go," Loretta cried, snapping her fingers so loud it made Trina jump. She stared at Loretta—that perfect oval of a face was all twisted up now and she wanted to put her hands on the lips and the brow and the cheeks to restore them to calm. "The two of you running off like children," Loretta said. "A busman's holiday. And I'm left holding the bag."

"We weren't together," Trina said. "I don't know where Charles is."

"What are you talking about?" Loretta demanded. "I can't understand a word you're saying. You're unintelligible."

Trina took a deep breath and then spoke very slowly. "Charles is gone. He sent me a letter. He's gone." She couldn't bear to look at Loretta; Loretta looked too stricken, too betrayed, even though she had been planning to fire him.

"What letter? Show me."

"I don't have it with me."

"You're lying."

"No."

Without warning, Loretta pounded on the Formica counter. "Stop trying to make a fool out of me!"

"What do you want?" Trina asked simply. "I don't have it."

Loretta put a hand up to her neck, and pressed her chin against the hand. She looked exhausted. "Tell me what was in the letter."

It was a while before Trina could reply. The letter seemed a long time ago, appearing in her mind as something ancient, found in ruins, puzzle pieces. "I can only tell you part of it," she said. She reached out for a dish towel and then, folding the cloth as she framed her next words, she felt like a woman of myth, whose tales are told to the spinning of flax or the miraculous pull of gold and silver thread. "He said that he stayed too long. He said he wasn't made to be so long in any one place. He said he couldn't say where he was going because he didn't know where he was going. But he said he'd carry a piece of us with him always, next to his heart. Like an amulet."

She laid the folded towel atop the one that Loretta had worked on. Loretta said nothing for a moment, but then she spat out words. "That fucking sick creep."

The words splashed over Trina like acid. She reached for another towel from the heap; there were so many that needed folding.

Loretta closed her eyes and shook her head in utter weariness and disgust. "I don't believe this," she said. "Do you know how long he's been here? And then he just disappears, without a trace. And who gets the job of explaining it? *I* do. *I'm* the one who gets that lovely job."

"Loretta . . ."

"First I have to make explanations to the parents. I have to try to explain why the people I hire disappear like thieves in the night or walk around like zombies waiting for their next dose of hemoglobin or hit little kids for no good reason at all . . ."

"You're making it worse than it is. You're—"

"Shut up," Loretta cried, the angriest Trina had ever seen her. "It *is* the worst. It's the biggest disaster going. And it's my job to explain it. And the only explanation I have is that I don't have the money to get any better. That's why I have to keep an eye out for people sitting on park benches because I just don't have the goddamn money! And then, when I finish explaining to the parents, I can start on the kids. I can try to tell them that people don't just disappear. Even though I know and you know that it's a crock of shit because people *do* just disappear. They disappear all the time. But I'll tell them the opposite, hoping they believe my lie, so that they'll maybe trust the next person who comes along, before that person disappears, and you know what, Trina? I'm sick of it. I'm goddamned sick of it!"

"I know you are. I'm sorry . . ."

"Do you know what it means to have someone leave you that way? It means that you can't count on anyone or anything. It means that you're going to be disappointed and even though you know you're going to be disappointed you can't help hoping that you won't be . . ."

Then she stopped herself. She looked at Trina and then she looked away. "It's not going to work out, babe."

"Loretta, please . . ."

"Uh-uh. It's not going to work out."

There was a silence. "Are you telling me you want me to go?" Trina asked.

Loretta couldn't look at her. "That's what I'm telling you."

"No," Trina whispered. "I can't."

Slowly Loretta turned away from the towels and faced her.

"I wish I had done everything right," Trina said carefully. "I owed it to you and I wish I could have given you that. But I didn't and I'm sorry."

Loretta shook her head slowly, from side to side.

"I don't want to leave," Trina said. "Let me stay."

"You're a riddle, Trina. You're a goddamn Chinese puzzle," Loretta said, her mouth all hard. "And I'm tired of it, Trina. It's made me so tired and it's given me such a splitting headache."

Trina reached right up and touched Loretta's temples. "I have to stay," she said, as she made light circles with her fingers.

It seemed too cold to Trina, but Darcy made such a fuss about going to the park that she and Darcy and Barry wound up taking the children out after lunch.

Walking to the sandlot playground, it felt to Trina like the Crusades, very near the end of it, after Constantinople or wherever it was, with only a few able bodies left.

"Where's Charles?" Hildy asked as they crossed Central Park West.

"He had to go on a trip," Trina said.

Hildy tried that one on and then threw it off. "Where did he go?" she asked, her question ending in a sharp whine, like the terminal strokes of a buzz saw.

"Not far," Trina lied, feeling helpless to do anything else. "Don't worry, OK?"

When they got to the playground, some of the kids complained they were cold but Darcy, acting like she was in charge, told them to run around.

"Maybe it is too cold," Trina said.

"It's cold enough for me," Barry admitted. "I favor indoor sports myself."

"Winter's coming," Darcy pointed out. "Let 'em get all the fresh air they can."

"Well, I for one am not going to freeze my cute little tush off," Barry announced. "I'm going over to the Three Brothers. Coffee, tea, or milk?"

Darcy didn't want anything, but Trina had to admit that a black coffee sounded pretty good. "Hurry back though," she said. "I don't want to be shorthanded here."

"I'm running," cried Barry, breaking into a jog.

"He's strange," said Darcy, as his small figure became even smaller, jogging off into the distance.

"Yes," Trina said, counting heads and then counting them again.

"That's the way the people is here," Darcy said. "Strange. Take Charles. He just go off and that's the end of it. Like you nearly done."

"I didn't nearly do anything," Trina replied.

"Loretta think you did. Said you and Charles run off."

"Loretta's wrong," Trina said. "And I don't want to be having this discussion."

"Bet you know where Charles gone off to," Darcy challenged.

She didn't want to be around Darcy. Darcy was a troublemaker. So she stood up and walked a few yards away, and that's when she heard crying and she knew it was one of hers. The playground was complicated—bridges, tunnels, lots of places to go unseen—but she followed the crying into the interior of a redwood pyramid that had slides going down its sides and there she found Caitlin, curled up and crying.

"Caitlin," Trina whispered. "What's the matter?"

But Caitlin just kept on crying. Trina scooped her up and carried her back to the bench. "Lemme have that girl," Darcy said, reaching out for her, and Caitlin reached for Darcy so Trina had to let her go. "Poor thing," Darcy said. "Her mama's gone to have her baby and she ain't likin' it one bit."

"Corinne's gone to the hospital?"

"Early this mornin'. God bless her, we just know everything goin' to be all right and you gonna have a nice little brother or sister to love."

After a while, Caitlin stopped crying, grew real quiet, seemed to fade off somewhere. Darcy sat her down next to her, in the cradle of her arm, and patted her gently, rhythmically, until she was asleep. "You see how good I am?" Darcy said. "I know just what to do. Just like peoples charm snakes—the same thing."

Trina wasn't listening to her. She counted heads. Hildy, Molly, Petey, Martha, Aaron, Olivier. And Caitlin. Seven kids, seven heads. She wished Barry would hurry back. She started counting heads again.

"Sure, I made mistakes but I learnt from them and now look at me," Darcy continued. "That's why I been tellin' you—peoples ought get second chances, no matter what they done."

Trina stopped counting heads and turned to look at Darcy. What was she talking about? What did she want?

"If peoples make a mistake, it don't got to mean the end of things . . ."

And then she figured it out. She wasn't fast but she wasn't entirely slow. "You mean Sybila," she said.

Darcy looked at her, pushed back her glasses. "That's right," she said, thrusting out her jaw.

"Darcy, I told you . . ."

"You know, you wasn't even suppose to be here," Darcy said darkly. "Everyone figured you for gone."

"Everyone was wrong," Trina said firmly.

"Loretta was suppose to come with us to the park today," Darcy said. "Not you."

Trina looked away from her to check on the children. When she looked back, she saw Darcy shaking her head dolefully, for somebody to see. Trina turned and there was Sybila, outside the fence. She looked better than Trina remembered. She'd gotten fixed up—washed, ironed, pins in her hair. "Look at her," Darcy said. "Don't she look sweet? I wanted Loretta to see her."

Just then Caitlin woke up with a whimper. "Pee," she said.

"Look at her," Darcy said again, gripping Trina's arm.

"Pee," Caitlin cried.

It broke the spell. "OK, baby," Darcy said, lifting her up. "Come with Darcy."

Trina watched Darcy carry Caitlin to the lavatory and then looked back at Sybila. They stared at each other. Sybila reached up to touch her hat, green velvet with a band of gold, and then smiled. "I remember you," she said. And then, when Trina was thinking of what to say, there was suddenly something else. A long howl. Oh God, it was a witch's day. Trina's eyes traveled, found Olivier hopping around, making a keening noise. She ran to him, found him with a bite taken out of his arm, and Hildy standing there, like Dracula, but scared too, knowing what she had done, and Trina wanted to smack her, hard, for thinking she could be like an animal.

"What did you do?" Trina cried, the wound not like something that a child should have made.

And then Hildy burst into tears and Olivier did his hopping kind of pain dance. All the noise and the crying—it made her want to scream too. Where was Barry? she wanted to scream. They had to get back to the Center. It was a bad bite: it needed attention.

"Petey," Trina said. "Go get Darcy. She's over there—in the bathroom. Tell her I need her," she said, as she tried to settle Olivier. "Go!"

Petey started across the playground and she turned back to the kids and the business of gathering them, telling herself that it was just one of those days and that it would pass. But there was so much crying and noise and the kids all set off in a chain reaction—she could hardly hear herself think as she got them lined up to move through the playground, supporting Olivier, who was still wailing, and urging along Hildy, who was beside herself with guilt and confusion.

She looked around the playground and saw Darcy, with Caitlin in her arms, waddling along. Cow, she thought furiously. Is that the fastest she could move? "Hurry up!" Trina cried, but Darcy moved at her own pace and when she reached Trina her breathing was sure and slow.

"What's going on?" Darcy demanded.

"Olivier. Hildy gave him a bad bite . . ."

"Girl!" Darcy cried, which only made Hildy cry more.

"Let's go," Trina said. She headed toward the entrance, the children in a line behind her. Goddamn Barry, she thought. Must have met a waiter. She got to the gate and looked behind her. Heads—counting heads—one, two, three, four, five, six. Wait. One two three four five six. Wait. Hildy Olivier Martha Molly Aaron Caitlin. Wait. She turned to Darcy. "Where's Petey?"

Darcy looked at her. There was fog on her glasses even though the day was cold.

"I don't know."

"What do you mean? I sent him to get you."

"I didn't see him."

Trina stared at her. Then she turned, looked around the playground. Tunnels, bridges. Ropes. Ladders. "Petey!" One two three four five . . . "Petey!" She looked back to Darcy—mouth open now, glasses all fogged up. "Stay here with the kids!" she cried.

She ran around the playground. The nannies looked at her. Thought she was wild/crazy. "Petey!" And she was—wild/crazy—her heart was up in her mouth. She ran around, up and down and back. Then she stood there. In the very middle. Looked up—saw a balloon stuck in a tree. Looked down. Looked past the fence. *I remember you.* She took a few steps going nowhere. Oh, she heard herself saying, making a fist out of her left hand and raising it up to the level of her shoulder. Petey, she whispered, wanting to scream it. "Petey!"

There were so many questions. But of course there had to be. Bill sat in Loretta's office with the two policemen, Ryan and Menestrello. They were almost young enough to be his sons, he thought. As he took Petey's picture out of his wallet, his hands trembled and he wondered what they would think of that.

"That's Petey. Three months ago. With his brother. Dennis."

"Dennis is how old?" asked Ryan, who looked like all the cops Bill had ever seen—Irish, blunt, big.

"Denny is almost eight," said Bill, looking at the picture, which showed the boys in athletic jerseys by picnic tables on the Jersey shore. Bill looked up. "Shouldn't you be out looking for him now?" he asked.

"First we got to take the report," said Menestrello, whose one large black eyebrow running across his face made him look angry or maybe he really was.

Bill nodded. He felt odd. Sick. They had called him out of a meeting to the phone. Loretta had been on the other end.

—Bill, I don't know how to tell you this but . . .

Petey's dead.

(He felt this large burning in his stomach and his intestine. He always had a nervous stomach but now, of course, it was even worse.)

—We think it's Sybila.

—I don't understand.

—Sybila was at the playground . . .

—I don't understand!

But he understood. He understood everything. The fatal condition of the human animal. What would she do to his boy? He knew about Satanic rituals. Every day in this city there were people—children—being tortured and murdered in the name of devil worship. Haitians killing fowl, smearing blood. "Help me find my son," he appealed to Ryan, whom he found the more sympathetic of the two. The other, he felt, even if he was wrong, judged him at fault in some way.

"Don't worry about your son, Mr. Dowell," Officer Ryan said. "Take my word. I've got a sixth sense about these things. He's going to be fine."

Bill took his word. Carefully, in his hands, like a magic egg. Then, as he held it—that magic word—Loretta came into the office. They looked at each other and then he looked away; he didn't want to see her.

"You got any enemies, Mr. Dowell?" asked Menestrello.

"Enemies?" Bill replied. Did he have any enemies? "I don't think so," he said. "No."

"But you and your wife are in a divorce situation?" Ryan asked.

"Yes. We're separated," he said quickly.

The two cops exchanged a look. "We're going to want to talk to your wife," Ryan said.

"She doesn't even know yet," Bill said, hearing the pleading tone in his voice and wondering what they would think of that. "I haven't even told her yet."

"Well, we'll still have to talk to her . . ."

"Of course," he said quickly. "But she's very . . . this will take its toll on her."

"We understand that, sir," said Ryan, "but still . . ."

"Of course," he said. "Whatever."

After the questioning, he sat there in the office and tried to collect himself. Loretta stood by, talking and talking.

". . . All the parents will be out helping. We'll make a net. We'll go through that park in teams, all night if we have to. You'll see, Bill. This will work itself out. I know it. I have faith in it. I can feel it, Bill . . ."

What was she saying? He looked at her as though she were speaking a foreign tongue, one that he couldn't understand. "Please," he said. "I have to make a call."

She looked as if she were about to say something but didn't. Silently she withdrew and then he was alone in the office. He looked around. There were pictures on the walls. A picture of the children at a picnic in the park. Petey. There. Why? he wondered. Why his? There were all those others. Why his? He picked up the phone and dialed; he got the Soames School switchboard. "Abigail Strong," he said. He waited a minute, then she picked up.

"Hello?"

She sounded just like Louise. High, fluting.

"Abigail, it's Bill."

"Bill. What's wrong?"

She knew. Always. She was a very instinctive woman.

"It's Petey. He's missing."

"What do you mean?"

"He was taken from a playground," Bill said, the words sounding fantastic to him, the stuff of nightmares. "He went there with the Center. We think he may be with a former employee of the Center, a woman named . . ."

He ran out of words. Very suddenly. He felt something come over him, like a very thick film, and he couldn't get his breath.

"Bill . . ."

"Stay with Denny. Please. Will you stay with Denny?"

"Bill, wait," she was saying, "what can I—?"

"I'll call back soon. I have to go. I have to," he said, hanging up.

He stood in the small office, pressing himself against a wall, his eyes closed. The room was spinning beneath his feet, like a carousel. He could hear, from somewhere outside, a wild peal of laughter. He stood like that for some minutes, then the ride came to an end. He felt exhausted and his limbs were trembling as he made his way to the front door.

There, by the front door, he saw her standing, waiting. She looked all pale—her hair, her skin, her eyes. She looked to him like a fish, and she was staring at him with these dead-fish eyes. He passed by very closely, without a word, and then, just past the door, he stopped and turned around.

"Did you want this to happen?" he asked her, in a whisper.

She stared at him and her mouth opened, like a fish's mouth, but he turned away from her, walked quickly down the street.

He stood at the glass door of the laboratory. He could see, through the glass, all the tools of her trade. She kept it all so neat. At home too. She was always neat. Even more than neat—she seemed to survive on so little. She had so few clothes. The hats—that's all. Ate so little. Left no crumbs. He could see, through the lab, the glass-partitioned cubicle at the other end. He could see the back of her head. She'd gotten her hair cut short. From her posture, he could tell she was writing something. A faint blue smoke curled up from her cigarette.

Silently he opened the door to the lab and silently he traversed it. When he was but ten feet from the cubicle, he stood there and watched her. She wrote, and he thought of her hand, so precise, the characters almost Japanese. He used to love getting letters from her. Now he watched as she brought the cigarette up to her lips and inhaled and then placed the cigarette back into the oversize glass ashtray that was made to look like tortoiseshell.

"Louise!" he called suddenly, at the top of his voice.

She whirled around, her face marked by panic. Then, seeing her, he let the anguish come into his own face and she jumped from her chair. Her legs were long and she moved fast and he remembered how she always beat him at tennis.

"What!" she cried, five feet from him now, her long white hands bent like paws in midair.

He was breathing very shallowly now, so that his chest rose and fell, rose and fell, rose and fell. Her hands turned into balls and she lowered them to her hips. She stared at him. Her eyes, which always bulged slightly, as if she suffered from a hypothyroid condition, which she did not, were even more so that way than usual.

"Tell me," she said, her tone impatient.

He licked his lips. "We can't find Petey," he said, watching her. "Sybila took him. At least that's what we think. From the playground. And the cops are out looking for him. Ryan. Menestrello. They'll want to talk with you. It's been two hours. Petey's gone two hours. Do you hear me, Louise? Do you?"

He watched a flush creep up her neck, move over her pale face, like a red shadow, and he was glad of it.

"Do you hear me? I said. Say something."

"I . . ." She touched her high domed forehead.

He kept up the breathing but then this room too began to spin. "Tell me how scared you are," he said. "Tell me. You're very scared. They may never find him. Petey. Our son. They may never find him. And you're very scared and I want you to tell me."

She put a hand over her mouth. He looked at the hand. It seemed unconnected to her body, as though she were going to scream and somebody had put a hand there to silence her and it was an ugly long white hand with no ring on it.

"Tell me!" he shouted at her.

She shook her head.

He looked around. He found a large glass jar. It was empty. He picked it up, raised it over his head, and then, with a grunt and a snarl, he sent it smashing down to the floor and it exploded. "There," he said, seeing her shock, glad for it, so glad, and then he fell to his knees, the glass all around him, and he began to cry.

She stood for a moment watching him. The flush had vanished; she was returned to her former paleness. The sounds of his crying—the awful childlike sounds—filled the laboratory.

"Petey," he cried. "Petey."

Slowly she walked to where he was kneeling, and she stood in front of him. He threw his arms around her legs and buried his face in her skirt. Slowly—very slowly—her hand descended and came to rest against the back of his head.

25

Fuck all the bad things
Fuckem
Fuck all the bad things
Fuckem

"Come on now. Breathe!"

Fuck all the bad things
Fuck all the bad things
Fuck all the bad things
Fuckem

"*Yankee Doodle went to town riding on a pony stuck a feather in his hat and called it macaroni . . .*"

She sagged back against the pillow. The sheets were wet. She was wet. Slick as a seal. And she was tired. She didn't have endless strength for this.

"You did great that time, honey," Patrick said, popping Parmesan goldfish down his throat. It seemed to her, when they were packing the Lamaze bag, that the thing he was being most scrupulous about was having sufficient munchies on board to stoke his fires.

"Could you get me a cold washcloth please?" she said, trying not to sound irritated.

"Sure, honey, sure."

He was looking around. For someone to hand him a cold washcloth. A nurse maybe, or an orderly. He was using up the time and she didn't have time. "Over there. By the sink."

He moved slowly. Lumbered. He had been up all of last night with her and he wasn't used to being up at night. All the caffeine was doing a number on his stomach. Already he had missed one whole contraction, sitting on the pot, trying to handle the coffee. She didn't know why he had to be so long on the pot. Just one of those kids who used to read his Marvel comics there hours on end. Never outgrew the habit. Now it was *Money* magazine and *Forbes*.

"Here, babe," he said, handing her the wet washcloth.

Thanks a bunch. You could apply that to me you know—gently to my brow. It's in the job description, bozo. She took the washcloth and held it to her lips. It felt so indescribably wonderful. Sucked it the way Caitlin used to—still—sucked washcloths in the tub.

"You want some lollipop?" he asked.

"OK," she nodded, licking her lips. "Root beer."

At least he did that right. Went to one of those gourmet treat shops and got the full assortment of lollies. So far she'd licked crème de menthe, banana, and passion fruit. It was the closest she'd come to licking a passion fruit in God knows how long. Now she was filling up with the need to taste root beer but he was lumbering again, getting off the cellophane, and then it was coming on again and she gave a noise like someone starting out on a roller-coaster and when he looked at her he looked surprised and she didn't know why he looked surprised.

"Another one?" he said, but she was too far into it to answer him.

> *Fuck all the bad things*
> *Fuckem*
> *Fuck all the bad things*
> *Fuckem*

And then she started to say it aloud but not so's he could understand it. She sounded like some snarling broken motor or a mad dog.

"OK, breathe," he said, getting down to business, and then, slowly but rhythmically, that song. "*Yankee Doodle went to town riding on a pony . . .*"

Stop it. I hate that stupid song I hate it.

"*Stuck a feather in his hat . . .*"

"Fuck all the bad things . . ."

"*And called it macaroni. Yankee Doodle went to town . . .*"

"Fuckem!" she cried, articulating the words, and his jaw dropped and what an oaf he looked, her poor little oafie.

"*. . . riding on a pony . . .*"

She started to laugh. It was funny. How he just picked up the stupid song again as though she hadn't just sworn a blue streak. Mr. Denial. The Master. Then it came harder and she began to whimper and he was leaning over her. "Breathe, honey," he was saying. "Look at me. Corinne. Look at me."

And she looked at him, and he was all wavy, as if she were looking through water.

"Come on, honey."

She gripped the sides of the bed. Fuck all the bad things, she thought. Wars. Boys dying. Cancer. Anna. Hunger. People whipping horses. Acid rain. Ivory poachers. Sick kids. Fuckem all. The bad things. Fuckem.

Then it was over and he was touching her face.

"I can't handle this anymore," she said, licking the root-beer lolly he had managed to get undone.

"The doctors think you can."

"Doctors kill people," she said, and it tasted so good.

"You can do it."

"It's going on twenty-four hours . . ."

"Hey now. All but maybe two of them were light labor."

"Light labor. Light for you."

He smiled. She loved his smile always did: it melted her. "I don't know," she said. "It's too much."

"You want a C-section?"

"No. I don't *want* a C-section . . ."

"Well, that's the alternative."

"Fuck you."

"Jeez. You've got a mouth on today . . ."

"Wonder why."

"The things coming out of that pretty little rosebud . . ."

"Oh, blow it out your blowhole."

"What do they call that disorder? The one where you've got uncontrollable profanity?"

"Being married to you," she snapped.

He let out that high-pitched hyena cackle. The one she loved right from the beginning. It made her smile. Always did always will. Went right into her funnybone.

"There's my girl."

"Stop it."

"Stop what?" he said, making gorilla noises that made her laugh when she was nine and that made her laugh now.

"Stop it!" she said, and then she felt it start up again, and there was the desperate edge in her voice. "Where's the doctor?"

"In the utility closet screwing the pretty Pakistani nurse."

"Get the doctor," she said.

"Hey. You're not going to be one of those . . ."

"Get him!" she cried, because she needed help so badly and he couldn't help her, no way could he help her.

"OK, babe," he said, in a different kind of voice, and as she heard him go down the hall, she went back to work, losing all her words this time, the precious words, at the will now of something bigger than herself.

"That's a good dog," Loretta said, leaning down to give Thomas, the golden retriever with one blind eye, a dog biscuit.

You don't have to feed him so much, Trina wanted to say. Every fifty yards Loretta stopped to reward him. It's the way to make a dog fat and they didn't need a fat dog right now. What they needed was a lean and hungry one.

It was just past dusk and they had a flashlight—a big heavy-duty one they had gotten from Loretta's janitor—and the dog Loretta had borrowed from a neighbor and they were in Central Park, south of the reservoir, and they were searching for Petey. They weren't the only ones out. All of the parents were out, on the streets, in the park, all searching for Petey.

"I know he's somewhere," Loretta said. "I know it in my heart."

Trina followed the beam of the flashlight, listened to the bighearted pant of the dog. She had never been in the park after dark, and it was darker than she could have imagined.

"She wouldn't hurt him," Loretta said. "I know it's not in her heart to hurt him."

How do you know what's in her heart? Trina wanted to say. Maybe her heart's a big lump of coal. "How do we know?" she said. "She could be dangerous."

"Don't keep saying negative things," Loretta told her. "You're creating a negative force. We want to create a positive force. We want to establish a whole field of positive transmissions."

It sounded like the language she had surrounded herself with for years, language she thought she had finally finished with, but Loretta was so convinced of what she was saying that somehow it didn't sound hollow. "I don't know if I can do that," Trina said. "I'm not feeling positive."

"Yes, you can," Loretta urged her. "You can if you want to."

Don't just say *you can* that way. Just because you say it doesn't mean somebody can do it. "I don't think I can," she repeated. "Not here. Not now."

Loretta stopped walking. The dog stopped along with her, panted, shook a little. Loretta told him to sit and he sat and got a dog biscuit for it. "You can do it anywhere," she said. "If you know how."

"Not here." Trina looked around. "It's scary."

Loretta put out her hand. "Take my hand," she said. Trina didn't want to. She wasn't comfortable touching Loretta or being touched by her. "Take my hand," Loretta instructed, in a voice that was firm, but not shrill, not unkind. She put out her hand and Loretta took hold of it. "There," Loretta said, gently. "You just have to be taught," she explained. "No one ever taught you, so you have to be taught."

Her mouth felt dry. "It's scary in here," she said.

"It's OK," Loretta assured her. "You have to find the positive force."

Then there was a click and the light went out. "What's that?" Trina cried.

"Just be still," Loretta whispered. "Let the positive feelings come."

What the hell was she doing? It was pitch dark. Here they were in this dark place, this dangerous place, dangerous people. Maybe Loretta didn't know about dangerous people. "Put the light on."

"No," said Loretta. "Not just yet."

"Put it on!"

"Not just yet."

Then there was the near-silence. Just the breathing of the dog, easier now. Easier than her own breathing. Loretta was trying to terrorize her. That was it. She felt this wave of anxiety—terror—take hold of her. "What are you trying to do?" she demanded. "You're scaring me. Why are you trying to scare me?" She tried to get her hand out of Loretta's grip, but Loretta was strong.

"Listen," Loretta said.

She listened. She heard the dog's breathing. A siren. Her beating heart. She heard Loretta's breathing.

"Let the positive feelings come."

What positive feelings? she wanted to scream. They were looking for Petey. A crazy woman took him. And it was her fault. She stopped counting heads. She lost his head. Nothing turned out right. She lost everything. Bill. Charles. Petey. Phyllis. The baby. She was going to bleed. It would all come out of her tonight. Thick red bright blood. Thick as jam. Full of broken cells. And then she would have nothing.

"Trust me," Loretta said. "I know what I'm doing. I've healed people."

It was so weird. The voice coming at her in the darkness. You couldn't see the tip of your nose and there were no stars. You had the feeling you'd never see stars again. In the distant dark only small spots of phosphorescence that disappeared once you stared at them.

"In our church," Loretta said, "I've laid on hands."

She felt stretched tight. Like she could break. Loretta held her hand tighter, put her other hand on her shoulder. Trina felt the hand on her shoulder and wanted it off.

"It's not crazy, Trina," Loretta whispered. "People have that power. Not all the time. Not for everyone. But sometimes. For some people."

The eye adjusted. It does that. She could make out the line of Loretta's jaw and, looking down, could see her fingers resting on her shoulder.

"It's my fault," Trina said. "If I hadn't told him to go get Darcy, he wouldn't—"

"Let the positive feelings come," Loretta said, cutting her off. "Only the positive feelings."

She stood there. She licked her lips. It was like she was being forgiven. Loretta wasn't blaming her. She could see more. The gold cross Loretta always wore around her neck. The dog. Thomas. The yellow bandanna around Thomas's neck.

"Shouldn't we look for him?" Trina said.

"We will."

He must feel so alone. What was Sybila doing with him? Where had she taken him? She couldn't be doing anything bad to him. She wouldn't do such a thing. No woman would do such a thing. Women were made to take care of children. A woman who would hurt a child—it was rare. One in a million. A million million.

"There," said Loretta. "It's coming."

The eye adjusted. She could see dark leaves high up on the autumn trees. She exhaled and heard cats and the sound of wings somewhere.

Loretta moved her hand from Trina's shoulder to her head. She ran her fingers through Trina's hair. "Don't worry," Loretta said. "Think only of good things."

She held her breath again. Loretta's fingers through her hair. Good things. Peter Pan. She let out her breath.

Loretta turned the flashlight back on. "Let's go," she said quietly. "I think we're going to find him now."

"I got money, boy."

He wished he did.

"Don' think I don' got money."

Was Sybila mad at him? Sometimes Sybila looked mad.

"What you want? You want a hot dog?"

Yes. He wanted a hot dog. "Yes. Please." Mommy said say please.

Sybila told him to sit there. Sybila went to the man and came back with the hot dog.

"I tol' you I got money."

He ate the hot dog. It was good. He was hungry. "I'm thirsty."

"So am I."

Sybila laughed. Then Sybila stopped and looked mad.

"I didn't say I got all the money in the world."

Sybila took a napkin out of the metal box. He wanted to. It was fun. He took out more napkins.

"Hey. Cut that. You want us thrown outta here? Eat your dog."

He ate his dog.

"I don' get to eat nothin.' You think I ain't hungry? But the children must eat. It's what God want. God don' want children go hungry. When I was a little girl I wasn't never hungry. My mama always feed us. She always treat us good. Always got food. That's why my sister grow fat."

Sybila laughed.

"You know who is my sister?"

No.

"Darcy. Big fat Darcy."

Sybila laughed.

"What's my name?"

He watched her.

"Children don' know nothin'. Don' even know my name. Children is stupid."

"Sybila."

Her eyes got big. Sybila laughed. "Oh now. Ain't that the cutest? You always been the cutest to me. Like a little yellow duck."

"I'm thirsty."

Sybila looked mad. "I tol' you I don' got money. Why you keep axing me?"

"Apple juice."

Sybila took a napkin from the metal box.

"Look. You got dirt on your nose."

Sybila was wiping his nose. Hard. He was crying.

"Shut it up now. Shut it. Children what cry is *bad*. I don' like no bad children."

"I want to go home."

"Why? I gives you a hot dog don' I? Children is ungrateful. I take you on a trip.

Wherever you want to go. I take you the beach. I take you Disneyland. I take you see the pope."

"I got to go potty."

"Shit."

Sybila stood up. "You got a bathroom here? Is for my boy."

She took him down a hall. It was dark. The bathroom was small. He stood in front of the potty.

"What you want?"

He pulled down his pants and sat on the potty.

"You ain't one of them what takes all day? I don't got all day. My time a precious thing."

He was thirsty. And she didn't have money. "I want to go home."

"Shit. I take you Disneyland. There is buses in this country will take you anywheres."

Sybila sat on the sink.

"You think they gonna be mad at me?"

"Why?"

Sybila stood up and looked in the mirror. "Ain't I pretty?"

He stood up. He pulled up his pants.

"You didn't got to go, huh?"

Sybila took his hand. She took him down the dark hall.

"Where are we going?"

"Goin' to Zion, honey."

"What's Zion?"

"Holy place."

Holy. He liked holes. He had a book with a hole in it. The book said to put your finger through the hole. Through Mommy's ring. When he put his finger into the hole, Daddy always grabbed his finger. He laughed. It tickled.

Then they were out of the dark hall and in the big place with the lights.

"How I wish I got money for coffee. I got money but I spend it all on you. That's 'cause God says so."

Sybila was talking. She didn't see the two men. He did. The policemen.

"Hey! You!"

They were running. At him. The policemen. He was scared. He was crying. Sybila said stop.

When they said don't push she didn't push. When they said push she pushed. She was going to do everything they said. That was the ticket. No sweat. Follow instructions. She was real good at following instructions. Big win for her on the aptitude tests. Look at the big guy. Scared shitless. Like an elephant with a mouse. Oh. Bad. A bad one. Bad.

—That's a girl.

—Hold on.

—Beautiful.

—Isn't she beautiful?

Mmmmnh. Mmmmnh. God. Oh. Push. Push down. Down. Look. My legs. Chinawoman. Look.

—Hold on. We're almost done.

We. Fucking doctors. Idiots. Residents.

—OK, Corinne. Hold on.

Breathe. Breathe. Idiots. Except for Dr. Waterman. She loved Dr. Waterman. Smart. Cute. Cute ears. Cute ass. Sugar voice. Wife pregnant. Send him gift. Tiffany. Three-ring rattle.

—Beautiful. Look at the job she's doing. What a job.

Talk. So much talk. Cheap. Look at the big guy. Wasn't made for this. OK Paddy. Hold on. Oh. Oh. A bad one. *Bad*.

—She's crowning.

—OK.

—Beautiful.

Oh. Oh. Jesus.

—Good. Good. You've crowned.

Fuck crowning. Queen for a day. Look at the big guy. Ate a bad clam. Right from here to the nearest bar sure's my name's Little Corinne McIver. Hit me with a double Dewar's fast Joe. And cigars. First time out was Robert Burns. This time it's your Montecruz specials. Two bucks a throw. What the hell.

"Oh."

It hurts. Jesus it hurts. Hurts good though hurts good. Look at me look. A Chinawoman. In a field. Look how I'm pushing. Look at my fucking legs how they're shaking. Oh Jesus. Women been doing this since birth of time. Look at my stomach. Filled up with baby.

—Now push. All the way.

Unnnnnnh. Unnnnnh. Oh big guy. Oh.

—All right. Now I'm doing the episiotomy.

Sugar voice. Hurts like hell. Sore for weeks. Sore forever.

—Corinne?

Hold on big guy.

Unnnnnh.

—Here it comes.

Go baby. Go for it. Go baby. Go. Go. Go. Go. Go. Go. Go.

"Oh."

Big guy. Look at him. Crying. Big baby. Look how he's crying.

—Hey! He's a pisser!

A boy. They know. A boy. Conrad. Oh God. A brother. Better. Better that way.

—Baby.

Kiss me. Yes. Kiss me.

—I love you.

"Paddy."

—I love you. He's beautiful.

"Is he . . ."

—Beautiful. Everything. Beautiful.

"I want to hold him."

—They're just getting him cleaned up.

"No. He's clean enough."

I'll lick him clean.

—What a job you did, Corinne.
Sugar voice. "Can I . . ."
—Another minute.
—Eight-ten.
A big guy. Eight-ten. All inside me.
—Whoa! That's some baby.
—We're talking Green Bay here.
Give me my baby.
—Here you go. Here's your baby.
Oh. Look. Paddy. Oh. A boy. Baby boy. A great big baby boy. Oh. Hold me. Oh.

"You don't have to do that now, Darcy," Loretta said, as Darcy ran steaming hot tap water over the children's's toys.

Darcy acted like she hadn't heard. Loretta looked to Trina and shrugged. The shrug was heavy and sad and there didn't seem to be any positive force in it. It made Trina feel scared.

The Center was very quiet and still. They had come in from the park over an hour ago and found Darcy sitting there, on the front stoop—she didn't have her key. When she saw them, she started to cry and swear and they brought her inside and gave her tea. Then, over the tea, Darcy told them everywhere she had looked—the laundermat where they did their laundry; the Gypsy fortune-teller to whom Darcy thought Sybila might have given Petey; the Chapel of Salvation and Deliverance. She was nowhere.

—She just disappears. She there but you can't see her.

Trina couldn't think of it. Petey, out there, with a phantom. All because of her—because she had looked away.

"Darcy, please," Loretta said, trying again. "Stop."

But Darcy had gone on a cleaning binge. "The toys is dirty," she said, reprovingly. "They got finger marks all over them."

Then the phone rang. Everyone stopped what they were doing. Loretta went to answer it. "Hello?"

Loretta had her back to them and Trina watched her shoulders for some sign. "What?" Darcy cried, also watching Loretta.

Loretta put out a hand to quiet her. "Yes? Yes? . . ."

(Let him be safe, Trina thought. He's only a child. He hasn't done anything.)

"Oh! Thank God!" Loretta cried. "Thank God!"

Trina felt something lift off her.

"Yes. Yes. Do the parents know? Oh, thank God. Yes. Thank you. Yes."

Yes. Thank you. Yes.

"He's safe," Loretta said as she hung up and turned to face them. "They found him at a luncheonette on Broadway. With Sybila." She looked at Darcy. "She didn't hurt him, Darcy. He wasn't hurt."

"I know that," Darcy said, in a strange voice, almost matter-of-fact. "She wouldn't hurt him."

"Well, she didn't," Loretta reaffirmed.

"I know that," Darcy repeated. She took off her rubber gloves and threw them in the sink. "She wouldn't hurt a fly," Darcy said, a bitterness leaching into her voice.

Trina and Loretta looked at each other.

"What's wrong with her?" Darcy said, mostly to herself. "Look what she done. Scared us half to death."

Loretta threw her red cape over her shoulders with the kind of bold toss that always reminded Trina of a bullfighter. "We have to go down to the stationhouse," she announced. "Come, Darcy."

Darcy sat there. "Look what she done," she said again. "I ought kill her. Then I wouldn't got these troubles."

"Darcy," Loretta said, "you've got to come."

"You go," Darcy said, refusing to move. "See where they put her. Then you let me know."

"Get up, Darcy. I'm tired. It's been a long night. Now get up."

Darcy just sat there. "When it's over you go to bed. Not me. I won't be goin' nowhere."

Trina watched Loretta, who looked like she was thinking of things to say. "Come on, Darcy," she said finally, very quiet, the way you do to someone on a ledge.

Darcy sat there another minute. Then she got up. "All my life I been doin' this," she said, putting on her coat. "And when I die she won't even spend the money to get me buried."

"I'll talk to you tomorrow," Loretta said to Trina, taking Darcy by the arm, leading her out the door.

Then Trina was alone in the Center. She didn't know what time it was: it was very late. She had never been here alone before. Most of the lights were out and everything was dim. The toys on the shelves—the puppets and the dolls and the play people—they had a poised quality, as if they were waiting to come to life as soon as she left the room or fell asleep. But she wouldn't fall asleep. It would be a night without sleep.

She got up and began to straighten things away. She was never a neat sort of person. She had no feeling for keeping a house spick-and-span. But tonight was different. She was taking up where Darcy left off. She took the toys from the sink to drain. She washed down the refrigerator. She swept the rugs, finding lost pegs and missing puzzle pieces.

She must have worked that way for an hour, and then she looked around and it looked good. Pretty. Like a toy shop. She didn't know why she felt so happy and sad. All of her feelings were crawling around right here beneath her skin— wriggling around—like those worms you get in the tropics who make their journeys just beneath the epidermis.

Finally, when it seemed time to go, she stood at the door, looked around one more time, turned off the light. Outside the night seemed darker still and now very cold. She had no coat. No cape. She walked quickly down the streets. Little Red Riding Hood. The forest. Her grandmother's house.

Then she was home. She turned on one light—just the one above the kitchen table. She didn't want too much brightness. She didn't want the night to end. It was a certain kind of night. A night of nights. The nights in summer when you first realized that summer had arrived and the opportunities were endless and you were young. The nights in winter when you've managed warmth and you think of all the creatures out there who haven't and there's a dry heavy steam and plenty of tea and the frost has made the windows opaque and you're glad not to see or be seen. And this night, with its good news, its resolution, the sense of peace. Close-fitting calm. A good night for miracles. Séances. Things without names.

Sitting down at the table, she took out her writing paper and a thin green pencil. "Dear Charles," she wrote. "How are you?"

Then, quickly, she put the pencil down. She felt the sudden heat—her stupidity flashing before her—and it burned her. She couldn't say why she had a green pencil. She couldn't think what that was about. But she made herself close her eyes, as she had been taught, and after a moment, when she opened them again, she could continue.

So much has happened here. I wonder what you would have done.

I'm not brave. I wanted you to know that. So now I know, she thought. Now I know. She put the eraser against her lips. She thought of him. How she had held him and how she would not be holding him again.

I was so scared in the park, Charles. It was so dark. I thought of Petey in there. Hurt. Hit with a rock. You know how they get when they bleed, Charles. The hardest time, when they bleed. How they call for their mommies and daddies and that's when they don't want us. I thought of him crying like that, Charles—bleeding—and I kept thinking I had done that to him. I kept wondering why I was made to do so many harmful things.

She put down the green pencil. She touched her forehead. She couldn't figure out why she didn't feel tired. Again she took up the pencil.

Loretta isn't what you think, Charles. You should have seen her with me. She was so kind. She did all the right things, Charles. I think you had her pegged all wrong. You didn't have to go away, Charles. Not because of her.

The light in the room flickered. At this late hour she felt entirely alone. She wondered where he was. In what state.

We made a baby, Charles. You and me. I think it's a boy. Can I call him Philip? No one knows. Just you and me. We're the only ones.

She held the pencil in the air. There was no more to write. She was done. The day was done. She had the feeling it was close to morning but though it would have been easy to find out, she didn't go to look. She folded the letter neatly, thinking that she must put it in a safe place, where it wouldn't get lost. But before she went to look for the safe place, she just sat there for a moment, in the kitchen, under the light.

They got out of the cab and Loretta checked to make sure they had everything. "You've got the cookies?" Loretta asked.

Trina nodded.

"And I've got the bear. Come, let's go."

Trina let Loretta walk on ahead. For a moment, she stood there, in front of University Hospital, and counted the floors. She wouldn't want to give birth in such a big hospital.

"Come on," Loretta said, turning around, hurrying her along.

They waited a long time for an elevator. One came, but there was only room for the doctors and the nurses so they waited for the next.

"Did I show you the teddy?" Loretta asked.

"Yes."

"Isn't it cute?"

"Yes."

"It's a Gund."

"Oh," said Trina, not knowing what that was.

"Gotta getta Gund," Loretta said absently, looking up to see which floor the elevator was on. "Damned elevators," she said, punching a button.

Trina sat down on a bench to wait. Even though she'd slept all day yesterday, she was tired. It had been a bad night. Twice she'd woken up—her mouth dry, her heart beating fast. Then she told herself it was over—they were safe—and she went back to sleep.

"Finally," Loretta said, when the elevator came.

They got off at the maternity floor. Trina looked around. She had never been here before. There seemed to be a lot of people smiling on this floor, and couples walking back and forth down the hall to help the labor along.

"Have you ever been here before?" Loretta asked.

"No."

"I meant to a maternity ward."

"No."

"I had Gregory at Beth Israel. He came out with a full head of oily black hair," she said, remembering. "My husband called him Victor Mature."

She stared at Loretta. It felt so strange being here.

"That's a joke. You're supposed to laugh."

She reached out and placed a hand on Loretta's arm. "I'm pregnant," she said quickly, so that it would be done.

Loretta stood there, not moving a muscle for what seemed a very long time. "Oh boy," she said finally, thinly, through her teeth.

There were the sounds of babies crying. Then the muffled sound of rubber soles on linoleum floors. *Do you at least know who the father is?* She looked down at the linoleum floor, which was made to look like marble. "It's Charles's."

Loretta folded her arms beneath the cape, so that it looked like she had enormous breasts.

"Did you hear me?" Trina said, looking up. "It's Charles's baby."

"Uh-uh," said Loretta, shaking her head. "It's your baby."

Crying. Why did they let the babies cry? She looked toward the swinging doors, where the sounds were coming from. Then she looked back at Loretta. "Don't you have anything else to say?"

Loretta looked up at the ceiling, then shrugged. "Gotta get another Gund."

What was the joke? Neither of them laughed. "Are you going to help?" Trina demanded to know.

She watched Loretta bite the inside of her cheek. "Sure," Loretta said. "I'll help. What do you want me to do?"

"I'm going to have the baby," Trina clarified, as if there might be a confusion.

"Of course you're going to have the baby."

They didn't speak; the crying babies filled the silence.

"Is it what you want?" Loretta asked.

It was a moment before Trina replied. "Yes," she said. "It's what I want."

Loretta nodded. "Let's go in."

They went through the swinging doors. The light was different on this side. Softer but somehow brighter. Trina saw the babies. The roomful of babies. Most of them were sleeping. A few were screaming. There was a Chinese baby screaming so hard it hurt Trina to hear it.

"Look," said Loretta, pointing. "McIver. Boy McIver."

Trina went up to the window, looking where Loretta was pointing. There, in the back row, second to the left, was the baby boy. Big face, red, big nose, bald. Fast asleep, all swaddled up.

"Looks just like his father," Loretta said, in a very full voice. "But we can't see his eyes. Maybe he's got Corinne's eyes."

She stared at the baby. Her fingertips went close to the glass.

"Eight-ten," Loretta said, reading the tag. "He got himself a real little bruiser after all."

She pulled her hand back from the glass, let it rest lightly against her stomach.

"Oh, there they are," Loretta cried, with a wave.

Trina turned. Walking down the hall were Patrick and Caitlin. They were holding hands.

"He's beautiful," Loretta called down the hall.

Trina turned back to the window. She had never seen this before. All the babies.

"Aren't they beautiful?" Loretta whispered, so close to her that Trina could practically feel the whisper against the back of her neck.

"Yes," Trina said.

They were very, very beautiful.